Green Ivy Publishing

1 Lincoln Centre

18W140 Butterfield Road

Suite 1500

Oakbrook Terrace IL 60181-4843

www.greenivybooks.com

ISBN: 978-1-943955-11-4

Thanks to Mike and Denise Novack and Vinnie Termini for their valuable feedback and encouragement. Special thanks to my wife Roberta for her patience and her tremendous editorial and sentence-tightening skills.

A FATEFUL REUNION

ALLEN FOSTER

PROLOGUE

Excerpts from a 2004 Rock and Roll Encyclopedia entry for the
Upper Hand:

HISTORY & HIGHLIGHTS:

The Upper Hand was a highly successful American rock and roll band in the 1970s and '80s. Formed in 1972 from members of several teen bands in and around Morristown, New Jersey, the Upper Hand built a substantial following playing in clubs and bars in northern New Jersey and New York City and landed a recording contract with Signature Records in 1974. Their first album, released in early 1975, sold over 1.5 million copies and yielded two hit singles. The band enjoyed consistent record sales and concert tour success until its abrupt demise in 1990 shortly after guitarist/vocalist Jeff Britton left the group mid-tour due to severe heroin addiction. No known attempts to reunite the band have been undertaken as of this writing in early 2004.

The Upper Hand released a total of ten studio albums, one live album, and a "Best Of" collection between 1975 and 1990, and charted twenty-two singles, including three number-one singles and twelve top tens. Although the band never suffered a significant drop-off in popularity while they were together, the peak of their success was certainly in 1980, when their fourth studio album, *Dangerous When Cornered,* sold over seven million copies, topped both the American and British charts for several weeks, spun off four high-charting singles, and served as the catalyst for a huge North American and European concert tour. The *Best of the Upper Hand* album, released in 1985, also found the top of the charts for an extended period. Several compilation packages have been released by their label since the band's breakup.

PERSONNEL:

The Upper Hand consisted of the same five members throughout its eighteen-year existence, apart from the emergency use of a number of fill-in guitarists to finish their last tour in 1990 after Britton's departure:

Mark Donahue (born June 8, 1954) — guitars, vocals

Jeff Britton (born February 20, 1954) — guitars, vocals

Anthony "A.J." Ramello (born February 1, 1953) — bass guitar

Dave Rowinski (born January 4, 1952) — keyboards, vocals

Steve Holmes (born September 29, 1952) — drums, percussion

MUSICAL STYLE:

The Upper Hand belongs in the category of classic, guitar-driven 1970s-era rock bands. The band's use of both electric and acoustic guitars, multiple lead singers, and frequent use of rich vocal harmonies invited comparisons to the Tom Johnston/Pat Simmons Doobie Brothers era (i.e., pre-Michael McDonald), as well as the more rock-oriented output of the Eagles. Keyboardist Dave Rowinski's adept use of a Hammond B-3 organ, and Mark Donahue and Jeff Britton's abilities to both trade off on fleet-fingered guitar solos and create memorable two-part harmonized guitar passages, also drew some comparisons to the Allman Brothers Band. Primary songwriters Donahue and Britton, who wrote separately, remained fairly true throughout the band's life to the basic blues/rock formula that brought them initial success. Rowinski, who typically wrote and sang lead on two songs per album, pursued a markedly different style, usually infusing his contributions with a soulful and/or jazzy vibe. Fans of the Upper Hand were known to be somewhat divided regarding the value of Rowinski's change-of-pace songs on the band's albums. The band's sole attempt to release a Rowinski-penned tune as a single in 1983 resulted in easily the weakest chart performance ever for an Upper Hand single. The band's rhythm section, particularly bassist A.J. Ramello, is still admired as one of the best of the era.

POST-UPPER HAND MUSICAL ENDEAVORS:

Mark Donahue has put together a successful career as a solo artist, releasing five solid if not spectacular selling albums and becoming a reliable concert draw at mid-size arenas and outdoor venues, performing a mix of solo material and Upper Hand hits he wrote and sang.

Dave Rowinski's attempt at a solo career has not been met with the same level of success as Donahue; his three solo albums sold modestly at best, each selling fewer copies than the previous release. He performs sporadically in clubs and small theaters and does some studio work.

A.J. Ramello, widely considered to be America's closest counterpart to the Who's John Entwistle as a virtuoso bass guitarist, has been the country's most sought after studio and touring bassist from the moment the Upper Hand dissolved. He has played on records and concert tours that are too numerous to list here.

Steve Holmes spent two years in the early and mid-1990s filling in for injured drummer Bill Shane in the Zachary Thomas Band after Shane was involved in a serious car crash. After Shane recovered, Holmes bounced around among a variety of bands, including two so-called "super groups" which never lived up to their hype. He now finds occasional road work with solo acts that need an experienced touring drummer.

Jeff Britton has remained musically dormant and totally out of the public eye since his drug-related departure from the band and lengthy rehab. It has been widely reported that Britton and Donahue, best friends since childhood and the core band members responsible for the creative direction and success of the Upper Hand, have had no contact with each other since the day Britton abandoned the 1990 tour and left the band.

CHAPTER 1

"*Fuck!*" Dave roared at the TV set. He pounded the sides of his clenched fists on his knees, grabbed a pillow from the sofa on which he was sitting, and threw it against the screen, where it landed with a soft thud and dropped harmlessly to the floor. "Fuckfuckfuckfuckfuckfuckfuckinggoddamnfuck!"

"What the hell are you yelling about?" Steve called out from the kitchen, where he was in the process of popping the caps on two more Sam Adams Lagers. "And stop throwing shit at my TV."

"You're lucky it was just a pillow and not a beer bottle."

"Bullshit. *You're* the lucky one. That TV cost me over two grand, and if you bust it, the replacement is going to cost *you* two grand, plus glass cleanup costs." Steve entered the family room holding the two beers but pulled the one intended for Dave close to his chest. "Now, are you going to use this bottle strictly for its proper and righteous purpose, or do I need to pour your beer into a plastic sippy cup?"

"OK, OK, give me the damn beer. I won't smash your precious TV. I promise."

"So, what was on that got you all wound up anyway?"

"Weren't you listening? They just announced that the Lobotomy Boys have gotten back together after eight years apart and have a thirty-city concert tour all lined up. They're going to be playing twelve to fifteen thousand-seat arenas, and tickets are selling like crazy. They mentioned the expected ticket sales gross, but I was yelling too loud to hear it. Probably just as well; the TV may have died a violent death if I had heard the number."

"Why does that bother you? They were a pretty good band. I thought you liked some of their stuff."

"*That should be us!*" Dave exploded, gesturing animatedly towards the television with his arms, spilling a couple mouthfuls of beer from the bottle in his right hand in the process. "Those guys weren't one tenth the band we were, and here they are getting ready to rake in a fortune on a concert tour."

Steve didn't reply but sat down next to Dave on the sofa and took a long pull on his Sam Adams.

"It's not just the Lobotomy Boys, either," Dave continued loudly. "Scarcely a week goes by anymore that some long-lost band that couldn't hold a candle to the Upper Hand dusts off their gear and makes a shitload of money touring behind their old songs, or even making a new album. There's no goddamn reason we shouldn't be out there doing the same thing!"

Steve grabbed the TV remote, turned off the set, and reached into the bowl of potato chips on the coffee table in front of the sofa, popping a few chips into his mouth and chewing them deliberately. He stared at Dave, who had his head back aggressively emptying his two minute old bottle of Sam Adams. "You know full well that's not true," Steve finally replied quietly. "There's a huge goddamn reason we're not out there doing the same thing."

Dave's silence served as acknowledgment of the hard truth behind Steve's declaration. Dave got up from the sofa and headed to the kitchen to get another beer. When he returned to the family room, the two of them sat wordlessly for over a minute, each one absorbed in thoughts of how amazing their lives had once been, how suddenly everything had imploded, and how dim the prospects were for a revival of the five-headed monster known as the Upper Hand.

It was April of 2004, a full fourteen years since the breakup of the band. Dave Rowinski was fifty-two years old, Steve Holmes fifty-one. They were sitting in the family room of Steve's comfortable apartment in the Greenwich Village section of New York City. (Steve never tired of claiming to visitors that the opening footage from the TV sitcom *Friends* proved that Ross, Rachel, Chandler, Monica, Joey, and Phoebe lived and hung out right there on the same block he now called home. The fact that these people were fictional characters, and that the show was recorded in California, was a minor administrative detail that never seemed to matter to Steve or his guests).

Dave, while almost as trim at five foot ten and 160 pounds as he had been during his time in the Upper Hand, looked very little like the rock and roll keyboard player seen on the band's album covers and posters. His hair, once thick, shaggy, dark brown, and cascading down to his shoulders, was still reasonably thick but almost completely gray and cut in a style that would fit in at a Boston law firm. His once ever-present droopy mustache was long gone, and his face, while retaining the angular shape of his band days, showed every one of his fifty-two years.

Steve, in contrast, looked like he just stepped out of an Upper Hand promotional photo circa 1985. His longish, carefully layered blond hair, powerful six foot, 195-pound drummer's physique, and clean-shaven movie-star-quality features were shockingly untouched by the hands of time. Steve's remarkable good looks had led the many photographers who shot Upper Hand publicity and album photos over the years to almost invariably place Steve front and center in the five-man group shots. Anyone unfamiliar with the personnel of the Upper Hand would certainly assume from these photographs that Steve was the leader and front man of the band. It didn't take the other members of the band long to realize what these photographers were doing, but none of them had the kind of ego to be bothered by it—and besides, they all knew that photos of Steve didn't hurt when it came to drawing female fans to the band.

The former bandmates sat silently on Steve's sofa, draining their beers and emptying the bowl of chips. While there was certainly some overlap in their thoughts about their days as members of a top notch, internationally successful rock band—the fame, the camaraderie, the wild, hedonistic lifestyle—the focus of Steve's musings was completely different from Dave's. For Steve, it was all about sex. He never had any problem attracting women and always seemed to have a stunning new girlfriend (or two...or three), even now that he was over fifty. But there was absolutely nothing to compare to life on the road with the Upper Hand. Steve's legendarily enthusiastic embrace of the groupie culture—"the incredible smorgasbord of lovely, willing young things" as he was once quoted in the 1980s—

brought a little smile to his face as he headed back into the kitchen to replenish the potato chip bowl and grab two more beers. *Damn, if only we could recapture those sweet days*, he thought longingly as he reentered the family room.

Dave's thoughts took him somewhere else entirely, to multi-million selling albums, mega-grossing concert tours, and lucrative television appearances—the financial rewards he had enjoyed as a member of the Upper Hand.

Dave's post-Upper Hand life was marked by deep disappointment and heartache, leaving him in 2004 with the stunning realization that his once seemingly inexhaustible financial resources were dwindling dangerously.

The disappointment involved his solo recording and touring career. Although Dave had been sincerely saddened by the demise of the Upper Hand, he was also convinced that the end of the group represented the removal of a barrier to his attainment of stratospheric rock stardom. The band and its record label had always seen Dave's key role in the Upper Hand as keyboardist and harmony vocalist, not as a lead singer or songwriter. No Upper Hand album, other than the last one, had ever included more than two of Dave's songs, and it took eight years and six albums—and a lot of cajoling on Dave's part to his bandmates and label executives—before one of his songs was released as a single. The failure of that record, a soulful, piano-based tune called "Tireless Dancer," stung and embarrassed Dave deeply, but he assured himself that the cause for the song's lackluster sales was simply a disconnect in the minds of fans between the Upper Hand name and his distinctive vocal and songwriting style. He wouldn't say it out loud, but he privately compared himself to George Harrison in the latter days of the Beatles, creatively stymied by Lennon and McCartney and just waiting to explode musically and commercially on his own, as Harrison so famously did with his landmark album *All Things Must Pass*.

But it didn't happen.

Dave's first solo album, rather self-indulgently titled *Out from the Shadows*, was released with considerable fanfare less than a year after the dissolution of the Upper Hand. Reflecting the style and keyboard-oriented arrangements of his Upper Hand songs, it sold a disappointing 300,000 copies, disappearing from the charts within six weeks. Neither of the two singles released from the album rose above number thirty on the CD singles charts. The twenty-five-city concert tour, featuring a backing band of high caliber studio musicians (but no former Upper Hand bandmates), barely broke even.

Alarmed at the less than triumphant start of his solo career, Dave allowed himself to be persuaded to adopt a harder, bluesy, guitar-based sound—that is, a more "Upper Hand-like" style—for his next album, which he recorded and released in 1993. It sank almost without a trace, and Dave Rowinski's dreams of solo stardom were finished. He managed to release one more album on a small independent label in 1999, but it fared even worse than the second one.

In contrast to his flagging professional career, Dave's personal life received a spectacular boost in 1991. Still seen as an important rock and roll musician with a promising solo career ahead of him, Dave was frequently invited to exclusive parties thrown by actors, sports stars, and other musicians. It was at one of these gatherings, on the Upper East Side in New York, that Dave met Sharon Van Horn, a breathtaking twenty-eight-year-old model who had graced the pages of virtually every fashion magazine and catalog imaginable, plus the *Sports Illustrated* swimsuit issue. Tall, blonde, and (almost) as intelligent as she was gorgeous, Sharon captivated Dave from the moment he was introduced to her. Luckily for Dave, he was at that time quite coolly confident about who he was and who he was about to become in the celebrity hierarchy, and managed to amuse and dazzle Sharon in return. They left the party together that night, becoming an inseparable couple from that day forward.

Dave and Sharon married in 1992. It was widely anticipated in celebrity circles that Sharon would bolt for greener pastures when Dave's solo recording career disintegrated the next year, but the gossips thoroughly misjudged this relationship. Theirs was a real marriage, not a celebrity pairing with a built-in expiration date.

Sharon delivered a baby boy, Justin, in July of 1996. The new parents' joy at the arrival of their son was soon clouded by the distressing news that Justin had cystic fibrosis, a chronic, incurable genetic disease of the lungs and digestive tract. Sharon responded to this blow with a fierce determination to give Justin a normal life, becoming an expert administrator of his challenging medicinal, dietary, and oxygen therapy requirements and exploiting her still considerable celebrity to advocate tirelessly for research on the disease while the equally supportive Dave struggled to resurrect his career in music. Dave's limited success in landing studio work or small venue gigs over the eight years since Justin's birth, combined with the loss of any potential for Sharon to resume her once lucrative career and the crushing expenses associated with Justin's care, meant that the impressive fortunes each of them had amassed prior to Justin's birth were being steadily eaten away. The very real possibility that Justin would need a lung transplant sometime during his childhood loomed as both an emotional and financial terror to Dave and Sharon.

It was Steve who broke the silence. "You know, it's funny," he said.

"What's funny?"

"For God knows how many years now, I haven't spent even two seconds thinking about the band reforming. I guess I'd just assumed that it was never going to happen. But your little tirade just now got my mind spinning."

"Oh yeah? What exactly are you thinking?"

Steve placed his beer bottle on the coffee table and turned to face Dave. "I'm thinking that fourteen years is enough of this horse shit. It's time for you and me to go put Humpty Dumpty back together again."

CHAPTER 2

Dave stared at Steve, absorbing what his friend had just said. "I'd ask if you were kidding, but I'm pretty sure looking at you that you're not," said Dave.

"Damn right, I'm not. You should have started throwing stuff at my TV years ago to wake me up about this. We've just sorta convinced ourselves that Mark will never speak to Jeff again. Well, I say it's high time we stopped accepting that. Neither one of them is going to make the first move. Mark is too stubborn, and Jeff has just given up, so we have to figure out a way to make it happen."

By now Dave was up out of the sofa, pacing around the room, shocked at Steve's unexpected determination to put back together something that everyone thought was shattered forever. "Steve, I'd do anything to get the Upper Hand back together. Nobody, and I mean *nobody*, wants that more than me. Hell, nobody *needs* it more than me. You know what's happening with Justin and the cost of all these medicines and oxygen machines and stuff. But do you really think it's possible?"

"Hey, we've been talking about it for all of about two minutes here. It's going to be tricky, for sure, and we have to put some serious thought into how to go about it. Let's start with the low hanging fruit first. We have to get A.J. on board before we can even think about working on Mark and Jeff."

"Low hanging fruit, eh?" Dave laughed. "Do you realize that rejoining the Upper Hand would probably represent a pay cut for A.J.?"

Steve smiled. "Yeah, but he's such a sweetheart that he'll do it anyway. Goddamn, though, he is doing great, isn't he? Couldn't have happened to a better guy."

Anyone who knew Anthony James (A.J.) Ramello would agree on two things: one, that he was the finest electric bass guitarist American rock and roll had ever produced, and two, that there was no nicer human being on the face of the earth. A musician with

A.J.'s phenomenal professional success and reputation could be forgiven for adopting a bit of a "rock star" attitude, but he remained one of the most unassuming and affable people in the business.

The ugly dissolution of the Upper Hand in 1990 dealt a heavy blow to A.J. on a personal level, and the damaged relationships among his friends and former bandmates stemming from that breakup upset him deeply. But professionally, A.J. Ramello became the hottest, busiest bass player in North America the day it was announced to the world that the Upper Hand was no more. His biggest challenge, especially during the initial post-Upper Hand years, was learning to say "no." He allowed himself to be booked into an exhausting, virtually non-stop whirlwind of geographically dispersed studio sessions and tour engagements, until finally his wife Cathy and their three children insisted that he cut back significantly on his commitments. In fact, the family developed its own "gig rating system" in 1996, where no studio or touring job would be accepted by A.J. until it had been scrutinized by all five family members (including then ten-year-old Stephanie, A.J. and Cathy's youngest child) on the basis of quality of artist, level of inconvenience to the family, and fee. An elaborate point system was established, and if a request for A.J.'s services didn't earn enough points from the five family members, the request was turned down. Not once since the system was set up did A.J. ever consider defying its results. With a devoted wife, three outstanding children, and, thanks to the "system," some much needed balance in his life, A.J. Ramello was a contented man.

If Steve Holmes was the striking, square-jawed poster boy of the Upper Hand, A.J. Ramello occupied the other end of the photogenic spectrum in the band. Short, chubby, with a prominent nose and otherwise nondescript features, A.J. was also cursed with frizzy, unmanageable hair and a receding hairline that could absolutely not be made to look even remotely stylish in the long hair days of the 1970s and '80s. He finally surrendered and began shaving his head in 1981, adding a goatee a year later.

Dave suddenly began chuckling loudly.

"What's so funny?" Steve inquired.

"You sound pretty sure that A.J. would happily jump back into the band, but guess what? It's not totally his call!"

"Oh, shit, that's right—the family point system! He must be the only world-class musician on the planet who lets his kids decide where he can play!"

"I wonder if that crazy system is still in operation. I mean, the two boys are in their twenties, and even Stephanie must be eighteen by now."

"Yeah, we won't be able to bribe them with lollipops, will we? Hey, maybe a couple of bags of pot!"

Dave, caught in mid-sip of his beer, let out an uncontrollable snort that sent beer flying from his nose and mouth onto the carpet. "Cathy would rip our lungs out!" He howled with laughter as he tried to mop up the wayward beer with his hand.

Dave and Steve immediately agreed that their conversation with A.J. had to take place in person, rather than by phone. Luckily, A.J. was home for the next couple of weeks. So, three days after Steve and A.J. exchanged e-mails to set up a get-together, Dave and Steve headed out of New York in Steve's silver Mercedes CLK500 convertible towards A.J and Cathy's home in Montclair, New Jersey.

Steve pulled his car into the long, azalea-bordered driveway and proceeded past the expansive, beautifully landscaped front yard to the turnaround area by the three-car garage. Steve and Dave hopped out of the car and walked up the brick walkway to the front door of A.J.'s spectacular stone mansion. Before either of them could ring the doorbell, the front door opened and they were greeted with a squeal of delight and hugs from A.J.'s wife, Cathy. While both Steve and Dave had been in regular contact with A.J. via phone and e-mail, they had not seen A.J. or Cathy in nearly a year.

A.J. and Cathy Ramello, both natives of Parsippany, New Jersey, began dating during their sophomore year in high school. It was widely assumed, and never refuted by A.J or Cathy, that neither of them had ever been in a romantic relationship with another person, either before or after their first date in 1969. They graduated from high school in 1971 and were married in 1976, just as the Upper Hand was becoming established as a seriously successful rock band. Their first son, Anthony Jr., was born in 1980, followed by Eric in 1982 and Stephanie in 1986.

Cathy shared A.J.'s remarkable affability and down-to-earth likeability as well as his utterly unremarkable physical appearance. Short, plain-featured, and possessed of a rather matronly figure even when she was in her twenties, she and A.J were truly two peas in a pod—two extraordinarily happy peas in a pod with eyes for no one besides each other. It surprised no one that Anthony Jr., Eric, and Stephanie were all engaging, well-adjusted, and popular kids, but there was some mild shock among A.J. and Cathy's friends (never expressed to the couple, of course) when all three of the children turned out to be highly physically attractive. While neither Dave, with his gorgeous, dynamic wife, nor Steve, still happily adhering to his lifelong "flavor of the month" dating lifestyle, would have wanted to trade places with A.J., they both greatly admired the relationship and life A.J. and Cathy had built together.

As Steve and Dave stepped into the foyer, A.J. appeared at the top of the winding oak staircase leading to the second floor of the house. "Hot damn, Cathy," he bellowed as he charged down the stairs. "I told you if you left that front door unlocked that all kinds of unsavory characters would come creepin' in!"

He hopped onto the polished oak bannister and slid down the last six feet of the staircase on his butt, leaping off at the bottom directly into a bear hug with Dave, followed by an equally exuberant embrace with Steve. "What a treat it is to see you guys! Wow, how long has it been?"

After two or three minutes of small talk and progress reports on the Ramello kids and Dave's son, Cathy knew the time had come for her to leave the boys alone because it was clearly time for the obligatory trip to the game room. A.J. had turned one of the expansive first floor rooms of the house into a truly awesome man cave, featuring a twelve-foot billiard table, a foosball table, two 1970s era pinball machines, a Space Invaders machine, and a dartboard. The room had a full bar including two beers on tap, and was set up with a sixty-inch wall-mounted TV and an eight-speaker sound system. In addition to six barstools lined up along the bar, there were ten chairs arranged throughout the room, every one of them a leather revolving recliner.

Although there was a serious agenda behind Dave and Steve's visit, they immediately turned into twelve-year-old boys, just as they always did when it was time for a visit to the game room. Eagerly following A.J. down the hallway toward the irresistible joys that awaited them, they passed by a collage of framed photographs of A.J., Cathy, and their three children on the hallway wall. Dave, gesturing toward the photos as he walked past them, remarked, "So, tell me, A.J., does it ever get boring living the most amazingly perfect life on planet Earth?"

There was absolutely no jealousy or acrimony in Dave's voice, just admiration, and A.J. laughed.

"Nope, no boredom whatsoever. Just a shitload of gratitude. I know, I know, things are going unbelievably well. I've settled into a pretty good routine that keeps things humming along. I don't see much reason to dick around with it."

Dave and Steve exchanged a quick glance. They were about to ask A.J. to dramatically "dick around" with his routine. Was he simply too content with his life as America's most in-demand freelance bass guitarist to jump back into the Upper Hand circus, let alone to put in the effort to piece the band back together?

As always, Dave and Steve were overwhelmed when they stepped from the hallway into the game room. A.J. drew himself a Sierra Nevada Pale Ale draft and let his friends wander around the room and fiddle with the toys. Eventually, A.J. and Steve settled in for a game of eight ball, and Dave contented himself with one of the pinball machines, each man refilling his beer glass as needed.

After a solid hour of game playing, beer drinking, and general bullshitting, it was Steve who finally pulled his head out of the game room-induced cloud and reminded himself of the real reason for the visit. He gave Dave a little poke in the side with his elbow and nodded his head toward A.J. who was lining up a shot on the billiard table. The two of them stepped closer to the table and waited for A.J. to finish his turn.

"A.J.," Steve began haltingly. "It's not like we, you know, Dave and me, need any excuse or incentive to, you know, uh, come here to see you. It's always a blast, and we don't get to see you often enough. But, uh, we did have sort of an extra reason to stop by today, and we'd kinda like to talk to you about it now."

A.J. furrowed his brow at Steve's obvious nervousness. "Is everything OK with you guys?" he asked, shifting his glance back and forth between his two friends.

"Yeah, yeah, sure, everything's cool, everything's fine. It's just that, well, Dave and I were thinking that, well..."

Dave couldn't take Steve's stammering and beating around the bush any longer. He raised his hand in Steve's direction to cut him off. "A.J., something near and dear to all of us, something we worked very hard at building into something great, has been lying broken for fourteen years, and Steve and I would like to know if you'd be willing to work with us to put it back together again."

A.J. laid his pool cue on the table, taking in what Dave had just said. He said nothing for a few seconds and then whispered, almost inaudibly, "Wow."

Wow? A.J.'s one syllable utterance provided no clue whatsoever to Dave and Steve what was going through his mind. They waited silently for a more telling response.

A.J. walked slowly along the side of the billiard table, distractedly sweeping the balls with his arm into the pockets. He turned to face Dave. His voice was subdued. "Remember before when you said my life was perfect, and I pretty much agreed? Well, there is one thing in my life that's extremely unperfect. Non-perfect? Imperfect? Ah, fuck, who cares? *Not* perfect, and that's the fact that two people I love and respect, two people who had loved and respected each other since they were still crapping their diapers, two people who played an enormous, fantastic role in my life, can't be in the same room together. I guess I just figured that if they haven't worked things out by now, they never will. I don't know what you guys have in mind, but if you've got a plan for getting the band back together, which means getting Mark and Jeff back together, I want to hear it."

CHAPTER 3

To fans of the Upper Hand, and to the rock and entertainment media that covered the band, Jeff Britton's abandonment of the group in 1990, and their breakup shortly thereafter, was a shock. Even the band members, left in the lurch, knowing what they did about Jeff's deteriorating condition, erratic behavior, and declining musical skills over the prior year, never allowed themselves to entertain the possibility that Jeff's problems would lead to the end of the band. In reality, though, conditions leading to Jeff's stunning departure, which occurred not only in the middle of a sold-out concert tour but right onstage during a concert, had been building for months.

By the jaw-dropping standards set by countless highly successful rock and roll bands of the 1970s and 1980s, the Upper Hand's record of alcohol and drug abuse was, prior to 1988, rather tame. Mark Donahue could put away prodigious quantities of vodka on a "good" night, and Dave Rowinski was similarly liberal with his consumption of Jack Daniels during the band's heyday. Both Mark and Dave experienced issues with cocaine on and off during the late '70s and early '80s, but at no time did their drinking or drug habits seriously compromise their abilities to function in the band.

Steve Holmes' top priority throughout his tenure in the Upper Hand, after any concert, in any city, was to bed the best looking female fan on whom he could work his formidable charm. He had no interest in hindering his sexual performance with drugs or excessive drinking, and would usually top out at two or three beers a night when on tour. A.J. Ramello was generally content to drink whatever was being offered on a given night, knocking back a few at post-concert parties to be sociable and feel like part of the gathering more than anything. For A.J., five beers and a couple of hits off a joint qualified as a wild night.

Jeff Britton was a beer man, a highly accomplished beer man. It was not at all uncommon for Jeff to polish off two six packs after a show and then pop out of bed the next day as if he'd been drinking herbal tea all night. Jeff and beer had what he liked to call a "beautiful relationship." He had no taste for other alcoholic beverages, and when it came to drugs, even pot let alone any of the higher octane substances constantly circulating among the band's inner circle, Jeff had no interest whatsoever.

Until 1988. Until Denise Blake.

Media accounts of Jeff Britton's heroin-fueled meltdown and subsequent disappearance from public life invariably referred to Denise Blake, if not always by name, as the "groupie" who turned Jeff onto heroin and was thus the catalyst behind the demise of the Upper Hand. While Denise's role in Jeff's transformation from a carefree, beer-swigging rock 'n' roller to a catastrophically strung out drug addict was undeniable, she was certainly no one-night-stand rock star lay, as the "groupie" label would imply. Rather, Denise Blake could be more accurately described as a serial rock and roll girlfriend, having exploited her dazzling physical assets and party girl persona to maneuver her way up from the lowest to the loftiest castes of the rock and roll road show world.

Denise was born in 1960 to alcoholic parents Stan and Sue Blake, in a small town in central Pennsylvania. Stan divorced Sue and abandoned the family when Denise was five. What followed over the next thirteen years for Denise was a dizzying parade of Sue's boyfriends and husbands, one more abusive than the next to both mother and daughter. Looking back as an adult on the time between the departure of her father and her escape from rural Pennsylvania at age eighteen, Denise could not definitively say how many of the uniformly drunken, lecherous men who shared Sue's house during those years had actually been married to her. Denise's best guess was three.

Denise, an indifferent student who never participated in any sports or other school-related extracurricular activities, was regarded by her high school administrators and most of her teachers as a willful, rebellious spitfire probably headed for nothing but trouble. These faculty and staff, along with virtually every female member of Denise's high school class, were thus shocked and appalled when

Denise was voted "Most Popular Girl" in her senior year. To the boys in her class who drove the results of that ballot, the choice of the pretty, voluptuous, and highly accommodating green-eyed brunette was no mystery at all.

Denise's eighteenth birthday and her high school graduation took place almost simultaneously in June of 1978. She had become bored with the queue of male high school classmates vying for her affections and hooked up in April with Ted, a twenty-year-old singer from a local bar band. Less than two weeks after Denise's graduation, Ted's band was recruited as opening act for a four-band bus tour of clubs and outdoor venues covering suburban towns in Ohio, Indiana, and Kentucky. Denise tagged along, never to set foot in her hometown again.

The tour lasted three months. During that time, Denise debuted the rock musician dating protocol she would use for the next two decades, "upgrading" twice by first dispatching her warm-up act singer boyfriend in favor of Spike, the second-billed band's bass player, and then trading Spike in for the headlining band's front man, Jake. She stayed with Jake for several months, joining him in his hometown of Akron when the tour was over, waitressing when she needed cash. But when Jake's band was invited to participate as a supporting act for a significantly more ambitious tour of the Midwest featuring far more established bands, his relationship with Denise was doomed. She worked her way right up through the tour hierarchy again, setting the stage for what would become a repeating pattern of tempestuous, six to twelve month relationships with ever more illustrious rock stars.

By the time Denise Blake and Jeff Britton sank their hooks into each other, meeting at an Upper Hand after-show party in St. Louis in August 1988, Denise was one of the rock world's most notorious squeezes. She gained frequent mentions in gossip and entertainment periodicals when seen with a new rock star love interest, managed to have photos of herself included in the sleeve artwork of several major artists' album releases, and even garnered a backing vocal and tambourine credit on a song from one big name musician boyfriend's album. She had also, by 1988, acquired a serious heroin habit.

No one, including Jeff Britton himself, could recall exactly when he allowed Denise to convince him to try heroin for the first time, but by the end of 1988 it was clear to everyone in and around the band that Jeff was under the influence of something other than barley malt and hops. Attempts by A.J. and Steve to offer friendly, concerned advice, sarcastic cracks from Dave, and an unending stream of lectures, pleas, and threats from his lifelong best friend Mark all failed to stop Jeff's slide into full blown heroin addiction.

Jeff and Denise withdrew deeper and deeper into their own drug-dominated world as the months of 1989 went by, particularly during a long-planned post-tour band hiatus that ran from May through July. The Upper Hand was scheduled to end their break by meeting throughout August to run through new material in preparation for the studio time they booked starting in September to record their next album.

The first rehearsal was set for 2:00 on a Monday afternoon in early August, at Mark's house in Caldwell, New Jersey. When Jeff finally showed up at 3:15, the rest of the band barely contained gasps of astonishment at his frighteningly sickly appearance. His complexion was a deathly gray. His normally well-tended long brown hair was a greasy, unkempt mess. His already lean frame looked at least fifteen pounds lighter than normal. There was little doubt how Jeff had spent his three months away from the band. Compounding the band's dismay, Jeff proved to be woefully unprepared for the session. Since a typical Upper Hand album would include five or six songs written by Jeff, he would always come to initial meetings like this one armed with at least seven or eight solid song ideas to present for band feedback. This time he brought just two completed songs that, by his past standards, would be considered mediocre at best. He also played three partial ideas for tunes that, at least in their current stage of development, were of no use to the band and seemed to Jeff's bandmates to be uniformly unpromising as candidates for further attention.

Dave, Steve, and A.J. tried to be diplomatic in their comments to Jeff on his weak offering of song ideas, but Mark was too livid to be subtle and ripped into Jeff as soon as he finished playing through his compositions. "What the fuck do you call this?" he bellowed, as the others looked on uncomfortably. "You look like a corpse, you've been as useless as tits on a nun all afternoon, and now you bring these piece-of-shit songs to us? What the hell is going on with you?"

Jeff made no real effort to defend himself. "Sorry, man, it's been a rough couple of months," he mumbled. "I'll clean these tunes up and have them ready to roll in a few days. I promise."

"You better clean yourself up, Jeff, before you start worrying about fixing your piss-poor songs. You gotta stop letting that whore Denise run you into the ground. Ditch her before you wind up dead!"

"She's not a whore, man. Maybe we've gone a little off the deep end lately, but we're working on it, and everything's gonna be cool. Don't worry."

Mark was tempted to continue laying into Jeff to try to convince him to send Denise packing but decided to let it drop for the time being and give Jeff some time to make good on his promise to straighten himself out.

Being back working with the band did help Jeff for a while. Over the course of the August rehearsals, at least some semblance of his old self appeared. Still, the group ended the four weeks of rehearsals with only two Jeff Britton-penned songs for the upcoming album, and in truth, these songs required so much tweaking and reworking from Mark and Dave that they should have received co-writing credits for them. Dave gratefully accepted the invitation from the rest of the band to help fill the gap by contributing four songs instead of his usual two. Six songs by Mark were chosen for the album.

In September of 1989 the band, with their girlfriends and wives, headed to Total Immersion for the recording of the new album. Total Immersion was a combination state-of-the-art recording studio and private hotel converted from a large old boarding house in rural Newton, New Jersey. It was not possible to simply purchase time at the Total Immersion studio; the owner only rented out the entire building. As its name implied, Total Immersion was created for recording artists who truly wished to focus on the project at hand,

and live "twenty-four/seven" within a flight of stairs of the top-notch recording facilities housed in the basement. When Total Immersion first opened for business in 1974, the living accommodations were quite Spartan, but as its popularity with East Coast recording artists grew, several improvements were made to the living quarters to make them attractive to major acts. By 1989, the two upper floors consisted of twelve well-appointed bedroom/bathroom/living room suites.

The Upper Hand had recorded their last five albums at Total Immersion. There was no question of going to a different studio for the new album. The band had had terrific success recording there; in addition, Mark, Dave, A.J. and Steve thought that the communal environment would help them keep an eye on Jeff and prevent further acceleration of his heroin use.

They were wrong.

Any improvement in Jeff's condition achieved in August quickly evaporated during the recording of the album in September and October. The Upper Hand had always been a thoroughly democratic band, with suggestions on arrangements, tempos, and effects—and sometimes even lyric and chord changes—expected and welcomed from all five members. As the recording sessions for the new album progressed, Jeff's input on creative discussions steadily declined and effectively ceased by the fourth week of the project. His guitar playing was uncharacteristically sloppy, to the point that Mark would frequently berate him in front of the rest of the band, chase him out of the studio, and record the guitar part that was intended for Jeff. There were also several instances where Mark would head back to the studio after a session with longtime producer Sonny McCrea or sound engineer Billy Cole and replace a substandard guitar track by Jeff with one of his own. Jeff's drug use also took its toll on his singing voice. Mark and Dave, after a number of private conversations regarding the unsatisfactory vocal tracks being performed by Jeff, developed and sang harmony vocal parts over most of Jeff's lead vocal lines, not because the songs really called for these harmonies, but more to mask the weakness of Jeff's voice.

The Upper Hand was booked for an extensive, highly anticipated concert tour in support of the new album (which was rather ironically titled *Better Than Ever,* after one of Mark's songs on the album) beginning shortly after the album's release in February of 1990. The rest of the band approached the first rehearsal for the tour in a state of deep trepidation, fearing on the basis of Jeff's pathetic performance during the recording of the album that this tour stood a frightening chance of turning into a disaster. Jeff, however, who had always found performing live to be the most exciting and rewarding part of being in the band, spoke enthusiastically about the upcoming tour and insisted repeatedly to the others that he was ready to deliver top-notch performances at these important concerts. His bandmates, clinging to any reason for optimism they could find, allowed themselves to be convinced that Jeff could pull it off. Still, Mark and Dave remained concerned enough that they worked out a series of signals between them to quickly cover for Jeff vocally or instrumentally if he faltered during a live performance. They also established a number of subtle cues with their tour sound people, to alert them if there was a need to lower the volume on Jeff's microphone or guitar amp in the event that they needed to drown him out with their own emergency fill-ins. A.J. and Steve knew of these contingencies and approved of them. If Jeff ever figured out what was going on, he never acknowledged or protested it.

The 1990 Upper Hand *Better Than Ever* tour was scheduled to stop in thirty-two cities across the United States over a four-month period. The first dozen shows, to the great relief of Jeff's worried bandmates, went well. The sold-out arena crowds scarcely noticed the rough edges in Jeff's singing and playing and even newspaper and magazine critics made only passing references to his miscues. But soon the party atmosphere surrounding the tour and the post-concert gatherings proved to be too much for Jeff and Denise, and their drug use began to spiral out of control. The pre-arranged signals worked out by Mark, Dave, and the sound crew were now being put into use at least two or three times per show, and their audiences as well as the rock press started to take real notice of Jeff's erratic performances. No amount of effort by Mark, Dave, A.J., and Steve to keep an eye on Jeff between shows or to get through to him regarding the damage he was doing to himself and the band, did any good.

The dam burst on April 23, 1990, at the second of two sold-out shows at the Omni Coliseum in Atlanta. Jeff's playing and singing were worse than ever, and Mark and Dave spent much of their energies desperately trying to anticipate Jeff's flubs and compensate for them with their own vocals or instrumental fills. The crowd couldn't help but notice that Jeff wasn't giving them their money's worth, and a vague audience murmur soon morphed into scattered catcalls and then into widespread boos when Jeff totally botched a guitar solo from one of the band's best-known hits. The band soldiered on for two more songs, and then, as the crowd once again erupted in protest at another horrendously misplayed guitar lead from Jeff, he suddenly stopped playing, stared blankly at the audience as Mark frantically stepped in to cover the part, and then slowly removed his guitar from around his neck, laid it down on the stage floor, and shuffled unsteadily offstage. The crowd went silent as Jeff's utterly shocked bandmates did their best to finish the song.

With Jeff now AWOL, there were still six songs, plus an encore, to be played. Dave made a hasty "he's been under the weather" excuse for Jeff to placate the crowd, but an enraged Mark, in no mood to sugarcoat Jeff's stunning walk-off, kicked Jeff's abandoned Stratocaster off the stage into the front row of the audience. When the lucky fan who suddenly found the guitar in his lap yelled up to Mark asking if he wanted it back, Mark snarled, into his microphone so the entire crowd could hear, "Keep it. The shithead who used to own it doesn't know what the fuck to do with it anymore anyway." The remaining four band members onstage, falling back on the contingency plans they had worked out weeks earlier, somehow managed to get through the rest of the show and recapture at least some of the audience spark. When they left the stage after the encore, the four of them rushed to the dressing room, led by a blindly furious Mark, to confront Jeff.

But Jeff was nowhere to be found. And no one in the band would have any idea where he was for the next four months.

CHAPTER 4

Simultaneous, almost audible sighs of relief came from Dave and Steve as they absorbed the meaning of A.J.'s reply to them in the game room. He was onboard with their as yet vague scheme to reunite the Upper Hand. The really difficult step—orchestrating a reconciliation between Mark and Jeff—still loomed, but having A.J. in their corner generated a wave of optimism in both of them.

"So," A.J. said to his two happy friends, "tell me what you guys have been plotting to get our wonderful band back together."

Dave and Steve glanced at each other, grimaced, and shrugged their shoulders. Dave could see that Steve wasn't about to offer any useful reply, so he dove in. "Well, we haven't really worked out all of the details yet."

"Tell me what you've got so far, and we can take it from there."

"OK. Well, actually, as far as we got was deciding to come here to talk to you."

A.J. howled with laughter, grabbed a nearby foam ball from a Nerf basketball set, and bounced it off Dave's head. "You lame-asses! I assumed you guys came here with it all figured out!"

Steve chimed in, "Aw, c'mon, A.J., don't bust our chops! We knew it was pointless to even try this at all if you weren't interested, so we had to make sure you thought it was worth chasing before we put a whole lot of effort into it."

"I believe Steve's phrase was 'picking the low hanging fruit first,'" offered Dave.

A.J. laughed again. "I gotchyer low hangin' fruit *right heah*," he spouted in his best Brooklyn accent, grabbing his crotch. Dave picked up the Nerf ball and fired it back at A.J.'s midsection.

Steve tried to steer the conversation back on topic. "Besides, you're a lot smarter than Dave and me, so we knew it made no sense to plan this without you."

"Oh brother, it's getting thick in here now! Flattery will get you nowhere, Steve!" A.J. paused, and his tone suddenly turned serious. "Look, guys, I get it, and I'm with you one hundred percent. Let's put our heads together and make this happen. Let's talk about Mark first. When's the last time you saw him or spoke to him?"

"Dave and I both saw him back in the winter, maybe January. I haven't spoken to him since. Have you, Dave?"

"Nope."

"How about you, A.J.?"

"I haven't seen him for at least six months, but I talked to him on the phone a couple of times over the past few months. Now, what are your impressions of how he's doing?"

"Seems like he's doing pretty good," replied Steve. "His last album sold well, and I think the tour he did last year was successful."

"That's not what I mean. Do you think he's a happy guy?"

"I don't know. I guess so. He seems all right when I see him."

"That's not what I see. I don't think Mark gives a shit about his solo career, as nice as it's been. He's just going through the motions. The Upper Hand, and the key roles he and Jeff played in it, were everything to him, and he's still so bitter about how it came crashing down that he can't even talk about it. Did you ever notice? Not only won't he mention Jeff's name in conversation, you can't even get him to reminisce about the great times we had in the band. He just changes the subject. I'm telling you Mark, to this day, is not over what happened. He misses the band, and I'm certain that he really misses his friendship with Jeff, although he's too full of lingering anger to recognize it."

A.J. paused and took a healthy swig from his beer. "And that's the key to getting Mark onboard here. It's not about how great it would be to get the band back together, and it's not about doing poor Jeff a favor by letting him off the hook. It's about making Mark realize that forgiving Jeff and letting him back into his life will make *him—Mark—*way happier than he is now."

"See?" Steve exclaimed. "I told you A.J. was smarter than us! I would have gone with the 'how great it would be' angle or maybe even the 'forgive poor Jeff' angle."

"Yeah, yeah, A.J.'s a fucking genius. I know," Dave replied with a chuckle, firing the Nerf ball at him again. "But I think you're right. Mark doesn't have the same spark he used to. We have to pound it into his stubborn head that he needs Jeff to get that spark back."

A.J. and Steve nodded in agreement.

"There's something else I think," said A.J.

"What's that?"

"We're all assholes for not having this discussion ten years ago."

Dave didn't care to ponder how different his life might be if the three of them had indeed made the effort to get Mark and Jeff to reconcile a decade earlier, so he quickly changed the focus of the conversation. "I think we should talk a bit about the other side of this coin, Jeff. Where do you think his head is at regarding Mark and the band?"

"Man, I just about want to cry every time I speak with him," said Steve. "He's still working in his brother's auto repair shop out there in Butt Fuck, West Virginia, pretty much doing nothing. He stopped trying to contact Mark probably eight or nine years ago now, maybe longer. Whenever I'm on the phone with him, he always, at the end of the conversation, asks real casually like he's just idly curious, how Mark is doing. It's so painfully obvious that he's hoping that I'll offer up some sort of indication that Mark's thinking about calling him. Ugh, I can't stand it. I don't speak with him as often as I should because it's just so depressing."

"Same here. They're not the most fun phone conversations I have," said Dave.

"Has anyone seen Jeff recently?" asked A.J.

"Nah, it's been years. It's not easy to get to that God-forsaken place," replied Dave.

"Me neither."

Steve added, "Same with me. Last time I was there, the closest hotel room I could find was more than twenty miles from that shitty little house he lives in."

"All right," said Dave. "Does anyone think that Jeff *wouldn't* immediately and gratefully accept any gesture from Mark offering to put an end to this crap?"

"Are you kidding me?" said A.J. with a small laugh. "He'd do backflips!"

Steve added, "Remember before when A.J. said that Mark is still too mad to realize how unhappy he is without Jeff? Well, Jeff knows exactly how miserable he is without Mark. He's dreaming of the day when they're friends again."

"So, our mission is clear. Not easy, but clear! We have to put the big push on Mark to make him *want* to reconcile with Jeff."

"Piece of cake," said A.J., rolling his eyes and grimacing.

"A.J., I have a question," said Steve with a grin. "Suppose we're wildly successful here, and Mark and Jeff come marching out together arm in arm, singing 'Kumbaya' and screaming for a reunion of the band. Do we have to worry about Cathy and the kids vetoing your return to the group with that gig rating system of theirs?"

"Hah! No worries. When it comes to the Upper Hand, there's only one vote, and that's mine!"

***

When Mark stormed into the dressing room of the Omni Coliseum following the band's short-handed encore, trailed closely by his frantic bandmates, there was little doubt in the minds of the three of them that they were going to have to intervene immediately to prevent Mark from physically assaulting Jeff. But what they found was not their drug-ravaged guitarist/vocalist, but a hastily scribbled note written on the side of a Burger King bag: "SORRY."

Mark snatched the bag off the table, held it up briefly for the rest of the band to read, barked, "What the fuck is this?" then crumpled it up, and threw it to the ground. "Where the hell is he?" he yelled at no one in particular, and when a young female dressing room attendant had the bad fortune to wander into the room at that moment, Mark screamed at her, "Where did that son of a bitch Jeff head off to?"

The attendant, too startled to reply, took a couple of steps back toward the entryway to the dressing room.

A.J. quickly stepped between Mark and the frightened young woman. "Mark! Calm down." He beckoned to the attendant to come back into the dressing room and gently spoke to her. "The other member of our band, Jeff, came back here about a half hour ago. Did you see him? Can you tell us where he went?"

"I saw him. He didn't look too good. He was—"

Mark broke in, snarling, "He's gonna look a whole lot worse when I—"

"*Mark!!* Put a sock in it, would you?" admonished A.J. He turned back to the attendant. "You were saying?"

"He was running around the room, stuffing his things into a gym bag. He kept saying to himself, 'I'm fucked. I'm so fucked up. I'm so fucked up.' I think he was crying. Then he ran out with the gym bag. He never spoke to me at all."

"He's probably back at the hotel. Let's get over there now," said A.J. "And, Mark, listen to me. I know you're pissed; we're all pissed. But just beating the shit out of Jeff isn't going to help anything, so when we find him, just control yourself, OK?" Mark nodded slightly in reluctant agreement.

When they arrived at the door to Jeff's hotel room, Steve knocked gently, with A.J. and Dave positioned behind him but firmly in front of Mark, ready to pull him back if he lost his temper and tried to attack Jeff.

The door opened, but it was Jeff's girlfriend Denise, not Jeff, standing in the doorway. A.J. and Dave, fully aware of Mark's absolute hatred of Denise, each instinctively grabbed onto one of Mark's arms and shot him a sharp glance to prevent either a verbal or physical confrontation.

"Where the hell is Jeff?" Denise demanded.

"Denise, we came here to ask you the same question," Steve replied calmly.

"Well, when I came back to the room about ten minutes ago, all of his clothes, his suitcase, everything, was gone. What's going on here? Wasn't he playing with you at the Coliseum?"

"So you weren't there to watch him?" exclaimed Mark. "What kind of girlfriend are you?"

"Fuck off, Mark. I saw the show last night, all right? That's probably why you can't keep a wife or girlfriend; you make them go to every goddamn concert you have."

Mark lunged toward Denise but was held back by A.J. and Dave.

"The both of you, just shut up, OK?" Steve admonished. "Denise, Jeff walked offstage right in the middle of the show, and we haven't seen him since. So you don't have any idea where he is?"

"I have no clue. I can't believe this. Look around this room. All of his stuff is gone. He just vanished and left me here!"

A.J. and Dave, who hadn't let go of Mark's arms yet, could feel the angry tension in him suddenly dissipate, replaced by a resigned slouch of his entire body. The icy fury in his eyes gave way to a defeated, empty downward stare. He shook his arms gently, and his two friends released their grip. He began to speak, quietly, in almost a monotone. "That's it. He's gone, and I don't give a rat's ass where he went. We have eleven more shows to do to fulfill our contract for this tour, and then this band is history. I'll call Eddie Sanchelli tomorrow to get him to fill in on guitar for the rest of the tour. Dave, you and I can meet tomorrow to figure out how to split up Jeff's lead vocals."

Dave broke in. "Isn't this a bit hasty? Shouldn't we try to find—"

"*No!* He's done, and when this tour is over I'm done. There's no Upper Hand without all five of us, and Jeff just flushed it all down the toilet." He reached into his back pocket, grabbed his wallet, and pulled out a few bills. He stepped over to Denise, shoved the money into her hand, and growled, "Here's two hundred dollars. Jeff's out of here, so you're out of here. Buy yourself a ticket to wherever the fuck you want to go, but don't let me see your face anywhere near this tour for these last eleven shows."

Denise, too stunned to respond, stepped back into the hotel room and slammed the door.

The remainder of the concert tour consisted of a series of emergency rehearsals with three different replacement guitarists, significant ticket returns, no-shows, and audience catcalls as word spread through the media that Jeff had walked off the stage in Atlanta and abandoned the tour. An overwhelming sense of gloom quickly enveloped the band and crew. Eddie Sanchelli, a longtime friend who played Jeff's guitar parts at four concert dates before departing to fulfill commitments to his own band, was quoted a few weeks later as saying the mood around the Upper Hand during those days was "like being at a five-year-old's funeral."

Dave, A.J., and Steve made numerous phone calls from the road in the first few days after Jeff's disappearance, trying to track him down, succeeding only in confirming through a call to Jeff's sister, that Jeff was safe. Mark, all but unapproachable through the waning days of the tour, made no effort to find out where Jeff was holed up. When the dispirited foursome limped home following the final show of the tour, no one felt like disputing Mark's declaration that the Upper Hand was no more.

CHAPTER 5

By the time Jeff reached the backstage dressing room, he wasn't certain, in his heroin-induced fog, if what he thought had just happened on the stage of the Omni Coliseum had actually occurred, or if it was some sort of weird dream. A splash of water on his face from the nearby bathroom sink to clear his head was just enough for him to recognize that his mid-song walk-off was quite real. As was described later to his bandmates by the female dressing room attendant, Jeff went into a full panic, sobbing, audibly berating himself, grabbing any personal objects he could find, scribbling his one word apology on a fast food bag, and fleeing the building.

Pulling a Yankees baseball cap low over his face to avoid detection by any Upper Hand fans he might encounter, he hailed a taxi and instructed the driver to take him to the Marriott where he and the rest of the band and crew were staying. Desperate to disappear from everyone for a while, including Denise, he was relieved to see that she was not in their room when he arrived there. He quickly packed and, after a moment's hesitation, grabbed half of the heroin stash the two of them had been sharing. He had intended to write Denise a brief note, but a combination of haste and an inability to decide what to say to her left the note unwritten.

Slinking past the front desk as inconspicuously as possible, he hopped into another cab and asked to be taken to the Atlanta bus station. There he purchased a ticket for the next morning's first bus to Baltimore. Spotting a Holiday Inn near the bus station, he checked in for the night under a false name, arousing concern from the check-in clerk with his drug and tear-reddened eyes, uncertain gait, and slightly slurred speech, but managing to secure a room without incident when he paid in advance with cash.

He boarded the bus the next morning, baseball cap still low on his forehead, and chose a seat near the rear of the bus as far away from other passengers as possible. Halfway into the eighteen-hour trip, seeing that the only passenger with a full view of him was asleep in the seat across the aisle, Jeff extracted a syringe from his gym bag and proceeded to shoot up. As he inserted the needle into his left forearm, the passenger, a middle-aged woman, awoke, glanced at Jeff, and gasped in alarm at the sight of the syringe. Jeff quickly whispered across the aisle to her with a smile, "Insulin; I'm a diabetic." She stared dubiously at Jeff for a second or two, then closed her eyes and feigned a return to her nap. Jeff finished dosing himself, then leaned back into his seat with a quiet sigh and swore to himself that he would find a way to eliminate heroin from his life.

From the Baltimore bus station, Jeff took a cab to his sister Betsy's house outside of Annapolis, arriving shortly after 4:00 a.m. He settled into a chaise lounge on Betsy's backyard patio and waited in the chilly April pre-dawn for signs of activity inside the house. At 7:30 the light to the bathroom went on. Jeff waited thirty more minutes, then walked around to the front door and rang the doorbell. Betsy, shocked not only at her brother's unannounced presence at her door, but also by his deathly appearance, quickly ushered him inside to find out why he was there and why he looked so ill.

Jeff made no attempt to sugarcoat the circumstances surrounding his surprise visit, readily admitting to his sister that he had allowed heroin to turn his entire world upside down, and describing in uncompromising detail his strange flight from the Omni Coliseum the night before. He begged her to allow him to hide out at her house while he figured out how to straighten himself out. Betsy, divorced, with no children, and living alone in a three-bedroom house, could easily accommodate him, and she agreed to let him stay with her and also reluctantly agreed to lie to anyone who might call asking if he was there—under two conditions: first, that he inform their parents in New Jersey and their brother in West Virginia that he was safe, and second, that he not bring any heroin into her house. Despite knowing full well that he could not live up to the latter condition, Jeff assented. He phoned his parents and brother, assuring them he was OK, but he refused to divulge his whereabouts, explaining that he needed time alone to "regroup after a tough stretch." To minimize any chance of being recognized by any of Betsy's neighbors, he chopped off his shoulder-length brown hair, replaced his contact lenses with dark plastic framed glasses, and shaved his dark, full beard.

The anticipated phone call from the Upper Hand came six days after Jeff's arrival at Betsy's house. Betsy dutifully followed Jeff's instructions, informing A.J. that yes, she had spoken to Jeff; no, she didn't know where he was staying; and lastly, that Jeff was deeply remorseful over what had happened and would be getting in touch with all four group members to apologize and try to explain his actions as soon as he could get his head together sufficiently to do so. A.J., still struggling through the rest of the tour with his remaining bandmates at the time of his call, reported the news from Betsy to the band and crew. Dave and Steve, while still stunned and angered, expressed relief that Jeff was safe. Mark offered no response at all.

It took less than three weeks for Betsy to uncover evidence that Jeff was continuing to use heroin. A tearful confrontation ensued, but thanks to Betsy's naïveté regarding the harsh realities of heroin addiction, Jeff was able to convince her that he was making significant progress and just needed a few more weeks to get himself completely off the drug. His living arrangement at her house was left unaltered.

After another month, and an obvious lack of headway by Jeff in weaning himself off heroin, Betsy reached the limit of her patience. She steeled herself to deliver a firm ultimatum to her brother: "Check yourself into a legitimate rehabilitation center within the next week, or I reveal to everyone—your family, your friends, your band, the media—that you're living here and still shooting up." It was perfectly clear to Jeff that his sister was dead serious with this threat and could not be persuaded to give him any more time. He was out of options. Four days later he walked into the reception lobby of a well-regarded private drug and alcohol rehab facility in Scottsdale, Arizona, where he would stay for the next three and a half months.

After six weeks in rehab, Jeff felt sufficiently clear-headed and was able to summon up enough nerve to write to Mark, A.J., Steve, and Dave. He painstakingly composed four lengthy, individualized, emotionally charged letters, sending them out simultaneously at the end of August. He also started to write a letter to Denise but soon realized that he had no idea where to send it.

Jeff's letters marked the beginning of a difficult, bumpy, but ultimately successful, process of reconciliation with A.J., Dave, and Steve. Mark, on the other hand, threw his letter in the trash without opening it and did the same with multiple follow-up attempts by Jeff to communicate with him. Through the gradual rebuilding of his relationships with his other three comrades, Jeff was made aware of the depth and apparent endlessness of Mark's bitterness toward him. He also received the disheartening news that the Upper Hand had disbanded.

Jeff's first round of rehab would not prove to be his last. It would take three cycles of relapse and treatment, once more in Arizona, once in the Bahamas, and once in Austria, before he was able to leave heroin behind, apparently for good, in 1995. He retreated to the small town in West Virginia, where his brother Bob lived with his wife and two sons, and began working in Bob's auto mechanic shop, drug-free but emotionally shattered.

CHAPTER 6

Dave, Steve, and A.J. were in agreement that A.J. would do most of the talking when their upcoming get-together with Mark turned to the topic of reconciliation with Jeff. Mark liked and trusted all three of them, but it was understood that Mark felt a special respect for A.J. that they felt would allow A.J. to get contentious with him if necessary without leading to Mark storming out of the room. They also recognized that the hard-line "enough is enough" stance they were prepared to take with Mark would have the most impact coming from the normally mild-mannered A.J.

Mark still lived in the same stately brick colonial house in Caldwell, New Jersey, where the Upper Hand frequently rehearsed in the 1980s. Twice divorced and currently only two months into a relationship with a new girlfriend, he lived alone in the five-bedroom house.

Just as Steve and Dave had kept the main purpose of their recent visit to A.J.'s house a secret, the three of them gave Mark no indication of what they had in mind when they arranged to meet. Mark was well aware that the four of them had not been together as a group in almost two years and readily agreed to a pizza and beer get-together.

A.J., Steve, and Dave arrived together at Mark's house early on a Friday evening in April armed with three pizzas from a local pizzeria and four six-packs of assorted high-quality microbrewery beers. As the four friends worked their way through the pizzas, sampled each of the beers, and engaged in the usual catching up and other small talk, the three visitors, by prior arrangement, made it a point to occasionally interject stories from their days in the band, to gauge Mark's response. True to A.J.'s prediction, Mark consistently attempted to steer the conversation away from anything to do with the Upper Hand. Dave, A.J., and Steve exchanged quick glances every time Mark withdrew from the band-related recollections or made an effort to redirect the discussion to a totally different topic. *Yes,* they silently communicated to each other, *this is a guy who still hasn't gotten over the demise of the band fourteen years ago, even if he was*

the man who declared it dead following Jeff's abandonment of the tour. The
task at hand, of course, was to somehow convince Mark that the only
way for him to free himself from his anger and sense of loss was to
let Jeff back into his life.

Mark did not have the kind of fantasyland game room that
A.J. had in his house, but he did have a nicely appointed billiard
room where the four of them gathered for the evening. As a lively
conversation regarding the prospects for the Yankees getting back
to the World Series in 2004 wound down, A.J. nodded slightly to
Dave and Steve to let them know that he was about to change the
mood of the gathering. Dave and Steve tensed up and fell quiet in
anticipation.

A.J. wasted no time getting to the point. "So, Mark," he began, "I
gotta ask you something. How much longer are you planning to piss
away your life as a bitter, angry man?"

Mark bolted upright from his casual slouch in one of the
comfortable chairs positioned around his billiard room. He was
taken aback, not only by the harsh and confusing question, but also by
the fact that it came from the most easy-going, non-confrontational
person he knew. Steve and Dave were knocked almost as off-balance
as Mark by the tone of A.J.'s opening query and exchanged quick
raised-eyebrow glances.

"Huh? What the heck are you talking about?" Mark replied
warily, his eyes darting among his three guests.

"I'll tell you what I'm talking about. You've locked yourself into
a sad little world where you can't allow yourself to embrace and
celebrate the greatest eighteen years of your life. You can't even
bring yourself to talk about them! You had an unbelievable run
of triumphs as a creative force in a world-famous rock band, and
you've erased it all from your life."

"What kind of crap is this? When did you become a psychologist?
Who gave you the idea that I'm bitter and sad?"

A.J. rose from his seat, strode briskly across the room to a long,
undecorated, billiard room wall, and smacked it loudly with the

palm of his hand. "Look at this! Look at this!" A.J. exclaimed. "This used to be the coolest wall I knew. Platinum albums, photos, framed magazine covers and newspaper clippings, tour T-shirts, you name it. This wall was its very own Upper Hand museum! I used to love coming over here to see what you'd added to it. What'd you do, Mark? Throw it all in a pile and burn it?"

Dave and Steve sat transfixed as Mark reddened. He was clearly provoked by this unfathomable verbal assault from A.J., but as they had hoped, Mark was unwilling or incapable of lashing out at A.J. in response. His reply was mumbled, defensive, and totally unconvincing. "I didn't burn anything. I...just thought that stuff was kinda old, and it was time to do something else over there."

A.J. kept up the pressure. "Something else, eh? Let's just take a look." He turned to face the blank wall and made an exaggerated outward sweeping motion with his hands. Still staring at the wall, he exclaimed, "Well, this is just gorgeous. I *love* what you've done with this wall. Tell me, does this stunning display represent all of your fondest memories and greatest achievements from your solo career?"

Mark, truly stung by this last broadside, tried to generate some righteous anger in his reply, but he could only sputter pathetically, "Jesus Christ, A.J., what's going on here? Why are you ripping me like this? And why are you shitting all over my solo work? I thought you liked my stuff."

A.J. turned away from the wall to face Mark. He spoke in a markedly softer tone. "Mark, I do like your solo music. In fact, I like it way more than you do."

"What the hell does that mean?"

A.J. wasn't ready to answer that question yet, so he changed the subject. "Mark, why do you think I'm giving you such a hard time here?"

"I have no fucking idea, but it sucks."

"I'm not enjoying this either, but we've got a situation that has to be addressed. It should have been addressed years ago, and I'm not going to shut up until I've said everything that needs to be said."

"You mean you're not done dumping on me?"

"I'm not going to dump on you. But I am going to tell you some things that you need to hear, and I want you to promise me something."

"Do I get to find out what it is before I make any promises? I still have no goddamn idea what's going on here."

"I want you to promise me that you won't try to cut me off unless I say something that is absolutely not true. You don't get to interrupt me just because you don't like what I'm saying."

"I...I don't know. How am I supposed to answer that? I'm in the dark here." He turned his attention to Steve and Dave. "Are you guys in on this? Do you know what A.J.'s digging at here?"

Dave replied, "Mark, just hear him out, OK? He—*we*—aren't just trying to bust your balls here."

Steve nodded in agreement. Mark took stock of the three pairs of eyeballs staring at him and decided he had little choice but to let his friend say what was on his mind. He let out a long sigh and asked resignedly, "Do I at least get to raise my hand to let you know when I figure out what the fuck I'm being grilled for?" His attempt to add a touch of levity failed to generate a smile from anyone, so he sank back into his chair and extended an upturned palm to A.J., beckoning him to speak.

"Mark, there are four guys in this room who lost a tremendously important part of their lives fourteen years ago. But for you, the loss was way deeper, way more painful, than it was for Dave, Steve, or me. I'm not trying to minimize the hurt that the three of us felt when the band blew up, but for you it was different. The Upper Hand was everything to you, and you took great pride in the fact that you, together with your best friend since you were in diapers, were the key creative force behind the incredible success we had."

Dave squirmed a bit in his seat at A.J.'s insinuation that his creative contributions to the band were incidental to the band's meteoric rise. Mark also became instantly uncomfortable at A.J.'s reference to Jeff, as it started to dawn on him where A.J. was going with his monologue.

"The fact that it was Jeff who caused the band to disintegrate, and the way it all went down, tore—"

Mark leaned forward. "I don't want to talk about him."

"I don't care. We're going to talk about Jeff, and we're going to do it now." A.J.'s voice was quiet but firm, and Mark found himself powerless to protest. Dave and Steve watched in awe at A.J.'s command over the strong-willed Mark.

"Mark, we were all infuriated with Jeff for turning himself into a heroin-addled mess and bailing out on us. The three of us have managed to come to terms with it, and to accept Jeff's apologies for what he allowed to happen. You haven't, which I know isn't news to you. But what I don't think you realize is that your continued refusal to let Jeff back into your life is hurting you as much as it is hurting him. You can't even bring yourself to talk about or think about those great years we had together in the group, and you've just been going through the motions in your post-Upper Hand career without your musical partner."

Mark jumped out of his seat. "Again with the dissing of my solo career! What the hell is this?"

"Put a lid on it, Mark. I'm not dissing your music, and you know it. But I want you to answer me honestly: all of the heart and soul you put into every Upper Hand record and performance, all of the pride you felt from the success we achieved, all of the outrageous fun you had being a part of all that, can you tell me that you feel anything that even remotely resembles those feelings from your solo years?"

Mark wanted badly to yell out "*Yes!*" and put an end to this bizarre confrontation, but the word was caught in his throat. He could feel himself choking up, and he knew that his eyes were moistening. He sat back down wordlessly, avoiding eye contact with his friends.

A.J. walked back over to the blank wall and touched it again, this time far more gently. His voice also became softer. "Mark, if I weren't right about everything I'm saying here, this wall would still be decorated with all those great Upper Hand mementos you so carefully compiled, and there'd be a whole new section devoted to your own stuff."

Mark had had enough. In a shaky but determined voice, he said, "OK, A.J., you've made it quite clear that you disapprove of my interior decorating choices. So what do you want from me?"

"I want you to do yourself a huge favor and reconnect with Jeff. You'll never be—"

"I thought that's where you were going with this. Well, forget it! It ain't happening."

"Mark, at least give it some thought. Can't you see what this has done to—?"

Mark cut him off again, this time more forcefully. "No, dammit, no! That guy earned a one way ticket out of my life, and that's the way it is, *period.*" He started to say more but felt a lump in his throat again and paused in an effort to conceal the anguish that was mixed in with his anger. After several seconds of heavy silence in the room, he took a deep breath and said softly, "Look, I think you guys should leave now. You know the way out." He strode out of the room without another word, and seconds later his three stunned guests could hear the sound of Mark's footsteps ascending the staircase to the bedroom level of the house.

Chapter 7

A.J., Dave, and Steve piled into A.J.'s imposing Cadillac Escalade and pulled out of Mark's driveway to begin the fifteen-minute trip back to Montclair. None of them had spoken a word since Mark suddenly cut off their visit and left them in his billiard room. All three of them were now replaying the intense conversation between A.J. and Mark in their heads. The car radio, set to North Jersey rock station WDHA-FM, was playing "No Excuses" by Alice in Chains at a barely audible volume. It was Dave who finally broke the silence.

"A.J., you were amazing back there. I could hardly believe what I was watching."

A.J. smiled ruefully. "I obviously wasn't amazing enough. This didn't exactly turn out the way we hoped."

Steve chimed in, "OK, so today didn't end well. But you definitely accomplished something, A.J. There's no doubt that you opened Mark's eyes to the fact that he's just wallowing in his own anger. That stuff about the wall was just brilliant. He was really listening to what you said. You just weren't able to convince him yet that reconciling with Jeff is the key to being his old self again."

A.J. turned east onto Bloomfield Avenue, the perpetually busy, store-lined boulevard that connected Montclair, Caldwell, and several other towns in Essex County, New Jersey.

"The problem," A.J. replied, "is that I have no clue where to go with this from here. He's obviously upset by what happened tonight, but what if he's so pissed off that he won't even want to speak to us? Geez, I hope he doesn't add us to his shit list. What do you guys think?"

Dave mumbled, "I gotta think about it a bit."

Steve, sitting in the back seat of the Escalade directly behind Dave, was about to utter something equally noncommittal when his cell phone rang. He fished the flip phone out of his jacket pocket and peered at the screen. "Holy shit, it's Mark!" he exclaimed, snapping the phone open.

Dave and A.J. fell silent, and A.J. quickly punched the off button of his car radio.

"Hey, Mark," Steve spoke into the phone, trying to sound as casual as possible, as if nothing of consequence had just occurred a few minutes earlier.

Mark matched the forced nonchalance of Steve's greeting. "Hey, Steve."

An awkward silence followed. Steve was aware that it was his turn to speak but had no idea what to say. To Steve's relief, Mark broke the impasse. "Where are you guys?"

"Bloomfield Avenue. I guess we're in Verona now, on our way back to A.J.'s house."

"Could I talk the three of you into coming back here to talk about, well, just to chat a bit?"

Steve sat bolt upright in his seat. Rotating the mouthpiece of his cell phone away from his mouth, he hollered, "A.J.! Turn around! Turn the car around!"

"What are you talking about? I'm in the middle of Bloomfield Avenue."

"I don't care. Make a U-y. Mark wants us to go back to his house."

He repositioned the phone to put the mouthpiece near his mouth again. "Mark, we'll be there in fifteen minutes. Bye!" He snapped the phone shut.

A.J. worked his way into the left lane of Bloomfield Avenue. "I'll turn around at the next traffic light. What did Mark say, anyway?"

"He wants to talk to us. We gotta get back there before his mood changes. Look at all this fucking traffic backed up at the light. We can't wait around for this bullshit. Flip around here."

"Are you out of your mind? There's a cement island here."

Dave chimed in, "Big deal. This Sherman tank you're driving doesn't care about any cement islands. Do it."

Steve and Dave began chanting in unison, "Do it! Do it! Do it!"

A.J. rolled his eyes. "You guys are nuts. You really think another five or ten minutes is going to make a difference?" By now they were stopped in a long line of cars, over a hundred yards from the traffic light.

"Do it! Do it! Do it!"

At that moment a break appeared in the westbound traffic. A.J. muttered, "For chrissakes," and turned the steering wheel hard to the left as his foot hit the accelerator. The impact of the Escalade's tires on the road divider was significantly more molar-rattling than any of them had anticipated, but within seconds they were on the left-hand, westbound lane of Bloomfield Avenue. A.J.'s first glance into his rearview mirror made it immediately apparent that his island-jumping maneuver had not gone unnoticed. A Verona police cruiser had pulled out from a side street near the spot where A.J. had executed his illegal U-turn and was now behind the Escalade with its red-and-blue roof lights flashing.

"Shit!" A.J. hollered. "So much for your brilliant time saving idea."

"What are you talking about?" asked Steve.

"Look behind us, dickhead," A.J. replied with uncharacteristic agitation as he began the process of pulling over from the left lane to the curb. "I swear, you knuckleheads are going to pay this ticket."

A.J. came to a stop in an open parking space, and the police cruiser pulled in behind him. The police officer exited his vehicle and walked toward the driver's door of the Escalade as A.J. fished around in the glove compartment for the documents he knew he was about to need. He rolled down his window as Patrolman Ernie Garrison, twenty-two year veteran of the Verona Police Department, approached.

"License and registration, please," Garrison began in his standard, polite monotone, but as A.J. turned to face the officer, Garrison immediately exclaimed, "Hey, you're A.J. What's-his-name! The bass wizard from the Upper Hand! Holy cow, you can play!"

"Thank you. Yes, that's me. How are you, officer?"

Garrison peered into the SUV to check out the other occupants. Pointing at the ageless Steve, he said excitedly, "You're from the Upper Hand, too! Aren't you the singer? Man, you guys are great! My wife and I have a bunch of your albums."

"I'm Steve Holmes, officer. Nice to meet you. I'm the drummer."

Dave awaited his turn to be recognized but was greeted instead with, "Who's this other guy? He doesn't look familiar to me."

Dave didn't appreciate the reminder that he no longer resembled the guy in the band's album cover photos and wasn't a big enough celebrity to be recognized now, even by an Upper Hand fan. He nevertheless replied amiably, "Hello, officer. I'm Dave Rowinski, keyboards and vocals. I guess my looks have changed a bit since you and your wife bought those albums."

Officer Garrison took a harder look at Dave, trying without success to connect the face before him with his vague memory of the band members pictured on his old albums. "You're the singer, eh? Wow, so you're the guy who does that great vocal on 'Circling the Drain?'"

"Uh, no, that one was sung by Jeff Britton."

"How about 'Crowbar' and 'Better Without You?' Those are still excellent tunes. Did you sing those?"

"Actually, those two were sung by Mark Donahue."

Dave silently berated himself for introducing himself as a vocalist in the band. He, as well as Steve and A.J., knew exactly where this conversation was headed. This cop was about to reel off the names of every Upper Hand radio hit he could think of, and poor Dave was going to have to acknowledge that he was not the lead vocalist on any of them.

Thankfully for Dave, A.J. did not want him to go through any further embarrassment, and chimed in to change the subject. Eyeing the patrolman's name tag, A.J. interjected, "Officer Garrison, we love chatting about the good old days in the Upper Hand, but we are in a tremendous hurry, and I'd like to explain to you why I made that rather unconventional U-turn back there."

"Yes, we do need to talk about that, don't we?"

"Well, here's the thing, Officer Garrison. I know that, as a big fan of the Upper Hand, you'd love to see us get back together and make some new music, right? And of course you're aware that our two guitarists, Mark and Jeff, haven't seen eye to eye for a long time."

In fact, Ernie Garrison knew nothing about any feud between members of the Upper Hand, but he nodded his head in assent.

A.J. continued, "Well, we just got a phone call a few minutes ago informing us that these two guys may be willing to patch things up, and we knew that we had to help them work it out as soon as possible, before the mood changed. That's why I made that desperate turnaround, to allow us to get back to Caldwell in time to put our band back together, so we can start playing for you and the rest of our great fans again!"

A.J. held his breath, hoping that Officer Garrison wouldn't closely analyze his tale of urgency and quiz him on why this mission to resurrect the band was so time sensitive. Dave and Steve also sat rigidly waiting to see if Ernie Garrison, the rock and roll fan, would gloss over A.J.'s bullshit story and prevent Officer Garrison of the Verona Police from writing A.J. up and further delaying their trip back to Mark's house.

"Well, I'd hate to see an opportunity for the reunion of a great band like yours to be wasted."

It worked! A.J., Dave, and Steve let out silent, simultaneous sighs of relief.

"Now, A.J., if I were to run your license through the system, what kind of driving record would I find?"

Fortunately, A.J. had the right answer. "Clean as a whistle, Officer Garrison, honest to God. I don't do stuff like this; I was just so anxious to get back—"

"O.K., O.K., I'll tell you what. Follow me when I pull out, and I'll escort you to the Verona/Caldwell border. Go and make those two other guys kiss and make up, and then come do a concert at the Meadowlands."

A.J. stuck his hand through the car window and shook Ernie Garrison's hand.

"Thank you, Officer Garrison. I appreciate this, the soon-to-be resurrected band appreciates this, and our fans appreciate this. When we come to the Meadowlands arena to play, I'll drop two tickets off at the Verona police station for you and your wife."

"No, no, don't do that! You'll get me in big-ass trouble. Just follow me, now. Good luck with the band."

With that, Garrison headed back to his patrol car, A.J. rolled up his car window, and the howling began.

"Holy shit, I can't believe that just happened," gushed Steve as A.J. pulled out behind his personal police escort.

"No thanks to you two douche bags," replied A.J., unable to suppress a grin.

Dave chimed in, "OK, so we were stupid to make you drive your car over that divider. But, oh, man, the way you smooth-talked your way out of that ticket was maybe every bit as brilliant as the job you did on Mark earlier. You totally convinced that cop that Jeff and Mark are sitting together in a room somewhere with an egg timer ticking away, and if we don't get there before the timer goes off, they're going to change their minds about reforming the Upper Hand, beat the shit out of each other, and prevent the band from ever reuniting!"

"Hey, Dave," said Steve, chuckling. "I think that cop thought you were our accountant or something. You gotta grow out your hair a bit, maybe dye it, or grow back your 'stache."

Dave just grumbled in response, not pleased with the reminder of his anonymity.

Steve turned serious. "I know that A.J.'s story to that cop was a crock of shit, but I really think that it does matter how quickly we get our asses back to Mark's house. A.J. got Mark's mind spinning, and I'll bet he's open to being persuaded to get in contact with Jeff. Otherwise he wouldn't have asked us to come back. But if we give him too much time to dwell on it, he may find a reason not to do it. So, A.J., stay right on our friendly cop's tail, and when he peels off at the Caldwell border, haul ass to Mark's house!"

"What are you, a member of the Slow Learner's Club? You already got me pulled over once. I'm not taking any more driving advice from you two clowns. The next cop is unlikely to be as accommodating as this one was. If you're so worried about Mark over-thinking everything before we get back there, then give him a call and tell him to watch cartoons on TV until we arrive."

Steve and Dave chuckled, promised to behave and to refrain from pressuring A.J. into any further illegal driving maneuvers, and waved to Officer Garrison when the patrol car turned off Bloomfield Avenue at the Verona/Caldwell border.

CHAPTER 8

Mark opened his front door to greet A.J., Dave, and Steve before they reached the top step of the porch. "Thanks for coming back, guys," he said with a small smile, his eyes appearing to be a bit red. "I want to apologize for running out of the room before. I may have been sort of unnerved by the way the conversation was going, but that was a crap way to handle it."

The three visitors responded with reassuring pats on the back and a variety of "no need to apologize" utterances as Mark led them back to his billiard room. As soon as they entered the room, A.J., Dave, and Steve stopped dead in their tracks. The empty wall that A.J. had used to drive home his point about Mark's self-destructive anger was no longer unadorned. Mark had hammered three picture hooks into the wall, from which he had hung an Upper Hand platinum album, a framed 1985 *Rolling Stone* magazine cover featuring the band, and a framed photo of the band in concert at Madison Square Garden in 1980. In addition, he had thumbtacked to the wall an unframed newspaper concert review from his first solo tour in 1991.

"I did a little decorating while you guys were on the road. It's not much, but I guess it's a start."

Dave, who was standing closest to Mark, threw his arm around Mark's shoulders from behind and, battling a lump in his throat, exclaimed, "It's absolutely beautiful, man."

"Excellent! Great to see," added Steve and A.J., as Mark moved toward the sofa and the others headed to seats near him.

What did this token display of memorabilia really signify? Mark's three friends sat silently for several seconds waiting for him to provide a clue.

Finally he spoke. "I don't know if I can do it," he said softly, staring at the floor.

"Sure you can," began Steve, but A.J. cut him off with a vigorous wave of his hand and a shake of his head.

Mark continued, "I don't know if I should be pissed or grateful that you made me think about all this stuff today. But now that I have, I guess I have to come to grips with the fact that I haven't put everything that happened in 1990 behind me as successfully as I liked to believe I had. You guys were right; this shit still gnaws at me, as much as I keep pushing it out of my mind. I understand why you're saying that the way to get past it once-and-for-all is to speak to Jeff, but I really don't know if I can make myself do that."

A.J., clearly established now in his uncharacteristic role as the leader of this three-man intervention team, broke in gently. "What's holding you back, Mark?"

"I don't know really. I just can't even imagine what I'd say to him when he picked up the phone, or what he'd say once he knew it was me. What if I get myself all wound up to call him, and he hangs up on me? It just feels really weird to even think about."

"Well, there's one thing I can tell you for sure that should help a bit. Jeff will *not* reject any attempt by you to speak to him. The three of us still talk with him often enough to know that he still dreams of the day when he'll hear from you."

"Really? Damn. Still, I'm not sure. I mean, I'm still so pissed off that I might just start yelling at him through the phone, or...Man, I'm so mind-fucked right now, I don't know what to think."

"Here's what I think. You should not call Jeff on the phone. After all this time, you should take care of this face to face."

"No, no, no. I couldn't."

"Yes, you can, and Steve, Dave, and I will come with you."

Steve and Dave looked at each other, and shrugged. "Absolutely!" they called out in unison.

Mark shifted his eyes among his three guests. "What if it goes shitty? What if I blow my top when I see him and slug him?"

A.J. smiled and said, "I honestly don't think that's going to happen, and I can guarantee that the three of us will make sure you don't hit him. And you know what? Even if your meeting with Jeff started with a fistfight, it would be an improvement over the way things are now."

***

Mark Donahue and Jeff Britton grew up on the same street in suburban Morristown, New Jersey, two houses apart. Having shared a playpen on countless afternoons while their mothers sipped cocktails and discussed the joys, as well as the trials and tribulations, of first-time motherhood, Mark and Jeff could say they knew each other their entire lives.

As small boys, they shared the usual interests that occupied the minds and imaginations of late 1950s and early 1960s grammar school males: baseball, dinosaurs, comic books, and World War II-replica toy guns, planes, and tanks. Mark and Jeff were inseparable from the time they were old enough to venture outside their homes unaccompanied and play with the other kids in their neighborhood. Both boys were avid followers of the New York Yankees and would pretend to be Mickey Mantle, Roger Maris, Yogi Berra, Whitey Ford, and other Yankee stars in the innumerable stickball games held in the streets and backyards of their neighborhood. Jeff briefly flirted with developing a rooting interest in the New York Mets in the spring of their inaugural season in 1962, but when Mark refused to pay any attention whatsoever to the fledgling National League ball club, Jeff quickly dropped them and resumed his devotion to the Yankees.

On Sunday evening, February 9, 1964, the world changed for Mark Donahue and Jeff Britton, as it did for countless other young people across the United States. Sitting side by side on the Britton family's living room carpet in front of the black and white nineteen-inch Zenith television set, the two nine-year-olds watched wide-eyed and wordless as John Lennon, Paul McCartney, George Harrison, and Ringo Starr captivated an America, still staggering from the recent assassination of President Kennedy, and shook it to its core.

The historic first appearance by the Beatles on *The Ed Sullivan Show* that night left the two boys' heads spinning. Jeff immediately proclaimed that he was going to be a guitar player like John, Paul, or

George. Mark initially voiced his desire to be a drummer like Ringo, but Jeff quickly convinced him that the two of them should stand front and center in any band they formed, the left-handed Mark with his lefty guitar, like Paul McCartney, and the right-handed Jeff positioned immediately to his left like George Harrison.

All of Mark and Jeff's prior youthful obsessions—sports, army toys, monster movies—instantly took a back seat to the Beatles and rock and roll.They began using their weekly allowances to buy Beatles records, never duplicating a purchase between them, choosing instead to build one shared collection. They started listening obsessively to New York's AM radio station 77 "W-A-Beatle-C" and its hit-playing disk jockeys "Cousin Brucie" Bruce Morrow, Dan Ingram, Harry Harrison, and Scott Muni. And most importantly, they began clamoring for guitar lessons.

Mark's father Warren, a crew-cut former Army captain and World War II veteran, initially resisted his son's sudden preoccupation with the raucous music of "those weird long-haired twerps," but the enthusiastic support of his wife, Claire, and Jeff's parents, Jack and Liz, for the boys' new interest wore him down. "I feel like a fart in a gale wind," Warren grumbled as Mark and Jeff climbed eagerly into Liz Britton's Ford Galaxie 500 station wagon for their first guitar lesson.

Mark and Jeff insisted on taking their lessons together, so their parents worked out a deal with a local guitar teacher to teach the two boys at the same time for one and a half times the fee for a solo lesson. To Mark's initial disappointment and later great relief, his teacher refused to teach him to play left-handed, wisely reasoning that by playing right-handed, Mark could always play other people's guitars and would have a far easier time finding the kinds of guitars he wanted, it generally being extremely difficult at the time to find left-handed versions of most guitars.

The boys progressed rapidly, practicing together for hours at a time and pushing each other to learn the guitar parts to the latest songs from the radio and their burgeoning shared record collection. As would remain true right through their time together in the Upper Hand, neither boy ever consistently took on the role of "lead guitarist" or "rhythm guitarist." Rather, their parts on any given song would develop naturally. It wasn't long before they instinctively began working out dual lead guitar parts for songs.

Mark and Jeff quickly outgrew their first, and then second, guitar instructor, and by the time they were eleven years old they were taking lessons from the best-known guitar teacher in Morris County, a local bandleader and studio guitar veteran named Butch Green. Butch immediately recognized the natural ability the boys had for working out complementary guitar parts and opened the boys' eyes to the possibilities of harmonized lead guitar passages, a revelation that inspired Mark and Jeff to develop a signature lead guitar style that later helped propel the Upper Hand to rock stardom. By this time the boys had also long since disposed of their cheaply made, rented, acoustic beginner's guitars, and were now proud owners of their first electric guitars—a Fender Mustang for Jeff, a Gretsch Corvette for Mark—and amplifiers. Their dual practice sessions were now far longer, more intricate, and much louder than ever.

In 1967, seventh graders Mark and Jeff took note of a bulletin board announcement at their junior high school regarding an upcoming student talent show. They had never even contemplated performing in front of an audience, or getting involved with any other musicians, but they mutually decided that this talent show was going to be the venue for their public debut. They quickly determined that they needed a drummer for this momentous occasion and recruited a classmate named Kevin LaRoche. Kevin claimed to know his way around his older brother's drum kit, which resided in his basement. Having never sung a note in their lives, Mark and Jeff briefly considered finding a vocalist for their new band but soon decided that, if they wanted this talent show performance to serve as the historic first step of their journey towards rock stardom, they would have to learn to handle the singing themselves.

The three boys convened in Kevin's basement for their first after-school rehearsal two weeks prior to the talent show. Kevin, a strong, stocky football player, proved to be much more adept at generating volume than accurate or consistent rhythm on his brother's drums, but Mark and Jeff simply turned their amplifiers up as loud as possible to be heard over Kevin's haphazard din and plowed ahead, much to the alarm of Kevin's mother upstairs. The boys did not own a microphone, so their vocals were hopelessly drowned out at this, and the subsequent five rehearsals they held before the show. Mr. Fortunato, the school's music teacher in charge of the talent show, assured the young trio, who dubbed themselves the Werewolves, that a microphone would be available to them at the show. Mark and Jeff practiced their vocals alone in Jeff's bedroom between the ear-splitting rehearsals with Kevin, choosing to sing together in unison as co-lead vocalists on every song.

Despite Jeff and Mark's ever-expanding talents in playing intertwining and harmonized guitar leads, they decided, because of their additional duties as singers, to confine themselves to simple rhythm guitar parts for their talent show performance. The Werewolves chose four straightforward, popular pop/rock tunes to learn for the show: "I Saw Her Standing There," "Last Train to Clarksville," "Gloria," and "Wild Thing."

The boys were deeply disappointed when, five days before the talent show, Mr. Fortunato announced to the eighteen participating acts that each performance would be limited to five minutes, meaning that the Werewolves debut would consist of only two songs. However, as the dress rehearsal the night before the show progressed, Mr. Fortunato came to realize that most of the piano players, gymnasts, baton twirlers, lip synching air guitar bands, and woodwind combos had no more than two or three minutes of "talent" to share with the world, and he gave the boys the good news that they could perform all four of the songs they'd learned.

By the time the dress rehearsal ended, Fortunato was left with no doubt that the Werewolves were easily the most entertaining act he had for the show, and so he chose them to close the evening.

Brimming with excitement and anticipation, Jeff and Mark didn't sleep much the night before the show. The day of the show, a Saturday, found the boys trying to keep themselves occupied by shooting baskets in Jeff's driveway and playing a few games of electric football in Mark's bedroom, but the day dragged on endlessly as they counted the minutes until it was finally time to head to the school auditorium.

At long last the time came for the Brittons and Donahues to gather up their kids and the boys' guitars to go to the show. Jeff jumped into the family station wagon with his parents and younger siblings Bob and Betsy, and Mark joined his sister Evelyn in the back seat of his father's Chevrolet Impala for the five-minute trip to the junior high school.

As soon as Mark and Jeff arrived at the school auditorium, they headed backstage to drop off their guitars, then found Kevin and joined him in the audience, several rows away from their families. The boys were far too excited to pay much attention to the assortment of acts that preceded them and were totally preoccupied with thoughts of their own upcoming performance, until Mr. Fortunato approached them between the fourth and fifth acts.

"Hey, guys, how's it going? Ready to knock 'em dead tonight?" he began. When the trio responded affirmatively, he continued, "Listen, I'm hoping you can do me a favor. A sixth grade girl piano player who was supposed to go on before you just called in sick, so I need to fill some time. Could you add a fifth song to your act?"

Since the boys had only rehearsed four songs together, Kevin began to decline the offer, but Mark quickly jabbed him in the ribs to quiet him. "Sure. We could do 'Good Lovin'' by the Rascals," Mark replied, and Jeff immediately agreed. It was a song the two boys had played together many times.

"Kevin, you know 'Good Lovin',' don't you?" Jeff said.

"I've heard it on the radio, but I've never played it," Kevin answered cautiously.

"It's simple. Come outside and we'll show you. Don't worry, Mr. Fortunato. We'll have that fifth song for you."

With that, Mr. Fortunato headed backstage, and the three boys retreated through the exit at the back of the auditorium, where Mark and Jeff proceeded to sing "Good Lovin'" and pound out the drumbeats on their thighs for Kevin. In less than five minutes, the threesome was back in their seats. They sat impatiently through several more mind-numbing displays of lip-synching, tumbling, and comedic "talent" until, with just three more acts to go before the Werewolves' public debut, Mr. Fortunato came to them once again. "Boys, I've got another problem. Susie Fredericks, the violin player who's supposed to go on next, has locked herself in a girl's room stall with stage fright and refuses to play. You have a sixth song for me?"

Kevin didn't bother to try to raise any doubts this time. He simply rose in unison with his bandmates to head outside again, this time to learn "Twist and Shout."

After what seemed like an eternity to Mark and Jeff, it was time for them to close the talent show. Their inevitable first-time performance jitters were dwarfed by eager anticipation and confidence as they stood in the wings with Kevin, guitars strapped on, waiting for a pair of sixth grade boys, one dressed as Sonny Bono and the other decked out in drag as Cher, to finish their ill-advised lip-synching performance of "I Got You Babe."

It did not escape the notice of Jeff, Mark, or Kevin that this was not going to be a difficult act to follow. As the duo left the stage to a polite smattering of applause, the student emcee announced to the audience of sixth to eighth graders, parents, grandparents, and siblings, "And now, ladies and gentlemen, our final act of the evening, performing for the first time ever anywhere, rock and roll's Amazing Werewolves!"

The three boys exchanged bemused glances as they propelled themselves towards the waiting drum kit, microphone and amps. *Amazing? Where the heck did that come from?* Mark hissed to the emcee as he leaned over to plug in his guitar, "Billy! What's with the 'amazing' crap? We're just the Werewolves!"

"Sorry, man, Mr. Fortunato wrote this stuff. I just read it."

The three boys took their places, each signaling that he was ready to go. Ironically, the two future rock stars, who were about to offer an impressive first glimpse of their musicianship and stage presence, had no concept yet of how to dress like rock and rollers. Years later, Mark and Jeff would cringe at the only known photograph taken of the Werewolves on this night. Mark was decked out in an olive green Ban-Lon shirt, glen plaid slacks, and cordovan penny loafers. Jeff's shirt, also Ban-Lon, was harvest gold, and topped a pair of herringbone slacks and black lace-up shoes. If possible, Kevin's attire may have been even less suited for a rock music performance. His mother forced him to wear a white dress shirt, blue striped tie, navy sports jacket (which he dispatched before taking the stage, explaining afterwards to his mother that it was too confining for drumming), khaki slacks, and brown lace-ups.

Mark stepped up to the microphone and offered a quick "Hi, everyone. We're the Werewolves." Then he counted off, "One, two, three, four!" and the Werewolves kicked into "I Saw Her Standing There." Jeff and Mark sidled up to the lone microphone and began pounding out chords and singing in unison, while Kevin thrashed away powerfully, if a bit randomly, on his brother's drums. Jeff, standing to Mark's right, jabbed Mark in the ribs with the headstock of his guitar a couple of times as they converged around the microphone, but they quickly figured out how to position themselves, facing each other to prevent additional such mishaps.

For almost everyone in attendance at the talent show, experience with a live rock and roll performance was limited to exposure to hot new bands on *The Ed Sullivan Show* and other TV programs, so seeing and hearing the blaring guitars and jackhammer drums in person, even from a novice outfit like the Werewolves, was an eye-opening shock. The kids in the audience, including the king-of-the-hill eighth graders, began clapping and yelling long before the first song was finished, and the applause at the end of "I Saw Her Standing There" was explosive. The boys grinned at each other, Jeff delivered a shy "Thank you" into the microphone, and they launched into "Last Train to Clarksville." From that moment, the event was transformed from an eighteen- (well, sixteen, accounting for illness and stage fright-related cancellations) act talent show to a string of tedious warm-up acts for the crowd-mesmerizing headliners.

By the time the Werewolves were into their sixth and supposedly last song, the crowd was on its feet, the applause was all but drowning out the band, and there were dozens of girls screaming. Even Mark's straight-laced father Warren, no fan of anything to do with rock and roll, couldn't help himself from clapping and whistling enthusiastically, although he knew he was watching his dreams of his athletic son making it to the major leagues vaporize before his eyes.

When the boys hit the last notes for the set-ending "Twist and Shout," the crowd immediately began chanting for more. Mr. Fortunato rushed to the stage and asked Mark and Jeff if they could come up with just one more song. They were all out of simple three-chord bashers but instantly decided to reach into their repertoire of harmonized guitar lead songs they had been learning with their guitar instructor, Butch Green.

Mark and Jeff quickly agreed to perform the instrumental "Walk Don't Run," a song for which they had worked out intricate harmony parts months earlier.

Jeff leaned over to Kevin so he could be heard over the din. "Kevin, do you know the song 'Walk Don't Run?'"

"No, but that doesn't seem to matter much with this group!" Kevin yelled in reply.

"The beat goes like this," Jeff said, tapping his fingers on Kevin's snare drum. "Just listen to the introduction without playing, and then come in when I nod to you, OK? You'll be fine."

"OK! I'm not sure anyone's going to be able to hear us anyway with all this screaming!"

Jeff counted Mark in with the usual "One, two, three, four," this time into the microphone to make sure he could be heard, and Kevin dutifully joined in when signaled. It took the audience only ten or fifteen seconds to realize that something different was happening onstage with this encore song. This wasn't just simple chord patterns being banged out like before; these boys were doing something *interesting* on those electric guitars, weaving single note lead lines around each other and creating instrumental harmonies that weren't even on the Ventures' original hit version of the song. The crowd went totally silent to listen to the performance. Mark and Jeff, initially puzzled by the sudden silence in the auditorium, soon realized that everyone in attendance was hanging on every note they were playing.

A thrilled Mr. Fortunato, now assured that his talent show would be seen as a great success, stood in the wings with a wide grin. He figured that the crowd couldn't possibly respond any more enthusiastically than they had during the Werewolves' first six songs, but he was wrong. When "Walk Don't Run" was brought to its conclusion, the audience exploded into a jumping, yelling, whistling frenzy. The ovation lasted over a minute, as the boys stood stunned onstage soaking it in. For Kevin, the joy of accomplishment and adulation was mixed with a touch of relief that this challenging evening was over. But for Jeff and Mark, whose eyes were welling with tears of absolute ecstasy as they stood side by side accepting the thunderous applause from their schoolmates, this was an experience they wanted never to end. In the minds of these two seventh graders, their destiny was set in stone that evening. There would be no turning back.

CHAPTER 9

Mark's head was spinning. As A.J.'s Escalade barreled southwest through Pennsylvania on Interstate 81, with Dave riding shotgun and Steve seated beside him in the back seat, Mark's emotions pinballed rapidly and relentlessly among optimistic anticipation, fear of disaster, and bursts of renewed anger over the long-ago events that made this trip necessary. He tried gamely to participate in the lively conversation being carried on by his three travel companions and to enjoy the line-up of classic '70s and '80s rock CDs A.J. had loaded into his car's stereo system, but he simply could not disengage his racing mind from what was supposed to transpire the next day in West Virginia. At several points during the road trip, he actually became lightheaded from the mental strain.

Once A.J., Dave, and Steve had successfully pressured Mark into a verbal (if not completely heartfelt) agreement that a face-to-face encounter with Jeff was Mark's only ticket to escape from his longstanding feelings of emptiness and anger, they quickly decided that a road trip from New Jersey was the way to go. While certainly more time consuming, traveling by car would be a more enjoyable and a better reconnecting experience than a flight to Pittsburgh, followed by a sixty-mile rental car trip to Shinnston, West Virginia, where Jeff lived and worked.

It was a beautiful day in May for a drive, seventy degrees and sunny. The plan was to drive directly from New Jersey to Morgantown, West Virginia, a lively college town with no shortage of decent hotels, spend the night there, and then make the thirty-five mile trip to Shinnston the next morning. Mark was adamant that his appearance had to be a total surprise, claiming that the chances for a successful reconciliation with Jeff were far stronger if Jeff wasn't anticipating the meeting. In reality, Mark made this demand to allow himself the chance to back out at the last minute if he decided that morning that he couldn't go through with it. A.J., Dave, and Steve had no problem with this plan and did not suspect Mark's real motive for it.

After much discussion in the days leading up to the trip, it was agreed that Dave would call Jeff's brother Bob to ensure that Jeff would be at the shop on the day they planned to be there. Bob would be told only that Dave, Steve, and A.J. were coming to visit. They also decided to instruct Bob not even to let Jeff know that the three of them were coming to visit; the trip was being orchestrated to be a pleasant surprise for Jeff, quickly followed by the blockbuster of Mark's presence.

As the Escalade neared the Pennsylvania/Maryland border, roughly one hundred miles from Morgantown, Steve took notice of Mark's apparent preoccupation and discomfort and patted him a couple of times on the shoulder. "You doing OK, my man?"

"Yeah, I guess so. I wish I knew how this was going to go. I have no idea how Jeff is going to react, and even less of a clue how I'm going to behave when I see him. What should I say to him? Should I wait for him to say something first? What if—"

Dave cut in from the front seat, "Mark, Mark, Mark! Chill out, please. You're overthinking this and making yourself crazy. Listen, I know it's been a long time, and the relationship is nowhere right now, but still, this is a guy you've known your whole life. The right things to say are just going to come out naturally. I'm sure of it."

"Easy for you to say," grumbled Mark.

Steve chimed in, "You know what? You need to take the edge off. There's a cooler, right behind us in the way back, full of Pete's Wicked Ales and Sierra Nevadas. Whaddaya think, A.J., shouldn't we let our buddy here knock back a brewski to calm himself down?"

"Are you kidding me? The last time I took advice from you morons to do something illegal in this car I got pulled over within fifteen seconds. It's only because the cop happened to be an Upper Hand fan that I, excuse me, I mean *you*, didn't get nailed with a big fine."

"Yeah, yeah, I know, but this is an emergency. Poor Mark is wound up so tight back here we should stamp "Titleist" on his forehead. We gotta chill him down or he's going to stroke out. Come on. No one's going to see anything."

"I could really use one," Mark begged.

A.J. groaned loudly then exhaled slowly. "OK, OK, grab yourself one, Mark, but keep it out of sight, will you? It's highly doubtful the next cop who pulls me over will give a shit that I played bass in a famous rock and roll band. And none for you, drummer boy! You can wait like the rest of us until we get to Morgantown."

Steve spun himself around in his seat, reached into the rear section of the SUV, pried open the lid on the cooler, and extracted two beers. As he turned back around again, A.J., eyeing him through the rearview mirror, admonished him, "Steve! Put that bottle back! I told you, I'll let Mark suck one back for 'emergency medicinal purposes,' but that's it."

"Man, it's like driving with my mother."

"Did your mother blast Pink Floyd through her ten-speaker sound system when she drove you to your soccer games?" A.J. replied, cranking up the volume of "Run Like Hell" to ear-splitting levels. The whole car, including Mark, erupted in laughter, and Steve reluctantly returned his beer to the cooler before popping the cap off Mark's and handing it to him.

After a few more deafening seconds, A.J. returned the volume on his car stereo to a reasonable level, and Mark began draining his Pete's Wicked. A minute later, during a lull in the conversation, Mark, his voice just above a whisper, said, "Hey, guys, I got a question."

Barely able to hear Mark over the music, A.J. punched the off button on the CD player. "Sure, Mark, what is it?"

"What if this goes well tomorrow, and—"

Steve blurted out, "It *is* going to go well, Mark. I'm telling you."

"We'll see. Anyway, if Jeff and I manage to patch things up, if I don't wind up screaming at him, and he doesn't wind up coming at me with a tire iron, do you think it's possible that we could... maybe...put the band back together again?"

Mark's question hit like a bolt of lightning through his travel mates. All three of them wanted to scream *Yes!* But they somehow managed to contain themselves, not wanting to give Mark the impression that the whole purpose of their effort to reunite him and Jeff was simply to resurrect their careers in the Upper Hand.

Dave responded first, revealing only a tiny fraction of the excitement he was feeling, and trying to react as though Mark had just raised a notion that Dave hadn't really thought about before. "You know what? I think that would be awesome. I'd definitely jump back in. What about you guys?"

"Count me in!" exclaimed A.J. as he surreptitiously smacked Dave on the leg in silent celebration.

"Me, too," added Steve.

"Good to know," Mark said quietly. At that moment, Mark, for the first time, committed himself totally to the task at hand the next morning. For better or worse, he was going to make the effort to reconcile with Jeff. There would be no more consideration of backing out at the last minute; he was going to meet Jeff face-to-face in about sixteen hours.

The foursome checked into the Clarion Hotel in Morgantown shortly after 7:00 p.m. A.J., who arranged and paid for the accommodations, decided against four separate rooms, choosing instead a two bedroom suite which he felt would help recapture the spirit of the band's early days on tour. They ordered dinner from room service, began their assault on the cooler of Sierra Nevadas and Pete's Wicked Ales, and settled into the living area of their suite to watch the first two *Die Hard* movies on pay-per-view. The feelings of camaraderie and good humor in the room were infectious, and even Mark found himself having as much fun as he could remember having in years. He spent little time during the evening brooding about the next morning's challenges.

The closing credits of *Die Hard 2*, the empty beer cooler, and the surprising realization that it was after 1:00 a.m. brought the evening's festivities to a close. A.J. and Mark retired to one of the bedrooms, Dave and Steve to the other. After a couple of minutes of general bullshitting about the terrific night the four former bandmates had just had together, Dave, pulling down the covers on his bed, called out to Steve, who was brushing his teeth in the bathroom, "Any predictions?"

Steve finished up at the bathroom sink and sat down on his bed, facing Dave. "Damn, I wish I knew. I'm excited and scared to death at the same time. I'll tell you what makes me feel good, though: Mark talking about getting the Upper Hand back together again. I think he has real incentive to make this work tomorrow."

"Yeah, I thought I was going to jump right through the moon roof when he asked us about possibly reforming the band. Still, I don't know if I'm going to be able to watch this unfold tomorrow. I'm just about puking with anxiety now."

"Me, too. But hey, we've done everything we can, Dave. If I had told you a month ago we'd be sitting here in West Virginia, making final preparations for a Mark/Jeff face-to-face, you'd have told me I was crazy."

In the other bedroom, the conversation didn't switch gears away from good-natured banter until after A.J. turned off the light on the night table between the beds. Mark broke the silence in the almost pitch black room with a simple, heartfelt, "Thank you, A.J."

"You're welcome, Mark, and that's from all three of us. Look, I know you're really struggling with all this, but I truly think tomorrow is going to be a great day. I just wish we'd all put our minds to this years ago."

A.J. could hear a faint chuckle in the darkness. "Nah, I think your timing is just about perfect. A younger me from a few years ago would have been way too stubborn to let you bozos talk me into this. Anyway, good night. I don't think I'll be getting too much sleep tonight, but I'll be ready to go in the morning."

CHAPTER 10

As he had predicted, Mark scarcely slept that night at the Clarion, kept awake by the unending barrage of possible scenarios for his meeting with Jeff running through his mind. After showering and dressing, he headed down to the main lobby level of the hotel and downed three cups of coffee as soon as he joined the others for breakfast in the hotel restaurant.

Mark could not help but notice the exuberant mood of the table as the four men dug into the breakfast buffet. Not only were A.J., Dave, and Steve clearly excited at the prospect of seeing Jeff for the first time in several years, it was also evident that they had high expectations for Mark's attempted reconciliation with Jeff. This optimistic vibe increased the pressure Mark felt to succeed. He ate quietly as his friends chatted happily and refilled their plates. At last the meal ended, and it was time to check out of the hotel and begin the one-hour drive to Bob Britton's auto repair shop in Shinnston.

Notwithstanding Steve and Dave's relentless belittling of Jeff's adopted hometown, Shinnston was a pleasant (if intolerably sleepy by New Jersey standards) little town of around twenty-two hundred residents in northern West Virginia, located close to the Maryland, Pennsylvania, and Ohio borders. A former coal, oil, and natural gas town, Shinnston had long ago transitioned to a service-oriented economy and boasted a small but thriving downtown.

Bob Britton's auto repair shop was located near the edge of town, in an old, two-bay cinder block building that had once served as a gas station. A slightly faded, eight-foot by six-foot painted sign at the edge of the road, featuring a smiling cartoon mechanic wielding a wrench, read:

BRITTON'S AUTO SERVICE

Since 1985

Oil Changes & Routine Maintenance

Engine, Transmission & Brake Repair

Proprietor: Bob Britton

As indicated by the date on his roadside sign, Bob moved from New Jersey to West Virginia in the mid-1980s, at age twenty-six, and immediately started his auto repair business. What the sign didn't reveal was that Bob's relocation to Shinnston had taken place only under duress. While still in high school, Bob began dating a girl named Connie McAllister, whose family had moved from rural West Virginia to Morristown just months before she and Bob met. Never comfortable with the faster pace of life in suburban New Jersey, Connie nevertheless accepted Bob's marriage proposal in 1979, two years after they had graduated from high school, and married him in 1980.

By 1984, Connie and Bob had two sons, and Bob was a well-regarded auto mechanic working at a Midas Muffler shop not far from Morristown. However, by this time it had become apparent that Bob's longstanding prediction that Connie would eventually become comfortable living in New Jersey was not coming true. Rather, Connie's sense of homesickness became more severe once she was home with their boys, and late that year she issued an ultimatum: relocation or divorce. The move to Shinnston took place within six months. Nearly twenty years later, Bob still missed certain aspects of life in New Jersey, and usually managed to sneak in a trip or two back there each year, sometimes with Connie and the kids, and sometimes alone, to visit with family members and old friends. But overall he was happily established as a West Virginia family man, successful business owner, and source of long-term refuge for his recovering addict older brother.

A.J.'s Escalade pulled into the front lot of Britton's Auto Service shortly before 10:00 a.m. It was another balmy, almost cloudless May morning. This time Steve was riding shotgun, and Dave was in the back seat, offering words of encouragement to a nervous Mark.

The doors to both of the garage's work bays were open to take advantage of the spectacular weather. In the right-side work bay a 1998 Ford Taurus sat unattended on the hydraulic lift, suspended seven feet in the air with its tires removed. In the left-side bay Jeff Britton, dressed in well-worn dark green mechanic's garb with "Jeff" embroidered on the shirt pocket, was bent over the open hood of a banged-up 1993 Dodge Intrepid. A red bandana kept his hair out of his face. He was wearing a three-day growth of salt-and-pepper beard.

Bob, who was on the lookout for A.J., Dave, and Steve's arrival, stepped in front of the SUV with a wave, and gestured for A.J. to pull up directly in front of the open bay doors. Mark slid down in his seat to avoid being seen by Bob.

A.J hopped out of the SUV first, quickly put his index finger to his lips to instruct Bob to stay quiet, and then grabbed him in a bear hug. Steve and Dave emerged next, also greeting Bob with hearty and silent handshakes and hugs. Confirming through whispers that the hunched-over figure with his head under the hood of the Intrepid was indeed Jeff, A.J. stepped into the work area, took a deep breath, and bellowed, "What the hell is going on? Why is my fucking Taurus still up on that goddamn lift?"

Dave, Steve, and Bob stifled their laughter as Jeff popped up from under the hood, his eyes wide, searching for the source of the outburst. As soon as he saw that the angry "customer" was A.J., his wrench fell from his hand with a loud clang, and he ran toward his grinning former bandmates, wiping his hands on a rag and yelling, "Ohmygod! Ohmygod! Holy shit! A.J.! Steve! Dave! Ohmygod! Holy shit!" They converged in a joyous, noisy embrace.

Mark, still hidden in the backseat of the Escalade, listened to the happy scene through the open back window. The sound of Jeff's voice shook him, and any remnants of fourteen-year-old anger melted away instantly. He now could hardly wait for an opportune break in the animated conversation, or a signal from one of the guys, to pop out of the back seat and make his appearance.

It took only a minute for an opening to present itself, an enormous if inadvertent cue from Jeff. Taking advantage of a brief pause in the lively chatter, Jeff's voice became noticeably more subdued as he asked, "So, how is Mark doing? Is he OK?"

A wave of stomach-knotting emotion surged through Mark as he absorbed Jeff's obviously sincere show of concern for him. Before anyone else could respond to Jeff's question, Mark opened the door of the SUV and stepped out into full view of the gathering in the work bay. With tears welling up in his eyes, he replied in a wavering voice, "Yeah, he's doing all right. Thanks for asking."

Mark and Jeff stood stock still facing each other, about ten feet apart, Mark wearing a crooked, nervous smile and fighting back tears, Jeff with his hand over his mouth in shock. Mark's still-muscular five-foot-ten-inch frame had added fifteen to twenty additional pounds since the last time Jeff saw him, while Jeff, a lean and athletic six foot one, looked considerably healthier than Mark had expected. The two men still shared essentially the same long, straight, center-part hairstyle they'd each worn more or less continuously since the mid-70s. Mark's hair was the exact same light brown color it had been all his life, thanks to frequent coloring sessions with his stylist, while Jeff's once dark brown locks were now a steely gray.

Wordlessly, they rushed toward each other and embraced. Both broke immediately into violent sobs, neither even attempting to talk for close to half a minute. Steve and Dave smiled at one another and shared subtle fist pumps as A.J. wept openly. A stunned Bob managed to utter to the happy threesome standing with him, "You sly dogs! You sly dogs, you!"

Jeff's first attempt to speak came out as a breathless, incoherent grunt, and Mark fared no better on his first try. Finally, Jeff was able to voice a simple "thank you" into Mark's ear, and then he repeated it over Mark's shoulder towards A.J., Dave, and Steve. The two released each other from their bear hug and began beating each other rhythmically on the chest with the outsides of their fists, a ceremonial gesture of triumph they had developed and used from the time they were in high school until Jeff's descent into heroin addiction. As soon as their three former bandmates witnessed the rebirth of the old chest pounding ritual, any lingering doubts about the prospects for the reconciliation of Jeff and Mark vaporized.

Jeff grabbed Mark by the shoulders and said, "Let's go talk," and led him to the back of the garage toward Bob's tiny office. "Smoke 'em if you got 'em," he called out to the foursome standing in the garage, as he ushered Mark into the office and shut the door.

Bob Britton's office looked exactly like the office of a rural auto repair shop was supposed to look—cluttered, messy, dusty, and devoid of any evidence that the year was 2004. A mere eight feet by seven feet in size, the office was furnished with a metal desk, a three-drawer file cabinet, a rolling office chair whose cushion consisted more of duct tape than its original black vinyl, and a single steel chair for visitors. Every square inch of the desktop was covered in seemingly random piles of pink, yellow, and white bills, invoices, and service orders, and the walls were overwhelmed with thumbtacked and taped photos, reminder notes, and miscellaneous paperwork. A 1997 Playboy Playmate wall calendar hung from the interior side of the door, providing visitors with a cheery smile and pose from that year's Miss September.

Jeff motioned for Mark to sit in the battered office chair, and took a seat in the equally age-worn visitor's chair. Jeff spoke first. "I'm trying to figure out how to squeeze both 'I'm sorry' and 'thank you' into my first sentence to you."

"You really don't have to—"

"Yes, I do, Mark. I've been waiting fourteen years to spill this. Look, ever since that night when we took the stage as the Werewolves and blew away that school talent show crowd, you and I were on a mission to steamroll the whole world the same way."

Mark nodded and smiled at the memory of their triumphant public debut as seventh graders.

"And we did it!" Jeff continued. "We worked our asses off, weeded out the weak links, got the right guys to join us, and conquered the world of rock and roll...and then I flushed the whole thing down the toilet. Goddamn, Mark, even after all these years, I can't come up with the right words to tell you how sorry I am for ruining what we built. I really became a different person that whole last year, a truly shitty person I can't even recognize now, and that miserable son of a bitch blew up a sensational rock band."

Mark, newly willing to forgive Jeff, yet unsure how to respond to this abject apology from his old friend, instead countered with a query. In as gentle, non-accusatory a tone as he could muster, he asked a question he had not once bothered to ponder during the fourteen years of their estrangement: "Jeff, how did it happen? How did that 'other person' take control?"

"I wish to hell I knew. All I can tell you is that I didn't realize it was happening until it was way too late. Heroin is tricky stuff, man. It draws you in nice and easy, but does not let go easy at all. Believe me, from the very next day after I totally lost my mind and left you guys high and dry in Atlanta, I wanted nothing more in the world than to stop using, and it took me five fucking years to become clean once and for all. *Five years!*"

Mark's face hardened suddenly as he uttered, "That bitch Denise. She's the one who got you started on—"

"Nah, I can't really blame it on Denise. Yeah, she introduced me to the stuff, but I jumped in with both feet and went overboard with it. If you remember, she never got anywhere near as bad with it as I did."

"Well, bully for her!" Mark cracked sarcastically. "Listen, I'm here today because I am finally able to get over being mad at you. If it's all the same to you, I'm going to hang on to my anger at Denise, OK?"

Jeff chuckled, "I'm not sure I really have a choice here, but OK."

"You're not in contact with her, are you?"

"I haven't spoken a word to her since the day of my meltdown. I have no idea where she is, or if she's even alive."

"Good."

Jeff did not agree with that sentiment but saw no point in expressing his regret at losing all contact with Denise.

Mark stood up and patted Jeff on the shoulder. "It's good to see you, man. Look, we're gonna need about twelve hours to catch up, but right now, there are three very good friends of ours out there biting their nails waiting for us. And you and I both need to give each of them a huge thank you, because they're the real reason I'm sitting here. They're the ones who jumped on my case and made me realize what a sour old hardass I was. We owe them big time."

"Let's do it, then," replied Jeff, jumping out of his chair and opening the door back to the work area.

Ten seconds later the five members of the Upper Hand were standing together for the first time since 1990, laughing, crying, and celebrating. Bob Britton stood a few feet away watching the happy reunion with mixed emotions. Genuinely pleased to see the key obstacle to his brother's total emotional recovery disappear, he nevertheless felt a heavy sadness at the certainty that Jeff's nine-year residence and refuge in Shinnston was about to end.

As the boisterous gathering in the garage of Bob's auto repair shop continued, one topic remained unspoken—the potential reconstitution of the band. A.J., Dave, and Steve each wanted badly to bring up the subject, but all three held back for fear of coming across to Jeff as being solely concerned with the reformation of the Upper Hand, not with Jeff's personal reconnection with his best friend. Mark, however, had no reservations in this area and, as soon as he found an opportunity to do so, proclaimed loudly, with his fist raised over his head, "I hereby declare the rebirth of America's greatest rock and roll band, the Upper Hand, effective immediately!"

While the rest of them began shouting and clapping in celebration, Jeff found himself once more almost dizzy with shock. He finally gathered himself sufficiently to say, "Guys, excuse me while I pinch myself to be sure I'm not dreaming. This is one of the greatest days of my life, a day I'd just about given up hope would ever come." He paused, and a sheepish grin came across his face. "There's just one thing, though. I haven't touched a guitar in fourteen years. I don't even own one. I might suck."

In response to this surprising revelation, Mark thrust his fist in the air again and announced, "I hereby declare that the aforementioned reunion of America's greatest rock and roll band, the Upper Hand, will be postponed for two weeks while I teach this knucklehead how to play guitar again!"

"You got a deal," Jeff replied. At that moment, Jeff's attention was drawn for the first time to his brother, who was still standing nearby. "Bob," he began, but Bob cut him off.

"Britton, you're fired!" he barked in the best fake angry boss tone he could muster. "Your crummy mechanic services aren't needed around here anymore—" His voice cracked, and he was unable to continue. The two brothers grabbed each other in a long embrace.

"I can never thank you enough for these last nine years," Jeff said.

"Get out there and conquer the world again."

CHAPTER 11

The thunderous response to Jeff and Mark's public debut as the Werewolves was the spark that ignited the two boys' fierce determination to make a mark for themselves in the world of rock and roll. They attempted to balance their passion for music with their continued interest and participation in sports, but with each passing year the balance shifted further and further toward their guitars and rock music. Both boys were excellent athletes, but their diminishing commitment to their high school soccer, basketball, and baseball teams became sources of increasing frustration to their coaches.

Jeff, tall, lean, and agile, was a promising soccer goalie, an All-County forward with a deadly outside shooting touch in basketball, and a slick-fielding first baseman with a smooth, powerful swing. Mark, solidly built like his former Army captain father, was an intimidating if inelegant presence as a soccer defenseman, a rugged, effective rebounder and inside scorer in basketball, and a fearsome fastball pitcher and home run hitting outfielder.

Excitement on the part of the Morristown High School coaches morphed into aggravation by the boys' sophomore year, as skipped practices piled up to accommodate musical commitments. By junior year, even the occasional game would be missed for a gig, infuriating the coaches and souring the boys' relationships with them. The hot-headed and rebellious Mark, in particular, began finding himself the target of these coaches' wrath, most often during gym class where he had no choice but to attend. The boys' hairstyles, which became more and more suited for rock musicians, and thus less and less appropriate for sports, did nothing to improve their rapport with their angry coaches.

At the end of their junior year, in June of 1971, Jeff and Mark decided to abandon high school sports entirely for their upcoming senior year. This decision of course further enraged their coaches, and also strained Mark's relationship with his father, who had not lost his ambivalence over his son's ever-growing passion for rock music. Warren Donahue had always taken great pride in the fact that Mark had inherited his considerable athletic talents. Each step Mark took away from sports in favor of his guitar felt like another smack in the face to Warren.

Their senior year in high school was marked by frequent harassment by coaches as well as former teammates who resented the loss of Mark and Jeff's considerable talents on the soccer field, basketball court, and baseball diamond. Mark was suspended from school twice during that year, once for a profanity-laced retort to one of his gym teacher's harangues, and once for punching out a former baseball teammate who made the mistake of taunting him about his long hair. Even the relatively mild-mannered Jeff earned himself a week's detention for shoving a hostile former basketball teammate against a locker. These conflicts only strengthened the boys' commitment to rock music, providing a sense of rebelliousness that dovetailed perfectly with the image they were cultivating.

As for their music during these years, the biggest challenge Mark and Jeff faced was finding suitable musicians to accompany them. Kevin LaRoche, the drummer for their debut as the Werewolves in seventh grade, did not share their enthusiasm for live performances and departed within weeks of the talent show. What followed over the next five years was a parade of drummers, none possessing anywhere near the level of talent or desire required to satisfy Mark and Jeff. Occasionally a sax player or keyboardist (usually armed with a cheap plastic organ that was more of a toy than a serious musical instrument) would make a cameo appearance, but would quickly be sent on his way. Bass guitarists in their age group were nowhere to be found, much to the boys' dismay.

Their band, such as it was, went through innumerable name changes as well, until they finally settled on "Incendiary," a term their guitar teacher Butch Green once used to describe one of their guitar duets. They played primarily at birthday parties, bar mitzvahs, and other private teen gatherings, as well as at youth events sponsored by local towns in Morris County. Most often the band consisted only of Jeff, Mark, and whoever the drummer *du jour* happened to be.

As is true of many rock bands who make it to the top, who beat the astronomical odds and achieve the fame and fortune that so many others only dream of, the Upper Hand could point to a single day, in this case a Saturday in May of 1972, as the fateful day that ultimately brought the acclaimed five-some together. A local event promoter had put together a Teen Rock Festival as a showcase for Morris County area bands with members under the age of twenty-one. The well-publicized festival, held at the Morristown Armory, a cavernous National Guard facility frequently utilized for trade shows, craft shows, and other exhibits, drew over two thousand local teens. Twelve bands, including Incendiary, were booked to perform thirty-minute sets, beginning at 2:00 that Saturday afternoon. The stage was set up at the far end of the huge, high-ceilinged cinder block building, and the perimeter of the open space was taken up by food concessions, as well as displays of clothing, jewelry, and other teen-oriented paraphernalia.

Incendiary was scheduled to be the fifth band to perform. The group on this day consisted of, Mark and Jeff and the latest in the never-ending string of mediocre drummers to pass through the band, a skinny, bespectacled junior named Eddie Phair, as well as a "bassist," a short, chubby sophomore named Bruce Schneider who lived on the same street as Jeff and Mark. Eddie had been with Incendiary for just six weeks, and Bruce, after begging Mark and Jeff for months to let him into the band, was finally allowed in just a month before the festival.

Bruce did not own a bass guitar. His instrument was a Fender Jaguar guitar strung with just the bottom four strings, with its tone control turned all the way down to minimize treble, and his amplifier similarly dialed in to give his guitar as bottom-heavy a tone as possible. It was only Jeff and Mark's desperation to present Incendiary as a full band at the festival that led them to accept Bruce and his makeshift bass into the group. When Bruce showed up the day of the festival wearing a white button-down shirt, paisley tie, and plaid slacks, Mark and Jeff began to regret their decision to add him to the lineup.

Incendiary took the stage shortly after 5:00 p.m. Mark's muscular frame was well displayed beneath a tight black T-shirt and black jeans, while Jeff wore an unbuttoned blue plaid flannel shirt over a T-shirt bearing the Rolling Stones tongue logo and faded blue jeans. Both wore bandanas to keep sweat and their nearly shoulder length hair out of their eyes. Eddie was decked out in jeans and a green-and-white striped T-shirt; Bruce had been coerced by his fellow band members to remove his tie and to undo the top button of his shirt. As would remain the case for the next eighteen years that they played together, Jeff was strapped to a Fender Stratocaster, Mark to a Gibson Les Paul.

Incendiary's seven song set consisted of three cover songs of recent vintage—The Allman Brothers Band's "Blue Sky," Creedence Clearwater Revival's "Up Around the Bend," and Led Zeppelin's "Rock and Roll"—plus four original compositions, two each by Jeff and Mark. Despite Eddie's wildly inconsistent drumming and Bruce's monotonous plunking on his improvised bass guitar, the group received an enthusiastic response from the young crowd.

By this time, Jeff and Mark had both developed strong vocal capabilities. Jeff had a smooth voice with a powerful upper range, and Mark could generate a distinctive, melodic growl. But it was their guitar work that really had members of the audience talking to one another. Their ability to deliver solos in the styles of Duane Allman, Dickie Betts, Jimmy Page, and John Fogerty, together with their inventive original work, completely overwhelmed the inadequacy of their rhythm section, and earned them by far the loudest ovations so far in the festival.

Paying particularly close attention to Incendiary's performance were two members of a band called Hatful of Dynamite, the band scheduled to go on two slots after Incendiary. "Shit, I'm glad we don't have to take the stage right after these two monsters," yelled twenty-year-old keyboard player Dave Rowinski into the ear of nineteen-year-old drummer Steve Holmes over the roar of Incendiary's guitars and drums. Steve nodded in agreement. "The rest of their band is pathetic, though."

"I know. Are you thinking what I'm thinking?" Steve's head nodded in assent again, and then the two of them went back to watching Mark and Jeff trade fiery guitar leads on "Blue Sky."

Dave Rowinski was raised in East Hanover, a pleasant suburban town less than fifteen minutes from Morristown. His start in music was not a happy one, and took place only under parental pressure. Like millions of boys growing up in the 1960s, Dave wanted badly to learn to play the guitar. He vacillated from day to day between wanting to become a raucous electric guitar slinger like Keith Richards, or an introspective acoustic guitarist/songwriter like Paul Simon or Bob Dylan, but there was no doubt in his mind that the guitar was his musical instrument of choice. However, his strong-willed mother had other ideas. She categorically vetoed Dave's request for guitar lessons, and forced him to take piano lessons instead, beginning in 1965 when Dave was thirteen.

Piano lessons represented nothing but a chore to Dave, and he progressed in his grasp of classical and jazz piano techniques more or less in spite of himself. Although there were certainly a number of important rock bands in the mid-1960s utilizing keyboards in significant roles—the Animals, the Rascals, and the Dave Clark Five, among others—Dave could see no connection whatsoever between his coerced mastery of the piano and the rock and folk music he longed to play.

Dave's attitude towards his piano lessons changed suddenly and irrevocably on a Wednesday afternoon in April of 1967.

Dave was taking a break from his tedious piano practice, listening to the radio, when the deejay dropped the needle on a brand new single from a band Dave had never heard of, the Doors. As Ray Manzarek's fleet-fingered, vaguely classical, and utterly unforgettable organ intro to "Light My Fire" filled the room, Dave's jaw dropped. He quickly grabbed a piece of paper and pencil to write down the name of the song and band and sat wide-eyed through the rest of the song. *Holy shit. That's how I'm going to turn these piano lessons into something useful!* He got his older brother Greg to drive him to a local record shop that evening and purchased not the "Light My Fire" single, but the Doors' first album, which, to his amazement when he first played it that night, contained not the brief edited single version of "Light My Fire" he had heard on the radio that afternoon, but rather the full seven-minute rendition featuring a stunning, lengthy organ solo by Manzarek.

As soon as the needle lifted off side two of his new Doors album, Dave marched downstairs from his bedroom to the living room of the Rowinskis' split-level house where his mother and father were both reading the *Newark Evening News*. He announced, to his mother's initial delight, that he was willing to double the amount of time he would devote to keyboard practice every week. Then he followed this pronouncement with his non-negotiable condition for fulfillment of this offer: that his parents buy him a Vox organ, and that he be allowed to spend half of his practice time playing the Vox. His mother, pleased to see evidence of enthusiasm from Dave regarding his piano playing (and clueless about the type of music Dave had in mind for the mysterious Vox organ he wanted), readily agreed. The purchase of the Vox that ensuing weekend sparked a passion for keyboard playing that would serve Dave extremely well for decades to come. His dreams of abandoning piano for guitar went out the window instantly.

Steve Holmes grew up one town over from East Hanover, in Florham Park. If rock and roll hadn't already burst into existence by the time Steve was a child, it would have had to be invented simply to accommodate the boy's incessant need to bang rhythmically on just about anything that didn't move: pots and pans with wooden spoons, tabletops with open palms, school desks with yellow Number Two pencils. The highly energetic Steve Holmes would pound away on almost any available surface, with almost any (or no) implements.

Strangely, no one in Steve's family ever thought about trying to channel the boy's energy and natural rhythmic sense towards proper instruments or instruction. Aside from a set of toy bongos given to him by his grandparents when he was six, Steve never encountered or contemplated playing real drums or other percussion instruments until the day he met high school classmate Dave Rowinski at the beginning of his junior year, in 1968.

East Hanover and Florham Park both funneled their graduating eighth graders to the same high school, Hanover Park High School. Dave and Steve, who had not had occasion to meet during their first two years in the same school, found themselves seated next to each other in Social Studies class in junior year. After watching Steve for two or three days as he pounded away on his desk with his bare hands or pencils in the minutes leading up to the start of class, Dave finally asked him, "Hey, man. Do you play drums?"

"Nah."

"Well, why the hell not? You'd be pretty good at it based on the way you bang on that desk."

Steve looked at Dave for a couple of seconds, shrugged, and replied, "I guess I never really thought about it."

"Listen, I play organ, and a friend of mine sings. We're looking to start a band, and we need a drummer. My older brother is in college, and he left his drums in our basement. You want to come over and try out your chops on some real drums?"

"Sure, why not? Might be fun."

That afternoon's basement session resulted in Dave and Steve becoming musical colleagues for over two decades and best friends for life.

Hatful of Dynamite, the band founded almost four years earlier in Dave's basement shortly after he introduced Steve to his brother's drums, also included Dave's childhood friend Phil Lanza on vocals, and guitarist Ron Blackwood, who had been with them for almost a year. Hatful of Dynamite had no bass guitarist; Dave handled bass duties on his Vox organ with his left hand.

Jeff and Mark finished packing up their equipment and accepting congratulations from friends in time to catch Hatful of Dynamite's set, which consisted of six cover tunes from popular contemporary rock bands ranging from the Rascals to the Doors to the Guess Who. Eddie and Bruce were not interested in hanging around for the rest of the festival, and left together.

Hatful of Dynamite launched into their first song, the Rascals' lively rocker "Come on Up." Jeff and Mark, immediately riveted by the sight and sound of a real drummer plying his craft, poked each other in the ribs with their elbows and pointed every time Steve executed another explosive run on his drums. Their attention was also drawn to Dave's considerable keyboard prowess and strong backing vocals, but they were singularly unimpressed with the band's other two members. Guitarist Ron Blackwood played nothing but the most basic of rhythm parts, even letting Dave provide keyboard solos where guitar solos should have been. Vocalist Phil Lanza, who did deliver a highly animated, strutting, rock and roll front man performance, was really just a shouter, not a singer. Still, Hatful of Dynamite was well received by the crowd and left the stage to hearty applause.

Twenty minutes after Hatful of Dynamite's performance, Mark and Jeff stood near a concession stand downing hot dogs and Cokes. Dave and Steve approached the two boys. Although there was only two year's difference in age between the Incendiary guitarists and the duo from Hatful of Dynamite, they looked like they were in entirely different stages of life. Mark was barely shaving, Jeff not at all; faint remnants of battles with acne were still visible on both their faces. In contrast, Dave already had the big droopy mustache he would soon become well known for, and Steve, while clean shaven, looked more like a twenty-five year old than the late teenager he was.

Steve began the conversation. "Hey, you two guys were amazing. I loved listening to you pound out those Zeppelin and Allman Brothers leads."

Before Mark or Jeff could thank Steve for the compliment, offer one in return, or introduce themselves, Dave added with a smile, "But the rest of your band sucks."

Jeff chuckled ruefully and replied, "No argument there. Good help is hard to find."

Mark chimed in, "I could say the same about your band." He turned to Steve. "You're a fucking killer on drums! Jeff and I were drooling watching you out there." He switched his gaze back towards Dave. "And you! You're a double threat—great keyboards, cool vocals. Hell, you should be the lead singer of your group. That guy you've got didn't hit one decent note during your whole set."

"Ahh, Phil's not so bad. He just gets a little bit worked up and starts hollering instead of singing sometimes."

"And what's with your guitar player? Is he just lazy, or does he really just know three chords? He left you to do all the solos on your Vox, which were awesome, by the way."

Steve stepped between Jeff and Mark and clasped one hand on each one's shoulder. "You're absolutely right, he's dead weight. That's why we'd love to have you two guitar slingers join Hatful of Dynamite."

Jeff and Mark stared wide-eyed at each other and then back at Steve and Dave. Mark, sensing that Jeff was about to immediately agree to Steve's proposal, replied, "I've got a better idea. How about if you two guys join *our* band?"

The next thirty seconds or so were taken up by Steve and Dave verbally battling Mark two-on-one over the relative merits, popularity, and viability of Hatful of Dynamite versus Incendiary until Jeff emitted a sharp whistle and yelled, "Shut up, all three of you! There's only one way to handle this. We're not joining your band, and you're not joining ours. Here's what's going to happen: the four of us are going to form a totally new, kick-ass band that's going to leave all of these other groups begging for mercy. Agreed?"

Dave, Steve, and Mark all nodded their heads affirmatively, but then Dave stopped and asked, "What about Phil?"

Mark quickly replied, "Are you kidding me? You, me, and Jeff all sing ten times better than that guy, and he doesn't even play an instrument. Adios to him. This band is gonna be great, and we can't be dicking around with guys like that, even if he's your friend."

"He's right, Dave," said Steve, and Dave murmured his reluctant agreement. Dave had known Phil since fifth grade, and this sudden parting of the ways was not going to be pleasant.

Jeff followed up on Mark's train of thought. "We need a fifth guy, but not a singer. We need a bass player. I heard you doing bass lines on your Vox, which was pretty cool, but if we're going to be serious, we need both of your hands playing regular keyboard stuff and a real bassist laying down the bottom end. God knows Mark and I haven't had any luck finding one. Do you guys know any good bassists?"

Steve replied, "I may have a solution for us. There's a band playing at this festival right after these guys setting up onstage now, called the Hell Raisers. We've seen them play at a couple of our gigs. They're pretty shitty, but they have this amazing—and I mean *amazing*—bass player, this funny-looking frizzy haired guy from Parsippany who'll knock your socks off. If we could nab him from that crappy group he's in now, we'd be set."

The four young musicians agreed to wait around to watch the Hell Raisers and try to get a conversation with their bassist after the performance. As they settled in to check out the band currently onstage, it dawned on Jeff that these two pairs of ambitious young rockers who were about to join forces to create a hot new band didn't even know each other's names. "Since it looks like we're going to be spending a lot of time together, it probably makes sense to introduce ourselves. I'm Jeff Britton, and this is Mark Donahue. We live in Morristown. We're graduating from Morristown High next month."

"Nice to meet you. I'm Dave Rowinski, and this drumming maniac here is Steve Holmes. We both graduated from Hanover Park in '70. Steve works at Robbie's Music, and I work at Sam Goody's at the Livingston Mall. I got the feeling that once we get this band up and running, Steve and I are going to be able to kiss those crummy jobs goodbye forever."

Once the introductions were done, Mark said to Dave, "Jeff and I write our own music. I'm sure you noticed that four of the songs we played today were originals. How about you? Do you write?"

Dave would regret his response for decades to come. The truth was yes, Dave had been writing his own songs for the past six months and had drafts for seven or eight compositions written down and recorded on cassettes. But he lacked confidence in the quality of his work, had never revealed to Steve or the other members of Hatful of Dynamite that these songs existed, and did not feel ready to expose them to the scrutiny of his soon-to-be new band. "No, I haven't really gotten into that yet," he replied, effectively handing over the roles of principal songwriters for the Upper Hand to Jeff and Mark before the band was even formed or named. By the time Dave gained enough faith in his songwriting to present his songs to the rest of the group, Jeff and Mark were firmly established as the Upper Hand's creative forces. Dave's contributions were never looked upon as anything more than change of pace diversions. Decades later, Dave was still kicking himself for his initial timidity regarding his compositional capabilities.

As the Hell Raisers took the stage to set up their equipment, Steve came across a small pile of single printed sheets bearing a photo and some information about the band on a folding table near the stage. He plucked one of the sheets off the stack, looked at it for a couple of seconds, and let out a low, "Oh, shit."

"What's wrong?" asked Jeff.

"The bass player and the drummer in this trio have the same last name, Ramello. They've got to be brothers. He's not going to leave his own brother to join up with us!"

Dave put his hand on Steve's shoulder and joked, "Well, Steve, that's a damned shame. Looks like the Ramello brothers are in, and you're out. Good luck to you!"

Steve was not amused. "Fuck you, man. Ain't nobody gonna keep me from being the drummer for this band!"

Mark offered, "How about a two-drummer line-up, like the Allman Brothers Band? If this bass player is as good as you say, it might be worth taking on his brother as well, not instead of you, Steve, but in addition."

Dave could see Steve bristling at the idea of sharing drum duties and quickly replied, "Nah, forget that. That drummer isn't any good. Believe me, the bass player is the only one we want; you'll see. I'm not so sure now that we're going to be able to get him, but we gotta try."

The Hell Raisers started their set, a collection of covers by hard rock acts including Cream, Vanilla Fudge, Iron Butterfly, and Black Sabbath. While not really deserving the "shitty" tag Steve had given to them, the Hell Raisers' drummer, Vinny Ramello, and their guitarist/vocalist, Richie Zarrillo, were adequate at best. But the quality of their performances was of no interest whatsoever to the four young men watching intently ten feet from the stage. They listened and stared as A.J. Ramello dominated the sound of the band with thunderous runs up and down the fretboard of his cherry red Fender Precision bass, at once awestruck by A.J.'s talent and disheartened by the realization that he would almost certainly not agree to leave a band that included his own brother.

When the Hell Raisers finished their set, A.J. stepped up to Richie's microphone to address the applauding crowd. "Thank you, thank you so much. Before we make way for the next act, a terrific band known as the Jersey Blasters, I have an announcement to make. Today's performance, sadly, will be the last for the Hell Raisers. My brother Vinny has joined the Navy and heads off for Virginia next month, and Richie here has been accepted at the University of New Hampshire and will be leaving for school in August. Richie, Vinny, and I want to thank all of our friends and fans for your amazing support over these past three years. Take care, and thanks again!"

Mark, Jeff, Dave, and Steve stared at each other in disbelief. "Unfuckingbelievable!" shouted Steve. "He's got no band! This is perfect!"

"Uh oh," called out Dave, pointing with his thumb toward a trio of teens talking excitedly among themselves about twenty feet away. "Those guys are from the band the M-80s. They played right after we did. They don't have a bass player, and there's no doubt that they're thinking the same thing we are. We gotta get to that guy before they do."

"Wait a minute," said Mark. "Jeff, those guys are the douche bags who zoomed around us and cut us off in the parking lot to get that great parking space today. Well, I got news for you guys, there is no way those jerk-offs are getting first crack at that bassist. Dave and Steve, you head over there by the stage and catch—what's his name, A.J.?—when he's through packing up his stuff. Jeff and I will take care of these guys. C'mon, Jeff."

At that Mark began walking briskly to intercept the members of the M-80s, who were already heading toward the spot where A.J. was sure to emerge. Jeff followed, unsure of what Mark had in mind.

Mark stepped directly into the path of the trio of rival musicians. "Where do you think you're going?" he challenged.

One of the boys, a short, chubby seventeen year old who played drums for the M-80s, retorted, "What's it to you?" He attempted to walk past Mark, but Mark aggressively blocked him.

"I'll tell you 'what's it to me.' You assholes cut me off in the parking lot this morning, and now I'm cutting you off. Turn around and get the fuck out of here."

The M-80s' keyboard player, also heavyset but taller than the first boy, began to protest, "You can't tell us—" but immediately found himself nose to nose with Mark, a fistful of his T-shirt balled up in the vise-like grip of Mark's left hand.

The cold menace in Mark's eyes and voice, together with the sight of his powerful arms bulging out of his skintight black T-shirt, paralyzed all three of the M-80s. "Listen to me, cocksucker, and you two dickheads, too. You're already due for a beating for that wiseass move in the parking lot, and I'm gonna deliver it right now if you don't get out of my sight in the next ten seconds. Do any of you doubt that I can and will beat the living shit out of all three of you? *Do you?*"

He released his grip on the boy's shirt and shoved him backwards. The three shell-shocked boys, trying not to look terrified but clearly unwilling to risk a physical battle with the brawny, black-clad fire breather staring daggers at them, slunk away, muttering insults under their breath.

Dave and Steve, who witnessed the entire encounter, stared in astonishment at Mark and then at each other.

"I think this guy's serious," deadpanned Steve.

"I think you're right. I'm glad he's on our side."

Jeff and Mark then strode over from the spot of the confrontation to where Dave and Steve stood. With a huge grin on his face, Jeff announced, "After a frank exchange of views, it was unanimously agreed that the M-80s will not be pursuing the musical services of Mr. A.J. Ramello. So, boys, let's go get us a bass player!"

CHAPTER 12

The five members of the about-to-be-reborn Upper Hand arrived at Mark's house weary but upbeat after the long drive from Shinnston. It had been enthusiastically agreed upon by everyone that Jeff would stay at Mark's house for the next two to three weeks to undergo an intensive guitar "boot camp" with Mark, and then the fivesome would convene at Mark's in-home studio, just as they had done so many times years before, to relearn and rehearse their old repertoire. Mark used his key to activate his electric garage door opener, and they all marched up the stairs from the garage to the main level of the house. It was 9:30 in the evening.

The group headed straight to Mark's billiard room, and raided the refrigerator for beers. No one took particular note of the fact that Jeff chose a Diet Pepsi. It took Jeff less than half a minute to notice that the wall of Mark's billiard room, which he remembered so well for its wide-ranging array of Upper Hand memorabilia, was now haphazardly adorned with just three framed pieces and a newspaper clipping. "Mark, what the heck happened to your amazing wall?"

Dave and Steve couldn't suppress chuckles, and A.J. just smiled.

"It's a long story, my man," replied Mark, "but for now let's just say that these boys here were not happy with my more recent minimalist approach to that wall. In fact, if you look over there, I think you'll see A.J.'s palm print of disapproval. Those four things hanging there now are just a groundbreaking for the restoration of the wall to its former glory. Maybe while you're here these next couple of weeks you can give me a hand with it."

Jeff, immediately grasping the connection between the status of the wall and the status of his relationship with Mark, eagerly replied, "You bet!"

When everyone had finished his drink, Mark stood up and announced, "OK, you clowns, I'm kicking you out now. Jeff and I gotta rest up so we can hit the ground running tomorrow at my special guitar boot camp. We'll be in touch in a couple of weeks, when I decide he's been whipped back into shape."

"Jeez, I hope I survive this."

Mark and Jeff gave each of their departing friends long, heartfelt hugs, and suddenly they were alone. Mark could sense that Jeff was preparing to issue another emotional apology or thank you to him, but he preempted him with, "Jeff, before you say anything, you and I have spent much of the past two days apologizing to each other for causing or extending the fourteen-year black hole in our friendship. What do you say we draw a line, right here and now, and just start focusing forward and doing what we can to make up for the lost time?"

"That would be fantastic." Jeff paused for a couple of seconds. "There's just one thing I need to ask you about. I know you got married again a few years back, and that it didn't work out. What was the deal there?"

With Jeff back in his life, it now seemed absurd to Mark that he could possibly have met, married, and divorced a woman whom Jeff had never met. Mark's first marriage to longtime girlfriend and Morristown native JoAnn Kelley lasted from 1978 to 1987 and produced a daughter, Gabriella, born in 1981. He met his second wife, a freelance reporter named Joanne Fisk, when she interviewed him for a local newspaper during a stop in Hartford on his third solo tour in 1996. They married in 1998 but split three years later. On rare occasions when he was in the right mood to do so, Mark would joke that Joanne had left him for blurting out JoAnn's name during sex.

Mark generally disliked talking about his failed marriages but felt comfortable answering Jeff's question thoughtfully. "I wasn't the best husband and father to JoAnn and Gabriella, you know that. Typical rock and roll bad boy stuff, which you were witness to. But with the second Joanne—yeah, her name is Joanne, too, Joanne Fisk—I really made an effort not to make the same mistakes I made the first time around. I never really understood why she bolted, but with all the stuff that's gone on these past couple of weeks, I think I may have just figured it out. I was probably just too goddamn cranky to be around. Joanne is a really upbeat, fun lady. You'd like her. Anyway, as has been made abundantly clear to me by our buddies Dave, A.J., and Steve, I have not exactly been a barrel of laughs since, well, you know."

Mark continued, but was now speaking more to himself than to Jeff. "Damn, I'll bet that's it. She just got tired of my bitching and moaning. Shit. She was a good one, too. I'd love to get a 'do-over' with her."

Suddenly he brightened, and planted a huge smile on his face to make sure that Jeff would understand that his next statement was a joke. "Hey, that means I can blame my second divorce on you!"

Jeff groaned and flung a nearby pillow at Mark's head. Then, turning serious, he asked, "How are things with you and Gabriella?"

"Depends on how recently her mother has reminded her of what a lousy husband and father I was to them. Right now we're pretty cool, although she's not thrilled with my new girlfriend Emily, because she's only about seven years older than Gabriella."

"You dog, you!"

"Yeah, yeah, you sound just like Gabby. Emily lives in Manhattan. You'll meet her soon."

"I look forward to it. And now that you've become Mr. Sunshine again, there's no way this one's gonna get away!"

The pillow was launched on a return trip back toward Jeff's face.

"Hey, Jeff, how about you? Is there a woman of significance down there in West Virginia that you'll be summoning up here sometime soon?"

"Nah. I dated a bit during my time in Shinnston, but I think I purposely avoided getting seriously involved with anyone. Even though I was there for what, nine years? I always felt like I was just visiting and wouldn't be around long enough to settle down."

"In other words, you were in a holding pattern, waiting for me to get my head out of my ass."

Jeff laughed softly. "Yeah, I guess so."

"Let me ask you something. If Shinnston never really felt like home, why didn't you come back to Jersey years ago? You certainly didn't need anyone's permission, including mine, to come back here. You weren't exiled."

"It's hard to explain, but in a way I did feel like I was in exile. As long as things weren't right between you and me, it didn't feel right to come back here and try to pick up the pieces of my old life. Besides, it's cheap to live in West Virginia, and I did at least have a job at Bob's garage."

"Are you OK financially?"

"Yeah, even I couldn't piss away all the money we made. The payments from all those greatest hits packages Signature Records has released over the past decade haven't hurt either. But still, it seemed like a prudent idea to just stay down there where it costs next to nothing to do anything and fix cars for Bob."

"Speaking of Signature Records, Stan Rabin is gonna cream his trousers when he hears that the Upper Hand is back together. That label is hurting without us. I think Stan keeps repackaging and re-releasing our stuff just to keep the business afloat."

"Yeah, I think you're right. We'll have to talk with Kevin, but I'm pretty sure the Upper Hand still owes Signature one or two more studio albums under the last contract." Kevin LaRoche, the drummer for Mark and Jeff's very first public performance as the Werewolves, remained friends with both boys after quitting the band, became the road equipment manager for the Upper Hand during their early years, and after graduating from Rutgers with an accounting degree, moved up to become the band's business manager.

"By the way," Jeff continued, "why didn't you stick with Signature for your solo albums?"

"I don't know. They were always pretty fair with us, but there's just something about that guy Rabin that creeps me out. Always dressed in a suit and tie, with those big bug eyes and that weasely little smile, it just felt right to go somewhere else for a change. Hey, how did you know my solo albums are on a different label?"

"It's not exactly rocket science. The name Waterfront Records is printed right on the back of the CD case on each of your albums, isn't it?"

"You mean you bought copies of my solo albums?"

"Sure I did. And I like them, too. Some real nice stuff on those disks."

"*Aarrgh!* Now I feel even worse about shutting you out for so long. Let's call it a night before you say something else to make me feel even more guilty."

The selection of breakfast foods available at Mark's house was decidedly uninspiring, so he and Jeff headed out the next morning to one of their favorite old haunts, the Tick Tock Diner, an iconic landmark eatery just off Route 3 in Clifton, New Jersey. Mark was clad in a black golf shirt, blue jeans, and deck shoes, Jeff in a pale green short-sleeved button-down shirt left open over a white T-shirt, jeans, and work boots. A weathered Yankees baseball cap perched on Jeff's head.

Still a frequent customer at Tick Tock, Mark was recognized and greeted by several of the waitresses, but no one took any particular notice of his companion. As they pondered the almost infinite choices on the menu, Jeff took a long sip out of his first cup of coffee, put down the cup, and said, "Mark, I've got a question for you. It's an incredibly cool thing for the five of us that the Upper Hand is getting back together, but do you think the world is going to care? We've been out of the loop for a long time."

Mark peered over the top of his menu. "If you listen to what Dave says, bands that were nowhere near as big as we were are reforming left and right, drawing huge crowds, and selling shitloads of new CDs. So that's encouraging."

"Yeah, but Dave really *needs* this reunion to be successful with all that expensive medical stuff his poor son has to go through. His perception might be skewed a bit by wishful thinking."

"Well, we won't find out unless we give it a shot, and we're going to give it a shot."

"Do you find it strange that in a place with all these people, nobody has paid any attention to us? When we used to come here back in the '70s and '80s, we'd be mobbed by fans, girls, autograph hunters, and rock wannabes looking for guitar-playing tips."

"Nah, don't fret about that. First of all, I'm a regular here, so nobody's gonna jump up and down when I show up. Second, we used to come in here after midnight, when the rock and roll crowd was hanging out. Look around you. It's breakfast time. Does this look like a rock and roll crowd to you? And third, with that gray hair of yours, you're damned near unrecognizable from our old band photos. You might want to look into doing something about that." In a conspiratorial whisper, he added, "I do."

Jeff glanced quickly at Mark's light brown hair and went back to his menu.

When they returned to Mark's house from the Tick Tock Diner, Jeff and Mark headed straight to Mark's studio. Two Gibson Les Paul Customs, one sunburst and one black, sat side by side on matching black tripod guitar stands, tuned up, and plugged in to practice amps. A pair of padded stools was positioned in front of the amps. Mark walked over to the amps, bent over, and turned each one on. He handed Jeff a guitar pick and gestured toward the guitars, inviting him to pick up whichever one struck his fancy. Jeff hoisted the black one, sat down on one of the stools, and began strumming some simple chord patterns. It was his first time touching a guitar since he had laid his on the floor of the stage in Atlanta in 1990. Mark did not pick up the other guitar to join in with Jeff, or even say anything to him, for several minutes, letting Jeff get reacquainted with the instrument at his own pace. Gradually Jeff moved on from simple strumming to some basic, and then not so basic, lead passages. At that point Mark plucked the sunburst Les Paul off its stand and began playing along. Jeff smiled broadly, and without a word, the two began recreating a few of the interlocking guitar parts that had helped make them famous.

As the hours passed in this initial "rehab" session for Jeff's guitar playing, it became apparent that, although he had most certainly not forgotten how to play the instrument, the extended time away had taken its toll. He still knew for the most part where he wanted his fingers to go, but getting them there with his accustomed speed and smoothness was another matter. It was clearly going to take some work to recover his once extraordinary dexterity. As for his memory of his parts in specific Upper Hand songs, he was disappointed to discover that he was only batting around .500.

During one particularly frustrating attempt to execute his lead guitar part from "Circling the Drain," one of his own best-known compositions, Jeff suddenly stopped playing and blurted out, "*Aarrgh!* That's it. I can't go on like this!"

Mark stared at him in alarm. "C'mon, you can't give up so soon. It's just your first day." He stopped when he saw Jeff's face break into a huge grin.

"No, no, no. That's not what I mean. I can't play any more on this plank you call a guitar. I want a Strat—now!"

A key element of the Upper Hand's tremendous success had been their instantly recognizable guitar sound, a combination of techniques and tones that remained remarkably consistent throughout their long recording and concert career. Most of their fans, of course, had no knowledge or interest in the equipment used by the band's two guitarists to achieve that winning formula; they just knew they liked what they heard and knew right away it was the Upper Hand when one of their songs was played on the radio. However, there was a sub-group of serious Upper Hand fans (virtually all of them young males, most of them guitar players themselves) which was fully aware that Mark Donahue always played Gibson Les Pauls, and that Jeff Britton was equally loyal to Fender Stratocasters. These highly devoted followers of the band had little trouble determining who played which part on any electric guitar-driven song in the Upper Hand catalog, thanks in large part to the significant contrast between the clear, clean twang of Jeff's Stratocaster and the darker, heavier bark of Mark's Les Paul. Jeff and Mark were well aware of this fanatical following and never risked disappointing them by straying from their weapons of choice. Occasionally in concert, one of them would teasingly ask the audience if they'd like to see the two guitarists swap axes for the next song, to the inevitable loud chorus of "*No!*" from the hard-core fans in the crowd.

Mark howled at Jeff's rude dismissal of his prized Les Paul Custom and exclaimed in response, "Sorry, pal, we don't keep any of those screechy Strat things around here. This is a Gibson household."

"Then there's only one solution: road trip. I've got to get myself a couple of Stratocasters before I play another note. Damn, the neck on this thing feels like a fucking two by four."

"To each his own, my man. Those skinny Strat necks feel like they belong on a ukulele to me. Anyway, it sounds like we're heading to 48th Street. Let's see, it's 2:00 on a Saturday afternoon; should be no problem getting into Manhattan by car if we leave now."

Just east of 7th Avenue on West 48th Street in midtown Manhattan was a group of music shops often referred to collectively and affectionately as Music Row. Manny's, Rudy's, and Sam Ash had together constituted New York's premier musical instrument destination since the 1950s and had become particularly well known for their spectacular offerings of guitars. Megastars and everyday players alike would bypass their local music shops to make the trip into New York City to ogle, test drive, and purchase their guitars from these landmark shops. Although there were several well-stocked music shops located within just a few miles of Mark's home in Caldwell, both Mark and Jeff felt compelled to cross the Hudson River into New York to acquire for Jeff his beloved Fender Stratocasters.

After checking out the street-level display windows of the three famous shops, each of which contained an awe-inspiring collection of new and vintage guitars, Jeff and Mark made the random choice to enter Sam Ash. As was typical for a Saturday afternoon, the shop was crowded with customers, almost entirely young and middle-aged males. A small number of them were actually there with the serious intent of buying an instrument; the rest had used the excuse of needing a new cable or set of strings to stop by and gaze upon, hold, and play guitars they would never own.

A forty-ish, heavyset man with long thinning black hair and dressed in a black Pink Floyd *Dark Side of the Moon* prism logo T-shirt was chatting about the relative benefits of two different brands of guitar strings with a young salesman behind one of the counters when Jeff and Mark's entrance into the store caught his eye.

"Hey, aren't those the guys from the Upper Hand? Mark Donnelly, or Donaldson, or something like that, and Jeff something-or-other?"

"Nah, it couldn't be. The one guy, Jeff Britton, is dead, I think."

Another forty-something customer who was standing nearby and had overheard this exchange broke in. "No, no, no, that's them for sure. Mark Donahue and Jeff Britton. Holy shit, those guys haven't played together in years! Maybe the Upper Hand is getting back together."

Within seconds an unmistakable buzz migrated throughout the store surrounding the arrival of the two renowned guitarists. Even customers who were not familiar with Mark Donahue or Jeff Britton quickly figured out that two important musicians had just entered the store.

Barry Lederman, the thirty-nine-year-old store manager on duty that afternoon, caught wind of the vibe of excitement coursing through the shop and peered up from a stack of paperwork he had been browsing through behind one of the display counters. His eyes went wide when he spotted Mark and Jeff, and he jumped out from behind the counter to greet them.

"Mr. Britton, Mr. Donahue, it's an honor to have you here! My name is Barry. How can I help you?"

Before either Mark or Jeff could respond, several customers clustered around them and started peppering them with declarations of admiration, as well as questions about the status of their famous band.

"Are you guys back together?"

"Is the Upper Hand going on tour?"

"Have you ended your feud?"

Mark held up his hands to quiet the gathering and said, "Hi, everyone. Thanks for the warm greeting. Yes, I'm happy to be able to say that the Upper Hand is indeed in the process of reforming, and we hope to be out on tour sometime soon. My man Jeff, here, has been away from the rock world for a while, so we're here to get him some guitars, so we can get back to playing those songs you want to hear."

As Mark attempted to field the continuing barrage of questions from the small crowd surrounding him, Jeff turned to Barry and began, "Hello, Barry, I'm looking for—"

Barry didn't need Jeff to finish his sentence. "Mr. Britton, we have the best selection of Stratocasters in the city. Follow me, and I'll set up an amp and a stool for you over where the Strats are displayed."

"OK, but you gotta cut out that 'Mr. Britton' shit. It's Jeff."

Barry, followed by Jeff, Mark, and several star-struck and curious customers, headed for the section of the store where over a dozen Fender Stratocasters hung from wall-mounted neck hooks. He pulled over a pair of stools and turned on and plugged in patch cords to, not one, but two nearby amplifiers. He then jogged over to the area of the store where Gibson guitars were displayed, plucked a gold-top Les Paul from its hook, and trotted back to where Jeff was already busy examining the selection of Stratocasters. He handed the Les Paul to Mark and said with a grin, "There's really no way to tell which Strat is right for Jeff unless he hears it played against a Les Paul, is there?"

Mark accepted the guitar with a smile. "You're a smart man. I can see why you're the manager here."

Over the next hour and fifteen minutes, the employees and customers at Sam Ash were treated to a spontaneous jam session, courtesy of Mark Donahue and Jeff Britton. The familiar feel of a Stratocaster, together with the energy generated by the small but enraptured crowd, enabled Jeff to quickly shake off a lot of the rust in his playing. Barry kept turning up the volumes on the amps, and before long a microphone was provided for vocals. Customers were banging on percussion instruments handed out by salespeople, and Mark and Jeff were fulfilling shouted requests for Upper Hand hits. The performances, especially Jeff's, were ragged, but absolutely no one cared, and loud applause greeted every song.

Finally, the impromptu performance came to an end, and Mark and Jeff profusely thanked and shook hands with their thrilled audience. Jeff chose two Fender American Deluxe Stratocasters, one black, the other one red, from the eight guitars he had tried.

Barry Lederman's great day at work got even better when Jeff suddenly announced to Mark, "Wait a minute. I'm gonna need acoustic guitars, too. Barry, you pack up these Strats, and then meet me in the acoustic room."

Forty minutes later, Jeff added a Martin six-string acoustic and a Guild twelve-string acoustic, both equipped with built-in electronics for live performance amplification, to his new arsenal of guitars. As Jeff was finishing the process of paying for his four new guitars, Barry held out his hand and said, "Thank you so much, Mr. Britton—sorry, *Jeff*—not just for your business, but for the coolest afternoon I've ever spent here."

"Hey, Barry, it was pretty cool for me too. It's been a long time, a *very* long time, since I've played, and this little session here today made me realize how much I missed it. Your clever idea to hand that Les Paul to Mark was absolute genius. I won't forget this. I expect to be needing a lot more equipment soon, and I'm coming straight to you to get it."

Barry's euphoria kicked up another notch. Figuring he was on an incredible roll, he turned to Mark and asked, "Mark, is there by any chance something I can help *you* with this afternoon?"

Mark smiled. "No, I'm pretty well stocked right now. Besides, I think you've bagged your limit for one day!"

As the happy duo stepped onto the West 48th Street sidewalk, each bearing two of Jeff's new guitars, Mark nudged Jeff with his shoulder and grinned. "Still worried that no one's gonna give a shit about the Upper Hand getting back together?"

As soon as they returned home, Mark headed straight to his refrigerator and pulled out two bottles of Belhaven Scottish Ale. After popping the caps on the beers, he headed to his comfortable TV room, where Jeff was busy tuning up his new acoustic twelve string. Mark offered one of the Belhavens to Jeff as he said, "Helluva cool afternoon, eh? Here, this is a fantastic beer that I'll bet my ass you can't find in Shinnston."

Jeff hesitated, then took the bottle from Mark's hand, pondered the label for a few seconds, and then placed the bottle on the nearby coffee table without taking a sip. "Mark, there's something you ought to know. I haven't had a beer in nine years, since my last go-round in rehab. They told me I needed to stay away from everything 'mind altering'—the ol' 'slippery slope' theory, I guess."

"Wow, even beer?"

"That's what they said to me. To tell you the truth, I've been thinking about it a lot over these past couple of days. Down in Shinnston, it wasn't all that hard to just drink Diet Cokes all the time. But once we get the Upper Hand road show going again, I don't think there's any fucking way I'm going to be able to just sit there sipping sodas while everyone else is pounding brewskis and Jack Daniels and whatever."

"Should I take this bottle away?"

"Nah. I think it's time to prove those rehab mopes wrong. What the hell, I'll just have one...or two."

CHAPTER 13

A.J. Ramello put up absolutely no resistance when offered the bassist slot in the as-yet unformed new band comprised of guitarists Mark Donahue and Jeff Britton, keyboardist Dave Rowinski, and drummer Steve Holmes. A.J., knowing that his current band was disintegrating due to the college and military commitments of his partners, had been scouting all of the other bands performing that Saturday at the Morristown Armory. He was fully aware of the guitar firepower (and weak rhythm section) of Incendiary and also knew that Hatful of Dynamite boasted an exciting keyboardist and powerful drummer, but little else. When the four talented musicians from those two bands approached him and told him of their plans, and presented their proposal to include him in those plans, A.J. could barely believe his luck.

Not until five years later, when the Upper Hand was firmly established as a top tier recording and performing rock band, was A.J. made aware by a reporter from the rock press of Mark Donahue's aggressive actions the day of the 1972 Teen Rock Festival to prevent the M-80s from getting to A.J. first to recruit him for their band. Somehow this story had never been told to A.J., and he reacted with shock. Rubbing his hand over his thinning frizzy hair, he confided to the reporter, "That's incredible! At that time the M-80s were a more accomplished band than either Incendiary or Hatful of Dynamite. I had no idea at that moment, of course, that my four current bandmates had just jettisoned their weak links and were planning to start a new band, so if the M-80s had gotten to me first, I'm sure I would have accepted. Wow, things might have turned out way differently if Mark hadn't cut those boys off at the pass!"

The evening after that interview, A.J. made a point of giving Mark a huge hug and thanking him for his decisive action back in '72 at the Armory.

A.J. Ramello's musical talent manifested itself early in his life, first via the flutophone in third grade, and then with the clarinet in junior high school, an instrument for which he was chosen to play in an All-Morris County band as a seventh and eighth grader. The chubby, hopelessly nerdy A.J. attempted to attain some semblance of "coolness" during his freshman year of high school in his hometown of Parsippany, New Jersey, by taking up the guitar. Despite becoming highly proficient on the instrument in a short period of time, he was unable to find anyone interested in forming a band with him as lead guitarist. Frustrated, he reluctantly agreed in 1969, during his sophomore year, to switch to bass guitar in order to join his younger brother Vinny, and Vinny's friend Richie Zarrillo, in the formation of the Hell Raisers.

Despite his initial feelings of disappointment at having to issue himself a self-imposed demotion from lead guitar to bass to get himself into a band, A.J. quickly drew inspiration from thunderous, assertive rock bassists like the Who's John Entwhistle, Cream's Jack Bruce, and Grand Funk Railroad's Mel Schacher and almost immediately became the dominant musical force in the Hell Raisers. A.J. remained in the Hell Raisers throughout their three-year existence, strictly out of loyalty to his brother. The timing of the band's dissolution in 1972 was highly fortuitous for A.J., providing him the opportunity to join forces with Mark, Jeff, Steve, and Dave. But even if the life-changing meeting at the Armory had never taken place, and Vinny and Richie had not decided to leave New Jersey for the Navy and college, A.J. soon would have found it necessary to find a higher-caliber band, having far outgrown the Hell Raisers.

A.J.'s parents had always been highly accommodating regarding the Hell Raisers' rehearsals and were equally amenable to having their roomy basement serve as the main practice site for their son's new band. The very first meeting of the new fivesome took place in that basement the Friday after the Teen Rock Festival that had brought them together. Over the course of the six days between the festival and this initial gathering, Jeff and Mark broke the news to Eddie Phair and Bruce Schneider that their services as the rhythm section of Incendiary were no longer required, and Dave and Steve delivered a similar message to Hatful of Dynamite's singer and guitarist.

Jeff and Mark's duties in disbanding Incendiary proved to be relatively painless, and Hatful of Dynamite's laid-back guitarist Ron Blackwood seemed pretty much undisturbed by Dave and Steve's abandonment of the band. But Phil Lanza, Dave's friend since grade school, reacted violently to the news that a new band was being formed without him. Steve had to restrain Phil to prevent him from physically assaulting Dave. Phil, more than a bit delusional regarding his prowess as a vocalist, rather fancied himself as Mick Jagger, Roger Daltrey, and Robert Plant all rolled into one as a rock and roll frontman. No amount of explaining or apologizing by Dave could get Phil to accept or understand how he could be cast aside. He eventually stormed out of Dave and Steve's apartment, where the breakup meeting took place, smashing a beer bottle on the kitchen floor as he exited. Fifteen years would pass before Phil and Dave would reconcile.

Neither Eddie nor Bruce ever attempted to form or join another rock band after Incendiary dissolved. Ron, too, left the world of rock and roll. Phil, however, tried mightily to latch on to several area bands but never succeeded in doing so.

One of Dave Rowinski's most valuable contributions to the Upper Hand took place during the first meeting in A.J.'s basement, before the band even had a name, and prior to one note of music being played by the quintet. The other four eager young musicians wanted nothing more than to set up their instruments, plug in, and begin jamming right at the outset of the meeting. Dave, however, felt it was important to discuss and establish certain "ground rules" and strategies for the new band, and proceeded to propose, and gain complete approval of, four key points:

1. This band would function as a pure five-way democracy. There would be no leader or leaders, and everyone would have an equal voice in any important matter concerning the band.

2. Any band member would be welcome to submit his own original songs to the group, and acceptance or rejection of such songs would be determined by band vote.

3. Ideas from all band members regarding instrumental and vocal arrangements, including suggestions regarding other members' playing or singing, were to be not only welcomed, but encouraged.

4. The band would start out playing mostly popular cover songs, with a handful of original compositions sprinkled in, as they built their popularity but would progress towards a mostly or totally original repertoire as soon as possible, depending on audience response to the original material.

The rest of the band thanked Dave for years to come for having had the foresight to think of these key guidelines and credited his suggestions for the long-term stability and lack of friction within the Upper Hand. Dave humbly accepted his partners' kudos. At the same time, he never once hinted to anyone that he had had another motive for generating the guidelines: to ensure that the brand new fivesome didn't quickly and irrevocably turn into the Britton-Donahue Band. He knew he had made a significant mistake the day he had met Mark and Jeff by concealing his own songwriting efforts and ambitions, and he desperately wanted the door left open to his creative contributions when he was ready to offer them.

The band's name was also established at the same initial gathering, almost by accident. Jeff raised the topic.

"What are we going to call ourselves? I guess anything is fair game except Incendiary, Hatful of Dynamite, or the Hell Raisers, right? We want an all-new name."

Steve replied, "We really need to give this some thought. You saw the overall level of local rock band talent around here at the festival last week. Our new group has so much more musical ability than any of those other groups. With the right name, we'll have such an upper hand over those guys that we'll be grabbing the plum slots at every club in the area."

"Wait—that's a cool name!" exclaimed Mark.

"What, the Plum Slots?"

"No, numbnuts, the *Upper Hand!*"

All five of them glanced at each other for a couple of seconds and then began repeating the name out loud: *The Upper Hand...The Upper Hand...That's not bad.*

A minute later Mark Donahue, Jeff Britton, Dave Rowinski, Steve Holmes, and A.J. Ramello held their very first band vote and unanimously agreed that they would be known as the Upper Hand.

Within three months the Upper Hand had fifty songs, more than enough for a full gig, in their repertoire. Thirty-eight of the songs were well-known crowd-pleasing cover tunes, many selected from the old set lists of Incendiary, Hatful of Dynamite, and the Hell Raisers. The other twelve songs consisted of five originals each from Mark and Jeff, and two originals from Dave, who had at last come forth with a couple of his compositions around six weeks after the band's first get-together. Lead vocals for the cover songs were divided more or less evenly among Dave, Mark, and Jeff, and each sang lead on his own songs. Dave, experienced at providing harmony vocals from his time in Hatful of Dynamite, proved to be a strong contributor in this role from the outset for the Upper Hand; the dynamic three-part vocal harmonies that would someday help define the band's hugely popular sound were not yet in evidence. Steve and A.J. did not sing at all.

A.J. had no interest in songwriting and never once gave it a try during his entire time in the Upper Hand. The same was not exactly true for Steve. Starting in the late 1970s, the Upper Hand's high-octane drummer, who had by then learned to play guitar for his own amusement, would occasionally present to the band a demo of an original composition, consisting of himself on guitar, his younger brother Drew on piano and vocals, and his other younger brother Wayne on drums. These songs invariably featured outrageously pornographic lyrics. The rest of the band would howl with laughter at the latest gleefully obscene song, Steve would react with mock disappointment when the offering was soundly rejected as a possible Upper Hand album track, and then he would happily add the demo to his *Holmes Brothers* collection, which he would play at parties for select groups of friends. Some of his best-loved audio-porn creations included such titles as "Grab Your Ankles," "Three at a Time," "Ass-Fault on the Asphalt," "Just Blow Me," and "Bite Mark."

Twice in the 1980s, the music presented on Steve's demo proved to be of such high quality that the band felt compelled to commandeer the music, toss aside the salacious lyrics, replace them with socially acceptable ones (written and sung the first time by Mark, the other time by Dave), and record the songs for inclusion on Upper Hand albums. Steve thus received two song co-writing credits during his time in the Upper Hand and got to play guitar on both songs as Jeff sat in behind the drum kit.

CHAPTER 14

A peculiar dynamic emerged between Dave and the band's other two songwriters, almost from the moment Dave first revealed himself to be a composer. This vague, unacknowledged, yet influential undercurrent remained in force throughout the life of the band.

Although all four of Dave's bandmates outwardly welcomed and supported his songwriting contributions, Jeff and Mark, both initially taken by surprise by the unexpected emergence of a third writer in the Upper Hand, never totally shook off feelings of ambivalence regarding the additional creative force in the band. While neither Jeff nor Mark could be accused of ever attempting to sabotage Dave's songs in any way, they certainly treated his songs differently, specifically regarding their guitar parts. From the day Dave presented his first song to the rest of the group in 1972, right through to the rehearsal sessions in 1989 for their last pre-breakup album, Mark and Jeff consistently nudged the instrumental arrangements for Dave's songs toward a strong keyboard orientation, dominated by Dave's organ, piano, or other electronic keyboard work, with the guitars relegated to subtle supporting roles in the instrumental mix. The stated purpose of these arrangement suggestions, of course, was always to "give Dave a real showcase in his songs for his keyboard wizardry," and Dave never shied away from the opportunities presented to dominate the instrumentation of his songs on record or in performance.

The real effect, however, was to make Dave's songs come across as distinctly untypical of the Upper Hand's signature style and, therefore, be regarded by fans (and record label decision makers) as mere change-of-pace offerings to be sprinkled in lightly among Mark and Jeff's guitar-heavy tunes. Thus, any chance that may have existed for Dave to become an equal contributor as composer and lead vocalist was eliminated.

By the end of August 1972, when they had enough material ready for a full evening's performance, all five members of the Upper Hand were jumping out of their skins to unleash their act in front of a live audience. Every one of them felt certain that the Upper Hand was a strong enough entity to skip over the local town-sponsored teen events they had depended on in their previous bands and to take the North Jersey club scene by storm. Nevertheless, they decided to take the path of least resistance for their debut and got a booking at a Rock and Roll Happening at the high school gymnasium at A.J.'s alma mater in Parsippany. Incendiary, Hatful of Dynamite, and the Hell Raisers had all performed at this event over the previous couple of years, and the organizers were more than happy to set aside a date for the new band, aggressively promoting the premiere with signs and flyers that read:

ROCK AND ROLL HAPPENING

PARSIPPANY HIGH SCHOOL GYMNASIUM

SATURDAY, SEPTEMBER 16   8:00 PM

Presenting

THE UPPER HAND

Morris County's brand new All-Star rock and roll band

Featuring top members from your old favorites

Hatful of Dynamite, Incendiary, and the Hell Raisers

The heavy promotion for the Upper Hand's first public performance drew the largest Rock and Roll Happening crowd of the year. The attendees were treated to a caliber of rock show never before imagined at the Parsippany High gym, as all five pumped-up musicians left it all on the temporary wooden stage set up below the basketball backboard at the far end of the gym. Most of the crowd, familiar with one or more of the now-defunct bands that had fed members into the new group, came expecting a similar type of performance. Their astonishment at the explosiveness, cohesion, and musicianship being delivered that evening led to a continually escalating audience response as the quintet tore their way through their set of popular rock covers and hard-hitting original tunes. Soon the crowd was hollering and clapping loudly during the songs as well as between them, and the band kept feeding off the electricity of the gathering and pushing themselves to ever-higher energy levels. By the end of the show the young crowd was in a frenzy, to the point that the people in charge of the event were briefly concerned that a riot might break out.

To the tremendous benefit of the five exhausted but triumphant young musicians, the show—and the overwhelming audience reaction to it—was witnessed by Denny Mosteller, a twenty-three-year-old "youth beat" reporter for the *Newark Star-Ledger*, one of New Jersey's largest newspapers. Mosteller wrote a glowing review that appeared in the following Tuesday's edition of the *Star-Ledger*. The publicity made Steve's prediction about "plum slots" becoming available to the band at virtually every rock club in Northern Jersey a reality. Dave, Steve, and A.J. all quit their mundane day jobs, and the Upper Hand eagerly accepted a heavy schedule of club performances, building a reputation as a crowd-magnet throughout the region. In early 1973 the bandmates moved in together, renting a rundown three-bedroom Cape Cod house with a fully subterranean (and thus reasonably soundproof) basement, in Randolph, a relatively sparsely populated town several miles west of their hometowns. The collective focus was now one hundred percent on making the band better and on expanding its audience.

***

Armed with his new Stratocasters, and thoroughly electrified and rejuvenated by the spontaneous performance at the Sam Ash guitar shop, Jeff quickly regained his formidable playing skills. Mark declared the "guitar boot camp" to be completed after just ten days and invited the rest of the band to his house the next day to rehearse and discuss logistics regarding the reformation of the Upper Hand.

That morning, as Mark puttered around his home studio preparing it for the first Upper Hand musical endeavor since 1990, he heard Jeff's voice behind him asking, "Well? What do you think?"

Mark turned around and was immediately transfixed at the sight before him. Jeff's hair was restored to its old dark brown color. His three weeks' worth of facial hair, still a month or so away from recreating his full bearded look of the late 1970s and early 1980s, was similarly transformed, although the skin still visible beneath the nascent facial hair was bright red.

"Goddamn, look at you! What a change, damn."

Jeff ran his hand through his hair. "Not bad, eh? But what a pain in the ass. Did you know that you gotta buy two different boxes of stuff, one for your hair and one for your beard? Maybe it's just marketing bullshit, and it's the same stuff in both boxes, but I didn't want to take any chances. But, damn, it took forever. At least you don't have the beard to deal with, but do you really go through all this nonsense for your hair?"

"Hell no. I have it done by my hair stylist when I get it cut. I'll introduce you to her next time you need it done. What happened to your face? You look like a fucking lobster."

"I think I made a mistake. My beard isn't all the way in yet, and I think when the goop didn't find enough beard to dye, it decided to dye my face instead. Probably should've waited a few more weeks. Anyway, I had to scrub the living daylights out of my face to get the brown crap off. Stings like hell too."

Mark laughed, "From now on, let the trained professionals do this stuff for you. Still, you look like *Jeff Britton: Rock Star* again. Maybe this will inspire Dave to do something. He looks like a goddamn Supreme Court justice with that short, gray hair."

"I know. Did you hear A.J. tell that story about the cop who pulled them over last spring? The guy was an Upper Hand fan and still couldn't recognize Dave even after he told the cop who he was."

"Yeah. That should have given Dave a message right there. Meanwhile, Steve and A.J. don't need to do anything for totally different reasons. Steve is still our poster boy, and A.J., well, A.J. is just A.J. There isn't an Upper Hand fan on the planet who doesn't want 'Ol' Kojak' to look exactly the way he does."

Jeff's newly darkened hair got the expected big reaction from Dave, A.J., and Steve, the latter two giving the change an immediate thumbs-up. Dave remained neutral in his comments, and as soon as

A.J. and Steve finished voicing their strong approval of Jeff's "turn back the clock" look, Dave felt four pairs of eyes staring at the top of his head.

"What are you guys looking at? Hey, Sharon likes my hair this way. She says it makes me look distinguished."

Steve snorted. "*Distinguished?* Fuck that. You're in a band again. Time to leave the Rock and Roll Witness Protection Program and grow out that hair. Bring back that big ol' mustache of yours. Maybe toss in some color like Jeff did. Our fans are going to want us to look like they remember us."

"I'll grow my hair out if A.J. does."

Loud laughter filled the room as A.J. rubbed his hand over his hairless scalp and exclaimed, "Sorry, boys, that ship has sailed."

Dave saw that his friends were still staring at his hair, and muttered noncommittally, "We'll see."

Once the initial distraction over hair color and length was mercifully brought to a conclusion, the fivesome got down to business. Much to Dave's relief, there was quick, unanimous agreement that the Upper Hand's return to the rock music world would take place first via live performances rather than with a new CD. Costs for the care of Dave's son had been escalating in recent months, and he truly needed the quick source of income that an arena tour would provide. A new album, on the other hand, could take half a year or more to write, record, mix, and release. However, Dave's suggestion that the band immediately schedule and announce a major U.S. tour was countered by a more cautious approach proposed by A.J. and quickly endorsed by the others. A.J.'s idea was to book a short series of local club dates to "blow off the cobwebs" and gauge the public's response before deciding how ambitious of a tour should be planned. Dave reluctantly went along with the go-slow option.

At last it was time to set up, plug in, and start playing. It did not escape the attention of the five musicians that this session bore remarkable similarities to the afternoon in A.J.'s parents' basement almost thirty-two years ago, the first time they played together.

Becoming acquainted with each other as musicians, debating and deciding on set lists, figuring out arrangements and cues—it was 1972 all over again as Jeff, Mark, A.J., Dave, and Steve dove headfirst into the session.

Another parallel to the experience of 1972 was the rapid redevelopment of their repertoire as the five veteran musicians quickly gelled and re-established the tremendous instrumental and vocal chemistry that had propelled them to stardom decades earlier. Inevitable memory lapses by individual band members regarding song details were instantly resolved by other members, and song after song came back to life, deemed performance-ready in short order. Within three weeks the Upper Hand had resurrected and tightened to perfection enough songs from their famous catalog to deliver a solid two-hour concert plus encores and a few spares to rotate in and out of the set: twelve Jeff Britton songs, eleven by Mark Donahue, four by Dave Rowinski, plus the Steve Holmes tune with Dave's lyrics in place of Steve's original sex-soaked ones, a song that allowed for a crowd-pleasing swap of instruments between Steve and Jeff.

By early July 2004 the band, bursting with confidence and anticipation, declared itself ready to re-conquer the rock world. Dave was even starting to look "rock-ready." Although he had not changed his hair color, he at least stopped getting it cut and was in the process of bringing back his big '70s-style mustache.

Jeff continued to live in Mark's house. Occasionally Jeff would make a comment about finding his own place, but Mark would immediately discourage any such thoughts. Jeff's re-entry into Mark's life delivered a reinvigorating jolt to Mark, and he was in no hurry to find himself rattling around his large house alone again. His relationship with his young girlfriend Emily was far from a serious one, so Jeff's presence in no way preempted any changes in living arrangements for the couple. Also, since the day Jeff decided to stop following his last rehab center's "total abstinence" edict, Mark liked being able to unobtrusively monitor Jeff's beer consumption. *So far so good.*

CHAPTER 15

It was the end of 1973, and the Upper Hand was a full year into their reign as the hottest, best-known, and busiest band working the North Jersey club circuit. Their hard-rocking stage show drew overflow crowds not only on weekends, but also during the week, and their appearance fees shot up accordingly. As Dave had prescribed back at the band's very first meeting, the Upper Hand's set list evolved from one consisting of mostly cover tunes to one about ninety percent comprised of original songs written by Mark, Jeff, or himself.

Yet a growing sense of frustration was beginning to envelop the quintet. All five of them knew—*knew*—that the caliber of music they were creating and delivering was high enough to merit a recording contract and a chance at not just local, but national stardom. But nothing developed for them during '73 that made them feel any closer to achieving that dream. Several times during the year they were approached in one of the clubs by some representative or self-described "president" of an "up and coming" record label, and their hopes would soar, but each time the label turned out to be nothing more than a wannabe's pipe dream. After one of these deflating episodes, an agitated Steve even began talking about giving up and getting a "real job," although the resounding chorus of *don't you dare!* from the rest of the group quickly defused the potential crisis. Also contributing to the uneasy mood of the group was the total lack of response from major record labels to which they had sent demo tapes. Adding to the sense of uncertainty concerning the Upper Hand's future, Mark and Jeff were receiving escalating pressure from their parents to cut back on their involvement with the band to attend classes at County College of Morris, the local two-year community college.

In early 1974, the Upper Hand made a strategic decision that would finally open the door to the worldwide exposure they were desperately seeking. They convinced themselves that the lack of interest shown in the band from the big record companies was due to the fact that, although the Upper Hand was a New Jersey-based band, they did not have (nor did they desire to have) the "Jersey sound." This was the rhythm and blues-flavored, horn-infused sound which was garnering tremendous attention of late, thanks to the explosive performances being delivered by Bruce Springsteen & the E Street Band and Southside Johnny & the Asbury Jukes along the Jersey Shore, eighty or so miles south of the Upper Hand's domain. The Upper Hand's new plan, then, was to look to the east, to New York City, to shed the "New Jersey" affiliation and expectations, and also to stand a better chance of being spotted by legitimate record label people.

Dave's older brother Greg was not only a proud fan of the Upper Hand, he was also a bartender at Club 14, a rock club and bar located on busy 14th Street in Manhattan, just north of Greenwich Village. Greg had been bragging about his kid brother's hot rock band to his co-workers at Club 14 for months, so when the Upper Hand expressed their interest in playing in New York, Greg had no problem convincing the manager of the club to book them for a try-out performance.

On Greg's advice, the five members of the band aggressively promoted their upcoming gig at Club 14 to their friends, and on the night of the show, the manager of the club witnessed not only an electrifying performance by the band, but also a big, raucous crowd and a healthy take at the bar. The Upper Hand was immediately booked for additional shows at Club 14.

Just as they had hoped, the band's successful appearances at Club 14 created considerable word-of-mouth exposure around town, and with some help from Greg Rowinski's connections with other bartenders and club managers in the area, they were soon getting dates at three other rock clubs, all in Greenwich Village. Then, at last, on a steamy August Saturday night at a Village club called Big Wally's, a bona fide record company executive introduced himself to the band as they were dismantling their equipment after another powerful, wildly received set.

Thirty-six-year-old Stan Rabin, a native New Yorker, started Signature Records in the early 1960s by recording and releasing albums by several Greenwich Village-based folksingers who patrolled the Village coffeehouse circuit during the folk music boom of that time. A few of those singer/songwriters attained a level of success as recording artists, providing Rabin and his new label with a springboard for expansion into mid-60's pop music. Rabin, no particular fan of the burgeoning pop/rock music scene of that period, nevertheless possessed an unerring ear for what would sell to young music listeners of the time, and Signature Records exited the 1960s as an undeniably viable, if still modest-sized, popular music record label.

Stan Rabin was doggedly determined to elevate his record company to the next level in the 1970s and knew full well that he needed to add a dynamic rock band to his rather stagnant stable of veteran folk artists and quickly fading pop stars to do so. He began scouting the rock clubs of midtown and lower Manhattan in search of a high potential, studio-ready rock act that had not yet caught the attention of the major record labels. He started hearing talk early in the summer of 1974 of a band from New Jersey called the Upper Hand that was filling clubs in and around Greenwich Village and decided to check them out that hot night in August at Big Wally's.

Despite the stifling heat inside Big Wally's, Stan Rabin spent the evening dressed in a pale gray suit, white shirt buttoned to the collar, and red striped tie, nursing scotch and sodas and chain-smoking Lucky Strikes at a table not far from the stage. (Decades later, not one member of the Upper Hand would be able to recall ever seeing Rabin dressed any less formally, or even with his collar button undone.)

Stan Rabin most definitely did not give the appearance of someone the members of the Upper Hand would have any interest in speaking to regarding a record contract. Tall and almost impossibly lean, he had thinning dark brown hair combed straight back and a narrow wedge-shaped face dominated by glasses with unfashionably thick black frames. But as the strange looking, dramatically overdressed, charisma-challenged record company executive introduced himself, and then proceeded to roll off the names of the various successful folk and pop artists signed to his label, the weary musicians quickly shook off the fatigue from the long hot night onstage and began listening intently to Rabin's every word.

The monologue ended with Rabin handing his business card to A.J. and saying, "I think you boys are ready to make some real waves in the rock world, and Signature Records is able and willing to help you make that happen. Two in the morning, in the middle of this furnace, is not the time or place to talk details, so give me a call next week, and we'll discuss how to make you famous and all of us rich." Without waiting for a response from the now adrenaline-charged band, he turned away and headed for the club exit.

As soon as the front door of Big Wally's closed behind the departing record label president, animated chatter commenced among the five thrilled band members.

"A.J., don't lose that fucking card."

"We gotta call this guy Monday, first thing."

"He's sort of a strange guy, isn't he? Kinda gives me the willies."

"Who cares? We don't want to date him. We want to get a record contract from him."

"Yeah, he's the real deal. Did you hear the list of people that label has?"

Dave held up his hand to quiet everyone down and announced, "Wait a second. Shouldn't we have a lawyer or something before we go in and sign anything? What the hell do we know about recording contracts?"

His question was met with murmurs of agreement from his bandmates until Kevin LaRoche, who was the band's equipment manager at the time, spoke up. "Hey, my sister Mary Ellen is a lawyer, works right in Morristown. I bet I can get her to help you out with your contract."

True to his word, Kevin convinced Mary Ellen to represent the Upper Hand in their contract negotiations with Signature Records for a significantly reduced fee, thereby permanently elevating Kevin's status within the band's soon-to-be-substantial organization. Less than a week after meeting Stan Rabin at Big Wally's, the Upper Hand was officially signed to Signature Records, and details were being worked out for the recording of their debut album.

At the time of the band's signing of its recording contract, Dave Rowinski had spent the previous year working feverishly to increase the quantity and quality of his songwriting output, in an effort to achieve equal footing with the band's other two composers. By the summer of 1973, he had managed to nudge his share of original songs performed at a typical show up to around twenty-five percent. As the band excitedly prepared for the studio sessions for their album, Dave held high hopes that the decision-makers at Signature Records would see fit to include a healthy number of Dave's keyboard-driven, slightly jazzy songs on the record.

He was bitterly disappointed.

Both Stan Rabin and Signature's in-house record producer, Larry Temple, immediately made it clear that the album would be built around Jeff and Mark's electric guitar-heavy rockers and acoustic ballads, and that the presence of Dave's songs on the disk would be limited. Rabin initially intended to include just one Dave-penned song on the twelve-song album. The entire group, including Mark and Jeff who, with their positions as primary composers for the band secure, found it easy to be magnanimous, protested, and a second Rowinski composition was added.

When the Upper Hand's self-titled first album and its two hit singles, one written and sung by Jeff, the other by Mark, launched the band to stardom, Dave's position deep in the shadows of Jeff and Mark was cemented. Ironically, Stan Rabin did develop a real appreciation for Dave's keyboard playing abilities and would enlist his services repeatedly over the years on other Signature Records recording sessions. But Dave would never forgive Rabin for pushing him into the background of the Upper Hand and carried a simmering antipathy for the label boss that would never fade.

CHAPTER 16

Mark, Jeff, Dave, Steve, and A.J. were scattered around A.J.'s wondrous game room, entertaining themselves with the various amusements available and conversing excitedly about the six Upper Hand concert dates that had been arranged at three of their favorite old New York club venues, including both Club 14 and Big Wally's. Club 14 was now owned by Dave's brother Greg, so the band of course agreed to begin the mini concert series there.

Also in attendance on this stormy afternoon in August of 2004 was the band's old pal, former equipment manager and now business manager, Kevin LaRoche. Kevin, now a successful accountant with his own busy practice in Morristown, was thrilled to see the Upper Hand reunited and in need of his services. His first significant duty for the band in years was to work out the financial details with the three clubs in New York for the six upcoming shows, which were scheduled over a two-week period in late August and early September. It was also Kevin's responsibility to assemble and pay a road crew to handle the band's equipment—a welcome change from the Upper Hand's last appearance at these clubs thirty years earlier, when Kevin *was* the road crew.

Peeling himself away from the Space Invaders machine and taking a healthy swig from his mug of Bass Ale draught, Kevin said, "Guys, I have to admit I never thought I'd see this day, and this little set of club dates to announce the rebirth of the band is so cool that I'm almost puking with excitement. It's also great to hear you talking about following this up with a good old-fashioned national tour of major arenas, which is going to be awesome! But have you figured out what you're going to do about Bryce Miller?"

The room went quiet for several seconds, and then Mark growled, "Fuck him."

Jeff, looking confused, asked, "What's the deal with Bryce?"

"He stole two fucking million dollars from us during our last tour in 1990!" Mark roared.

"I never heard anything about this before."

"Well, you were...indisposed at the time," offered Steve.

"There is no way in hell that Bryce Miller is going to be our tour manager again. He's a goddamn thief."

"Look, guys, we went over this years ago," replied Kevin. "We can't prove that Bryce took that tour receipts money. It looked suspicious, for sure, but the record-keeping for those receipts was so convoluted and tangled that I couldn't tell how that two mil disappeared. I even got another accountant to look at everything, remember? She couldn't trace it back to Bryce either. And the bottom line is, he has a signed contract from the Upper Hand that guarantees him one more go-round as the band's tour manager."

Dave spoke up. "Don't you think Bryce arranged for those records to be such a mess on purpose to cover his tracks?"

"My opinion? Almost certainly. But we have no hard proof. Same thing with those smaller amounts we found later on that seemed to have disappeared from the receipts from some of your previous tours."

"He built himself a huge house down in central Jersey—a two million dollar house. How's that for a coincidence? Six months after the tour ended. There's no doubt involved here at all!" Mark exclaimed, his arms waving. "I will not go on tour with that asshole as tour manager. We can just go make albums and become the fucking house band for Club 14 for the rest of our lives before I'll let Bryce Miller make or steal another nickel off us."

Dave felt a knot in his stomach at the thought of losing the income from the prospective tour but knew better than to try to change Mark's mind at that moment. Instead, he replied, "Hey, it's been fourteen years. Bryce lives in Tennessee now with his rich new wife, right? Maybe he won't even give a damn about organizing a rock tour anymore."

"I hope you're right, but I doubt that money-grubbing weasel will pass up the chance to rob us blind again. Who let that glad-handing, phony bastard into our organization, anyway?"

"Uh, that would be you, Mark," Jeff replied, and the others nodded their heads in agreement.

"Good God, you're kidding! Really? What the fuck was I smoking?"

"You want an itemized list? Could take a while," chortled A.J., bringing some brief much-needed levity to the room. Even Mark couldn't help but laugh.

Mark was indeed the member of the Upper Hand who had introduced Bryce Miller to the rest of the band and had first proposed that Miller take over the tour management responsibilities for the group. It was 1977, and it had become widely known in rock music circles that the Upper Hand, whose first two major American concert tours in 1975 and '76 had been plagued by multiple organizational foul-ups, were seeking new tour management for their upcoming third tour.

Bryce Miller, born in 1949 and thus just a few years older than the members of the Upper Hand, desperately wanted the enormous boost that his fledgling tour management company would receive by adding the fast-rising rock band to his meager client list of pop and comedy acts. Before setting out on his own, he had worked for two years for a Boston-based tour management company. Although he had been little more than a low-ranking go-fer in that firm, the smooth-talking Miller managed to convince prospective clients of *BDM & Associates Concert Tour Logistics, Inc.*, including Mark Donahue and then the rest of the Upper Hand, that he had been the key tour organizer responsible for the success of many of the Boston company's biggest concert tours.

Bryce Miller could best be described as a latter-day snake oil salesman, a born conman and bullshitter with a big smile, even bigger voice, and genial backslapping demeanor. Tall, burly, and blond, he knew instinctively how to create a larger-than-life, confidence-inducing impression.

A native of Dover, Delaware, Miller began his checkered career while still a student at the University of Delaware, spinning wondrous tales about the amazing virtues of such questionable products as "therapeutic" copper magnetic bracelets, "healing" crystals, and nutritional supplements of unknown origin, selling huge quantities of each. In 1974, the latest addition to his line-up of "magical" health supplements managed to sicken dozens of customers, and the twenty-five-year-old Miller barely got out of Delaware ahead of charges for fraud and reckless endangerment. He headed to Massachusetts and used his well-honed salesmanship skills to obtain his job at the Boston tour management firm.

Mark's initial encounter with Bryce Miller in early '77 was by all appearances a chance meeting, not far from the studio in Manhattan where the Upper Hand was recording its third album. But in reality Miller had very carefully monitored the comings and goings of the members of the band around the recording facility, making sure he would soon find himself in the right place at the right time to strike up a conversation with one or more of them. He easily engaged Mark in casual banter while Mark was ordering a sandwich at a deli around the corner from the studio and quickly convinced him that BDM & Associates was the answer to the Upper Hand's tour-related headaches. Within two days, Bryce Miller's fanciful description of his rock band tour logistics experience and his bold pronouncements regarding his vision for the Upper Hand's concert appearances landed him a contract to handle the band's next tour.

Despite his lack of real experience as a concert tour manager, Bryce Miller proved himself capable of the job and eventually managed to gain a multi-tour contract from the Upper Hand in 1988 that covered their next three tours—one of which had still not taken place as of 2004. Because of his undeniable competence as the Upper Hand's tour organizer, the band and other members of their inner circle managed to tolerate Miller's braggadocio and over-the-top personality. His noisy presence became particularly trying during the tours themselves. He accompanied the group on almost every tour stop, attended every post-concert party, and attempted to out-drink, out-snort, and out-debauch everyone else there. On several occasions he would cross the line and receive a reprimand from one of the band members, most notably at a 1985 tour post-show gathering when he loudly proclaimed to a female party attendee that he was "the sixth member of the band." This outrageous claim earned Miller an angry and embarrassing rebuke from Dave and Jeff.

The Upper Hand would have been far less solicitous of Bryce Miller's antics if they had known that he was skimming money from the band's tour receipts right from the very beginning of his tenure as their tour manager. Expert at inventing phony or inflated expenses as well as creating complicated and indecipherable webs of financial records that effectively covered his tracks, Miller kept the monetary sums of his thefts modest enough to go unnoticed—fifty thousand here, seventy thousand there—until the closing weeks of the band's ill-fated 1990 tour. As the Upper Hand spiraled toward imminent dissolution after Jeff abandoned the tour, Miller upped the ante and arranged for two million dollars in concert fees to disappear. In the chaotic weeks and months following that tour, no one in the band was in any position to examine the financial results of their time on the road, as Miller had anticipated. But business manager Kevin LaRoche noticed the shortfall and phoned Miller in July of 1990 to get an explanation. Miller's crazy-quilt financial records and practiced conman double-talk deftly sidestepped Kevin's accusations, leaving the frustrated business manager convinced of Miller's thievery but unable to pin it on him. Miller's last words to Kevin that day were a sickeningly cheery reminder that he held a contract for the management of the band's next tour, whenever that might be.

Miller used the two million dollars he pilfered from the Upper Hand to build a mansion in exclusive Far Hills, New Jersey. With no Upper Hand activity during the 1990s, Miller's tour logistics business and his interest in it waned, and he set his sights elsewhere. In 1998 he met Anna Mae Hightower, a slovenly, dim-witted, but fabulously wealthy daughter of a Memphis-based televangelist and quickly became both her husband and "manager" of the wide-ranging financial assets her father had given her over the years to keep her occupied and out of trouble. Miller sold his Far Hills mansion and moved to Tennessee immediately following their wedding in September 1998. By 2000 he had also managed to secure himself a highly public and lucrative marketing position within his televangelist father-in-law's empire.

CHAPTER 17

The Upper Hand's six-show mini-tour of Manhattan was nothing short of a spectacular success for the reformed band. Overflow crowds spilled onto the sidewalks. Fans lucky enough to get inside and witness the performances raved about the undiminished power of the band after their long hiatus. Once the word of mouth spread regarding the shows, the rock press descended on the clubs. Aside from an awkward moment after a show at Club 14, when it was discovered in the nick of time that the attractive young brunette Steve was in the process of seducing was club owner Greg Rowinski's daughter, Dave's niece, the two weeks unfolded flawlessly.

"For chrissakes, Dave, why didn't you let me know your niece was in the audience? That could've gotten dicey."

"Man, you're still incorrigible, aren't you? It's a good thing we caught that in time. It would have been a damn shame to have to have you killed just when things are starting to come to life for the band."

The phone call from Bryce Miller came less than two days after the end of the Upper Hand's triumphant and breathlessly reported return to action in New York. Television, radio, and newspaper coverage of the surprise reunion of the long-dormant band was incessant over the course of the two-week run. Miller, absorbing the news from the magnificent home outside of Memphis he shared— with as little actual contact as possible—with Anna Mae, took particular note of several quotes from the happy, exhilarated band members promising a huge U.S. tour of major arenas in the near future.

Mistakenly thinking that his strongest ally within the Upper Hand camp was Mark Donahue, he dialed Mark at 10:00 a.m. on the Tuesday morning following the last New York gig.

Mark was alone in his kitchen, dressed in sweat pants and a Doobie Brothers T-shirt, working his way through an English muffin and coffee. He was greatly enjoying an article in the *Star-Ledger* praising the Upper Hand's Saturday night performance at

Big Wally's when the phone rang. Jeff was out of the house running errands.

"Hello?"

"Well, greetings there, Mark! Long time no speak. I'm just tickled to death that you boys are back in the saddle again where y'all belong." Miller's booming voice required no upfront identification, even if it now carried a disconcerting Southern drawl.

Mark's relaxing morning with his newspaper came to an abrupt halt, and he felt an instant fury rise through his body and into his reddening face.

"What the fuck do you want, Bryce?"

"Now, now, is that any way to greet your ol' buddy and business partner after such a long time apart?" The syrupy, overly cordial tone of Miller's voice, combined with the newfound country accent, just fed Mark's rage.

"Don't hand me that 'buddy' shit, and don't you dare call yourself a business partner of ours. You stole two fucking million dollars from us."

"Mark, Mark, Mark, where did you get that misguided notion? Why, your business manager Kevin and I—nice man, that Kevin—we talked this all out years ago, and he agreed that there was absolutely nothing to it."

"Bullshit! Kevin just said that you were too damn clever with the paper trail for him to be able to put together the proof we needed to throw your thieving ass in jail. And why are you talking like a fucking hillbilly, anyway? You're from Delaware, for chrissakes!"

"Oh, do I sound a little different these days? I guess it just naturally rubbed off on me from living down here in God's country for the past six years. But look here, Mark, that business manager of yours, Kevin, is a smart boy. If I'da done something crooked with your money, he would've found proof of it for sure. So, let's forget about all this unpleasantness and start talking business. I hear you boys are planning a bodacious new concert tour."

"Forget about it, Bryce! We're not letting your sticky fingers anywhere near our new tour. Go find someone else to rip off."

Suddenly, the nauseating sweetness in Miller's voice, along with most of his "naturally acquired" Tennessee accent, disappeared. "It doesn't work that way, Mark. I have an ironclad contract to manage the next Upper Hand tour, and it won't do any of us any good if you try to renege on it. I've got very good lawyers down here. Don't make me use 'em."

"Screw yourself, Bryce!"

Miller replied, "You're making a huge mistake," but Mark had already slammed down the phone.

The band, plus Kevin, was scheduled to meet at 2:00 that afternoon in Steve's Greenwich Village apartment to begin discussions regarding a full-fledged U.S. tour. Fresh from their wildly successful set of club performances and the tremendous national publicity generated by the shows during the past two weeks, the rest of the band arrived at the meeting full of optimism and eager to put together a massive, coast-to-coast tour. Even Jeff, who was already in Manhattan that morning and did not speak to Mark prior to the meeting, had no idea that his friend was about to dramatically alter everyone's mood.

Mark wasted no time delivering the news of his morning phone conversation.

"Well, I said it would happen, and sure enough, it did. That son of a bitch Bryce called me this morning."

A collective series of groans and expletives followed.

"I think I know the answer to this, but what did he say?" asked Steve hesitantly.

"God, I was so pissed. If I could have jumped through the phone lines, I would have strangled that cocksucker. He's all super-friendly, denying everything, even claiming that Kevin agrees he didn't take any money—"

"He *what?*" exploded Kevin.

"Oh, yeah, this guy's unbelievable. He'll say anything. Anyway, his tone changed when I told him there was no goddamn way we were going to let him have anything to do with our tour. He started talking about the contract, his lawyers, shit like that. I slammed the phone in his ear, but you know he's not going away. This puts the kibosh on the whole tour idea."

Dave immediately leaned forward in his chair. "Wait a minute, Mark. You can't just—"

"This guy ripped us off for two million bucks, Dave. Going out on a tour managed by that crook is out of the question."

Dave's face began to redden. "Just like that? You're going to throw away the chance to launch the Upper Hand back to the top over this?"

"Look, Dave, I know that you have some real money issues because of your son's medical expenses, but—"

Dave jumped out of his seat, his face now crimson. "You leave Justin out of this! You've got a fucking nerve! It's real easy for you to just piss away this fantastic opportunity for all of us, isn't it? You're sitting on your pile of songwriting royalties, so you don't give a shit. You and Jeff worked it out with Stan Rabin from the very beginning to make sure that all of our albums were loaded up with your songs, and now you're just riding the royalty gravy train."

Jeff, Steve, and A.J. squirmed uncomfortably in their seats as an angered Mark stood up to confront Dave. "What the fuck are you talking about? Nobody worked anything out with anybody. And I got news for you, Dave—those albums supposedly 'loaded' with songs by Jeff and me did pretty goddamn well. You got a problem with the thirty-five million albums we sold? We had a formula for success, and all five of us did quite well with that formula, and you know it. Didn't our experience with 'Tireless Dancer' show us—?"

As soon as the words left his lips, Mark knew he had gone too far by mentioning the unsuccessful 1983 Upper Hand single written, sung, and instrumentally dominated by Dave. The next fifteen seconds consisted of an almost incoherently furious verbal explosion by Dave, interspersed with equally vociferous but defensive rebuttals by Mark, as well as an attempt by Mark to steer the argument back to the Bryce Miller issue.

"SHUT UP, BOTH OF YOU, AND SIT DOWN—NOW! SIT DOWN, I SAID!"

For the second time in six months, the mild-mannered A.J. stepped dramatically out of character and seized control of the band. Dave and Mark, both shocked by the outburst by their normally non-confrontational friend, fell silent immediately and retreated to their chairs. A.J. was standing, his face a mask of distress and anger. Jeff, Steve, and Kevin, equally stunned, sat stock-still in their chairs.

A.J. turned toward Mark. "*You,*" he began, his voice strangely calm now but with an unmistakably hard edge to it, and his normally warm, cordial eyes boring holes into Mark's. "You just chose, all by yourself, to ditch our plans for our comeback tour? What the hell is that? This band has never operated that way and *never will.* We make these decisions together, and don't you forget it. This Bryce Miller thing is a problem, and we have to figure something out, but you just deciding to punt on first down and fuck us over to spite Bryce doesn't cut it."

He now switched his focus to Dave. "And *you*—what's with the conspiracy theories? Nobody in this band plotted with Stan Rabin or anybody else to keep your songs off our albums. Stan did what he thought was right in those early days to maximize our chance for success. And guess what? That bug-eyed bastard was right. Every one of us—not just Mark and Jeff with their songwriting royalties—*every single one of us* made a shitload of money from being in this band and enjoyed a lifestyle most people can't even dream of. So toss that back-room-deals crap out of your head; it's not helping anyone."

Mark and Dave remained silent, as if awaiting permission from A.J. to respond. A.J. turned next to the band's business manager.

"Kevin, I have a question for you. If we were to go out on tour with Bryce as tour manager—"

Mark began to protest, but A.J. immediately cut him off. "Cool your jets, Mark, and let me finish. Kevin, would you be able to oversee the receipts and expenses during the tour to make sure— *one hundred percent* sure—that Bryce doesn't rip us off again?"

"Absolutely. He only got away with it back then because nobody suspected anything, so nobody was watching. He wouldn't be able to skim off two bucks for a cup of coffee without me knowing it next time, if there is a next time."

"Good to know. OK, guys, here's what I propose." All eyes were riveted on the still standing A.J.

"None of us has had time to really digest this news about Bryce waving that old contract at us, so it makes no sense to make any kind of decision today on what to do about it." He was staring straight at Mark as he spoke these words. Mark exhaled heavily but said nothing.

"All of us should spend the next couple of days thinking of ideas on how to deal with this. We're six pretty smart guys. There has to be an answer out there that one of us can come up with. Let's reconvene at my house on Thursday and see if we can solve this."

A.J.'s suggestion was greeted with affirmative head nods all around, although Kevin arranged to have the meeting at A.J.'s house pushed back to Friday to give him a chance to show Bryce's tangled paperwork from 1990 to another colleague.

Dave and Mark did not speak to one another as they left Steve's apartment, each harboring a combination of residual anger at the other and embarrassment at himself for the ugly scene that had just taken place.

CHAPTER 18

The mood in A.J.'s game room that following Friday afternoon was undeniably tense. For the first time ever, a group of males was gathered in that room without anyone availing himself of the many amusements offered there. Steve had not yet arrived, and the rest of them had agreed not to start the discussion regarding any solutions to the Bryce Miller situation until all were present, but it was apparent from everyone's subdued demeanor that no one had come up with any bombshell breakthroughs. The only counterweight to the grim atmosphere in the room was that Dave and Mark had greeted each other upon their arrival with a friendly handshake and appeared to have put Tuesday's bitter confrontation behind them.

Just as the group's attempts at casual conversation were fizzling out, Steve burst into the game room, dripping wet from the steady rain that had served to further darken the atmosphere. He was carrying a large canvas bag and grinning broadly as he greeted the gathering with a wretched rendition of the Mr. Rogers theme song.

"*It's a beautiful day in the neighborhood, a beautiful day for a neighbor. Would you be mine? Could you be mine?*" he warbled as the guys stared at him curiously. "Lovely day, isn't it, boys?" he said, apparently oblivious to his dripping clothes and the slate gray sky visible through the windows of the game room.

"What's with you, drummer boy?" groused Jeff. "You're acting like you just got laid by a Victoria's Secret model."

"No, no, no—well, actually, yes I did—but that's not why I'm in such a sunny mood. Who wants to guess why I'm so happy today?"

Nobody was in the mood to play guessing games, so Steve carried on.

"Such a grouchy-looking bunch. Let me guess. No one here came up with a solution to our Bryce problem, did they? Kevin, did your accountant friend figure out a way to dig through all the paperwork shit to pin the missing two mil on Bryce?"

"No, I'm afraid not," admitted Kevin.

"No brainstorms from any of you other guys? Well, it's a good thing your ol' buddy Steve is on the case, isn't it?"

"You got something on Bryce?" Dave asked hopefully.

Steve responded with an even bigger smile.

"How much do you guys know about what Bryce has been up to since he married Miss Piggy and moved to Tennessee?"

"I just know she's filthy rich, and he's living in some huge mansion down there that makes the house he built up here with our tour money look like a garden shed," offered Mark.

"Yeah, well, I did a bit of digging around online, and here's where it gets interesting. That rich little toad he married is the daughter of one of those ridiculous TV preachers they have down there. That's where her money comes from. Daddy fleeces his dumb-as-shit TV flock, and he doles some of it out to her. Bryce has jumped headfirst into the whole fundamentalist religion thing, no doubt to keep daddy happy and the money flowing to the daughter."

"OK, but how does this help us?" asked Dave.

"Wait, it gets better. Bryce is now working in a high profile, very visible job for his preacher father-in-law, helping promote the old man's whole ultra-conservative fire and brimstone playbook. Can you even imagine how much money he's skimming out of that organization, working from the inside?"

"Makes me want to puke, but so what?" grumbled Mark.

"Oh, ye of little faith! Just hold on. All will be revealed. Now. Back in our touring heyday, who was the number one most wanton, lecherous, shameless hound patrolling our after-show parties?"

"*You were!*" came the instantaneous, unanimous cry from around the room, leading to several seconds of hoots, howls, and barking noises.

"Oh, man, you guys are harsh," replied Steve. "OK, OK, who was the *second* worst hound dog at the tour parties?"

"That would be Bryce," admitted A.J. to general agreement from everyone else.

Steve grabbed the canvas bag he had brought with him, pulled six vinyl-covered photo albums out of the bag, and spread them across A.J.'s billiard table. Each album had several yellow Post-It notes sticking out of its open side.

"As you guys may remember, I used to be fond of photographing the hilarity and general goings-on at these little late night gatherings. As luck would have it, our good friend Bryce is prominently featured in quite a few of these photos." Steve began opening the albums, using the Post-It notes he had earlier placed on the appropriate pages for guidance, as everyone gathered eagerly around the billiard table. They were treated to a wide selection of pictures of Bryce engaged in various forms of "un-Christian-like" behavior, including groping and cavorting with young women in various stages of undress, leering drunkenly into the camera holding emptied bottles of liquor, and partaking of marijuana joints and lines of cocaine. Steve was smothered in hugs, backslaps, and gleeful congratulations as the group pored through the photo albums.

"Boys, what do you say we give ol' Bryce a phone call and chat about some of the wonderful mementos we have of him from those Upper Hand tour parties? I happen to have his phone number right here," suggested Steve, patting his shirt pocket.

"Hey, guys, I have a speakerphone in my office," chimed in A.J. "We can all listen in. I think Steve should do the honors of breaking this spectacular news to Bryce, don't you?"

A chorus of affirmative responses delegated to Steve the pleasure of leading the upcoming phone conversation.

The six now decidedly happier men filed out of the game room and headed to A.J.'s office down the hall, each stopping at the game room bar first to pour himself a draught Guinness or Bass Ale. The office contained a modest-sized circular table surrounded by four chairs; the speakerphone sat on the table. Dave, Steve, Jeff, and Mark settled into the four chairs. The only other chair in the room was A.J.'s desk chair. Kevin deferred to A.J., but A.J. firmly insisted that

Kevin take the chair and stood near the round table. Steve arranged the photo albums to display a few of the most incriminating photos of Bryce, as A.J. leaned over the table to dial Bryce's number.

"Hello?"

"Hello, Bryce? Steve Holmes here." Steve spoke in a disarmingly friendly tone of voice.

"Steve Holmes, well, how the heck are you? Good to hear from you." Bryce's voice carried the same phony country accent he used during the first part of his conversation with Mark three days earlier.

"Actually, Bryce, I'm on a speakerphone. The whole band is here, and so is Kevin LaRoche."

"Well, that's just wonderful. Hello, boys!"

No one bothered to return Bryce's greeting. Mark extended his middle finger in the direction of the speakerphone.

Bryce continued, "So, are we all gathered here to talk a little business—Upper Hand tour business?"

"Yes, we are, Bryce, but first we'd like to talk a little religion with you. We understand you're now a big mover and shaker in the TV Jesus business."

"Why, that's right, Steve. Yes, I was fortunate enough to meet my wonderful wife, Anna Mae, and her dynamic father, the Reverend Orvis Hightower, several years ago. Reverend Hightower is doing a spectacular job of delivering the word of Jesus to the good people of Tennessee. He has graciously asked me to assist him in his work. I'm really just doing God's bidding here, doing what I can to help Reverend Hightower spread the good word."

Kevin had to wave his hands frantically at the members of the band to keep them quiet, as their barely stifled laughter and gagging gestures approached audible level. Mark reprised his middle finger salute to the phone.

Steve composed himself enough to reply. "Well, listen, Bryce, we heathens up here think we have something important to communicate to your righteous new family and friends down there. After all, you've only been living in Tennessee for a few years. I don't think the folks down there know the real Bryce Miller. We want to help."

Bryce hesitated for a second or two. "I'm not sure I know what you mean," he replied cautiously.

"Well, Bryce, back in the day when the Upper Hand was touring all over the world, partying and carrying on like we did, I became really interested in photography, remember? Yeah, I was a real shutterbug. Took pictures of all kinds of shenanigans, just for fun."

Bryce started feeling uneasy about the direction the conversation was taking and simply replied, "OK."

"Well guess what, Bryce? You're very well represented in these photos, and I think the righteous people of Tennessee—especially your lovely wife and her Bible-squeezing preacher daddy—would enjoy learning more about what makes Bryce Miller tick by getting a look at these great photos."

Bryce felt a sudden sinking feeling in his stomach, and his mouth instantly became too dry for him to utter a reply.

Steve continued, his voice even cheerier than at the beginning of the call. "Now, this first photo I'm looking at here is a terrific example. There you are, sitting on a big old sofa, looking all happy, with a nice-looking girl on either side of you, one blonde, one brunette. Wholesome, Christian-looking women in my estimation. Funny thing is, they seem to have misplaced their blouses and bras, but you're right there to the rescue with your left hand on the blonde's left boob and your right hand on the brunette's right boob. That's right, all you God-fearin' people of Tennessee. Bryce Miller is always ready and willing to lend a helping hand."

Bryce was starting to feel dizzy, and his forehead was drenched in sweat.

"Now, here's another heart-warming photo, Bryce. There you are, on your hands and knees, wearing nothing but your skivvies—oh, wait, you've got socks on, too. And this pretty young thing is riding you like a pony, wearing nothing but your shirt. Yes, folks, Bryce Miller is the kind of guy who'll give you the shirt off his back!"

Jeff, Mark, A.J., Dave, and Kevin were now biting the fronts of their shirts to keep from howling, and Bryce was wiping his face with a wadded-up ball of tissues.

"Now, this next one is so perfect that I have to wonder if you didn't know twenty years ago that you were going to be living in Tennessee. There you are, spread-eagle on the floor, with a big old smile on your face. It's hard to tell for sure if you're conscious or not, but guess what you're holding in your hand? An empty bottle of Jack Daniels! Now, I ask you, what's more 'Tennessee' than that?"

A reflexive, audible groan came through the speakerphone, but Bryce was still unable to pull himself together enough to deliver a coherent reply.

"Given Tennessee's complex and difficult history with race relations, I think you're going to be especially pleased about this next shot. There's you dancing with a very attractive young black girl, and by golly, she's lost most of her clothing, too. But you're holding her gently around her naked little waist and staring tenderly into her, well, it's not really her eyes you're looking into, but you're definitely staring very meaningfully at parts of her. I think Tennessee is hungry for this kind of open-mindedness from its church spokespeople regarding interracial couplings, don't you?"

Bryce finally managed to blurt out hoarsely, "What is this all about? What do you want?"

Mark barked into the speaker phone, "You know damn well what this is about, Bryce. You're going to rip up that contract for our next tour and stay out of our lives forever, or everyone in the state of Tennessee, starting with your holy-roller wife and in-laws, is going to find out what a phony piece of shit you really are."

Bryce no longer cared the least bit about the Upper Hand's upcoming tour. "What about the photos?"

Steve happily replied, "Oh, you want a set, Bryce? They were taken on a good quality camera, so I can have them blown up to banner size if you'd like."

"Fuck you, you son of a bitch."

"Oh, my, that didn't sound very Christian."

Bryce's Southern accent was nowhere in evidence now. "I don't give a damn what it sounded like. If you want that contract voided, I want assurances that those fucking photos never see the light of day."

Kevin got out of his chair and leaned over the speakerphone. "I hear you've got some top notch lawyers working for you down there, Bryce. You get one of them to put together a formal dissolution of this contract. You sign it and get it notarized and have it on my desk by next Friday. You can put in a clause about the photos if you want. Just be damned sure the Upper Hand is officially free from that contract by the end of next week."

"Or these photos get turned into posters and T-shirts!" yelled Mark. "I'll personally see to it that your wife gets the size XXL shirt she needs with the picture of you and the two topless girls on it."

Bryce slammed down the phone, and a wild celebration commenced at A.J.'s house. They returned to the game room, but this time the room was abuzz with activity. Steve was hugged and grabbed and pounded on the back so many times that he had visible bruises the next morning.

As the celebration neared its end several hours later, Jeff called out to Kevin, "OK, Kev, you've got a big assignment. Find us a legitimate tour manager, and sign him up. We have a tour to plan."

CHAPTER 19

With the thieving Bryce Miller and his contractual grip on the Upper Hand's touring plans now permanently in the band's rearview mirror, a seemingly inexhaustible energy now drove the group in its preparations for its nationwide comeback. By the end of September 2004, a mere three weeks after Steve's brilliantly conceived and executed disposal of Miller, Kevin had a respected, veteran tour management firm picked out, thoroughly vetted, and signed to handle the winter-spring 2005 concert tour. The band dubbed it the *We Were Dead...But We Got Better* tour.

By early November, thirty-eight arena shows in twenty-eight cities were booked over an eleven-week period beginning in early February. The tour would start in Jacksonville, Florida, concentrate on southern and western cities during February, and then spread throughout all major regions of the U.S., plus Toronto and Montreal, in March and April. Demand for tickets was so great when the tour dates were announced that fifteen additional shows were quickly added, and the tour was extended through May. In their own New York/New Jersey backyard, the band's original plans for two shows at Manhattan's Madison Square Garden, one at Long Island's Nassau Coliseum and two at New Jersey's Continental Arena grew to four shows at the Garden, two at Nassau, and three at Continental.

The hyper-energized band rehearsed tirelessly in the weeks leading up to the first concert in Jacksonville. By mid-January, they had thirty-five vintage Upper Hand songs fully ready for public performance, enough to allow them to significantly vary their two-hour show from night to night.

Mark and Dave showed no outward signs of lingering animosity following their explosive confrontation back in September. However, the emotional issues raised that day were never really addressed following that skirmish and sat dormant below the surface of the band's current state of excited anticipation.

Mark, still bothered by some of Dave's bitter comments, but not willing to reopen any old wounds by revisiting those complaints with him, instead offered an olive branch to his sensitive colleague at the end of a rehearsal in late January.

The group had ended that day's rehearsal at Mark's house with a run-through of "Tireless Dancer." Mark happened to find himself alone with Dave as the rest of the band departed for the evening.

"Nice job on the 'Tireless Dancer' vocal today, Dave."

"Thanks, man, I appreciate it."

Mark hesitated a second or two. Then he decided to say what was really on his mind.

"Listen, Dave, I want you to know that I have always thought that 'Tireless Dancer' is a terrific song, and I wish fans had appreciated it as much as they should have."

"That's nice to hear. Thank you."

"And, I've never said this to anyone before. In a way, I think I'm partly to blame for that song not being a monster hit for us."

Dave tilted his head and stared at Mark quizzically. "Huh?"

"Back when we were figuring out the instrumental arrangement for 'Dancer,' I had this idea in my head for a really cool, really big guitar part that would have fit that song perfectly. But you know how things were back then—*hey, it's a Dave song; keyboards rule, guitars hang back*—and I just kept my mouth shut. Thinking back, I guess we did that with all of your songs; I'm not really sure why. I'm wondering now if maybe we weren't doing your tunes any favors with that philosophy. Anyway, I wish I had played that idea of mine for you guys."

Dave, both moved and somewhat taken aback by Mark's comments, did not wish to dwell on the broader implications of the suggestion that his bandmates had held certain attitudes regarding the arrangements of his songs which may have weakened those recordings, so he simply asked, "Do you still remember that guitar part?"

"Actually, I do. Believe it or not, every time I hear or play that song, that phantom guitar part goes through my mind, even though I've never actually performed it."

"Would you play it for me now?"

"Sure, I'd like you to hear it."

Mark plucked one of his Les Pauls off its tripod stand, plugged it into his rehearsal amp, and flicked the amp's on switch. Dave settled in behind his electric piano, turned it on, and began to play. As soon as Dave finished the intro sequence to "Tireless Dancer" and launched into the first verse, Mark joined in with the powerful yet melodic lead passages he had held in his head for over twenty years. Within seconds Dave's eyes were wide with shock at how Mark's inventive guitar work transformed his song without overwhelming it. Mark, seeing Dave's expression, smiled broadly in acknowledgment, and the two of them played the song all the way through.

When the song was over, Dave ran a hand through his hair, looked over at Mark and his *well, whaddaya think?* expression, and exclaimed, "Mark, I hardly know what to say. That was brilliant. Fucking brilliant!" He paused a second and grinned. "I oughta strangle you for keeping that under your hat for all these years."

"I'm glad you like it, and I am really sorry I wasn't smart enough to break our old habits and offer this up in 1983. Should we play it for the guys at our next rehearsal?"

"Are you kidding me? I have no intention of ever playing this song again without that guitar part."

To the puzzlement of the rest of the band, Dave and Mark insisted on starting the next Upper Hand rehearsal with "Tireless Dancer," even though they had performed it flawlessly at the end of their previous get-together. As Mark strapped on his Les Paul to begin the practice session, Jeff called out to his co-guitarist, "Why do you have an electric in your hands? You said you wanted to begin this session with 'Dancer.' Shouldn't you be playing an acoustic along with me?"

"We're going to try something a little different. Just play your normal part and see what you think."

The band followed Dave's lead into "Tireless Dancer," and before long A.J., Jeff, and Steve were furrowing their brows, and then simply staring with utter surprise at Mark's *tour de force* enrichment of the song's instrumental arrangement.

"What the hell was that? Goddamn, that was amazing!" opined Jeff when the song wound to a close.

"Where did that come from? I've never heard this song sound so hot," added A.J.

"Wow! Are we going to play it that way on the tour?" asked Steve.

"You bet your ass we are," replied Dave.

"Mark, when did you come up with that part? That was sweet," said Jeff.

"Way back in 1983 when Dave first brought the song to us. I just never said anything about it because, you know, it's a pretty big part, and...it's a Dave song."

A.J., Steve, and Jeff nodded their heads in immediate comprehension, to Dave's bewilderment. *So Mark's comments a couple of days earlier about the instrumentation of Dave's songs were true.*

"What was there, some kind of unwritten rule that my songs couldn't have strong guitar parts in them? Did I ever say anything suggesting I wanted the guitars toned down in the stuff I wrote?"

The guys looked at each other and shrugged their shoulders.

Jeff said haltingly, "I don't think there was any *rule* or anything. It just sorta seemed...actually, I don't know where it came from."

"Me neither. But I guess I always just kind of assumed...how about you guys?" said Mark, looking to quickly deflect the discussion to A.J. and Steve.

Steve immediately tossed the hot potato to A.J. with, "Hey, I'm just the lowly drummer."

A.J offered, "I can't remember anyone ever saying a word about it, but I do agree that somehow an assumption developed that Dave's songs were going to be big on keyboards, not so big on guitars."

"Well, wherever it came from, I want to declare it officially dead. For any song I've written or will write going forward, I want you guys to feel free to bring on the guitars. Stuff like this 'Dancer' part Mark's been sitting on for two decades shouldn't go unheard."

Dave spent the remainder of the rehearsal preoccupied by everyone's comments about his old songs. Had he somehow unconsciously influenced Mark and Jeff over the years to under-contribute instrumentally to his songs, perhaps to guarantee a stronger focus on himself? Or had these arrangement decisions originated with the other members of the band...or maybe record label boss Stan Rabin? *Had Dave's chances at achieving true recognition and stardom as a songwriter and singer been torpedoed by these arrangement choices?*

CHAPTER 20

Opening night of the Upper Hand's *We Were Dead...But We Got Better* tour—Friday, February 4, 2005, at the sold-out, 15,000-seat Jacksonville Veterans Memorial Arena—arrived at last. Every member of the band was in top form musically, mentally, and physically as he eagerly awaited the cue to take the stage:

Mark Donahue, fifteen pounds lighter and looking fitter than he had in a decade, after agreeing at the behest of his young girlfriend, Emily, to watch his diet and do some jogging in preparation for the rigors of the tour.

Jeff Britton, his hair and full beard now professionally trimmed and colored, bearing little resemblance to the strung-out wreck from the disastrous 1990 tour.

Steve Holmes, timelessly trim, powerful, and irresistible to women.

Dave Rowinski, his hair still slate gray, but now nearly shoulder length and accompanied by his familiar bushy mustache, looking just like...a fifty-three-year-old rock musician.

A.J. Ramello? Well, A.J. was A.J. Having inexplicably shaved off his goatee late in 2004, he now bore an uncanny resemblance to Uncle Fester. But there wasn't an Upper Hand fan on the planet who was looking to A.J. Ramello for eye candy anyway. All they ever watched were his two hands working their magic on his four- and five-string bass guitars.

The wildly enthusiastic and welcoming audience consisted of a healthy mix of veteran Baby Boomer followers of the Upper Hand and younger fans who, being familiar with the band's extensive collection of hits through their continued strong presence on classic rock radio, were now getting a chance to see them live for the first time. As the quintet took the stage to a roaring standing ovation, Mark stepped to his microphone and greeted the crowd with, "Hello, old friends and new friends. I can't begin to tell you how great it is to be here tonight. We are the Upper Hand. As you may have heard, we used to be dead...BUT WE GOT BETTER!" With that, A.J. kicked things off with his rumbling bass introduction to one of Jeff's well-known songs, "Shoulda Cut and Run."

The concert was a raving success. The show, originally planned for two hours plus a two song encore, stretched to close to three hours as the crowd kept screaming for more, and the band happily accommodated them by reaching into their supply of extra songs to extend the evening.

The story was much the same at every stop during the first seven weeks of the tour: sold-out arenas, rapturous crowds, blistering performances, and total harmony among the band members both onstage and off. The happiest man of them all during February and March was Dave. Night after night, the newly punched-up "Tireless Dancer" received deafening applause and standing ovations from the crowds. After the fourth concert of the tour, A.J. addressed the rest of the group during the after-show party back at the hotel.

"Holy smoke, the new version of 'Tireless Dancer' is driving people wild at every show. Way to go, Dave! And, Mark, you're a frickin' genius. I'll tell you what we gotta do. We need to get a top-quality in-concert recording of the song, as soon as possible, and get the label to rush release it as a live CD single."

"Sweet idea!"

"Excellent."

"Let's do it at the next show, in San Antonio."

"Do you think Rabin will go for it?" asked Dave. "He's not exactly a huge fan of my stuff."

Mark replied, "He'll do it. First of all, he's starving for anything to release from the Upper Hand. How many more 'Greatest Hits' packages can he conjure up? And second, if he balks, I'll kick his scrawny ass."

Stan Rabin, having attended the band's second show of the tour to gauge the band's popularity—and thus its prospects for creating and delivering a hit album after the tour—did not need any persuading. The San Antonio performance of "Tireless Dancer" was recorded, edited, and released as a single in early March. It received immediate heavy nationwide FM radio airplay and climbed to number two on the Billboard CD singles chart by the end of the month, decisively outperforming the original 1983 studio single release of the song.

Rabin and the Upper Hand each quickly agreed to put up fifty percent of the upfront money required to reserve six weeks' time at the band's favorite studio, Total Immersion, to record an all-new Upper Hand album, beginning in August.

The first half of the 2005 comeback tour was truly an idyllic time for the Upper Hand. The band was completely on top of its game, delivering blazing, ecstatically received and reviewed performances at every stop. Just as importantly, the atmosphere surrounding the tour in February and March was, if certainly far less raucous and hedonistic than in the 1970s and '80s, overwhelmingly positive. Dave's wife Sharon, who hadn't met Dave until after the band's 1990 breakup, arranged to join the tour for several stops to get a first-time taste of the band's life on the road, leaving their fragile eight year old son Justin in the capable hands of her parents. A.J.'s wife Cathy and Mark's girlfriend Emily also flew in when they could, further enhancing the comfortable, congenial vibe of the tour. Steve picked up right where he had left off in the 1980s, finding himself a gorgeous date at every city they visited. Jeff's nightly beer consumption, unobtrusively monitored by Mark, was, at least by Jeff's historical standards, relatively modest, generally topping out at four or five bottles per night.. Everyone associated with this career-resurrecting tour was enjoying it immensely, and it seemed like nothing could derail the Upper Hand Reunion Train as it sped towards April.

That is, until March 30, in St. Louis.

It was 4:30 on a Wednesday afternoon, an off day before the next evening's concert. The band was seated in the restaurant of the Renaissance St. Louis Grand Hotel, chatting idly, and nursing beers. Having just completed an interview with a reporter from *People* magazine for an upcoming feel-good article about the Upper Hand's headline-making return, all five of the band members were seated facing the now empty chair where the reporter had been sitting, with their backs to the restaurant door. None of them witnessed the entrance of the striking brunette wearing the form-fitting red and black blouse, equally figure-revealing black Capri pants, and red heels.

Turning heads as she strode over to the unsuspecting quintet, she came to a halt immediately behind them, and purred to the backs of their heads, "Well, well, would you look at this? The old gang's back together. I never thought I'd see the day."

Conversation screeched to a halt, and the five men sat motionless for a second. Not one of them had to turn around to know who had just shattered the serenity of their gathering.

"Uh oh," muttered Steve under his breath.

Oh, shit, was the first thought that entered Dave's mind.

For A.J. it was, *this can't be good.*

The sound of that voice hit Jeff like a taser. His eyes went wide as he was instantly overwhelmed by a wave of intense, conflicting emotions.

Mark's reaction was far simpler and required virtually no time at all to process: a deep, ear-reddening surge of pure hate.

Jeff was too shocked to be the first to spin around and respond, so Mark did the honors.

"*What the fuck are you doing here?*" he hissed.

The venom in Mark's voice and the unmistakable fury in his eyes were enough to make almost anyone take two steps back in alarm, but the target of his malevolence stood her ground and coolly replied, "It's nice to see you too, Mark."

It was Denise Blake.

Mark began to spew more invective at Denise, but Jeff, standing up now to work his way around the grouping of chairs to get to her, quickly barked, "Enough, Mark! Just shut the hell up."

Mark sat steaming as Denise, using the few seconds of time Jeff needed to reach her to greet the rest of the group, said, "So, how have you boys all been?"

Dave, Steve, and A.J. weren't exactly thrilled to see Denise, but none of them carried the intense hatred for her that Mark did, so each managed a semi-affable response.

"Doing OK, Denise."

"Doing fine. What's up with you, Denise?"

"Hello, Denise. How are you doing?"

Mark shot baleful glances at all three of them for their cordiality.

Jeff and Denise now stood directly face-to-face. Jeff's mouth was open, but no words were forthcoming. Denise gave him a smile and held out her arms, and an instant later they were locked in a tight embrace. Jeff could only manage to sputter, "What...where have...I mean, how…" before Denise placed her fingers gently over his mouth and said softly, "I'm so glad you've emerged from your backwoods hiding place. We have unfinished business."

Glancing over at the four sets of eyeballs staring at them, Denise took a step back from Jeff and whispered, "I have a room here. Let's get away from these inquiring minds."

Jeff, powerless and totally without incentive to resist, turned toward his friends with a sheepish smile, and let Denise lead him by the hand out of the restaurant. Mark gritted his teeth and spit out, "Christ! This can't be happening. This fucking cannot be happening."

Steve, in an effort to calm Mark down, offered, "This might not be as bad as you think. I mean, she looks good. I'm willing to bet that she hasn't been near heroin for a long time."

Dave added, "Who knows? Maybe this is just a one-day drop-by. She may have a flight out of here tomorrow."

Mark exhaled glumly. "We can only hope, but don't bet on it. Did you see the two of them standing there? We're going to need a crowbar to separate them. In fact, if you go get me one, I'll be happy to go take care of it right now."

CHAPTER 21

Denise slid the plastic room key in and out of the slot in her hotel room door and opened the door to a luxurious, spacious suite. Jeff, taking in the grandeur of the accommodations with a nod of his head, said, "Well, this answers one of the questions I had for you. Apparently you've been doing all right for yourself."

Denise closed the door, pulled the still somewhat stunned Jeff close to her, kicked off her red high heels, and after giving him a long kiss, said, "We have an enormous amount of catching up to do, both conversationally...and between the sheets. Which would you like to start on first?"

Jeff's smile left no doubt what his first instincts were regarding the choices just provided him, but after a brief pause he took a small step back and replied, "I can hardly believe I'm saying this, but I have so many things rushing through my head right now that I need to ask you—and tell you—that I think it's better that we sit down on that cushy sofa over there and talk to each other first. Believe me, we'll get to part two of your catch-up plan very soon."

"Ahh, you always were a rational man. Come, let's have a drink and sit." She grabbed two glasses from the suite's kitchen counter, opened the refrigerator's freezer door, and pulled out a bottle of Grey Goose L'Orange vodka. As she began to pour the vodka into the first of the glasses, Jeff asked, "You wouldn't happen to have any beer in there, would you?"

"Beer is for teenagers and football players, darling. Here, take a sip of this deep-chilled ambrosia, and you'll leave your Joe Six Pack days behind for good."

Jeff accepted the glass and sampled the flavored vodka. "Whoo, that is so cold I can't even taste—oh, wait a minute, there it is. Hmm, not too shabby. Orange-flavored vodka, eh? What will they think of next?"

By this time Denise had already downed her first helping, and was busy pouring herself another. They walked over to the massive sofa and sat down close together. Denise had her refilled glass and the bottle within easy reach on the coffee table. She topped off Jeff's half empty glass.

"So, who wants to go first?"

"I guess I will. Where did you go when I had my meltdown and stranded you in Atlanta? I've never stopped thinking about where you were or how you were doing."

"It's strange, isn't it? Neither one of us had any idea where the other one was from that day forward. I'm willing to wait my turn here to ask you where you disappeared to that night, but the bottom line is, you and I really had no way to get in touch with each other. So, let's just call it even and declare both of us innocent of abandoning each other, OK?"

"Deal," replied Jeff, and the two of them clinked their vodka glasses together.

"Anyway, once I found out that even good old A.J. had no clue where you were hiding out, I just sort of drifted around the country for a while and then took off for Europe in 1993. I lived in Portugal for a few years, then Spain, then Denmark, before coming back to the States two years ago. There's no one place significant enough to talk much about. I guess I've really been a restless wanderer over these past, what is it, fifteen years?"

"If you don't mind me asking, how are you doing money-wise? This suite certainly suggests that you're not suffering, but are you OK?"

"You know me. I'm a survivor, babe. You don't have to worry about me."

"One last thing, Denise. Are you, well, you know...?"

"Clean? Absolutely. I haven't touched heroin since 1992." She reached over to the coffee table and poured another sizable drink from the bottle of Grey Goose L'Orange. She held her glass aloft in front of her, as if giving a toast. "This is how I take the edge off now. Much easier to come by, and a whole lot friendlier to the system."

Denise's decidedly vague description of where and how she had spent the past fifteen years was entirely by design, and if Jeff had pressed her for any details about her personal or financial endeavors during that time, she had a supply of fabricated stories at the ready. It was true that she had gotten in touch by phone with A.J. about two weeks after Jeff vanished in Atlanta, and equally true that she began "drifting around the country" as soon as she learned that nobody knew where Jeff had gone or how to contact him. What Denise neglected to mention was that her city-to-city wandering took place in the company of another touring rock band, a successful southern California-based group called Nuts & Bolts. In classic Denise fashion, she easily latched onto the Nuts & Bolts tour when they passed through Atlanta, first by attracting the attention of the group's lighting director, and then quickly moving on to the band's lead guitarist, Lenny Adamsky.

Denise also conveniently forgot to talk about her entrepreneurial activities during and after her time traveling with Adamsky and his band. The members of Nuts & Bolts and their entourage were extraordinarily heavy users of cocaine, heroin, and just about every other illicit substance known to the world of 1990s rock. It took the ever-resourceful Denise almost no time to recognize and exploit the Nuts & Bolts traveling road show's insatiable need for drugs, and she quickly set herself up as a reliable and discreet go-between for the tour's many drug users and each concert city's eager suppliers. Her skill at providing this much-needed service proved to be extremely lucrative, and by the end of the Nuts & Bolts tour in August of 1990, Denise had amassed over $200,000 in cash.

Denise quickly dumped Adamsky when the tour wound down, using the many connections she had established around the country to expand the scope of her underground drug procurement business to other touring rock bands. Her hidden wealth swelled to almost $1.5 million over the next two and a half years.

Denise's claim to Jeff that she had not used heroin herself since 1992 was true. In September of that year, a careless mistake Denise made during a drug transaction very nearly caused her to be knifed by a rogue cocaine dealer. She attributed her lack of judgment that day entirely to having dosed herself with heroin a few hours earlier and swore that night never to touch the drug again. As of the early spring of 2005, she was true to her vow.

By early 1993, Denise sensed that the viability of her underground business was quickly coming to an end. Too many people knew about the services she was providing, and an apparent law enforcement crackdown had led to the arrest of several of her connections. When one of her most trusted suppliers informed her that one of his other customers had been asking questions about her, Denise correctly deduced that undercover DEA agents were nosing around, trying to build a case against her. Without advance word to anyone, Denise pulled up stakes and flew to Lisbon, Portugal, in May of 1993, mere days before the DEA was planning to bring her in for questioning. Her choice of Portugal as her destination was almost random, influenced by little more than recent magazine ads she'd seen touting the pleasures offered there as a tourist stop.

Denise's offhand, almost dismissive recap to Jeff of her years in Europe also excluded a number of details that would have raised the hairs on the back of his neck. In Lisbon, Denise happily exploited her glamorous looks and drug-generated wealth to integrate herself into the social circles of the city's party class, discovering quickly that she could be fully understood and welcomed by this crowd as an English-only speaker. Less than a month after her arrival in Portugal, she was introduced at a party to a charming, wealthy, and physically frail eighty-two-year-old retired British shipbuilding executive now living on the Portuguese coast. Jeremy Bradley, twice-divorced with three children in their fifties from his first marriage, was immediately enraptured by the gorgeous and highly attentive Denise, and before long she was seen at his side at every important social event Bradley attended. Bradley's daughter and two sons, each still living in England and each of whose relationship with their father was difficult at best since his long ago trade-in of their mother for his second wife, were appalled when they learned of their father's dalliance with the American woman nearly fifty years his junior. They were positively apoplectic when Jeremy Bradley and Denise Blake married in November of 1993.

Despite the considerable tongue-wagging amongst their acquaintances and the fury of Bradley's children, the marriage offered considerable benefits to both Denise and her elderly new spouse. To Bradley, his stunning young wife provided doting attention, companionship, and no small measure of a sensation of restored power and virility when seen in public with Denise on his arm. He also took a certain satisfaction in torturing his spoiled offspring by rubbing their noses in his newfound bliss. For Denise, being wed to Jeremy Bradley meant a luxurious, carefree lifestyle in a magnificent seaside mansion, many valuable social connections, and relatively few demands of her time or affections. Marriage to Bradley meant only minimal interruption of Denise's own personal, social, and clandestine romantic pursuits.

Jeremy Bradley's already fragile health began to deteriorate dramatically in early 1996. Bradley had promised Denise shortly before they were married that he would make sure that she was well taken care of when he was gone, but she had no idea *how* well taken care of until after his death in July of 1996. At the reading of Bradley's will that October, attended by Denise as well as Bradley's three hostile, stone-faced offspring, there were audible gasps from Bradley's sons and a barely muffled shriek from his daughter when it was revealed that Bradley had left his spectacular house and half of his twelve million British pound—eighteen million dollar—fortune to his young widow, and just one million pounds to each of his children. The rest was bequeathed to several of Bradley's favorite charities. The children loudly vowed to challenge the will, but Bradley, predicting such a response, had instructed his lawyers to include ironclad proof that Bradley was of sound mind when he made the will, and had inserted several other safeguards to ensure that his wishes were fulfilled. Bradley's sons and daughter had no choice but to bitterly accept their father's unequivocal declaration of who he felt most deserved to inherit his wealth.

Freed from having to tend to her elderly and ailing husband, Denise eagerly anticipated stepping into her new role as the desirable, openly available young widow and heiress. However, she soon found herself in the frustrating position of having to fend off the relentless advances of a seemingly endless stream of unappealing, lecherous old men, many of them acquaintances of her late husband, who fervently hoped to persuade Denise to share her abundant physical and financial assets with them. By the summer of 1997 she abandoned Portugal for Barcelona, Spain, where she spent the next two years serially seducing and discarding a string of suitors, not one of whom was as much as a day older than she. Having exhausted the supply of young men in Barcelona to toy with by the fall of 1999, she relocated to Copenhagen, Denmark, similarly running roughshod over that city's most eligible thirty-something males. By this time, she had also developed a tremendous capacity, and need, for alcohol.

Finally, in the spring of 2003, Denise, correctly assuming that ten years out of the country was enough to make the DEA lose interest in her, returned to the U.S., choosing Chicago as her new home. As she reflected on the parade of men she had allowed into her life between the time she escaped western Pennsylvania in 1978 and her latest escapades in Copenhagen, she came to the realization that the only one she had any desire to reconnect with was Jeff Britton. It had been widely reported by 2003 that the former Upper Hand guitarist was a recovering heroin addict living and working with family members in West Virginia, apparently retired for good from the music industry, so Denise knew she could locate him easily if she so desired. However, she envisioned the Jeff Britton of 2003 as a hollowed-out, fragile shell of his former self, and decided against making any effort to contact him.

Everything changed when Denise caught the press reports of the unexpected reunion of the Upper Hand in late 2004. She was astonished to see a healthy, vibrant Jeff talking confidently and enthusiastically on TV about the band's ambitious plans for 2005. She obtained a copy of the *We Were Dead...But We Got Better* tour schedule as soon as it was published, made some inquiries of some old contacts from her days as a rock and roll tour follower to get information on the hotels where the band would be staying, and plotted her surprise March 30 appearance at the Renaissance St. Louis Grand Hotel.

The bottle of orange-flavored vodka, full when Denise retrieved it from the freezer, was now empty. Jeff had just finished encapsulating the last fifteen years of his life—his desperate bus trip out of Atlanta the morning after he walked offstage mid-show, his refuge at his sister's house in Maryland, his multiple stints in rehab and his eventual success in kicking his heroin habit, the boredom, but much needed serenity, of his nine years working for his brother in West Virginia, his long and painful estrangement from Mark, and the gallant efforts of A.J., Steve, and Dave to reunite Jeff and Mark and resurrect the Upper Hand—and now his head was spinning from the vodka. Denise was also obviously feeling the effects of her own significant role in the draining of the three-quarter liter bottle, and the two of them sagged towards one another on the sofa. Within seconds, they both passed out. The "between the sheets" portion of their reconnection would have to wait a couple of hours.

CHAPTER 22

Mark, Dave, A.J., and Steve were seated around a circular table in Steve's hotel suite, with various sheets of paper spread across the table containing typed and handwritten lists of Upper Hand songs. Plates full of bagels, muffins, and pastries were arrayed along a nearby serving table, along with containers of coffee and juice. It was 10:00 the following morning, the day of the band's St. Louis concert, and the group was gathering for its usual pre-concert assembly of that night's set list.

Steve had stuck a washcloth between the doorjamb and the door to his room to keep it unlocked. Jeff came through the door into the suite, ambled a bit unsteadily over to the serving table, and grabbed a pastry and a cup of coffee. He then stumbled over to where his bandmates were seated and plopped himself heavily into the remaining chair, a crooked smile plastered on his face. He took a bite out of his pastry and a long gulp of his coffee, and suddenly noticed that no one in the room was speaking. Everyone was staring at him.

"What?" he blurted out, shrugging his shoulders and gesturing with his palms skyward.

"Look at that shit-eating grin," teased Steve, poking Jeff in the arm. "Your little rendezvous with Denise went well, did it?"

"Hey, I don't kiss and tell...but yeah, I guess you could say that."

Steve, Dave, and A.J. chuckled, but Mark was not the least bit amused.

"I don't give a rat's ass if you got laid or not. Look at you. Your eyes are all bleary. You come in here all but caroming off the walls. That bitch isn't even back a day yet, and you look like you're using already."

"Go fuck yourself, Mark." Jeff stood up, pushed up the sleeves of his sweatshirt over his elbows, and displayed the fronts of his forearms toward Mark. "Look—no needle marks. Satisfied? Or should I drop my pants and let you inspect my ass, too? I wasn't using, and neither was Denise. She's been clean for something like thirteen years. So get off my case."

Mark was not convinced. "She tells you she's clean and you just take it as gospel?"

"Yeah, that's right. I do."

"Well, if you two weren't shooting up, then why do you look like you aged ten goddamn years overnight?"

"Not that it's any of your business, but I may have overindulged in chilled orange vodka."

"This is a joke, right?"

"No, Denise had a bottle of this Grey Goose orange vodka in her freezer, and, well, the bottle's not there anymore. Tasty stuff, by the way."

"You dumb fuck! What are you doing drinking that high-octane stuff? You're a beer drinker, for chrissakes."

"What are you griping about? You used to pound vodka like a maniac."

"Yeah, but I didn't spend five years in and out of drug rehab. Your rehab counselors told you not to drink at all, remember? You may be able to handle a few brews, but if you let that bitch—"

"Stop calling her a bitch! I mean it."

"If you let that *sweet angel* pour eighty-proof vodka down your gullet, you're gonna wind up just as fucked up as you were when she hooked you on heroin."

"I'm through talking about this. We have a set list to put together. Besides, I have an announcement. You're not going to like it, Mark, but tough shit. Denise is going to accompany me on the rest of the tour. Yes, we're back together again, and no, heroin will not be a part of our lives."

If Jeff was hoping for at least a token positive reaction from A.J., Steve, or Dave, he didn't receive it. They sat silently, staring blankly and waiting for someone else to say something as Mark banged his forehead repeatedly on the table.

"Jeez, don't all jump up and down at the same time," Jeff grumbled.

"Are you sure about this, Jeff?" offered Dave. "If you are, then I guess it's cool. Just be careful, OK?"

"There's nothing 'cool' about it," growled Mark, pulling his head back up off the table. "I'm going to get the fuck out of here before I say what I really feel about this insanity. I trust you boys to put together a great set list. I'll see you at sound check." With that he rose from his chair, grabbed a muffin off the serving table, and strode out of the room without another word to his stunned bandmates.

The concert put on by the Upper Hand that evening in St. Louis at the sold-out, nineteen-thousand seat Scottrade Center delivered the same top-caliber, crowd-pleasing instrumental and vocal performances the band had been providing throughout the tour, and no one would claim that the fans went home dissatisfied. But to Dave, Steve, and A.J., and perhaps a handful of true die-hard veteran followers of the band, there was a disconcerting difference between this show and virtually any previous Upper Hand concert, a difference that the band's keyboardist, drummer, and bassist felt had to be addressed immediately.

Mark and Jeff's in-concert guitar histrionics were always accompanied by a great deal of interactive showmanship—face-to-face guitar duels, egging on the crowd to cheer for each other's solos, humorous demonstrations of mock one-upmanship—and they would frequently dash over to one another's microphones to sing harmonies together into one microphone. But at the St. Louis concert, the two guitarists all but ignored each other throughout the performance, standing near their own microphones or strutting off away from the other to play to the crowd individually.

The following morning, there was a knock on Jeff's hotel room door. Jeff and Denise were packing for that afternoon's trip to the next tour stop, Indianapolis. Jeff opened the door, and was greeted by A.J., Dave, and Steve.

"Hey, Jeff, got a minute?" asked Dave rhetorically, as the three marched past Jeff into the room.

"I guess I do," shrugged Jeff, following the visiting trio into the living area of the suite.

"Hi, Denise," said Steve. "Listen, sorry to bother you, but we have some band business to go over. Would it be possible for you to step out for a cup of coffee for a few minutes?"

"Wait a minute, wait a minute," protested Jeff. "Denise shouldn't have to leave the room. She's inner circle now."

Dave shot Jeff a crooked scowl. "*Inner circle?* What the hell are you talking about? There's no inner circle except the band itself when there are important matters to discuss, and you know it."

Denise, not wishing to become any more of a divisive figure in the band than she already was, said, "That's OK, babe, I can entertain myself at the shops downstairs. Knock yourself out, boys. How long do you need?"

"Ten, fifteen minutes tops. Thanks, Denise."

She gave Jeff a kiss, grabbed her purse and room key, and sauntered out of the room.

Jeff turned to face his visitors. "OK, what's going on? And where's Mark? I thought we had some important band stuff to talk about."

Dave ignored Jeff's question about Mark. "What did you think about last night's performance?"

"I thought it was fine. Why?"

"Well, it wasn't fine. Matter of fact, it pretty much sucked. And do you know why it sucked? Because you and Mark behaved like a couple of feuding schoolgirls who refuse to go to each other's birthday parties."

Jeff knew it was pointless to try to deny the lack of interaction between himself and Mark at the concert and just mumbled defensively, "It wasn't that big a deal."

"Bullshit!" exclaimed Steve. "It's a damned big deal. The back and forth stuff between you two guys is an important part of the show, and what happened last night can't happen again. You have to fix this, Jeff, *now*."

"Why is it up to me? Mark is the one who went off the rails yesterday."

It was A.J.'s turn to pitch in. "Come on, Jeff, get real. How did you expect Mark to react to Denise reappearing out of nowhere? You know full-well what he thinks about her and her role in your drug problems. Are you really surprised he thinks the same shit is going to happen again?"

"Well, he's wrong. Don't you guys agree he's overreacting?"

"Well, the three of us are willing to give you the benefit of the doubt, although I don't mind telling you that we're more than a little concerned, but it's your job to convince Mark that—"

A.J. stopped speaking suddenly, as his glance happened to fall upon an open, one-third-empty bottle of vodka, dripping with condensation from having been recently removed from the freezer, and two half-filled glasses, resting on a desk.

Oh, fuck, here we go, thought Jeff as his eyes, as well as Dave's and Steve's, followed A.J.'s toward the glaring proof that Jeff and Denise had been downing vodka before 10:00 in the morning.

Steve was the first to react, exploding, "Are you fucking kidding me? What the hell are you doing? *Trying* to prove Mark correct?"

Dave was next. "I don't believe this! You got a problem, Jeff. Something goes haywire when you and Denise get together, and you better do something about it."

"It's not a problem. I promise. It's still only been two days since we've been together again after a really long time apart. Things will calm down once we're settled in, OK?"

"You expect us to believe that?" replied Steve. "Listen, Jeff, no more crap about Mark overreacting. He's dead-on right, and now you've got the three of us to deal with too. Go patch things up with Mark today, before we leave for Indy, and start using your head about joining Denise in her party habits."

Jeff continued silently cursing himself for leaving the vodka bottle in plain view. He could feel the chances of Denise being fully accepted by his three friends fading away.

"OK, OK, I'll talk to Mark. And I don't need you guys babysitting me. Denise being back is good for me. You'll see."

Dave, Steve, and A.J. filed out of the suite, each issuing words of warning to Jeff as they passed by. Jeff sat gathering his thoughts for a minute regarding how to approach Mark, then stood up to head down the hall to Mark's suite. Passing by the vodka bottle and glasses, he paused, took one step away, then backtracked, topped off his glass, and emptied it in three quick gulps. He grabbed his room key off the desk and exited the room.

CHAPTER 23

Mark was reclining on the king-size bed in his suite, watching predictions for the 2005 baseball season on ESPN, when he heard the knock on his door.

"Hey," he said simply when he saw it was Jeff at the door.

"Hey. Can I come in?"

"Sure."

The stilted exchange was followed by an awkward silence as the two friends found themselves in the almost surreal position of not knowing what to say to each other. Mark's abrupt, angry departure from the previous day's set list meeting, and their non-communicative performance at the concert that evening, hung over the room. Jeff took a seat in a plush armchair, and Mark perched on the edge of the bed.

Jeff broke the ice. "You got a minute to talk?"

"I guess so, but unless you're gonna tell me that Denise is on a one-way trip to Timbuktu, I don't know what the hell we're going to talk about."

Jeff's face reddened. "So that's it, then? As long as I'm with Denise, you won't even talk to me?"

Mark's voice got noticeably louder. "I'll talk to you, but it's pretty goddamn obvious that you won't listen. I can see exactly where this is headed—anyone with half a brain can see it—and yet you think it's just wonderful that Denise-fucking-Blake has materialized out of nowhere and wants back into your life. What is she, hard-up for money or something?"

"Will you get it out of your stubborn head that Denise is some sort of parasite that swoops in, jabs heroin syringes in my arm, and merrily skips off when she's done? That's not how it was, and it's not how it is now, Mark. We had a terrific relationship, and it came crashing down because of my fuck-ups, not hers. And now we have a chance to put the really good things about our relationship back together. But that doesn't fit in with your whole 'Denise as demon' view, does it?"

By now both men were standing, gesturing emphatically with their hands as their voices continued to rise.

"You want my view? Here's my view: we lost fourteen prime years because of Denise Blake, and now I'm watching it happen all over again. It makes me sick."

Jeff became even more agitated. "Will you stop with the *fourteen years* horse shit? Listen, I'll take the fall for the first five years, but those next nine years are on *you* and your stupid grudge. So take your victim act and shove it."

Mark, truly stung, and unable to think of anything to say in rebuttal, quickly changed the subject. "If you're so convinced that you and Denise are such perfectly matched lovebirds, then why did she just hop aboard the Nuts & Bolts tour right after you flamed out in Atlanta, screwing her way all the way to the top, right up to Lenny Adamsky himself?"

"What the fuck are you talking about?"

"Oh, she didn't bother to tell you about that, eh? Well, you may have some sort of delusional vision of Denise sitting around in a long black dress and veil, mourning your departure, but guess what, pal, she was off and running in no time. She turned into a pretty damned good drug supplier for those boys, too, from what I heard."

"You lying prick."

"I'm not lying. I toured with those guys in '93, and I'm just telling you what they told me."

"Yeah, and of course you're going to believe everything you heard from those drug-addled clowns? For chrissakes, at the very depths of my addiction I was Donny Osmond compared to those lunatics in Nuts & Bolts. You can toss every stupid rumor about Denise you want at me, and it doesn't matter. In fact, Denise is the exact same thing to me that your second wife Joanne is to you."

"What?"

"You told me that Joanne is a terrific woman that you wish you could have another shot with, a chance to make up for the mistakes you made with her the first time. That's how it is for me and Denise, and now I have that second chance to make it right."

Mark exploded, "Don't you *dare* compare Joanne to that drug-pushing whore!"

Mark's insult sent a blinding flash of rage through Jeff's semi-inebriated brain. Screaming "You bastard!" Jeff threw a wild, roundhouse right-hand punch that caught Mark square on his left eye, sending him sprawling to the floor by the foot of the bed. By the time Mark's head cleared, and he was able to prop himself up on his elbows, Jeff was out of the room, slamming the door loudly behind him.

A.J. unlocked the door to his hotel suite, returning to his room shortly before 1:00 p.m. after having grabbed a quick lunch with Dave and Steve at a casual restaurant not far from the hotel. Checking his cell phone, which he had left in the room, he saw that there was a voice message from Jeff. Hoping to hear that Jeff had met with Mark and at least cleared the air to prevent another sub-par performance at the next evening's concert in Indianapolis, A.J. instead found himself listening to a strange, rambling message from a clearly distracted, and apparently drunk, Jeff.

"Hey, A.J., it's Jeff. Uh, listen, I've decided...that is, Denise and I are going to...well, we're going to ride in the equipment bus with the roadies to Indy, so, uh, I won't see you guys on the band bus, OK? Uh, you probably know why...or maybe you don't, but you will soon enough...but I think this is the best thing for now. You might not see me before tomorrow's show, but I promise I'll be there when the curtain goes up...well, I don't think they have a curtain, but you know what I mean, right? Well, OK, I guess that's all...uh, I was going to say something else, but...uh, no I guess that's it. Later."

A.J. listened twice more to the message, saved it to his cell phone, and immediately called Dave. "Dave, did you receive a phone message from Jeff?"

"No, why?"

"I got one on my cell while we were at lunch, and it's pretty weird. Meet me at Steve's room, and I'll let you guys listen to it."

Ten minutes later, Dave and Steve were staring at A.J.'s cell phone as the voice message played through the phone's tiny speaker for the third time.

"Well, what do you make of it?" A.J. asked.

"First of all, it sounds like he dipped a little deeper into that bottle of vodka after we left," offered Steve. "Also, it doesn't sound like things went very well with Mark, does it?"

"Maybe he chickened out and didn't go to see Mark at all, and that's why he jumped on the roadies' bus—to avoid catching shit from us," said Dave.

"There's only one way to find out," replied A.J. "Let's head over to Mark's room and see if he knows anything."

They filed out of Steve's room and headed down the hall. Dave knocked on Mark's door. Instead of simply opening the door, Mark called out in a wary-sounding voice, "Who is it?"

Steve called out in reply, "It's Moe, Larry, and Curly. Who were you expecting, Jack the Ripper? Open up."

"Is Jeff there?"

"No."

Mark's door opened, and all three of his visitors gasped and physically recoiled at the sight before them. Mark stood facing his friends, expressionless, an ice cube-filled washcloth in his left hand. His left eye, horrifically swollen and entirely shut, was ringed by a grotesque array of purple, red, and black splotches. The left side of his face was wet from the washcloth.

It took A.J., Dave, and Steve several seconds to recover before A.J. finally blurted out, "Good God, what happened?"

Mark's reply was delivered in a strangely flat, detached tone. "There'd never been a punch thrown between Jeff and me in our entire lives before. Not when we were toddlers, not when we were eight, not when we were teens. It took Denise Blake to bring us to this. I don't know. I just—" He stopped speaking, let out a deep, sad sigh, sat down on the bed, and applied the cold washcloth back to his eye.

A.J. was too upset to speak, fighting back tears at the gruesome sight of Mark's disfigured face and thoughts of what had transpired to cause the injury. Dave's reaction was a sick feeling of panic in the pit of his stomach, his personal feelings regarding Mark, Jeff, and the band intermingling with new fears about the financial implications of the Upper Hand's possible implosion.

Steve, in contrast, was spitting mad. To confirm his suspicions that this had been a one-punch fight with no physical provocation from Mark, he asked, "Mark, did you take a swing at Jeff before he clocked you?"

Mark's voice remained somber. "No, no. We were going at it pretty heavy verbally, but this came out of the blue. The topic of the 'discussion' was Denise, which I'm sure doesn't surprise you, and he just lost it and cold-cocked me. He was gone before I even got my shit together to figure out what had happened."

"Goddammit, that dumb sonofabitch has lost his fucking mind! A.J., give me your cell phone. I'm gonna set his ass straight right now."

A.J. hesitated. "Are you sure that's the right thing—"

"C'mon, A.J., give it to me. Punch in Jeff's cell number, and hand me the phone."

A.J. complied, and Steve stepped out of Mark's room into the hallway. Jeff, assuming A.J. was on the other end, answered on the second ring.

"Hey, A.J."

Steve roared into the phone, "This ain't A.J. It's Steve. What the fuck is the matter with you? We ask you to patch things up with Mark, and this is your idea of how to do that? You're acting like a lunatic junkie. Are you back on heroin again?"

"No, God no. Look, I feel bad enough about what happened—"

"No, I don't think you do. Mark's eye is a horrifying mess. I don't even know if he's going to be able to play tomorrow. Where the hell are you right now?"

"I—we—are on the equipment bus with the road crew. I promise I'll be ready to go at tomorrow's show. Listen, Steve, Mark was downright verbally abusive today, and while I know I shouldn't have—"

"I don't give a fuck what he said to you today. What you did was insane. You've put the whole rest of this tour in jeopardy, not to mention the whole future of the band. You're gonna be in deep shit with all of us if you fuck this up. You better think of a way out of this, and soon. Got it?"

"Got it. I...I just need some time to think through how to do it."

"Think fast." With that Steve ended the call and went back into Mark's room. He walked in to see Dave and A.J. trying unsuccessfully to convince Mark to see a doctor, Mark insisting that all he needed was time and plenty of ice to get the swelling down around his eye. He also made it perfectly clear that he had every intention of playing at the next day's concert in Indianapolis. No one dared to bring up the subject of Mark and Jeff sharing the stage at that show.

CHAPTER 24

Mark, Dave, Steve, and A.J. were scattered around Dave's suite at the Crowne Plaza Union Station Hotel in Indianapolis, halfheartedly trying to put together the set list for that evening's concert. Jeff was totally incommunicado. He had not checked in to the Crowne Plaza, and his cell phone was turned off. It was late morning on a dreary, rainy day in Indianapolis, and the mood of the four band members was as dismal as the weather.

The swelling around Mark's eye had subsided slightly, but the ghastly rainbow of dark ugly colors around it was, if anything, more pronounced than the day before, and Mark was still unable to open the eye at all. He continued to hold cold compresses against it to try to further reduce the swelling.

Steve's frustration at Jeff's absence and the unresolved clash between Jeff and Mark boiled over. "You know? Fuck it. Why are we sitting here, jerking around with the set list, when we don't even know if Jeff is gonna be there? Let's just go with the San Antonio set list and hope he decides to grace us with his presence."

"Fine with me," sighed Dave. "Mark, you and I will have to sit together to discuss how to cover Jeff's vocal and guitar parts in case he no-shows."

Mark pulled the ice cube-laden washcloth from his ravaged eye. "Can you fucking believe this? It's 1990 all over again, covering up for Jeff."

A knock on Dave's hotel door interrupted the conversation. Dave hopped out of his chair and opened the door to find Benny Ramirez, Mark and Jeff's guitar tech, a man to whom the two guitarists had been trusting the care, maintenance, and tuning of their road guitars since the late 1970s. Benny had also long since become a valued friend to the entire band.

After an exchange of greetings, Benny, clearly not his usual jovial self, addressed the room. "Hey, guys, I don't know what's going on with Jeff, but he—" He stopped short when he caught a glimpse of Mark's eye. "Oh, my God, what happened to you, Mark?"

"Three guesses," grumbled Mark.

"Damn, so that's why Jeff is acting so squirrelly. He and Denise rode on the equipment bus with the road crew—I guess you knew that—but he never said why. Anyway, he asked me to come here to get tonight's set list, and to tell you that he will definitely be there for the show. He said he can't make it for the sound check, though. He asked me to stand in for him."

A.J. asked, "Where is he now, Benny? He never checked in here."

Benny hesitated. "I...don't know."

Steve challenged, "Then how are you going to get the set list to him?"

"He told me to just tape it to the stage floor by his microphone stand. Maybe he'll call me this afternoon and have me read it to him if he wants an advance look at it. I don't know. This whole thing is really weird."

"Tell us about it. Anyway, we're using the set list from the San Antonio show. Do you have that list somewhere?"

"Yeah, no problem."

"OK, then, we'll see you at sound check. And if by some chance you do see or hear from Jeff beforehand, tell him to turn on his fucking cell phone. We need to have a little chat with him."

"Will do. See you guys later. Sorry about your eye, Mark." With that, Benny left the room.

As soon as the door was closed, Dave asked, "Do you guys believe Benny when he says he doesn't know where Jeff is holed up?"

"Nah, he's covering for him," replied A.J. "But let's not hassle Benny over it. Jeff probably made him swear on a stack of Bibles that he wouldn't tell us. I don't think we have any choice now but to head to the arena at our normal time later today, hope to hell that

Benny is right about Jeff showing up, and then straighten out this nonsense afterwards."

Virtually no one familiar with the Upper Hand's live shows would dispute that the band's April 3, 2005 performance at the Conseco Fieldhouse in Indianapolis was the worst concert ever put on by the group, with the notable exception of the night in Atlanta fifteen years earlier when a strung-out Jeff walked offstage and out of the band mid-show. The negative vibe of the show was set at the very outset by Mark's horrendously discolored and closed eye, which was disturbingly visible not only to fans in the nearby floor seats, but to all attendees via the high quality projection screens in the arena. The video crew was soon instructed to minimize Mark's time onscreen and to try to shoot him only from the right side, but the murmurs had already started and intensified throughout the evening as the joyless performance of the band further distracted the fans. Mark's refusal to acknowledge or explain his injury, together with his total lack of engagement with the audience during the show, just fed the crowd's discontent.

True to Benny Ramirez's word earlier that day, Jeff did make it to the show, appearing onstage out of nowhere just as the rest of the band approached the stage from the dressing room. He managed to function vocally and instrumentally throughout the concert but appeared to be drunk and performed sloppily and listlessly. He provided absolutely no interaction or eye contact with his bandmates or the fans. His microphone was placed as far away from the rest of the band as possible, sparking widespread conjecture throughout the arena that Mark's black eye had come courtesy of Jeff.

Dave, the only other band member with a microphone, tried his best to whip up crowd enthusiasm during the first part of the concert, but as Mark and Jeff's lifeless performances steadily sapped the energy out of the building, he eventually gave up and began playing as perfunctorily as the two guitarists. The mood onstage and in the crowd was contagious, and it didn't take long for A.J. and Steve's playing to be similarly dragged down.

At the end of the set, as the band—with Jeff standing conspicuously apart from the rest of the group—gamely took bows to half-hearted cheers from those fans who weren't already heading for the exits, no one needed verbal confirmation that there would be no encore for this show. Both Dave and Steve planned to immediately confront Jeff and drag him backstage physically if necessary as soon as they were through acknowledging the crowd, but when they straightened up from their last bow, Jeff was gone.

The atmosphere in the dressing room after the show was grim.

"I've never been this embarrassed in my whole musical life. That was just awful," lamented A.J.

"I can't believe what just happened out there," added Steve. "And where the hell did Jeff disappear to after his so-called performance? I was going to grab him after the bows, but he vaporized."

"Me, too," said Dave. "I didn't want him to just slip away, but he managed somehow. Mark, were you OK out there? It looked like you were really struggling."

Mark was sitting with a bottle of beer in his hand, alternately drinking from it and holding it to his eye. "I apologize, guys. Some of that train wreck out there tonight could have been avoided if I'd stepped up. But it was tough to see out of one eye, and the fans were just pointing and staring at me like I had two heads or something. The damn thing still hurts like hell too. And Jeff was like eighty feet away, damn near off the side of the stage; there was no way to connect with him during any of the songs. Not that he would have responded even if I tried. The son of a bitch was drunk, too, that's for sure. Still, I should have done a better job. Sorry."

No one in the room was of any mind to put much of the blame on Mark for the disaster they'd just been through, regardless of what he may have said to Jeff to provoke the attack. A.J. just felt that the whole situation was profoundly sad, while Steve and Dave were becoming increasingly angry at Jeff, and Denise, with each passing hour.

Dave gave Mark a quick pat on the shoulder and said, "This isn't your fault, Mark. But we've got a real problem on our hands now. My guess is the local press is gonna rip us a new asshole over this show. We're playing in a huge media market, Chicago, in five days. We *cannot* have a repeat of what happened here tonight."

"Amen to that," replied Steve. "But how can we prevent it if we can't corral Jeff to knock some sense into him? His disappearing act tonight tells me that he's planning to pull the same crap in Chicago."

"Well, the only good news is that we have five days to figure something out. Put your thinking caps on, boys."

CHAPTER 25

Dave sat on the sofa of his suite at the Intercontinental Hotel, cursing to himself as he read the *Chicago Tribune*. His wife Sharon, who had flown into Chicago the night before to see the next night's show at the United Center, sat nearby sipping coffee and also glancing through the paper. It was 9:30 in the morning of April 7, four days since the disastrous concert in Indianapolis, and one day prior to the next show in Chicago.

"Shit, it just keeps on getting worse," he railed, waving the newspaper in Sharon's direction.

Dave had good reason to be upset at the press coverage the Upper Hand had been receiving since the Indianapolis show. The onslaught began with the review of the concert in the April 5 *Indianapolis Star*. It was to the band's misfortune that the reviewer, a veteran rock reporter named Hugh Gentry, was a longtime follower of the Upper Hand who knew how an Upper Hand concert was supposed to look and sound. Beyond Gentry's scathing remarks regarding individual performances and the total lack of enthusiasm and electricity generated by the band, the most damaging commentary in the review was Gentry's conclusion that the Upper Hand had nothing more to offer the world of rock and roll and had regrouped simply for a money grab:

> In recent years a tremendous number of defunct rock bands from decades past, including some of the greats, have put aside whatever the reasons were that led them to disband, and have reformed for a nostalgic concert tour and/or a new album. Some of these reunions have been fabulously successful, and the bands have come back as strong and vibrant as ever. Unfortunately, many more of these resurrections have served only to confirm that the band's time has passed, and the new endeavor is quickly exposed as little more than a lame effort to cash in one more time on past glories. Sadly, the Upper Hand appears to fall firmly into this latter category. This was a truly disappointing performance for a once top-notch act

returning with all five of its original members. I expected
much more.

Things got worse the next day when Gentry's review was reprinted nationally in *USA Today,* published alongside a companion article and a candid photo of Jeff and Denise taken in an Indianapolis hotel lobby on April 3. The article mentioned Denise by name, rehashed her well-known 1988-1990 relationship with Jeff and her generally accepted culpability in Jeff's addiction, and put forth the question of whether Denise's presence on the current Upper Hand tour signified Jeff's inevitable return to a drug-dominated lifestyle.

The gossip column fare in the April 7 *Chicago Tribune,* now being brandished angrily in the air by Dave, positively identified Jeff as the source of Mark's black eye. Further, it confirmed that Denise Blake and her drug-filled past—and perhaps present—were behind the tension between Jeff and Mark. The article also spewed forth a series of rumors regarding a relapse by Jeff back into heroin addiction, his apparent estrangement from the rest of the group, and the impending collapse of the tour and band. The same photo of Jeff and Denise from the previous day's *USA Today* piece accompanied this article.

For Dave, already agitated by bad news from Sharon regarding expected future medical expenses required for their ailing son, this gossip column was the straw that broke the back of his patience.

"Goddamn it, Sharon, this whole Jeff-and-Denise-and-Mark-and-black eyes-and-heroin-and-hide-and-seek nonsense is going to sink this band, not to mention our financial health. I've got to find that moron Jeff and straighten his ass out before he ruins another show."

"God, I wish you could. This is excruciating. But how are you going to find Jeff in a huge city like Chicago? Heck, you're not even certain he's in town."

"I think he's going to try to pull the same appear-out-of-thin-air act he did in Indy, with Benny's assistance, and I'm gonna lean on Benny to tell me where he's hiding out."

"Didn't Benny say he doesn't know where Jeff is?"

"Yeah, but that was A.J. asking him. A.J.'s too trusting. I'm gonna put the screws to Benny to get the answer. I have to go take care of this now, or my head is going to explode. Do me a favor, babe, would you? Call Steve and A.J.—umm, Mark too, for that matter— and make sure they read this latest bullshit in the papers about us. They ought to know what's going on. But don't tell them where I'm going, OK? There's no point in getting anyone else involved until I find out where Jeff is."

Dave stuffed the newspaper articles into the back pocket of his jeans, exited the suite, and took the elevator down to the floor where Benny and the rest of the tour crew were staying. He found Benny's room and knocked on the door.

"Hey, Dave, what's happening?" greeted Benny when he opened the door.

The tone of Dave's response left no doubt that he was in no mood for small talk. "Benny, where is Jeff?"

"I don't know, man."

The urgency in Dave's voice kicked up a notch. "Benny, I know Jeff well enough to know that he would insist on seeing that Indianapolis set list before he stepped onstage that night. You knew where to meet him in Indy, and you know where to meet him here. If we have another catastrophe in Chicago like we had in Indy, this band is finished, understand? *Tell me where he is!*"

Benny stared silently at Dave for a couple of seconds and then stammered, "I...he made me promise...I could get fired."

Knowing now that Benny could tell him where Jeff was, Dave eased up on him a bit. "Benny, think about it. If we don't get to Jeff and set things right between him and the rest of the band, especially Mark, there isn't going to be a band for you to get fired from. You saw that horrible show in Indy. Do you want to see a repeat of that tomorrow?"

"No, I certainly don't."

"Besides, you work for both Mark and Jeff. Mark wouldn't let you get fired for this. Anyway, I won't even let Jeff know I found out from you where he's hiding."

Benny exhaled audibly, and said, "I hope I'm doing the right thing. He and Denise are at the Omni Chicago Hotel, just a block up from here on North Michigan, room 1212. You won't tell him I told you this, right?"

"Right. But tell me this, Benny, what the hell is going through his mind? Does he think he's going to go through the rest of the tour like the Invisible Man, popping up onstage at the last minute to give a shitty performance and then disappearing again?"

"Nah, I think he knows his day of reckoning with you guys is coming soon, but he doesn't seem to be able to get his shit together to come to you voluntarily. He seems pretty liquored up when I see him, so that's probably not helping, either. Hey, at least he didn't no-show in Indy, and I know he's planning to show up again tomorrow, so give him credit for that."

"Are you fucking kidding me? I'm not giving him any *credit* for anything. A no-show would have been way less damaging than that pile of crap he put out there the other night."

"Sorry. I just...oh, man, I don't know what to think. Things were going so great, and now this. Are you mad at me?"

"I am beyond mad, Benny, but not at you. Jeff put you in an impossible position. But I am going to put an end to this idiocy now."

Dave left Benny's room, pulled his cell phone from his pocket, and called Steve.

"Hey, Dave."

"Meet me in the lobby. Now."

Dave's abruptness startled Steve. "Whoa, whoa, what's going on?"

"I know where Jeff is. I need you to come with me."

"How did you find out where he is?"

"Doesn't matter. This bullshit ends now. Come on. Get down here."

"What do you want me to do?"

"You're going to help me drag his ass back here to deal with the mess he's made, in case he puts up a fuss. You're also going to prevent me from strangling the S.O.B. when he opens his door."

"OK, OK, anything to fix this lunacy. What about A.J.? Should he come along, too?"

"No, no. A.J. would be a whole lot more reasonable than I intend to be."

"So, I'm just the hired muscle, eh?"

"This is no joke, Steve. I need your support, but I really need to handle this my way to keep this band from disintegrating. You with me?"

"Yeah, I'll be right down."

As Dave and Steve walked along North Michigan Avenue towards the Omni Chicago Hotel, Dave became more and more furious as thoughts of the events of the past week swirled through his mind. They entered the lobby of the hotel and proceeded directly to the elevators. Getting off at the twelfth floor, they approached the door to room 1212. Resisting the urge to pound aggressively on the door with his fist, Dave instead knocked lightly, and stepped to the side of the doorway, silently gesturing to Steve to follow him out of the line of sight of the peephole. Denise's voice called from inside the room, "Who is it?"

Dave put his fingers to his lips to prevent Steve from responding. The door opened six inches, the chain lock of the door engaged, and Denise peered out, calling out, "Who's there?"

Dave stepped into view, demanding, "Let me in, now."

Denise attempted to slam the door closed, but Dave, anticipating this less than warm welcome, raised his right leg and drove his leather-booted heel into the center of the door. The receptacle of the chain lock was ripped from the frame, and the door flew open, smashing into Denise's shoulder and forehead.

She screamed in pain as Dave barreled into the room, then she yelled, "Are you crazy? You can't just come barging in here!"

"*Shut the fuck up!*" Dave spat back with a viciousness that sent a jolt of fear through Denise. She expected this type of verbal venom from Mark, but not from Dave. She stood silently holding her bruised head and shoulder as Steve followed Dave into the room. Dave switched his gaze into the main area of the suite, where he spotted Jeff, dressed in a T-shirt, jeans, and socks, but no shoes, rising from a chair near the far window of the suite.

"What the hell are you—?"

"*Shut your mouth!*" Dave roared, jabbing his finger in Jeff's direction as he approached him. "You don't talk. You *listen*. Put on your shoes *now*. You're coming back to the Intercontinental with us to repair this colossal mess you've made."

"Can't we just—"

"*I said clam up, Jeff. I mean it.*"

Dave was now so violently keyed up that, aside from Jeff and Denise now fearing for their personal safety, even Steve was concerned that Dave might lose control of himself at any moment. Still unsure of exactly what he was supposed to do at this point, Steve thought better of interrupting Dave while he was in this state. He stood by passively as Dave continued to bark out orders to Jeff.

"I do not want to hear one goddamn word out of you until the five of us are in a room together. Put on those shoes, or I'll drag your ass out onto the street in your socks."

Jeff complied, and as he was lacing up his sneakers, Dave spotted a now all-too-familiar sight on the coffee table near where Jeff had been seated—a glistening, defrosting bottle of Grey Goose L'Orange vodka and two glasses. He grabbed the bottle by its long, thin neck, yelled, "*Godfuckingdammit!*" and hurled it against a framed floral painting over the head of the bed. The impact snapped the neck off the bottle and tore a jagged hole in the painting. The neck of the bottle ricocheted off the painting, skipped off one of the night tables alongside the bed, and dropped to the carpeted floor. The rest of the bottle landed with a dull thud on the unmade bed, leaking rapidly onto the sheets. Jeff, Denise, and Steve all stared in stunned silence as the broken bottle continued to empty its contents onto the bed.

If Jeff had any fleeting hope that the shock of Dave's violent smashing of the vodka bottle would somehow defuse his fury, that hope was quickly dashed. After casting a chillingly malevolent glare toward a now cowering Denise, Dave turned back to Jeff and growled, "Let's go. Now."

The three men marched through the entryway of the suite toward the door. Jeff, feeling like a prisoner, glanced helplessly at the distraught Denise as he passed by. Dave offered no acknowledgement of Denise's presence or of the damage done to the doorway and painting. Steve, still trying to absorb what had just taken place, also exited the room without a word or gesture to Jeff's traumatized girlfriend.

CHAPTER 26

Not a word was spoken among the three men as they rode the elevator down to the ground floor of the Omni Chicago Hotel, strode through the lobby, and exited through the revolving doors onto North Michigan Avenue. Dave's clenched jaw and intense look in his eyes made it perfectly clear to Jeff that any efforts at conversation with him were pointless, and Jeff didn't even dare try to speak to Steve for fear of incurring even more of Dave's wrath. Steve, whose natural impulse was to talk to Jeff during their walk to the Intercontinental, was also unnerved by Dave's scalding rage and decided to stay quiet as well.

As soon as they reached the sidewalk, Dave pulled out his cell phone and dialed A.J.

"Hi, Dave."

Dave was still too wound up and adrenaline pumped to engage in anything resembling pleasant conversation, even with an innocent party like A.J.

"A.J., meet me in Mark's suite in five minutes. It's important."

"Huh? What's going on, Dave? You sound wired."

"I'm with Steve and Jeff. We're headed back to Mark's room now."

"Jeff? You found Jeff? Where was he? Did he call you?"

"Don't worry about that now. Just be there so we can take care of this."

Dave hung up before A.J. could ask any more questions. He placed the phone back into his pocket, and the threesome continued their silent walk along North Michigan Avenue, none of them taking note of the beautiful, sunny, sixty-degree day.

The tension in Mark's suite was almost unbearable as Jeff and Steve took their seats, joining Mark and A.J. in the living area. Dave remained standing, and his demeanor left absolutely no doubt as to who was going to orchestrate the proceedings of this gathering.

Mark's eye, still dramatically discolored and swollen, was now partially open. Jeff, getting his first clear look at the damage he had done, grimaced at the sight. The two did not speak or otherwise acknowledge one another when Jeff, Dave, and Steve entered the room, yet they were more prepared to move past their violent altercation than anyone else in the room would have guessed. Both men still harbored tremendous anger over the incident—Jeff for Mark's relentless and uncompromising verbal attacks on Denise, Mark for Jeff's sudden physical assault—but each man was also highly troubled by his own role in the clash and wanted nothing more than to figure out a way to bury the hatchet.

But brokering a reconciliation between Jeff and Mark was not the number-one item on Dave's agenda. He pulled the folded newspapers out of the back pocket of his jeans and held them aloft for everyone to see.

"Look what's happened to us in just one week's time—*one week's time!* We've gone from being the hottest tour act in the country to *this*—" he shook the newspapers first at Jeff, then at Mark "—gossip-page fodder and objects of pity. Look at this. *Look at this!* An article, reprinted nationally in the fucking *USA Today* and God knows where else, telling the whole country that the Upper Hand is a washed-up lame-ass band out for one last paycheck."

He shoved the article with the photo of Jeff and Denise six inches from Jeff's nose. "How about this, Jeff? Did you know you and Denise made it to the gossip pages?"

Jeff's eyes widened in horror at the sight of the photo and the article headline, which read, *"New Drug Troubles for Upper Hand Guitarist?"* He desperately wanted to see what had been written about him but didn't dare make any move to take the paper from Dave's hand.

Dave pulled the article away from Jeff's face and continued, "Whether or not you and Denise are shooting up again, America now thinks you are. Oh, yeah, there's all kinds of interesting shit in this article. According to this, we're going to be breaking up any day now. There's even a 'Yoko Ono' reference to Denise in here."

Dave slammed the newspapers onto a nearby table as he glared first at Jeff and then at Mark.

No one else in the room moved a muscle or made a sound. Even Steve and A.J., non-targets of Dave's vitriol, sat paralyzed.

Dave's voice got quieter but, if possible, even more intense. "But that is not happening. There is no fucking way this band is dissolving now. Steve, A.J., and I worked too hard to make this reunion happen, and all five of us worked way too hard to whip ourselves back into top form. We can't piss it away now. I swear to God I'll eviscerate anyone who breaks up this band again." Jeff, Mark, Steve, and A.J. weren't exactly sure what "eviscerate" meant, but it sounded bad, and no one was of a mind to find out for sure the hard way.

"But here is what *is* going to happen." He spun on his heel to face Jeff. "First of all, you are going to send Denise home on the next plane out of here and keep her the fuck away from this tour. Got it?"

An alarmed Jeff could only mumble in reply, "She lives here in Chicago."

"Well, isn't that wonderful. You just saved yourself the price of a plane ticket. But you get her the hell away from this tour, *today.* This toxic gossip-page rumor shit has to stop, and it won't if she's still seen around us. The tour ends at the end of May, and then we don't reconvene until early July for the new album rehearsals. That gives you and Denise over a month to hang out together all by yourselves. I suggest you use that time to learn how to be with her without getting sucked into her bad party habits."

Jeff peered at A.J. and Steve to see if there was any sign that they might provide support if he tried to resist Dave's call for Denise to be exiled from the tour, but all he saw was both men's heads nodding in agreement with Dave.

A.J., ever the diplomat, erased all doubt about where he stood regarding Denise's continued presence on the tour when he broke his silence to say, "Jeff, look at this as an opportunity. Let's face it, your brief time together with Denise so far hasn't worked out so good. Focus on getting yourself back on track for these next few weeks, finish the tour on a high note, and then you and Denise can really reintroduce yourselves to each other without the pressure of the tour weighing on you. Trying to do it in the public eye, with all these rumor mongers circling around, is just too tough."

Steve weighed in with, "And for chrissakes, stay away from that goddamn frozen vodka Denise has been giving you. You can't handle that shit. If Dave hadn't smashed that bottle in your room today, I would have."

Mark and A.J. exchanged curious glances, wondering just what had gone on prior to Dave and Steve ushering Jeff into the meeting.

Jeff, realizing he had no choice, looked at Dave, threw up his hands, and said, "OK. She won't be with me when we leave for Detroit."

Dave now turned his attention to Mark. "Mark, you have to help out here, too."

Mark, startled by his sudden appearance in Dave's spotlight, sat up straight and replied warily, "Huh? What do I have to do?"

"You need to stop with the constant insults toward Denise: 'Denise-fucking-Blake,' 'that bitch Denise.' Stick a sock in it, all right? When this tour is over, all of us, and I mean *all* of us, are going to keep an open mind and give Jeff every chance to prove that he can be with Denise without going off the rails. Your incessant carping about her isn't helping, and if I were a gambling man, I'd bet that shot to your eye was immediately preceded by one of those insults."

For the first time since their fight five days earlier, Jeff and Mark made direct eye contact, each raising his eyebrows in silent acknowledgement of Dave's assertion.

Mark, still looking directly at Jeff, took a deep breath and said, "OK, Jeff. Prove me wrong. Nothing would make me happier. I'll give Denise a big ol' kiss on the lips if you show us that you can actually be with her without turning into a drug- or booze-addled wreck. Hey, you know what? If you do that, I might even let her blow me."

A flash of horror shot through Dave, Steve, and A.J. as their heads swiveled instantly toward Jeff to see how he was reacting to Mark's verbal grenade. But Jeff detected the mischievous, tongue-in-cheek tone in Mark's voice, saw the tiny smile on his face, and recognized, as only someone who'd known Mark since playpen days could, that the outrageous quip was Mark's weird idea of a peace offering.

Jeff actually grinned and replied, "How the hell did I ever manage to go fifty years before slugging you?"

"I don't know, but can you hold off another fifty before you do it again? This thing hurts."

There was a collective exhale of relief in the room as the mounting tension of the past week, starting from the moment Denise showed up in St. Louis, magically dissipated. Without a single word of apology or forgiveness uttered by either of them, Mark and Jeff stood up, shared a simple fist bump, and just like that, the crisis was over, or at least, the can was kicked down the road until after the tour was done.

A now remarkably less stern Dave addressed the gathering again. "OK, guys, let's get back to doing what we do best. We gotta absolutely knock 'em dead tomorrow night."

The group responded with cheers and handclaps.

"One last thing." Dave looked straight at Jeff. "The happy ending to this meeting is not a 'Get Out of Jail Free' card, Jeff. You're going to have your work cut out for you when this tour is over. Don't come back to us after your month with Denise all fucked up on vodka or heroin or whatever. I guarantee you that Mark will have to get in line to kick your ass if that happens. OK?"

"OK. Message received."

Steve chimed in, "As soon as I leave here, I'm going to head to the nearest liquor store and buy you a six-pack of Bass Ale to wean you off that flavored vodka shit."

"Can you make it a twelve-pack? I'm gonna need it after telling Denise she's been voted off the island."

"I'm not gonna buy you a twelve-pack if you're planning to drink the whole damn thing in one day. Can you promise me you'll make it last a couple of days?"

"Yeah, yeah, for sure. No problem."

"OK, then you've got a deal."

The meeting was over. Jeff rose from his chair and shook hands with each of his friends. When he got to Dave, he said with a small smile, "You're mean when you're angry. You know that? It seems strange to thank someone who just kidnapped me and terrorized my girlfriend, but I guess I can't argue with the results. So, thanks." He then left to deal with Denise.

Mark walked over to Dave and said, "I'm still not exactly sure what just happened here, but I know that you just pulled off a major miracle. Nice work, my man."

Dave patted Mark on the shoulder, and then he, Steve, and A.J. exited Mark's room together. As soon as they were in the hallway, A.J. turned to Dave and said quietly, "I can hardly believe what you did here today. You just saved this band. My God, you scared the piss out of *me*, and I wasn't even the guy you were skewering. You handled Mark just brilliantly too."

Steve added, "You're my hero, man. That took guts. I honestly thought you were about to totally lose control in Jeff's hotel room, but you knew exactly what you were doing the whole time."

Dave managed a small smile. "Thanks, boys. Desperate times call for desperate measures, and believe me, I'm desperate to keep this band intact."

CHAPTER 27

It was late morning, April 10, a day and a half after the Upper Hand's concert in Chicago. Dave stood looking distractedly out the window of his suite at the Detroit Marriott at the Renaissance Center, vaguely monitoring the ominous storm clouds approaching from the west. In his hand was a small slip of paper with a phone number handwritten on it. Twice he took a couple of steps away from the window toward the night table where his cell phone lay, but both times he stopped himself, changed his mind, and retreated to the window.

The show had been a *tour de force*, a complete and triumphant turnaround from their dysfunctional effort four days earlier in Indianapolis. Anyone who had read the review of the Indianapolis show before attending the Chicago concert would have concluded that reviewer Hugh Gentry had lost his mind.

The group had agreed, in the dressing room before the Chicago concert, not to make any attempt during the show to address the various rumors about them floating around the media, deciding instead to let their performance do the talking. This strategy proved to be a wise one, as it became apparent by the end of the first song that no one in the audience was distracted by Mark's injured eye, rumors of Jeff's possible relapse into heroin addiction, or any possible internal band friction that could cause the Upper Hand to break up again. The band was in top form, Mark and Jeff were back to delivering crowd-pleasing, high energy, interactive showmanship, and the crowd was on its feet throughout the evening.

Jeff had successfully dispatched Denise from the tour, with a minimum of angst. After the jarring incident in the Omni Chicago Hotel, plus the revelation that she and Jeff had become targets of the gossip press, Denise offered no resistance to the notion that she was better off staying away from the band while they remained on the road and in the public eye. Jeff and Denise made plans for the two of them to take up residence together in Manhattan when the tour ended.

When Denise made it clear that she did not require any financial assistance from Jeff to secure a suitable place for them to live while he continued on the tour, questions about the source of Denise's apparent wealth popped into Jeff's head. Mark's claims regarding Denise's drug dealing in the early 1990s raced briefly through his mind, but he quickly rejected them and chose not to dwell any further on the status or history of Denise's finances. *What does it matter? I'm back with the only woman I've ever really felt a connection with. And so what if the two of us take a bit more comfort from alcohol than the guys think appropriate? It's a hell of a lot better than heroin, isn't it?*

Dave had every reason to feel good on this stormy morning in Detroit, and indeed his sense of satisfaction over the events of the past couple of days was strong. It was only through his bold—if perhaps borderline maniacal—actions that the band was again operating on all cylinders. Mark and Jeff weren't at each other's throats, and, on a strongly related note, the volatile and dangerous Denise Blake issue had been put aside, at least for the next seven weeks. He basked in the expressions of deep appreciation he had received over the past two days from all four of his bandmates, including Jeff, the principal target of his fury. Jeff had even paid for the damages to his hotel room at the Chicago Omni and never voiced a word of complaint to Dave about the bruises Denise incurred when Dave kicked the door and smashed it into her.

Dave felt confident that his demonstration of take-charge leadership at that critical time, together with the stunning success of the recent CD single of the live "Tireless Dancer," put him in position to secure a significantly bigger singing and songwriting role on the upcoming Upper Hand album. *No two-song limit this time. Maybe even another single!*

But there was still something digging at him, a nagging irritant that was dampening his overall feeling of relief and accomplishment. He strode over to his cell phone a third time, and this time he did not stop. He dialed the number on the slip of paper.

"*Indianapolis Star.* How may I direct your call?"

"Yes, Hugh Gentry, please."

"I'll transfer you. Please hold."

Gentry was at his desk, groggily working on his third cup of coffee, trying to come up with the right terms of derision to use to describe the late night, multi-band death metal concert he had attended the night before, when his phone rang.

"Gentry."

"Hello, Hugh, this is Dave Rowinski. I play keyboards for—"

Gentry's fatigue vanished in an instant. "Dave Rowinski? The Upper Hand's Dave Rowinski? Are you really him?"

Dave chuckled. "Why, are people going around lately pretending to be me?"

"Sorry. You just took me by surprise. A long night last night. Anyway, what can I do for you, Dave?"

"Well, I'd like to speak to you about the show we put on there in Indy last week."

Gentry closed his eyes and braced himself for the expected tirade for the harsh review he had written about that show. "OK," he replied warily, pulling the phone away from his ear in anticipation of a loud outburst of abuse from the other end of the line.

But no verbal onslaught was forthcoming.

"I wanted to let you know that you were absolutely right about us in your review of that concert, but you were also wrong."

Gentry placed the phone back against his ear. "Uh, that's going to require some clarification."

"You described a thoroughly shitty performance, totally unworthy of a band of our caliber and reputation, and equally unworthy of the amount of money the fans paid for those tickets. And I couldn't agree with you more."

"OK, so I was right about that show. I wasn't happy to have to write that, by the way. I've liked you guys for a long time and have seen you really rock out in concert plenty of times over the years. So, what was I wrong about?"

"Hugh, that show was a terrible, embarrassing, one-time aberration for us. You figured after watching us that night that the Upper Hand is a washed-up old dinosaur, but I promise you we've never given a show like that before and never will again. I know from your review that you noticed Mark Donahue's eye that night. Without going into a whole lot of detail here, let me just say that the band had a rough couple of days leading up to that show. And let me also guarantee you that most of the shit that was written about us in the days after your review, especially regarding Jeff Britton and heroin, is totally untrue."

"Isn't Jeff back with Denise what's-her-name? That's why my review got picked up by *USA Today*, to go along with that article and photo of her and Jeff."

"Yeah, just our luck that yours is the review from the tour that goes national. Yes, Jeff and Denise have reconnected, but there are no drugs involved."

"Jeff didn't look so good at the Indy show."

"Like I said, there was some unpleasant stuff going on, and Mark's eye was the most visible souvenir, but Jeff just had a bad night at that concert. There's no new heroin crisis, and both Mark and Jeff are already back on track. We kicked ass in Chicago a couple of nights ago."

"Glad to hear it. But what do you want from me? I can't unring the bell, Dave. The review is out there."

"I'd like you to come see another Upper Hand show, and just write what you see."

"Are you guys coming back to Indianapolis?"

"No, not on this tour. I was hoping you could come see us in Detroit tomorrow, or maybe Cincinnati or Cleveland."

"I'm a local guy, Dave. The *Indianapolis Star* won't pay me to travel to other cities to see a concert."

"I—we—would happily pay all your expenses to have you come to one of these other shows."

Gentry was taken aback by this offer. *Jeez, this guy really wants me to review his band again.*

"Sorry, Dave, but I can't do that. My credibility as a reviewer would be shot if it was discovered that a band I reviewed paid my way to get to the show. Plus, the *Star* has no interest in printing reviews of shows outside the Indy area."

It was dawning on Dave that this call to Gentry was not the greatest idea, but in an effort to salvage something from the conversation, he blurted out, "Tell you what. Just tell your readers that we in the Upper Hand feel that we didn't give a performance to our Indianapolis fans that was anything close to what we always deliver. So, on our next tour, when we come to Indy, we're going to offer free tickets to any fans who present their ticket stubs from the April 3, 2005 show. We'll give them the show we should have given them the first time."

"You're serious about this?"

"You bet I am. I don't want *anyone's* impression of our band to be based on that shitty show last week."

"OK, then, I'll be happy to write that."

It only took about thirty seconds after he hung up the phone for Dave to start having second thoughts about having called Hugh Gentry, and as he began to replay the conversation in his mind, he quickly developed a sinking feeling that he may have made a big mistake. *Shit! Why did Sharon have to go home yesterday? She would have talked me out of this for sure.*

Dave now recognized that he came across as desperate, and perhaps a bit pathetic, in his attempt to lure Gentry to another Upper Hand concert and get him to announce to his readers that his initial opinion about the band's vitality was misguided. But that part of the phone call was little more than a source of minor regret to Dave. The real problem concerned the last moments of the call, when Dave, in his hasty zeal to erase the damage done to the Upper Hand's reputation, made a significant commitment to provide free concert tickets to dissatisfied fans. Worse, he had made the offer without the knowledge or approval of the rest of the band.

Dave paced the room, debating whether to allow himself to look even more foolish to Gentry by calling him back to rescind the ticket stub offer. By the time he decided to do so, Gentry had left the office for the day to catch a few hours' sleep before another concert assignment that evening. There would be no stopping the free ticket offer from being made public in Indianapolis the following morning.

The next morning, the five band members gathered in A.J.'s suite at the Detroit Marriott for their usual pre-show set list meeting. Dave, preoccupied by thoughts of how to break the news to the others about his Indy offer without getting his head chewed off, contributed little to the discussion. Finally, during a lull in the conversation as everyone paused to grab some breakfast pastries and coffee from the food cart brought in for the meeting, Dave said, as casually as possible, "Hey, guys, what do you think about, on our next tour, giving our fans in Indianapolis who saw us there a chance to see us for free? You know, to make amends for the crappy performance we gave them, and rebuild our reputation there."

His question was greeted with several seconds of silence, and then Steve replied, "Why would we want to do that?"

Mark added, "Yeah, Dave, we just want people to forget about that show. Why give them a big fat reminder about it?"

"Well, don't forget the review of that show went national, so there are people all around the country who think that we can't rock out anymore. This would be a good public relations move to let the country know that the Indy show was not typical of us. We'd get great publicity for the gesture, and even more for the great show we'd put on that night."

A.J. weighed in with, "Nice sentiment, Dave, but how would you even pull this off if you wanted to?"

"Just have people send in their ticket stubs from that concert. Heck, most people throw those stubs out anyway, so we wouldn't be on the hook for all that many freebies."

It was Jeff's turn. "No, you'd wind up with a shitload of counterfeits and photocopies. It would be a nightmare to handle. Look, I know I'm a big reason why that show sucked, and why those lousy articles are floating around out there, but I'm with Mark, man. Let's just let it go, and allow all our other performances to drown out that bad one. That Indy show will be long forgotten by the time we go on tour next, as long as we don't keep bringing it up."

Mark, A.J., and Steve all voiced their agreement, and Dave knew he was sunk. There was no option but to rip off the Band-Aid right there and then, and get it over with.

"Uh, there's just one problem, guys. I did a dumb thing, and sorta told the reviewer from the Indy paper that we'd offer free tickets to stub holders from last week's concert the next time we're in Indy. It's in today's *Indianapolis Star*."

The reaction was immediate and explosive.

"*You what?*"

"*You're joking, right?*"

"*Are you serious?*"

"*Tell me you're kidding!*"

"I'm sorry, guys, I got caught up in a moment while I was talking to the reviewer from the Indy paper, trying to figure out a way to undo the impression he gave everyone about us."

Mark jumped in first. "What the hell were you doing talking to that guy anyway?"

"I know, I know, it was stupid. I was trying to get him to see another one of our shows on this tour so he could see—and tell everyone—how good we still are."

"And instead you offered everyone free tickets?"

Jeff, feeling a strange mix of legitimate outrage at Dave's foolish unilateral move and relief at suddenly not being the band member in the crosshairs, exclaimed, "The shittiest part of all this is that you made this ridiculous offer without talking to any of us first and then tried to get our buy-in after the fact. We're a democratic band, Dave, remember? Hell, you're the guy who insisted back in frickin' 1972 that all five of us have an equal voice in any important band-related stuff. What is this? Just because you pulled the band's chestnuts out of the fire a few days ago, now you get to call the shots?"

Dave felt as though he were physically shrinking under the reproach of his bandmates. "No, no, I didn't intentionally leave you guys out of the loop. I...guess I've been overreacting to that Indy show and the newspaper articles that followed it and just didn't think things through very well yesterday. It won't happen again."

Mark piped in again, "Damn, I don't mean to pile on here, Dave, but we could be talking about a million dollar give-away here!"

A.J. felt it was time to move past this unpleasant detour in their meeting. "Look, if this offer is in the paper, then we're stuck with it. Dave, you've just made Kevin's life during our next tour a lot more interesting. You better start figuring out how many steak dinners you're going to have to buy our faithful business manager to make up for the hassle he's going to go through arranging and authenticating those freebies. I think we'll leave it to you to break the wonderful news to him. OK, boys, back to the set list."

There was no further discussion or overt lingering bad feelings during the remainder of the set list meeting regarding Dave's ill-conceived ticket offer. Nevertheless, Dave walked away from the meeting totally deflated. The intoxicating sense of confidence he had held just one day ago, the feeling of certainty that he had achieved an elevated status within the band that would translate to a more prominent role on the new Upper Hand album, was crushed.

As soon as Dave returned to his suite, he grabbed a drinking glass from the bathroom and hurled it in fury at a mirror in the living area. Not only did he smash the mirror, he also injured himself when the drinking glass, which miraculously did not break when it struck the mirror, bounced off the wall and smacked him in the mouth, chipping one of his bottom teeth. Dave Rowinski, who had never before in his life damaged a hotel room, had now done so twice in four days. This time, Jeff wasn't there to pick up the pieces and pay for the damages.

CHAPTER 28

The five band members were lounging around the billiard room in Mark's house, relaxing after their traditional kickoff meeting to present, discuss, and choose songs for their upcoming new album. It was a hot, humid, rainy day in early July, just after the Fourth of July holiday, and at the moment a wicked thunderstorm was raging outside.

It was the first such meeting for the Upper Hand since the one that initiated preparations for their 1990 album *Better than Ever*, when Jeff had shocked his bandmates with his unhealthy, disheveled appearance, wasted demeanor, and pathetic song offerings. Mark, Dave, Steve, and A.J. all found themselves mentally comparing the Jeff of that meeting fifteen years ago to the Jeff sitting with them on this stormy day in July of 2005. By virtually any relevant measurement, the present-day version of their guitarist/vocalist/composer was in dramatically better shape than at that long ago gathering. He came to this kickoff stone-cold sober, presented seven well-constructed songs, six of which were chosen by the band for inclusion on the new album, and—apart from an ugly, two-inch scar on his forehead and a noticeable limp in his stride—appeared healthy. Yet, undercurrents of suspicion and doubt about how Jeff had really fared during his weeks living with Denise in New York were swirling through the room as the five men sat chatting and watching the lightning flashes through the windows.

Dave and Steve shared skepticism regarding Jeff's story about a slip and fall down wet, slippery New York subway steps as the explanation for his head and leg injuries, but both men were grateful enough to see Jeff fully functional that they chose to sweep their concerns under the rug. A.J., however, knew better. Nine days prior to the meeting, his eyes had happened to catch a glimpse of an item in the police blotter of his local newspaper. The blurb described the arrest of Denise Blake, 45, of New York, for DUI and reckless driving after she crashed her BMW into a telephone pole at 2:30 in the morning, Sunday, June 26, on a side street in Roseland, New Jersey. She was reported to have failed field sobriety tests and to have registered a Breathalyzer blood alcohol content of .17, over twice the legal limit. While Denise was said to have emerged from the wrecked BMW physically unharmed, an unnamed male passenger in the vehicle was described as having suffered non-life threatening injuries in the crash. A.J., after long debate with himself regarding what to do with this alarming piece of news, decided not to share it with Mark, Dave, or Steve, and not to confront Jeff with it—for now.

Mark had spent the entire afternoon watching Jeff like a hawk, and he didn't like what he saw. Yes, Jeff was clearly sober throughout the song presentations and discussions, but through the eyes of someone who had known him for fifty years, Jeff appeared unnaturally tense, fidgety, and distracted. Mark was convinced that the story of the tumble down the subway steps was total bullshit but did not wish to start an argument with Jeff at this important meeting by challenging him on his tale. Mark's undiminished, visceral dislike of Denise had kept him from making any attempt to get together with Jeff over the five-week hiatus between the end of the tour and the kickoff meeting. Genuinely worried about the implications for his friendship with Jeff if the Jeff-Denise relationship actually turned into a long-term, stable one, Mark studiously avoided saying anything that could risk aggravating Jeff at the meeting.

In reality, Mark and A.J.'s concerns were well founded. Jeff's five weeks with Denise in and around New York City had been a wild roller coaster ride, including a major derailment. Denise, as she had done so easily years before in Europe, quickly charmed her way into multiple groups of wealthy, hard-partying socialites in Manhattan, Long Island, Westchester County, and northern New Jersey. By the time Jeff finished the concert tour and joined Denise in the gorgeous apartment she had landed on Manhattan's tony East 82nd Street, the couple's calendar for the month of June was jam-packed with parties and other social events with semi-famous and wannabe-famous New Yorkers and New Jerseyans. Jeff, weary from four months on the road and in need of time alone to compose new songs for the soon-to-be recorded eleventh Upper Hand album, was nevertheless energized enough by being with Denise to dutifully, and even enthusiastically, accompany her to nearly all of these events.

The various party cliques Denise had worked her way into had one thing in common: they were all filled with copious drinkers.

Some of them were also liberal users of drugs. Although Jeff did not once witness any heroin use at any of the parties he attended with Denise, cocaine, pot, and hashish use was rampant at several of these gatherings. On at least two occasions during the month of June an inebriated Denise suggested to Jeff that they "see what all the fuss is about" with cocaine, but Jeff managed to resist the temptation and talked her out of it.

Jeff was far less successful in keeping his alcohol consumption under control in these hard-core party environments. In general these were not beer-drinking crowds, and he found himself slipping back to vodka and other high-octane spirits. Jeff quickly became immersed in cycles of several consecutive days of extraordinarily heavy vodka intake, followed by a few days of resolve—either no drinking at all or gearing back to a few beers—and concentrated songwriting, and then back again to another round of excessive vodka drinking.

The June 26 auto accident on the way home from a party in New Jersey, Denise's arrest for DUI as a result of the wreck, and the injuries to Jeff's head and leg, shook Jeff badly. The trauma of the accident itself, combined with the knowledge that the Upper Hand would be reconvening in just over a week and would be intensely scrutinizing his condition and behavior, shocked Jeff into avoiding all alcohol, including beer, from that night right up to the kickoff meeting. It was this extended, self-enforced abstinence from alcohol that was giving Jeff the jitters during the meeting—an appearance of vague unease and stress that did not escape Mark's attention. Mark also couldn't help but notice that, when the meeting was over and the five band members were relaxing in the billiard room, Jeff's demeanor improved markedly after quickly downing three bottles of beer. Mark did not know exactly what to make of this, but he was convinced that Jeff was going through some sort of struggle with alcohol and that Denise's presence was contributing to the problem.

The remainder of the month of July 2005 was devoted to rehearsals and arrangements of the new songs in preparation for the recording sessions that would begin in August. The album was to consist of six songs each from Jeff and Mark, and four from Dave. True to Dave's dour, private prediction after his Indianapolis free-

198 A Fateful Reunion

ticket offer *faux pas*, he did not come into this new album project with any semblance of enhanced status within the band. In fact, Dave's bandmates seemed automatically programmed to expect that the new album would include the usual two compositions from him. However, the five songs he brought to the kickoff were of undeniably high quality, and he made it clear that he envisioned a strong guitar presence in every one. Lobbying aggressively, he successfully broke through the rest of the group's old "two Dave songs per album" mindset and managed to get four of his compositions accepted for the album.

Jeff, knowing full well that he could not stay away from alcohol for more than a few days at a time, and even then only with great difficulty, carefully orchestrated his party schedule with Denise to ensure that he was adequately dried-out in time for each Upper Hand rehearsal. As the rehearsals progressed, Jeff found it increasingly curious that none of his friends had yet really inquired as to how he was doing living with Denise, yet he knew all four of them were analyzing every move he made in their presence. He was not going to give them any grounds for badgering him about Denise's influence over his drinking habits.

Finally, as rehearsals were coming to an end, Mark decided to ask Jeff, in as non-confrontational a way as possible, how things were really going for him sharing the apartment in New York with Denise. He waited until the two of them were alone in his house.

"So, Jeff...you doing OK there in New York? You haven't really seemed like yourself these last few weeks."

Jeff's initial instinct was to vehemently deny that anything was amiss, or even to feign indignation at the insinuation. But he heard genuine concern in his old friend's voice, and so instead he paused and responded thoughtfully and candidly.

"I'm getting a real lesson in what it means to be an addict, Mark. It really is forever, man. Heroin's not an issue. Don't worry about that. But I have good days and not so good days with alcohol now. I guess those rehab counselors weren't kidding. I know you'll want to blame Denise for this, but it's not her. It's just me."

"Look, Jeff, I promised back in Chicago—or I guess, Dave made me promise—to give you a fair chance to show us all that you could jump back into a relationship with Denise without spiraling down the drain again. And I'm holding to that promise. But you're not making it easy. This cuts both ways, Jeff. If Dave, A.J., Steve, and I are going to have open minds about this, then you have to have open eyes. I don't know how you spent those five weeks after the tour ended, but if it was just a bunch of partying and drinking with Denise, then you better smarten up and try something different."

You don't know the half of it, thought Jeff, suddenly taking notice of the lingering aches in his leg and forehead. But he was in no mood to confess to Mark the details of Denise's alcohol-fueled auto accident or his recent bouts of out-of-control drinking. His level of candidness dropped significantly as he responded, "Don't worry. We're already well on our way into settling into a calmer, saner lifestyle. It's going to get easier and easier. You'll see."

Mark, dubious of this optimistic prediction, but lacking anything to counter it with, just replied, "I hope so. All four of us are watching."

CHAPTER 29

For the seventh time in their career, but the first time in sixteen years, the Upper Hand descended upon the rural northern New Jersey town of Newton to take up residence at the combination recording studio/private living quarters known as Total Immersion. It was mid-afternoon Monday, August 8, and the first recording session for the new Upper Hand album was just hours away. In keeping with a longstanding band tradition, a catered dinner buffet party was being set up to celebrate the start of the project.

The converted old boarding house that was now Total Immersion consisted of three floors, plus a full basement. It was in the basement that the spacious, state-of-the-art recording studio was situated. The first floor was wide-open living space, with plenty of comfortable seating and various amusements for the occupants, including a large screen TV, a surround-sound stereo system, and billiard, foosball, and air hockey tables. The two floors above contained the well-appointed living quarters. Recording artists who rented out Total Immersion were serious about focusing on the project at hand and about getting their album recorded expeditiously with minimum outside distraction.

Dave and his wife Sharon watched happily as Steve offered pointers to their nine-year-old son Justin, who was banging away on Steve's drum kit. Steve's striking, brunette, twenty-something-year-old girlfriend Melissa stood nearby, sipping a glass of white wine. (Few attendees had yet bothered to memorize the name of Steve's female companion, knowing full well from previous album recording projects that she was just the first of at least three or four young women who would be spending nights with Steve at Total Immersion over the course of the recording sessions.)

Sharon had never been to an Upper Hand recording project before, having met Dave after the band's 1990 breakup. But, having heeded the advice of A.J.'s wife Cathy, Sharon made it clear to Dave that she had no intention of staying cooped-up in Newton for the entire five to six weeks that the band would be recording. Rather, she would be doing plenty of back and forth commuting from home, sometimes with Justin and sometimes without him. Cathy didn't even need to tell A.J. that she would also be spending a significant portion of the time away from Total Immersion. As Cathy had counseled Sharon, the creation of a new album is a thrilling, intense, invigorating, all-encompassing endeavor—*for the participants.* For spouses and other spectators to the process, it quickly becomes about as exciting as watching paint dry.

Mark's relationship with his young girlfriend Emily did not survive the extended road trip of the spring tour, and he was unattached at the moment. He took advantage of his current nonexistent romantic life to invite his twenty-four-year-old daughter, Gabriella, to come to the party and to stay at Total Immersion for the first few days of recording. Gabriella, who was now a beautiful, tall, willowy blonde with a promising modeling career, happily accepted—not just for the chance to connect with her father, but also to glean any career tips she could from former supermodel Sharon Van Horn Rowinski.

Signature Records' president Stan Rabin was also on hand for the start of the recording project. Rabin's label was languishing and in desperate need of a new album from the long-dormant superstar act in his aging stable of recording artists. He had been through the full gamut of emotions over the past fifteen months—gleeful surprise and anticipation at the announcement that the Upper Hand had reformed, deep disappointment at the band's decision to embark on an extensive nationwide tour before recording a new album, renewed enthusiasm at the tremendous fan response to the band's return and the stunning success of the "Tireless Dancer" live single, despair and anger over the debacle in Indianapolis and the media field day that followed it, and relief over the band's rebound from the Indy-related problems and the strong finish to the tour. Aside from Dave, nobody associated with this new album was feeling anywhere near the same level of financial motivation to make it a commercial success as Stan Rabin.

Accompanying Rabin to witness the first days of recording was his twenty-six-year-old nephew Victor. Standing next to each other, watching the preparations for the evening party, Stan and Victor not only didn't look like they could possibly be related, they scarcely appeared to have come from the same planet. Stan, formally dressed as always in an immaculately tailored suit and tie, his now white and thinning hair still slicked back severely from his narrow, bespectacled, and perpetually frowning countenance, brought to mind a caricature of the miserly, mean old man who shakes his bony fist in fury at the neighborhood kids who dare run across his lawn. Victor, short and muscular, was clad in shredded black jeans, an equally battered black T-shirt adorned with the logo of death metal band Meshuggah, a black leather vest, and heavy black boots. His arms, knuckles, neck, and torso were decorated with an uncountable array of exotic tattoos, and his ears, eyebrows, nose, and untold other body parts bore an astounding number and variety of piercings. His longish, jaggedly cut black hair was studiously unkempt. The extreme contrast in appearance between uncle and nephew drew snickers from the others wandering around the main floor of Total Immersion.

As a favor to his younger brother—Victor's father—Stan had hired the rudderless Victor to Signature Records over a year earlier, purportedly to help Stan uncover and evaluate new, young musical groups. In reality, the primary purpose of giving this job to Victor was to sharply reduce his poorly spent free time. A single-minded devotee of extreme metal music, Victor shared none of his uncle's undeniable talent for recognizing commercially viable musical acts and had contributed nothing of significance to the label so far. Unbeknownst to Victor, his father was now kicking in half of his Signature Records salary to prevent Stan from firing him. Stan brought Victor with him to Total Immersion to give the young man some exposure to a truly professional recording act in the hope that it would leave him with some level of understanding of what it takes to be a platinum-selling rock band.

By 4:00 p.m., everyone, except for Jeff and Denise, who was expected for the party and evening recording session had arrived at Total Immersion: Mark and his daughter Gabriella, A.J. and Cathy, Dave, Sharon and Justin, Steve and date *du jour* Melissa, Stan and Victor Rabin, business manager Kevin LaRoche and his wife Wendy, two longtime Upper Hand recording colleagues, producer Sonny McCrea and sound engineer Billy Cole and Total Immersion founder and owner, seventy-seven-year-old Sid Coulter. Most of the attendees were now gathered on the main floor, chatting and sipping at the various available beverages.

The door to Total Immersion's main entrance opened, and Frank Parducci, owner of local eatery Frank's Italian Kitchen and frequent caterer to guests of Total Immersion, entered carrying several containers of food for the party. Right behind him, also carrying supplies for the buffet, was a short, thin young woman dressed in a cropped, bare midriff, gray tank top decorated with a skull and crossbones, a pale pink miniskirt, and clunky, black, high-heeled shoes. Her long uncombed hair was dyed a shade of pink that matched her skirt. The assortment of tattoos and piercings that adorned her from head to toe more than matched that of Stan Rabin's nephew.

Mark was the first to spot Frank as he began setting up the trays of food. "Frankie, my man, long time no see!" he yelled, trotting over to give the affable, popular restaurateur a hearty handshake. A.J., Dave, and Steve quickly joined in, and soon the five men were heavily engaged in nostalgic small talk about the band's hijinks at Total Immersion in the 1980s.

A.J. then inquired, "Frank, how's that adorable daughter of yours…Angelina, right? What a little cutie she was, helping you set up the dinners. What was she, maybe seven or eight the last time we were here? She must be all grown up now."

Frank gave A.J. a crooked smile, gesturing with his thumb toward the pink-haired, tattooed, and pierced young woman busily arranging cutlery on a nearby folding table.

"*No!*" cried A.J., Mark, Dave, and Steve in unison, unable to mask their shock. "*That's* Angelina?"

Frank exhaled heavily. "Yep, that's her. Angelina! Come over here and say hi to your old friends, the Upper Hand."

Angelina turned away from the table and bounced over to greet the four wide-eyed musicians. "Hi, Mr. Donahue, Mr. Ramello, Mr. Holmes, Mr. Rowinski. How are you? It's nice to see you."

Steve managed to stammer, "Hello, Angelina. We, um, didn't recognize you at first. Uh, hey, you're, um, an adult now. You can call us by our first names."

"Oh, cool, thanks!" She paused. "Except I don't think I know your first names."

Dave grimaced and mumbled to himself, "I think I just aged ten years." He then turned to Angelina and said, "Oh, that's all right. You can stick with 'mister' then."

"OK. Good to see you all. Gotta get back to work." With that Angelina returned to her set-up duties.

Frank saw the expressions on the faces of the four men standing with him and said, "Don't ask. I really have no idea what's going through her head with all these tattoos and shit. Her mother has worn out her rosary beads praying for her. But, hey, she's a good kid, works hard, and has mostly stayed out of trouble. I don't like the dipshits she hangs out with, but what are you gonna do? She's twenty-three!"

Frank headed back toward the entrance to gather more food and supplies. Just then Victor Rabin descended the stairs from the living quarter's level to the main floor. His gaze fell on Angelina setting up serving trays across the room, and he stopped in his tracks. Angelina turned toward the staircase, and their eyes locked.

Steve nudged A.J., Dave, and Mark with his elbows and whispered animatedly as he nodded toward Victor and then Angelina, "Oh my God, look at this. Talk about a match made in heaven, or maybe hell. Those two will be closely inspecting each other's tattoos before this day is over."

The four musicians watched with suppressed giggles and snorts as Victor all but sprinted across the room to introduce himself to the smiling Angelina.

CHAPTER 30

Fifteen minutes before the scheduled 5:00 start of the dinner buffet, Jeff and Denise appeared in the doorway of Total Immersion's ground floor. Heads turned as they made their way into the room, and instantly all conversation ceased, replaced by muffled gasps and murmured exclamations. Denise was hobbling on crutches, a hard plaster cast extending from the base of the toes of her right foot to just below her knee. Her nose was clearly broken, the horizontal bandage placed across it failing to obscure the deep discoloration below her eyes. Jeff's limp, which had almost disappeared by the end of July, was now more pronounced than ever, and his soft cast-encased right forearm and wrist was suspended in a sling.

Everyone immediately launched themselves towards the new arrivals, greeting them with a barrage of questions. Jeff held up his uninjured left hand to quiet the gathering, and announced, "Sorry to have to make such a dramatic entrance. We got into an auto accident last Thursday night, in Paramus."

The queries flew. *"What happened? Was there another car involved? How badly are you hurt?"*

"It was late at night, on a dark road. I swerved to avoid hitting a damn deer and wound up in a ditch. Denise's ankle and nose are broken. I got a hairline fracture in my wrist and re-injured the leg I hurt back in June, and we're both sore as hell all over."

Stan Rabin blurted out the number one question on everybody's mind. "Can you play guitar with that wrist injury?"

"Unfortunately, no. Not for a week or two. I know this is going to screw up our recording plans, but we'll figure a way around it. I'll have to dub in my parts later."

Additional questions and expressions of sympathy and concern poured forth from the gathering, and Jeff and Denise busied themselves in addressing them. But Mark and A.J. had a very different reaction to this shocking entrance by Jeff. Mark was familiar with busy Paramus, New Jersey, and had never seen a deer on any road in that town. Jeff's story wasn't sitting right in his mind, and he was convinced that alcohol was the main factor behind the crash. A.J., the only person in the room who knew about Denise's serious accident and DUI in late June, was also having difficulty buying Jeff's story.

Tired of tiptoeing around the issue, Mark knifed through the general conversational din with a sudden, "Were you drunk when this happened?"

The room fell silent, everyone's eyes darting back and forth between the deliverer and the target of this loaded question.

"No, Mark, but thanks for asking," Jeff sneered. He paused, debating whether to continue, and then added, "And the State of New Jersey would be in agreement with me if they hadn't dropped the fucking DUI Breathalyzer threshold from .10 to .08 a couple of years ago. I blew a .09 into the damned thing."

"Beautiful. Just fucking beautiful. Did you lose your license?"

"Yeah, for ninety days."

"Well, Denise sure as hell didn't drive here with that busted right foot. How did you get here today?"

"Very carefully."

"Jesus Christ, Jeff, are you trying to wind up with your ass in jail? Hire a goddamn limo!"

As Mark and Jeff continued their verbal sparring, A.J. suddenly took notice that Denise, who was wearing a spaghetti strap top, bore a pronounced, diagonal, two-inch-wide red bruise along her left shoulder. Anger building up inside him, he stepped between Mark and Jeff and commanded, "The two of you, shut up for a second." Both of them immediately complied.

Turning and pointing at Jeff, his face reddening, A.J. shouted, "You're lying. You're covering up for Denise."

Jeff, in total shock, stammered, "What...what are you talking about?"

His voice rising, A.J. bellowed, "That's a *driver's side* seat belt bruise on Denise's shoulder. She was driving." He stepped up to Jeff, slid his fingers inside the neck of Jeff's T-shirt, and yanked it down, exposing a similar bruise on Jeff's right shoulder.

"I know all about the auto accident and Denise's DUI in June, and it was no .09 either, it was a whopping .17!" Jeff's and Denise's eyes went wide in horror, and everyone in the room was suddenly staring daggers at Denise.

"That story about you hurting your leg and forehead, falling down the subway steps, was total bullshit. Denise damn near killed you in a drunken car crash then, and now you've allowed her to do it to you again. And you switched seats in the car to take the rap for her? What is the matter with you?"

A.J. pivoted to confront Denise. "And what kind of remorseless, selfish manipulator are *you* to stick Jeff with *your* DUI?"

The normally brash, thick-skinned Denise could conjure up no defiance in the face of A.J.'s searing exposure of her two reckless, drunken car crashes, and meekly mumbled, "It was Jeff's idea to switch seats before the cops came."

"Yeah, and I'll bet you protested mightily against it. Goddamn it, Denise, I've been trying really hard to stay positive about you being back with Jeff, but this is just too much. You're nothing but trouble."

Jeff started to protest, but it was obvious that A.J.'s fury was contagious, and hostility toward Denise was filling the entire room. He quickly decided that a hasty retreat was the best option for the time being, until he could figure out a way to repair the damage.

"Look, I don't want to talk about this anymore right now. Denise and I are really banged-up, hurting, and exhausted. We're just going to head up to our room. We'll have food sent up. I will be down for the recording session at seven. I know I can't play, but I can still offer advice and suggestions." If he was hoping for an encouraging response from his bandmates to his announced plans to attend the recording session despite his inability to contribute instrumentally, he didn't receive it. He grabbed the key to his room from studio owner Sid Coulter, arranged with Sid to have his and Denise's suitcases delivered to the room, and then he and Denise worked their way laboriously up the stairs.

As soon as Jeff and Denise were out of earshot, the main room erupted in a loud crossfire of conversation about the departed couple. Mark, Steve, and Dave descended upon A.J., preparing to pepper him with questions regarding Denise and Jeff's June accident—and to press him on why he didn't tell them about it a month ago—when a clearly agitated Stan Rabin approached the foursome.

"I don't believe this," he sputtered. "That lunatic broad is going to kill him. Do you realize that? This band, and all the hard work you've put into getting it back together, goes right down the tubes if Jeff winds up dead from drugs, booze, or getting wrapped around a fucking tree. You gotta do something!"

"What do you suggest, Stan?" countered Steve. "They're not kids. We can't order them around or slap a curfew on them."

"You better think of something. There's too much at stake here." Rabin stormed off, muttering to himself.

Dave waited until Rabin was across the room. "Rabin's still a creepy guy, but he's right. This whole Denise problem has taken an ugly and dangerous turn. Jeff really is liable to wind up dead if he hangs around with her much longer. What the hell should we do?"

Dave's question was met with shrugs and head nods, until Mark replied, "You know what? I'm sick and tired of worrying about it. I'm taking a break. The buffet is open, and I haven't had Frank's outrageous lasagna in over fifteen years." He headed over to the buffet line, closely followed by the other three men.

When recording a song for commercial release, some bands build the final track one piece at a time, often recording the drums first, then the bass, followed one by one by the other instruments and vocals. Others, like the Upper Hand, preferred the "live in the studio" feel, which could only be fully realized by playing the song together as a unit. The Upper Hand's longtime recording method was to first record a basic track including all five musicians playing as a band. Then separate instrumental overdubs were recorded and added as needed, sometimes replacing parts of the original basic track. Vocals were added last.

When the dinner buffet was finished, the band and production team retreated to the basement studio to begin basic track recording of a song by Mark tentatively titled "Seemed Like a Good Idea at the Time," a hard-rocking number with lyrics that could be interpreted by anyone paying attention as containing a few subtle references to Jeff's history with Denise. The soundproof studio control room was jammed with spectators: Sharon Rowinski and her young son Justin, Mark's daughter Gabriella, Steve's date Melissa, Kevin and Wendy LaRoche, and Stan Rabin and his nephew Victor. Cathy Ramello, who had witnessed many of these inaugural recording sessions over the years, begged off. To no one's surprise, the crippled and generally reviled Denise was nowhere in sight. Producer Sonny McCrae and recording engineer Billy Cole, who knew from long experience that this distracting crowd would surely dissipate before too long, did their best to ignore the intruders in their control room.

Since there would clearly be no vocal work required this early in the recording process, the injured Jeff had no real role in the session. His attempts to describe how his guitar part would mesh with the rest of the instruments, and his suggestions regarding how the rest of the group might want to alter their parts to accommodate his phantom instrumental work, quickly proved to be awkward and unproductive. Sensing the growing frustration of his bandmates and Sonny McCrae at his largely unsuccessful efforts to be useful, Jeff soon ceased trying to contribute and sat glumly silent as the rest of the group completed work on the basic track of Mark's song.

The original plan had been to move on to one of Jeff's compositions next, but Jeff requested, and everyone else readily agreed, that work on his songs be postponed until he could guide the band through them with his guitar. The other four band members were just beginning to set up for basic track work on one of Dave's songs when Billy Cole's voice broke in over the studio intercom. "Sorry to interrupt, guys, but there's a phone call for Jeff. I was told it's important."

A puzzled Jeff left the main studio area, entered the control room, and accepted a cordless receiver from Sid Coulter, who had taken the call on Total Immersion's phone line.

"Hello?"

"Jeff, it's me." It was his brother Bob.

"Hey, what's happening, Bob?"

"I couldn't reach you on your cell, so I called the studio. Good thing I remembered the name of the place."

"Yeah, we're recording. I had to turn my cell off. What's going on? Is everything OK?"

"No, not exactly. Fred died last night, Jeff. Heart attack, right in front of Trudy. She's a wreck. Connie's a wreck."

Jeff slumped into a chair, as Sharon, Kevin, Wendy, and the other spectators in the control room watched his face go ashen.

"Oh, damn...damn. Bob, I'm so sorry to hear this."

Fred and Trudy McCallister were Bob Britton's in-laws, his wife Connie's parents. Native West Virginians, Fred, Trudy, and Connie had relocated to New Jersey in the 1970s for Fred's job, leading to the meeting, courtship, and marriage of Connie and Bob. When Fred retired in 1993, he and Trudy moved back to West Virginia to be near their daughter and grandchildren. During Jeff's nine years working at Bob's auto repair shop and living in Shinnston, Jeff became very close to the McCallisters. The sudden death of seemingly healthy, seventy-eight-year-old Fred McCallister was a sad shock to Jeff.

"Jeff, the wake and funeral will be here in Shinnston on Wednesday and Thursday. I know it might not be possible for you to come down here—"

"Are you kidding? For Fred? And Trudy and Connie? Of course I'll be there. I'll fly in tomorrow." What Jeff didn't bother to add was that, because of his injured wrist, he was feeling useless and unwanted in the studio anyway, and his absence for a couple of days under the circumstances wasn't going to bother anybody.

"That's good to hear, Jeff. Trudy and Connie will really appreciate your presence. Get me your flight info, and I'll pick you up at the Pittsburgh airport." Bob paused for a second. "Uh, one other thing, Jeff."

"Yeah?"

"It would really be better if you came alone."

"What do you mean?"

"I know you're back together with Denise Blake, and you might have been thinking about having her join you here, but I don't think either Connie or Trudy would be particularly comfortable with that."

Geez, does everyone I know hold a grudge against Denise? Jeff thought to himself.

"That's OK, Bob, Denise injured her leg recently and wouldn't be able to fly anyway. I'll pick another, less stressful time to introduce them to Denise so they can stop feeling weird about her."

"Good, good. See you tomorrow."

212 A Fateful Reunion

CHAPTER 31

Basic track recording of Mark's and Dave's songs continued on Tuesday, Wednesday, and Thursday in Jeff's absence. Predictably, spectator interest in the proceedings quickly waned, and producer Sonny McCrae and recording engineer Billy Cole had the control room pretty much to themselves during the recording sessions. Cathy Ramello left Total Immersion on Wednesday, as did Steve's young distraction Melissa. Unbeknownst to her, Steve had another date scheduled to arrive Friday evening for the weekend. Stan Rabin departed Thursday morning. Victor, on the other hand, who had become intimately familiar with every one of Angelina Parducci's tattoos and piercings, wasn't going anyplace. He attempted to justify his continued presence with frequent "educational" visits to the studio during the sessions.

Sharon Rowinski was planning to leave for a few days with her son Justin on Saturday or Sunday; Mark's daughter Gabriella was certain to follow suit once her unofficial modeling career advisor left the premises. Business manager Kevin LaRoche was enjoying being witness to the making of the new album, but his wife was beginning to pressure him into heading back home. Denise, largely cooped up in Jeff's room, recuperating from the accident and avoiding the icy stares of the other inhabitants of Total Immersion, made it clear to Jeff before he left for the funeral that she planned to spend the next few weeks of her recovery back in New York. Reluctantly, Jeff agreed to arrange for her transportation back to their apartment if she still felt the same way when he returned from the funeral in West Virginia.

The recording sessions themselves were proving to be less than satisfactory to Sonny and the four participating band members. Although they were uniformly relieved to have the non-playing "consultant" Jeff out of their hair for a few days, they quickly came to the realization that they really missed the contributions of normal, guitar-playing Jeff. Laying down basic tracks as a quartet while trying to imagine how Jeff's part would fit in was confusing and tedious. Mark and Dave in particular found themselves having to develop and play multiple alternate versions of their parts to accommodate the different possible requirements that Jeff's part would create. If it had been up to them, the band and Sonny would have opted to postpone the sessions until Jeff's wrist was healed. But since Stan Rabin had put up half the money for the non-refundable studio time at Total Immersion, this option did not exist. Rabin strongly rejected the idea of postponement in a brief meeting with the band shortly before he left, and he implored them to be adaptable and to make good use of the expensive studio time.

Jeff, having heeded Mark's admonition to utilize limos while his license was suspended, arrived back at Total Immersion from Newark International Airport shortly before 9:00 p.m. on Thursday, August 11. As he entered the main floor of the building, he could feel the pounding of Steve's drums and the deep throb of A.J.'s bass, and hear Mark playing a searing lead guitar line over Dave's powerful B-3 organ accompaniment. The day's recording session was quite evidently still in progress. He briefly contemplated heading straight downstairs to the studio to catch up on what he'd missed over the past three days but decided instead to go to his room first to see Denise. His injured leg was even more bothersome than usual after the confinement of the plane trip as he lumbered up the stairs to the second floor.

Entering the room, Jeff found the lights on, a *M.A.S.H.* rerun playing on the TV set across from the king size bed, and Denise, clad in a T-shirt and terry cloth shorts, lying on her back on the bed. A largely untouched dinner sat on a tray on a nearby table.

"Hey, babe, you awake? How's your ankle today?"

Getting no response, Jeff leaned over the bed to gently jostle Denise awake, then suddenly recoiled in shock. Denise's eyes were half open, peering blankly at the ceiling over the bandage on her broken nose. There was a visible red puncture mark on the inside of her right forearm. As panic swept over Jeff, his gaze fell upon a hypodermic syringe and needle as well as a small re-sealable plastic bag full of white powder on the night table next to the bed.

Oh, my God, no! No! Oh, my God! Jeff was too petrified to touch Denise to confirm what was already obvious; Denise was dead.

Jeff grew lightheaded as he stood facing his girlfriend's body and then began pacing the room as he tried to clear his head enough to figure out what to do. He soon came to the realization that he could not think straight enough in his current state of mind to handle this situation on his own. He bolted out of the room and down the stairs, heading for the studio.

The sound of guitar, bass, organ, and drums pulsating through the walls, and the red light over the door to the studio, indicated that a take was being recorded as Jeff approached. He rushed through the door, surprising his bandmates, and causing them to abort the take. They began to offer welcome back greetings and were prepared to give Jeff a little good-natured harassment for bursting into the studio and ruining a perfectly good take, but it became instantly clear that something was seriously wrong with their returning friend.

"Jeff, what's happening? You OK?"

Jeff, out of breath from his adrenaline-driven mad rush down two flights of stairs, his injured leg burning in pain from the exertion, gasped, "You gotta come upstairs! Denise...Denise...she's dead! I went into the room...and she...she's lying on the bed...and she's dead! Oh my God, I can't believe this!"

After absorbing Jeff's stunning news, the four musicians dashed out of the studio and up to Jeff's room. Jeff, unable to run any further on his damaged leg, was assisted up the stairs by Sonny and Billy.

By the time Jeff, Sonny, and Billy reached the room, Mark, Dave, Steve, and A.J. were standing in a semi-circle around the foot of the bed, staring alternately at the lifeless Denise and the syringe and plastic bag on the night table, muttering to themselves but otherwise speechless. An anguished Jeff turned to his friends, waiting for someone to decide what to do.

"We gotta call 9-1-1," Steve finally said. The others nodded in agreement, and Dave pulled his cell phone out of his pocket and made the call.

Jeff pointed to the syringe and bag, cried out, "We have to get rid of that!" and took a step towards the night table.

"*Don't touch that!*" commanded A.J., and Jeff stopped in his tracks. "Jeff, did you know that Denise was using again? Did you have anything to do with that heroin being in this room?"

"No! This is insane. She wasn't using. Look at her arms. There's just that one needle mark. Why the hell did she shoot up while I was gone? It makes no sense."

"I don't know, but right now it's important to keep the drugs confined to Denise. They're going to figure out that there's heroin in her system when they check for cause of death. If that syringe and baggie aren't there, they're going to come back asking you a lot of questions and trying to tie you into the stuff being here, or at least screw you over for obstructing their investigation. They'd probably also turn this whole building inside out looking for more. So don't touch anything."

As Jeff slumped into a nearby chair, his head buried in his uninjured left hand, Mark spoke up. "You know, A.J. has a good point. If any of you guys have any illegal shit in your rooms, this might be a good time to go flush it down the toilet." Sonny and Billy looked at each other and slinked out of the room together.

Ten minutes after Dave's call, two uniformed Newton patrolmen arrived at Total Immersion, followed closely by two emergency medical technicians. A.J., who was waiting near the main entrance to greet the responders, led them up to the second-floor room. The EMTs quickly determined that there was no point trying to resuscitate Denise and were about to move her body onto a stretcher when one of the patrolmen, six-year veteran Rick Smithers, spotted the syringe, plastic bag, and puncture wound on Denise's forearm. "Wait, wait, don't move her. Looks like we got an O.D. here. We're going to have to get a detective in here to go through this room. Don, who's on duty tonight?"

"I think it's Jerry," replied rookie Patrolman Don Mackie.

"Call the shop and tell them to send him here."

Mackie pulled out his cell and called the Newton police station.

"Benny? Hey, it's Don. Listen, is Jerry on tonight? OK, tell him to come join us here at Total Immersion. This isn't a routine body grab. The woman is young, maybe forty or so, and there's evidence that C.O.D. is an overdose, probably heroin…OK, we'll be waiting."

Smithers turned to face the five band members. "Detective McDougal will be here in a few minutes to ask some questions and thoroughly check out this room. I don't think I have to tell you that the syringe and bag full of white powder over there have drawn our attention. While we're waiting for Detective McDougal, can any of you tell me who this woman is and if she was staying in this room alone?"

Dave replied, "Her name is Denise Blake, and yes, she's been alone in this room for the past three days."

"Whose men's shirts are those in the closet then?"

Without looking up or removing his hand from his face, Jeff said in a near whisper, "They're mine. I was away for three days and just got back tonight. I'm the one who found her."

"Can you prove you were not here in this room over those three days?"

Jeff sat up straight, eyes blazing. "What the hell are you talking about, 'prove?' I've been out of state since Tuesday and got back here less than an hour ago. So go fuck yourself."

A.J., seeing Smithers' nostrils begin to flare, jumped in to defuse the situation. "Officer, Jeff was in West Virginia attending the funeral of a relative and is now dealing with the death of his girlfriend. He's obviously distraught. It would be appreciated if you lightened up a bit."

Smithers stared at A.J. for a second, then at Jeff, and decided to back off and let McDougal handle the real digging. "OK, then can someone tell me the story behind Ms. Blake's broken leg and bandaged nose?"

Wanting to prevent Jeff from interacting any further with Smithers, all four of his friends quickly replied, "She was in an auto accident." A.J. added, "Jeff's arm injury is from the same accident."

Patrolman Smithers spent the next few minutes gathering basic information from the five musicians. His partner, Patrolman Mackie, who had left the room to greet the detective at the front door, soon returned with McDougal in tow.

Smithers and McDougal huddled together outside the room, Smithers filling the detective in on all he had learned so far. After two or three minutes, the two policemen stepped into the room.

Approaching Jeff, McDougal introduced himself. "Mr. Britton, I'm Detective McDougal. I understand Ms. Blake was your girlfriend." Jeff winced at the word *was*.

McDougal continued, "I'm sorry for your loss, Mr. Britton, but I hope you understand that I need to ask you some questions, and I will also have to treat this room as a crime scene. That bag of white powder over there is going to test out as heroin, isn't it? I need to find out how it wound up here with Ms. Blake. Were you aware that Ms. Blake was using heroin?"

"Absolutely not. I'm still trying to get my head around this."

"Were you using heroin, or did you leave any in this room before you left on your trip?"

"No!"

"Have you or Ms. Blake ever used heroin before?"

Jeff paused. "We were both users once. But that was a long time ago."

"So it shouldn't be a total shock to find her with this syringe and this plastic bag then."

"You're wrong. This is an unbelievable shock to me."

"Well, if you don't mind, I'd like to do a thorough search of this room and its contents to get a better sense of what transpired here."

Steve exclaimed suddenly, "Jeff, you don't have to let him rummage through your stuff without a warrant. That powder hasn't even been positively identified as anything illegal, so I don't get this 'crime scene' bullshit."

Jeff, with considerable effort because of his throbbing leg and immobilized arm, stood up from his chair.

He spoke forcefully, staring directly at McDougal. "No, I *want* you to go through the room. Because these are the facts, Detective. I haven't used heroin, or even seen heroin before tonight, since 1995. Denise had been clean even longer, by two or three years. I have no fucking clue how she got it, where she got it, and most of all, why she got it. If you find something in this room to help explain any of this to me, I'd like to hear it." His eyes shifted over to the bed and Denise's body, and his composure melted. "I...I...Denise..." His eyes filled with tears, and he collapsed heavily back into the chair.

"OK, Mr. Britton, we're done for now. Just one more question before I check through the room and arrange to have Ms. Blake's body sent to the Medical Examiner's office. Who is Denise Blake's next of kin?"

Jeff wiped his eyes and peered up at McDougal. "This may seem strange, but I have absolutely no idea. I'm not even sure she has any."

CHAPTER 32

Detective Jerry McDougal's search of Jeff and Denise's room turned up no additional signs of heroin, other illegal drugs, or hypodermic syringes. Nor did McDougal uncover anything among Denise's personal effects that offered any clue regarding her next of kin. However, he did find tucked inside Denise's wallet a plain white card, the size of a typical business card, on which there was a typewritten message:

IN THE EVENT OF MY DEATH, PLEASE CONTACT THE LAW OFFICES OF SILVA, CALISTO, AND PEREIRA. ASK TO SPEAK WITH OSCAR PEREIRA.

A twelve-digit phone number was provided, beginning with the U.S. exit code 011; this law firm was evidently not located in the United States. McDougal held the card in his hand for several seconds, contemplated turning it over to Jeff, but then decided that he would call the firm himself.

When McDougal awoke the next morning, he went online to find out which country had the telephone country code 351, the first three digits after the exit code in the number provided on the card he found in Denise's wallet. When he learned that the phone number was from Portugal, where it was already mid-afternoon, he quickly downed his cup of coffee and headed to the Newton police station.

Jerry McDougal was fifty-one years old, a career veteran of the Newton police force who was less than two months away from retirement. A dedicated cop throughout his long tenure on the Newton force, he now found himself counting the days until he could collect his pension and tend bar at his brother's sports bar in nearby Sparta, New Jersey. Newton, a pleasant, small town in hilly, largely rural Sussex County at the northernmost tip of the state, certainly qualified as a low-crime area, and McDougal's career had been fairly routine. However, over the past couple of years the town of Newton had seen a disturbing rise in drug-related crime—possession and sales of illegal drugs, trafficking in and theft of prescription painkillers, burglaries by addicts—and the Chief of Police was leaning hard on his police force to crack down on the perpetrators of these felonies and chase them out of his town. The heroin overdose death of Denise Blake was just going to cause the Chief to ramp up the pressure that much more. This was not how Jerry McDougal envisioned winding down his law enforcement career.

McDougal went straight to his desk at the station, pulled out the card and dialed the number. To his relief, the woman on the other end of the line answered in perfect English. Yes, Oscar Pereira was available, and the receptionist transferred the call to his office.

"Oscar Pereira here."

"Hello, Mr. Pereira. I am Detective Jerry McDougal, calling from the United States."

"Hello, Mr. McDougal. Detective, you say? How can I help you?"

"Mr. Pereira, I got your name and phone number off a card found among the possessions of a woman named Denise Blake. Do you know Ms. Blake?"

"Yes, yes, I do. Ms. Blake isn't in trouble, is she?"

"I'm afraid it's beyond that. She was found dead yesterday, here in Newton, New Jersey."

"Oh, dear. That's terrible news. Can you tell me how she died?"

"Our investigation is just underway. Her body was discovered only twelve hours ago. But I can tell you unofficially that there is reason to believe her death was drug-related."

"How distressing. But I'm glad you found that card, Detective. We have explicit instructions from Ms. Blake on how to proceed in the event of her death. If you would be so kind as to fax me the police report confirming Ms. Blake's death, I can set these instructions in motion."

McDougal, relieved that he wouldn't have to spend time digging around trying to find Denise's next of kin to deal with the disposition of her remains, assured Pereira that he would have that document promptly. Almost ready to end the conversation, McDougal had to satisfy his curiosity on one point.

"Mr. Pereira, your firm is located in Portugal, is that correct?"

"Yes, in Lisbon."

"Why then was my call answered in English? I thought I was going to have a tough time getting anyone to understand me."

"Ahh, yes, I can imagine that was a bit of a surprise to you. We operate internationally, Detective, with clients of various native tongues. We have five main phone numbers here, one for English-speaking clients, one for Portuguese clients, and three others for Spanish, German, and French. Ms. Blake wisely put the English number on that card you found."

"Impressive. How many of those languages do you speak, Mr. Pereira?"

"All of them, actually, plus Italian. English is probably my third best."

Damned impressive! thought McDougal as he hung up.

After an almost sleepless night spent in a spare bedroom, a disconsolate Jeff was kept company Friday morning by a steady stream of inhabitants of Total Immersion. Sharon and Gabriella each cancelled their plans to leave in order to be of whatever assistance or comfort to Jeff they could and to occupy him enough to keep him from drowning himself in vodka or beer. Even Kevin LaRoche's wife Wendy, who had been itching to get back home since mid-week, agreed with her husband that it was important to stick around for the next day or two. Steve called off plans for his next girlfriend's weekend visit, and the day's scheduled recording session was cancelled.

While no one at Total Immersion besides Jeff could be said to be really mourning Denise's demise, Jeff's obvious despondency cast a pall over the entire gathering. Jeff's emotional state was roiled by more than simple grief over the unexpected death of his girlfriend. The toxic emotional mix spinning through his mind included deep anger at Denise for having slipped back into heroin use, bafflement over why she did it, intermittent bouts of guilt for not seeing the signs himself and leaving her alone in an essentially hostile environment at Total Immersion for three days, and confusion regarding what he was supposed to do next and who would be responsible for Denise's funeral arrangements.

Shortly after noon, as Jeff tried to give himself a mental break with a nap, his cell phone rang, jolting him back to the grim reality of the day.

"H'lo?"

"Yes, may I speak with Mr. Jeff Britton, please?"

"This is Jeff."

"Mr. Britton, my name is Oscar Pereira. I am an attorney representing Denise Blake. Or, sadly, it is more accurate now to say I am representing Ms. Blake's estate. Am I correct in assuming that you are aware of Ms. Blake's recent passing?"

"Yes. I am the one who found her—" Jeff choked on the word "—dead."

"I'm sorry, Mr. Britton. I take it you and Ms. Blake had a...close relationship?"

"Yes. Yes, we did. I'm still having trouble speaking about it in the past tense. Mr. Pereira, how did you get my name? I never even knew Denise had a lawyer."

"Our firm has worked with Ms. Blake since shortly after her husband died, and one of our contracted duties is to see to her wishes regarding her estate as well as her remains."

Jeff shook his head in astonishment. *Estate? HUSBAND? What the fuck else don't I know about Denise?*

"Mr. Pereira, can you refresh my memory for me? When was Denise married?"

"Umm, let me look through her file here. Oh, yes...she married Jeremy Bradley in 1993, and he died in 1996. Ms. Blake first came to us in early 1997."

"Mr. Pereira, where is your law firm located?"

"We are in Lisbon, Portugal. Ms. Blake and Mr. Bradley were of course living in Portugal throughout their brief marriage, and Ms. Blake remained here for a while after Mr. Bradley passed away."

Well, there's a detail Denise left out of her recap of her years in Europe.

"OK. How did my name come to your attention?"

"Ms. Blake made you the principal beneficiary of her estate around three months ago. Did she not inform you of this?"

There appears to be no shortage of things Denise didn't inform me about.

"No, this is news to me."

"There are some...unusual conditions attached to your status as beneficiary of this estate, Mr. Britton. Do you have the time now to go through them? They involve the disposition of her body."

"Certainly. Not knowing what was going to happen to her as far as funeral arrangements has been weighing on me all day. I'm glad to hear she left directions on what to do."

"Oh, indeed she has, Mr. Britton. They are quite specific and more than a bit...imaginative."

"OK, let's hear them."

"As you may know, Ms. Blake had no close blood relatives, at least none who had any recent role in her life, and therefore none who will have any part in these arrangements. She was never clear regarding whether her parents are living or not, or even if she knew. But she was quite clear that she had no relationship whatsoever with either of them. Also, she had no siblings, and made no mention of any aunts, uncles, or cousins."

"Same here, Mr. Pereira. Denise had no family that I'm aware of."

"Anyway, the first part of her instructions is pretty straightforward. She wished to be cremated, and assuming you concur with the rest of the instructions, she called for you to take possession of her cremated remains."

"OK, I can do that."

"Here's where it gets interesting, Mr. Britton. Ms. Blake grew up in a small town in the state of Pennsylvania. Isn't that somewhere near New York?"

"Yeah, not too far."

"Well, her experience growing up in that town was evidently not a happy one. She went through the trouble to find out precisely what the latitudinal and longitudinal coordinates are for her hometown. She then pinpointed the spot on Earth that is exactly opposite that town. Ms. Blake wishes...wished...to have you scatter her ashes at that location, as far away from her childhood home as possible."

"You're serious about this?"

"I most certainly am. It is all spelled out in Ms. Blake's will."

"So, where is this place I would have to go to do this?"

"In the Indian Ocean, several hundred miles southwest of Australia. Ms. Blake's instructions are for you to travel to Western Australia, arrange for a ship to carry you to that exact latitude and longitude, and scatter her ashes there. You can bring anyone with you whom you wish; all expenses are to be paid out of Ms. Blake's estate."

Jeff was struggling to absorb this bizarre send-off Denise was asking him to execute. "Geez, this sounds like a major effort. Did Denise have enough money to pay for something like this? I'll do my best to cover any shortfall. I want her to have her wish."

Pereira suppressed a laugh. "Mr. Britton, rest assured money is not an issue here. The last time we checked, Ms. Blake's investment balances came to—here, let me convert it to U.S. currency—just over twelve million dollars."

"Excuse me?"

"Twelve million dollars, Mr. Britton. You can charter yourself any ship you'd like. Aside from a few relatively modest bequests to a handful of charities, that money is yours...*if* you agree to fulfill Ms. Blake's wishes regarding the disposition of her ashes."

Jesus Christ, did I really know this woman at all?

"I...I...of course I'll...this is really legit? Twelve million? American dollars?"

"That is correct, Mr. Britton. All yours if you follow these instructions."

"Just curious, since I fully intend to carry out Denise's request— what would have happened to all that money if I had refused to do this?"

"I'm highly pleased that you are agreeing to carry out these wishes, because the other option would have been highly challenging to execute, not to mention incredibly puzzling and enormously wasteful."

"What was it?"

"If you had declined, it would have fallen to our firm to use the entire twelve million dollars to purchase a shipload of something called Grey Goose L'Orange vodka, a product with which I am not familiar, and arrange to have her ashes and the entire shipload of vodka dropped overboard at that remote spot in the Indian Ocean. Thank you for saving me from having to figure out how to make that happen. Between the logistics and the legalities, I honestly don't know how I would have done it."

For the first time since discovering Denise's body, Jeff found a reason to smile. He would be sure to drop a bottle—*one* bottle—of Denise's favorite libation into the Indian Ocean with her ashes.

After Jeff ended the call with Oscar Pereira, his brief feelings of mirth were overtaken by dizzying astonishment over the revelations that had come out of the phone call. *Denise was a widow. She had twelve million dollars stashed away. She had recently made him her beneficiary—if he agreed to deposit her ashes in the middle of the Indian Ocean. Twelve fucking million dollars!*

It was all too much to take in. Jeff gave up on his nap, limped his way out of his room down to the main floor, grabbed a six-pack of Sam Adams Lager out of the refrigerator, and brought it back up to the room. If he'd had a second functioning hand, he would have grabbed two six-packs.

CHAPTER 33

Jerry McDougal was relaxing in his recliner in the living room of his tidy, one hundred-ten-year-old Victorian-style house in Newton, watching the previous night's Mets game on his VCR. It was 3:00 p.m. on Saturday and, to McDougal's delight, he had no particular plans for the rest of the day. He was in the process of fast-forwarding through the commercial break between the bottom of the third and the top of the fourth innings of the Mets game when his cell phone rang. Hitting the pause button on his VCR remote, he rose from the recliner to answer the phone.

"Jerry McDougal here."

"Detective McDougal? Hi, my name is Dr. Rohinish Patel. I don't believe we've met, but I am a forensic pathologist at the Sussex County Medical Examiner's Office. I'm sorry to be calling you on your day off."

McDougal's dealings with the SCME were fairly infrequent, since deaths considered suspicious or traumatic in Newton were relatively uncommon. Patel's name did not ring a bell with him.

"How are you, Dr. Patel? Can I assume that you're calling with information regarding Denise Blake?"

"Yes, that is correct. We've learned several things about Ms. Blake's death that we thought you'd want to hear about right away."

"OK. I'm all ears."

"Let's start with the basics. The cause of death here was cardiac arrest due to an overdose of heroin. Time of death is estimated at somewhere between 6:00 p.m. and midnight on Wednesday, August 10."

"About a day before her body was discovered by her boyfriend."

"Yes, and I see from the police report that the boyfriend was out of state all day Wednesday. You'll understand the significance of that by the time I'm through telling you what we now know."

"Is that right? Then please continue."

"There are several pieces of evidence here that make it quite clear that this was no self-inflicted accidental overdose. First of all, your report states that Ms. Blake had a history of heroin use back in the 1990s. That means she had knowledge of how to administer the drug, and how much to take. Well, she had enough heroin in her system to drop a rhino, and the entry wound from the needle shows that it was jammed straight into her forearm at a ninety degree angle. No one doses themselves in such a crude, painful manner."

All McDougal could come up with in reply was, "Whoa."

"There were no fingerprints on any part of the syringe. If Ms. Blake had injected herself, her thumbprint would have been on the end of the plunger. Also, the needle mark was on her right arm. A wristwatch found on Ms. Blake's left wrist suggests that she was right-handed. Most righty injectors use their right hands to guide the needle into their left arms."

"Was there any sign of a struggle? There was none apparent when we arrived at the room where she was found."

"No, but there's a reason. She had a significant quantity of flunitrazepam in her system."

"The 'date rape' drug, eh?"

"Yes. She was in no condition to offer any resistance. If she was conscious at all at the time the needle was jabbed into her arm, it was barely."

"So...bottom line...this was a murder."

"I see no other explanation based on these findings."

"Well, this certainly changes things. Thanks for the call, Dr. Patel."

McDougal hung up and switched off his VCR and television set. *There goes my Saturday afternoon. Hell, there goes my gentle seven-week drift into retirement. If this doesn't get solved quickly, they'll probably pressure me to stay on until it's put to bed. Shit!*

He retrieved his cell phone, and dialed Newton's Chief of Police, Roger Kehoe.

"Hello, Chief, it's Jerry. Sorry to bother you on your day off."

"Hello, Jerry. You caught me on the golf course. I just shot a 44 on the front nine at Farmstead, my best all year. Just about to tee off on number ten. I hope you're not calling me with something that's going to drag me out of here when I have a chance to finally break 90."

McDougal gulped, and replied apologetically, "Well, I just got some info from the SCME regarding our female O.D. that you need to know about. This was not a self-inflicted overdose, Chief; everything about it came back looking like murder."

"Damn! The mayor was up my ass just yesterday about drug-related crime in town. When he hears that this one is a homicide, he's going to blow a gasket. Listen, Jerry, this obviously changes everything. Call Skip, and the two of you meet me at the station in an hour. I need both of you on this."

"OK, see you at 4:30. Sorry about wrecking your golf game, Chief."

McDougal snapped his cell phone shut, muttering to himself, "Just what I needed—to be spending my waning days on the force working with Skip fucking Priefer."

Albert "Skip" Priefer was the other detective on the Newton police force. A young go-getter with eight years on the force and three as a detective, Priefer was certain to embrace this upcoming homicide investigation as the most exciting endeavor imaginable and pour every ounce of energy he had—and he had plenty—into it. Which was fine as far as McDougal was concerned, except for the fact that Priefer's zeal to please his superiors with quick resolutions of important cases too often resulted in hasty and ultimately time-wasting interrogations, arrests, and occasionally indictments of innocent people. McDougal sighed and reopened his cell phone to summon Priefer to the 4:30 meeting with Chief Kehoe.

Chief Kehoe leaned forward over his desk, still wearing his golf attire. Jerry McDougal and Skip Priefer sat side by side across the desk from him.

"OK, Jerry, tell us what you know about the cast of characters hanging out there at Total Immersion."

McDougal pulled out his notes from the night Denise's body was discovered. "You've heard of the Upper Hand, right? Big-time Jersey-based rock band from the '70s and '80s. Well, they're staying at Total Immersion to record a new album. One of the band members, Jeff Britton, was the boyfriend of the victim. He was out of town from the day before until the day after the vic's estimated time of death, so he's not the perp."

Priefer cut in, "Maybe he was conveniently out of town while he had someone else dose her?"

"Unlikely. His absence was sudden—death of a family member in West Virginia—and his grief over Denise's death felt real. Anyway, there are four other members of the band. Two of them, Dave Rowinski and Anthony Ramello, had their wives staying with them, although Ramello said his wife had gone home sometime Wednesday. Another band member, named Steve Holmes, had a girlfriend staying there, but she also left Wednesday. The fifth band member, Mark Donahue, had his adult daughter staying there."

Priefer blurted out, "I'll bet it was one of the other band members. Some kind of rock and roll love triangle thing."

Kehoe saw McDougal roll his eyes, and replied firmly to Priefer, "Cool your jets, Skip. I do not want this investigation to be derailed by gut feelings. Yes, I need this case solved fast to get the mayor off my butt, but I need it done right. No quick and dirty assumptions that lead nowhere. Facts. Facts! Get over there to Total Immersion and get the facts."

"Of course."

McDougal continued, "There were other people staying at Total Immersion beyond the band and their families. There are two men involved in the making of the band's album. One's name is Sonny McCrae, and the other's is Billy Cole. I got the feeling that both have been associated with the band for a long time. There was also the band's business manager staying there. His name is Kevin LaRoche, and I was told his wife was there as well. I think LaRoche is also a long-timer with the band. Lastly, there was a man named Stan Rabin, who was described as some major mucky muck, maybe the head guy, at the company that sells the band's CDs. He and his nephew Victor, also an employee of the company that makes the CDs, were staying at Total Immersion, although I was told that Stan left on Thursday. Oh, yeah, the guy who owns Total Immersion, Sid Coulter, has also been around. Skip, we've got a shitload of people to talk to."

The Chief leaned back in his chair. "OK, boys, your mission is clear. Talk to everyone over there at Total Immersion, and then let's reconvene. You know as well as I do that Mayor Carruthers is going to be screaming for constant updates on this, so I'm going to be all over you guys for progress reports. Clear your calendars for a while. Meanwhile, I now have the indescribable pleasure of calling Carruthers to let him know that a drug-related murder has been committed in Newton."

CHAPTER 34

Total Immersion was located less than three miles from the Newton police station. Jerry McDougal and Skip Priefer had a quick dinner at a local Thai restaurant after their meeting with Chief Kehoe and then made the brief trip to Total Immersion in a Newton patrol car. Priefer was behind the wheel. When they were less than half a mile away from their destination, Priefer said, "I'll bet you twenty bucks that one of the band members murdered Denise Blake."

"What? Are you kidding me?"

"No, I mean it. I haven't met any of these people yet, so I obviously have no inside information, but I'm telling you, it's going to be one of the members of the Upper Hand. A rock and roll murder!"

"I don't want to bet on this. I just want this fricking case solved quickly, so I can glide ever so gently into retirement. The last thing I need is you hounding all of the band members and ignoring any other possible suspects, stretching this case into November if it turns out you're wrong."

"Shit, is my reputation really that bad around here? Hey, when I arrest someone, there's a pretty damned good chance they're going to be proved guilty."

McDougal made a quick mental checklist of Priefer's more notorious "sure-thing" arrests that turned out to be wrong but decided not to stir things up by mentioning them. "Yeah, yeah, you're a regular Columbo without the raincoat and glass eye. I'll tell you what, I'll take your dumb bet, but if you wind up arresting one of the band members, and it turns out that the guy is innocent, then you owe me triple. Sixty bucks."

"What? That sucks!"

"Take it or leave it. If you're right, I'll be happy to cough up the twenty bucks for a quick resolution to the case. But if you lead this investigation down a long, useless path that fucks up my retirement plans, I want you to pay."

"You're on. You watch. There will be a famous rock musician in custody soon, and he will prove to be the perp."

Priefer pulled the patrol car into the Total Immersion parking lot, and the two men exited the vehicle and walked to the main entrance. It was 6:30 Saturday evening, almost two full days since Jeff discovered Denise's body.

The door to Total Immersion was unlocked. McDougal grumbled as he and Priefer stepped into the reception area, "Shit. This isn't what I wanted to see."

"What's that?"

"If this door is kept unlocked, then anyone could have waltzed in here Wednesday night and attacked our vic. This investigation would be a lot tidier if visitors needed permission to get in here."

The reception area was empty, so McDougal and Priefer proceeded into the main living area. Sharon Rowinski, her son Justin, Gabriella Donahue, and Wendy La Roche were relaxing among the many comfortable seats in the room, watching a DVD of *March of the Penguins* on the widescreen TV.

Sharon hit the pause button on the DVD player when she spotted McDougal and Priefer. "Hello, may I help you?" she greeted them with her dazzling supermodel smile, and both detectives' thoughts were instantly filled with decidedly non-job-related ways in which Sharon could help them.

"Good evening, I'm Detective McDougal and this is Detective Priefer, from the Newton Police Department. We have some important information regarding the Denise Blake investigation that we need to share with everyone who has been staying here the past several days." McDougal pulled out his notepad.

"Let's see," he continued, poring through his notes from two nights earlier. "Can I assume that you three ladies are Sharon, Wendy, and Gabriella, and that this young man is Justin?"

Justin chimed in, "Yep, that's us. We're watching *March of the Penguins*. It's really cool. Do you want to watch it with us?"

"We'd love to, Justin, but I'm afraid we're sort of busy tonight. Can you ladies tell us where the rest of the guests here—the band, the other men—are? We really have to gather everybody here to do what we need to do."

Gabriella replied, "Feel that thumping? That's the band recording downstairs in the studio. Everyone's down there."

Gabriella led the two detectives downstairs to the studio. The band was between takes, so Gabriella opened the door to the control room, and gestured to the two visitors to enter. Sonny and Billy were at their usual posts behind the massive control board, and Victor Rabin and Kevin LaRoche were seated on a couch at the back of the room, each nursing a beer. Through the glass window separating the control room from the main room of the studio, Mark, Dave, A.J., and Steve could be seen readying themselves for another take of the song they were working on that evening, an uncharacteristically hard-rocking song by Dave. Jeff, who had been coaxed into attending the session, if only to take his mind off Denise—and give the women upstairs a break from having to babysit him—sat quietly in a corner of the studio. His mind was focused more on trying to decide when, how, and in how much detail he would reveal the stunning news from his conversation with Oscar Pereira than it was on trying to be useful in the recording session.

Gabriella announced the visitors to the occupants of the control room. "Hey, everyone, these are Detectives McDougal and Priefer. They need to speak to all of us upstairs."

Sonny, Billy, and Victor's eyes all but popped out of their heads at the word "detectives," and Billy slid his hand as inconspicuously as possible onto a flat surface of the control board to scoop up three joints that were lying there.

"Good evening, gentlemen," Priefer said to the four men in the control room. "Can the guys in the band hear us from in here? We're sorry to have to interrupt your work, but as the young lady just mentioned, we need to pass on some information to everyone. It concerns Denise Blake."

Sonny pressed the intercom button and summoned the band members to the control room. Seconds later the entire gathering was marching up the stairs to the main floor. Through whispered curses, Sonny, Billy, and Victor each made it abundantly clear to a chagrined Gabriella that they were less than thrilled with the unannounced arrival of two cops in the studio.

When everybody was seated, McDougal requested that Justin leave the room. Sharon brought him up to their second-floor room, set him up with the *March of the Penguins* DVD, and returned to the main floor.

McDougal prepared to address the attentive group of eight men and three women. Priefer positioned himself so that he could observe the facial expressions of the five band members as his partner revealed the results of Denise's autopsy.

"We have received the report from the Sussex County Medical Examiner's Office regarding the death of Denise Blake. As we had anticipated, cause of death for Ms. Blake was an overdose of heroin. However, the examination also indicated, without doubt, that this was no accidental, self-administered overdose. I do not intend to reveal all the details of what the forensic pathologists found, but it is absolutely clear that Denise Blake was purposely and brutally injected with a fatal dose of heroin sometime Wednesday night. This was a homicide."

Although Priefer had intended to watch all five band members' reactions to the revelation that Denise's death was a murder, his eyes involuntarily became locked on Jeff, who reacted as though poked with a cattle prod. Ignoring the intense pain in his leg as he launched himself out of his chair, Jeff stood wide-eyed, his gaze shifting wildly back and forth over the other occupants of the room.

"Murdered?" he bellowed. "Denise was *murdered?* Someone in this room killed her while I was out of town and tried to make it look like she was some sort of junkie O.D. victim?"

"We do not know that anyone in this room was involved, Mr. Britton," Priefer said, as Jeff's eyes spit flames at everyone in the room.

Ignoring Priefer, Jeff screamed, "You people hated Denise, never gave her a chance! I wouldn't be surprised if the whole fucking bunch of you were in on this. I'm not hanging around here in a nest of goddamn murderers. I'm out of here." He limped painfully towards the staircase leading to the second floor.

"Mr. Britton, we're going to have to speak to you tonight—"

Jeff turned around at the bottom of the staircase and hissed, "I've told you all I know. You have my cell number. I'll be in New York. Call me when you find out who did this."

Jeff was followed up the stairs by futile pleas from the others in the room. *C'mon, Jeff. You know it wasn't us! Stick around and help them figure out what happened!* McDougal and Priefer knew it was useless to try to talk with Jeff any more that night, and so they turned their attention to the rest of the gathering.

"It is vital that Detective McDougal and I speak with each of you individually tonight. Please understand that none of you is a suspect at this point, and no one is under arrest. We just need to get as much information as we can regarding what each of you were doing and what you may have seen last Wednesday. We do request that all of you continue to stay here at Total Immersion, or if you cannot do so, then give us your contact information so we can be in touch later on if need be. Any questions before we begin?"

Ten faces stared blankly back at Priefer, so he said, "OK then. Let's proceed. Mr. Holmes, why don't we start with you? We passed a small side room before that can give us some privacy. Let's head over there."

Steve shrugged and followed Priefer and McDougal for the start of a long evening of interviews by the two detectives with the occupants of Total Immersion.

CHAPTER 35

"OK, gents, show me what you've got. Please tell me you have a solid lead, because now that this damned story is in the papers, Mayor Carruthers is just insane."

It was late Monday afternoon, almost four days since the discovery of Denise's body, and two days since the determination that she had been murdered. Chief Kehoe leaned back in his office chair, looking expectantly at Detectives McDougal and Priefer.

McDougal exhaled slowly and replied, "Well, we certainly have a lot to fill you in on, but no one stands out as the primary suspect yet."

"That's not what I was hoping to hear."

"Sorry, Chief. Anyway, let's start with the boyfriend, Jeff Britton. I'm going to tell you two things about Britton, and when I do, you're going to think we've lost our minds."

"Jesus, I can't wait to hear this."

"Britton item number one: he is the primary beneficiary of Denise Blake's estate. I spoke with Denise's lawyer this morning, and he informed me that Britton stands to walk away with close to twelve million dollars as a result of her death."

"Well, that certainly qualifies as motive for murder, doesn't it? What's item number two?"

"We don't consider him a suspect."

"C'mon, you're kidding."

"No, we're really convinced he's not involved."

"Then you're right. I think you've lost your minds."

"Don't forget, Chief, Britton was in West Virginia when the homicide took place, and he had no opportunity to plan in advance to be conveniently out of town and hire someone else to kill Denise. He was called away suddenly to a funeral."

"OK, but maybe the out-of-state funeral alibi was incidental. He could have set this 'accidental overdose' up days before without planning to leave town. I mean...twelve million bucks!"

"There's more. Britton went berserk when we announced that his girlfriend's death was a murder, and he all but accused everyone else there of being involved. He became too freaked out to stay at Total Immersion, knowing that someone there he knows may have killed Denise, and rushed out of there Saturday night while we were still interviewing. We both feel that his reactions are genuine. To top it all off, Denise's lawyer is one hundred percent convinced that Britton knew nothing of this inheritance prior to her death. By the way, we got Britton on the phone this morning. He's staying in New York, and he was considerably calmer and more cooperative than on Saturday but didn't offer much to help us narrow down the list of possible killers."

"Do you think he might be protecting someone? I assume his bandmates are also friends of his."

"No. He's hoping it's not one—or worse yet, more—of his friends behind this, but if that's how it turns out, he wants them strung up."

Kehoe sighed heavily. "It still seems strange to discount someone as a suspect who's benefiting to the tune of twelve million dollars. But let's set Britton aside for now, and tell me about the others staying at that place."

Priefer took a turn recapping their impressions from their interviews. "One thing that's absolutely clear is that Denise Blake was not a popular presence at Total Immersion. Everyone there felt that Blake was a horrible influence on Jeff Britton. I don't know how familiar you are with the Upper Hand, Chief, but they broke up fifteen years ago because Britton became a drug burnout casualty, and Denise Blake was blamed by just about everybody for getting Britton hooked on heroin. The band has only been back together for about a year, and Blake reappeared on the scene just a few months ago. She managed to get into two recent car crashes while drunk, injuring Britton both times, and—get this—even got him to claim to be the driver the second time so she wouldn't get a second

DUI. Her heavy drinking habits were also apparently rubbing off on Britton. Bottom line: no one associated with this band, besides Britton, is weeping over the fact that she's gone. If her death had remained perceived as a self-inflicted overdose, it would have been hard to find anyone who didn't think the band's long term prospects were a lot better without her around—even if most of these people are either too polite or too nervous about raising suspicion to come out and say it."

"So, anyone who has a significant stake, financial or otherwise, in this band's future could be seen as having a motive to kill Blake and have it look like an accidental drug death."

"That's what it feels like," replied McDougal. "There is another possibility, although we think it's a long shot."

"What's that?"

"Denise Blake was a heavy heroin user back in 1990, the other time she accompanied the Upper Hand to Total Immersion. She could have run afoul of some local drug supplier or fellow user back then, maybe even someone who works at Total Immersion, and this could have been a revenge killing for some past indiscretion. They're pretty bad about locking that place up at night. Maid service people and food delivery people come and go at all hours without being checked at all, so anyone could have snuck in there to slip the date rape drug into her meal and then load her up later."

"Sounds possible, I guess, but I'd focus on the 'ditch Denise to save Britton and the band' angle for now. Tell me about the people who were known to be at Total Immersion on Wednesday."

Priefer jumped in quickly to offer his views on the members of the Upper Hand. "Two of Britton's bandmates, Steve Holmes and Anthony Ramello, feel like low probability candidates. Yeah, they both think Blake was a shitty choice of girlfriend for Britton, just like everyone else does, but neither one of them comes across as especially motivated to do something this drastic. Ramello's wife left Total Immersion during the day Wednesday, so forget her. Same with Holmes's female companion. I wouldn't even call her his girlfriend; he had trouble remembering her last name. Not worth pursuing."

"OK, what about the other two band members?"

"First, Mark Donahue. This guy absolutely hated Denise Blake, blamed her totally for the breakup of the band back in 1990, and was convinced she was going to ruin Britton again. By the way, that assessment comes largely from Donahue himself. Most of the others we interviewed were way milder in their description of Donahue's feelings for Blake than he was."

"Well, if he is the killer, he may have felt it was better to acknowledge his disdain for Blake right upfront rather than have you guys dig it up and confront him with it later. The others could be trying to cover for him."

"Certainly a possibility. Now, the other Upper Hand guy, Dave Rowinski, is interesting to us for a different reason. It's hard to imagine these rich rock and roll stars needing money, but that's the case with Rowinski. He has a sick kid. I forget what disease he has, but it's chronic, expensive, and likely to get more expensive soon. Possible organ transplant-type of stuff. Anyway, Rowinski *needs* this band to stay together and be successful. It's not hard to picture Rowinski watching Jeff Britton getting wrapped around a couple of telephone poles—and being turned into a drunk besides—and deciding that Blake has to go to protect his income source: the band."

"All right, so we've got two people who need a closer look. Anybody else seem interesting to you?"

McDougal took his turn in the tag-team recap. "Well, the band's business manager, Kevin LaRoche, fits sort of in the same category as Ramello and Holmes—didn't like Denise, has incentive to keep Britton and the band going, but there's nothing in particular pointing to him, or his wife. Rowinski's wife Sharon and Donahue's daughter Gabriella are there, too. It's possible that, if Rowinski is our guy, his wife helped him. Same with Donahue's daughter if he's the killer."

"Does either one of them seem like the type who might get involved in something this extreme?"

"We didn't get much of a read from Donahue's daughter, but Sharon Rowinski is fiercely protective of her sick son. If her husband decided that Denise Blake had to be taken out of the picture to keep the band going and the money coming in for the kid's medical expenses, who knows?"

"Anybody else I need to hear about?"

"Oh, yeah, Chief, we're not done here yet," replied McDougal, knowing that Priefer's interest in anybody besides the band members was all but nonexistent, and that he, McDougal, would be delivering most of the rest of this progress report. "A couple of the other people we told you about at our first meeting still need to be looked at. First, there's Stan Rabin. We've now confirmed that he is the president of the Upper Hand's record label. So he certainly has a financial motive to keep this band operational and successful. He left Total Immersion on Thursday morning, less than a day after Blake's murder. We caught him on the phone this morning, and he told us that he left earlier than he had originally planned because he couldn't stand watching the way the recording sessions were going. Britton's hand had been injured in the recent auto accident with Blake, and he couldn't play his guitar, and I guess the recordings weren't going very well without him. Rabin made several references to the expense of renting out Total Immersion, how Britton's injury was screwing things up, and how the band had to get their act together fast. He denied having anything to do with Blake's murder but actually came right out and said that whoever killed her did the band an enormous favor. He came across as a pretty strange guy on the phone, so I don't know if his attitude toward Blake's death implicates him in any way, or just means he's a cold, dollar-driven guy. He was overheard yelling at Donahue, Ramello, Holmes, and Rowinski that they had to 'do something' about Blake when she and Britton showed up all banged up from the car crash. Rabin says that he just meant that they had to convince Britton to dump her. So, we still have more digging to do on Rabin. He's a pretty old man to have pulled something like this off, but he could have paid someone else to do it, which brings us to his nephew, Victor Rabin."

"You should see this joker, Chief," piped in Priefer. "More tattoos and piercings than Friday night at a Mississippi biker bar."

"Hmm, sounds like someone who'd know how to get his hands on heroin and a syringe."

McDougal replied, "Yeah, you could say that's true of Victor, as well as the recording guys Sonny McCrae and Billy Cole, and Sid Coulter, the owner of Total Immersion."

Priefer countered with, "Don't forget, this is a rock and roll recording studio. There are all kinds of characters flitting in and out of there. Anyone who decided they wanted a bagful of heroin on short notice could probably figure out how to get it."

McDougal chuckled, "Skip is so convinced that one of the other band members is the murderer that he crinkles his nose at anything that could point elsewhere."

Priefer scowled, flashed the finger to McDougal below desktop level, out of the Chief's eyesight, and protested as McDougal suppressed a laugh, "I'm open to all possibilities here. I just think that Donahue has the strongest motive from the emotional angle, and Rowinski the strongest from the financial standpoint."

Kehoe said, "OK, Jerry, give me your take on these last four guys you mentioned."

McDougal replied, "We don't know if any of them are heroin users, but they're all potheads for sure. Victor Rabin has no particular motive we're aware of, but his uncle could have been pulling his strings. McCrae and Cole were there fifteen years ago the last time the Upper Hand recorded at Total Immersion, so maybe they could tie into our 'revenge for an old Denise drug rip-off' scenario. Nothing else pops up. Same with the owner, Sid Coulter. So, that's your cast of characters."

"One more thing, Chief," said Priefer. "Trash pick-up at Total Immersion had already taken place by the time we learned this was a murder, but our boys went digging at the garbage dump and found a charred pair of latex gloves among Total Immersion's garbage. By the way, give Jimmy and Stu some Chiefly love when you see them; sifting through trash is not one of the job highlights. Anyway, our murderer was careful enough to use gloves and burn them, and as you know, we haven't found any helpful fingerprints anywhere in the room or on Blake. On the other hand, he wasn't quite clever enough to make the death look convincing as an accident."

"So, what's next?"

"Well, now that we know it's a murder, the forensics people are taking another peek at Blake's body and clothing, hoping for that TV crime show '*aha!*' bit of trace to link to someone at Total Immersion. We're also going to be talking to our guys who have been chasing the local drug dealers around town, to see if we can determine where the heroin and the date rape drug came from. We'll start re-interviewing everyone, even the low-interest people like the band manager and his wife, to try to jar some memories regarding last Wednesday night."

"OK, get to it. The sooner this gets solved, the better...for all of us."

CHAPTER 36

At the same moment that Detectives Priefer and McDougal were wrapping up their Monday afternoon meeting with Chief Kehoe at the Newton police station, Jeff Britton was sitting in the living room of the Manhattan apartment Denise had picked out for them three months earlier, twirling his cell phone over and over in the palm of his uninjured right hand. In "honor" of his murdered girlfriend, he had with him a sizable glass of deep-chilled Grey Goose L'Orange. He took a long sip from the glass as he debated whether or not to use the cell phone rotating in his hand.

Jeff had received and ignored multiple phone calls from Mark, A.J., Dave, and Steve over the past two days since he had fled Total Immersion. His mind was consumed by an ever-growing wave of possible scenarios surrounding Denise's murder, ranging from the depressingly plausible to the outright bizarre, as he tried without success to dismiss the possibility that one or more of his friends could have been responsible. Like Detectives McDougal and Priefer, Jeff recognized that, by any objective standards, Mark and Dave had to be looked at as possible suspects. But, remembering A.J.'s furious outburst when he figured out that Denise had been behind the wheel for the second car crash, Jeff was not as ready as the detectives were to rule out A.J. as a suspect. *Or, A.J. could have talked Steve into doing it. Or maybe they did it together. Or maybe all four of them were behind it. Maybe it was the fucking Martians teaming up with al Qaida terrorists! Shit, this can't be happening. Jesus, just let it be anyone besides the band!*

After several more minutes of spinning the cell phone in his hand, draining the glass of Grey Goose L'Orange, and driving himself crazy trying to figure out who was responsible for Denise's death, he speed dialed Mark's cell phone.

"Jeff!"

"Hey, Mark."

"Are you doing OK?"

"I've been better."

"Yeah, I understand. Are you coming back here?"

"No, I can't do that, Mark. Someone in that building murdered Denise, and I can't—I won't—associate with anyone there until the cops figure out who did it."

"You don't think I killed her, do you?"

"Mark, I don't *want* to think that *anybody* I know could do this. But somebody did. This was no random attack by a stranger, and you know it. I'm not accusing anybody in particular, but I'm not in position to rule anybody out, either. Someone stupidly figured that things would be better for the Upper Hand if Denise were to 'accidentally' O.D. on heroin. Well, I hope that asshole is happy, because his idiotic plan backfired. I'm just glad the cops were able to figure out that Denise's death was no accident. I wasted two days being angry at her for falling back into heroin use, and all that time, whoever killed her was fucking laughing at me behind my back."

"I'm sorry for what you're going through, Jeff."

"Mark, here's my message for you to pass on to everyone there at Total Immersion: To those of you who had nothing to do with Denise's death—and I still hope against hope that that's all of you—I look forward to the day when I can apologize to each of you for doubting your innocence. And to anyone there who is found to be responsible, rot in hell!"

Jeff hung up without waiting for any response from Mark. Mark sighed, snapped his phone shut, and headed from his second-floor room down to the studio, where he, Dave, A.J., and Steve were about to make their first attempt to record since Saturday's announcement that Denise's death was a homicide. The specter of a possible murderer in the building, along with Jeff's furious departure and uncertain return, cast a heavy pall over the entire project. No one was in any mood to create music under these circumstances, but Stan Rabin, angered when he called and found out that no recording had taken place on Sunday, elicited a promise from the four active band members that they would get back to business Monday evening.

Mark was the last to enter the studio. A.J. was tuning his Fender Precision bass, Dave was seated behind his massive Hammond B-3 organ going over notes on the composition by Mark they were planning to record that evening, and Steve was lounging in the control room, sipping a Harp Lager while Sonny and Billy shared a joint. Victor was taking a night off from his session observation duties to rub tattoos with Angelina.

Mark greeted the group with, "Hey, guys, Jeff called me."

"How's he doing?" "Is he coming back here?" "What did he say?" "How's his wrist?" came the simultaneous replies.

"No, he's staying away until this whole Denise thing is resolved. He promises to apologize to everyone not involved in her death once they catch whoever did it, but that's about it. I never even got to ask how his wrist is doing. As far as his guitar playing is concerned, I guess it doesn't much matter, does it? If they don't find out who killed her, who knows when the hell he'll come back. Shit, it makes this recording session sorta pointless, doesn't it?"

A.J. replied, "No, we gotta keep plowing forward. I still believe things will work out, and Jeff will be back in the fold before long. Plus, with Stan breathing fire over the studio time being pissed away, we don't have much choice."

Steve growled, "Fuck him! He has no clue what it's like trying to make an Upper Hand-quality record under these circumstances. Shit, I'll bet that S.O.B. is the one who offed Denise anyway."

Steve's outburst was met with an awkward silence. With everyone at Total Immersion under at least somewhat of a cloud of suspicion, there had been virtually no conversation regarding who may have been responsible for Denise's death, and nobody in the studio felt comfortable delving into the subject by reacting to Steve's broadside at Stan Rabin.

Finally, Dave broke the silence. "While we're on the subject, Mark, we got a call from one of those detectives while you were upstairs talking to Jeff. They're coming back here tomorrow morning to ask some more questions."

"Wonderful. They didn't get their fill of busting our balls on Saturday?"

"I guess not. Anyway, let's play some rock and roll and take our minds off this bullshit."

"Yeah, OK, let's do it. Goddammit, Denise is proving to be a bigger pain in the ass to us dead than she was alive."

Skip Priefer arrived at the Newton police station at 9:00 Tuesday morning to review his notes before heading over to Total Immersion. Jerry McDougal was scheduled to be in court all day to testify on an unrelated domestic violence case, so Priefer would be handling the day's interviews solo. Just as Priefer was about to get up from his desk and grab a patrol car for the short drive to Total Immersion, he was approached by Mike Camp, a sergeant on the Newton police force.

"Morning, Skip. How goes it with Newton's *Crime of the Century?*"

"Hey, Mike. Ahh, we're plugging away. I know it's one of the band members, but we haven't found anything yet to point to which one."

"Listen, I may have something of use to you. You know that scumbag Derek Underhill, the dealer we've been tailing forever? We caught him on one of our surveillance cameras last Tuesday night, less than a quarter mile from that studio where your murder took place. Are there any blonde women involved in your case?"

"Yeah, there are two staying at the studio. Why?"

"Well, the little bastard Underhill stayed in the shadows, so the picture quality is terrible, but the surveillance video shows him meeting with a woman with long blonde hair, and some sort of transaction takes place. That could be the source of the heroin used in your case—the date rape drug, too. This clown deals in everything. The only reason we haven't nabbed him already is we're trying to get him to lead us to his sources."

"Hot damn, this is huge, Mike! Thanks. One of the blondes is the daughter of one of the band members, and the other is the wife of another band member. I knew it was one of those two guys. So either Mark Donahue sent his daughter out to get the drugs, or Dave Rowinski sent his wife. Hot damn! Now I've got something to focus on when I head over there, instead of just sniffing around."

"Don't you want to see the video before you go there?"

"Oh, yeah, sure, let's go take a peek."

"You're not going to be able to make out any facial features or anything. This little meeting took place right at the outer edge of the camera's range, in a spot where the street lights don't hit."

"That's OK. It sounds like there's enough there for me to be able to lean on those two women to see which one of them bought the drugs. By the way, does this punk, Underhill, put his heroin in small plastic bags with blue and yellow zip-lock closures?"

"Yeah, that's his routine."

"Bingo! That's exactly what we found in the room where Denise Blake was killed."

Camp led Priefer to a small room set up with four metal folding chairs, a rectangular table, and a wheeled cart on which sat a twenty-inch TV set and a VCR. Camp grabbed the two remote controls, switched on the TV and the video player, and inserted the tape. He fast-forwarded to a point on the tape where the time/date monitor in the lower right-hand corner of the picture read TUE AUG 9 2005 10:36 PM. The fuzzy, black and white image of Derek Underhill standing on the sidewalk near the façade of a nail salon, facing the camera, filled the screen. A female figure with long light-colored hair and wearing dark clothing then appeared from the right edge of the screen, turning immediately to face Underhill, away from the camera. Her image was equally blurry and indistinct.

"Shit!" growled Priefer. "If only they'd met about fifteen feet closer, where the light is better, or if she hadn't turned so quickly away from the camera, we'd be able to see who she is."

The video then showed Underhill reaching three times into his shirt pocket with his right hand, accepting something from the woman with his left hand, and then handing the contents of his pocket to her. The entire transaction took less than half a minute, and the two parted in opposite directions. The woman disappeared out of camera range without ever facing the camera. The picture quality was too poor to be able to make out exactly what either person had handed to the other.

"Well, Mike, it's not gonna win an Oscar for cinematography, but it gives me an excellent lead. Thanks! I'm gonna go grill me a couple of blondes now."

"Have fun. They good-looking by any chance?"

"Are you kidding? They're both models! One's a frickin' former Sports Illustrated swimsuit issue supermodel."

"Lucky you. The highlight of my day today is gonna be helping evict a toothless, three-hundred-pound woman with eight cats from a shithole apartment on High Street."

"Sounds exciting. See you later."

CHAPTER 37

Detective Priefer entered the reception area of Total Immersion just before 10:00 a.m. It was Tuesday, August 16, the fifth day since Denise was found dead. This time there was a receptionist to greet Priefer. He asked to see Gabriella Donahue.

"Let me see if she's downstairs yet." The receptionist poked her head through the doorway to the main living area, and then announced, "No, she must still be upstairs in her room. I can ring the room for you. Who should I say is asking for her?"

"I'm Detective Priefer, from the Newton police. I believe everyone staying here is aware that I would be stopping by this morning."

The receptionist reached Gabriella in her room, and two minutes later the young blonde model appeared in the reception area. "Good morning, Detective," she greeted Priefer.

"Ms. Donahue, let's have a seat in the same room where we spoke on Saturday."

"OK. But I already told you everything I know."

"Well, we'll see. I have some more questions for you."

The two proceeded to the small side room off the living area, and Priefer shut the door as Gabriella took a seat. Priefer took a portable recording device out of his pocket, uttered, "Gabriella Donahue, August 16," into it, and placed it on the table between him and Gabriella. He wasted no time getting to the point of the interrogation.

"Ms. Donahue, where were you last Tuesday night, the ninth?"

"I was here, at Total Immersion."

"Did you leave the building at all that evening?"

"Tuesday? I'm not sure. I don't think so."

"Well, we have good reason to believe that you did, around 10:30 that night."

"I don't remember if I was out at all that night, and if I was, I'm sure I was back before 10:30."

"Let me refresh your memory for you, Ms. Donahue. Corner of High Street and Halstead Street, buying drugs from a local pusher. Ring a bell?"

Gabriella's eyes went wide. "What? I don't use drugs."

"I didn't say you did. I said you were seen *buying* them."

"Why...why would I buy drugs if I don't even use them?"

Priefer's voice went up a notch in intensity, and he leaned aggressively forward in his chair. "That's what I'm trying to find out. Did you buy them for your father to use to kill Denise Blake?"

The color began to drain out of Gabriella's face, and her hands started shaking visibly. "No! This is some kind of mistake!"

"Listen, Gabriella," said Priefer coldly, dropping the "Ms. Donahue" formalities, "I'm willing to be convinced that you played no part in the actual killing of Denise, and just maybe I can be made to believe that you didn't know what the drugs were going to be used for. But if you don't want to be tied directly to that murder, you have to tell me *now* who sent you out to buy them, and who you gave them to. Was it your father?"

Gabriella's eyes began to water. "No! My father didn't kill Denise!"

"Then who did?"

"I have no idea."

"Then how can you be so sure it wasn't your father? If you're going to tell me Mark Donahue definitely had nothing to do with this, then you must know who did. Who did you give those drugs to?"

"I don't know...I mean, nobody...I didn't buy any drugs! I just know my father couldn't have done this."

"Well, for someone who's insisting she doesn't know anything, you're sure bobbing and weaving like you've got something to hide. Why are you coming apart here if you had no involvement in any of this?"

"Because you're accusing my father and me of murdering Denise and saying you know I bought drugs, and I'm scared!"

"I'm going to give you one last chance to separate your actions from this murder, Gabriella. Buying a bag of heroin doesn't put you in anywhere near as much trouble as being involved in a homicide. Who put you up to this drug purchase?"

"I said I don't know—damn, I mean, I never had any drugs to give anyone! I'm not answering any more questions. I just want this whole Denise thing to go away!" She dissolved into tears with her hands over her face. Priefer could see that he wasn't going to get anything else of use from Gabriella for the time being.

"This 'Denise thing' isn't going to go away until you come clean with me. You can leave this room for now, but when I'm through talking to other people here, I'm going to bring you back in here and give you one final opportunity to cooperate. Don't leave this building until I say it's OK, got it?"

Gabriella replied with an incoherent sob and fled the room. Priefer spent a minute reviewing the interrogation in his mind before exiting the room. He couldn't decide whether Gabriella's inability to hold up under his accusations pointed to her involvement, or if it was just because she was so intimidated by the aggressive questioning. *Let's put Sharon Rowinski through the wringer, too, and then listen carefully to the playback of this one if necessary. It's gotta be one of these two.*

When Priefer emerged from the interview room into the living area, he encountered a still-weeping Gabriella being embraced by her enraged father. Dave, Sharon, Steve, and Kevin and Wendy LaRoche were also in the room, each one staring at Priefer with pure loathing.

Mark let go of Gabriella and took an aggressive step toward Priefer. "What the hell do you think you're doing, you pencil-dicked son of a bitch?"

Priefer jabbed his index finger in Mark's direction and growled, "Stay right where you are, Donahue."

Mark ignored the order and took another stride toward the detective. "You're fucking clueless about what happened here, so now you're badgering my daughter to cover your sorry ass."

"*I said stay where you are!*" Priefer barked, sliding his hand to his right side, nudging back his suit jacket and exposing his holstered pistol. "You take one more step towards me and you're under arrest. Denise Blake's murderer was obviously a violent person. You're doing a great job of convincing me that you're the one."

Mark glared at Priefer but stopped advancing toward him. "I repeat, your pathetic inability to solve this murder doesn't give you the right to harass my daughter," he shot back defiantly.

"You don't get to tell me how to run this investigation, Donahue. Stay the hell out of my way until I call you to answer my questions. Wise up or you'll be answering them in handcuffs at the station."

"Eat shit, Priefer," Mark spat as he returned to comfort his daughter.

Priefer turned towards Sharon, and with his adrenaline-charged voice carrying a bit more edge than he intended, said, "Mrs. Rowinski, I need to speak with you next."

Dave started to protest, but Sharon immediately placed a finger over his mouth and whispered, "Don't worry." She then strode past Priefer and entered the interview room. Priefer followed her, shut the door, and once again started his portable recorder, speaking Sharon's name and the date into it.

"Mrs. Rowinski, I need you to account for your whereabouts on the evening of August ninth, last Tuesday."

"Last Tuesday? Let's see, that was our second night here...I was here at Total Immersion all evening, with my son."

"How about after he went to bed?"

"No, I didn't go anywhere that night."

"Well, I have reason to believe that you did leave later that night, around 10:30, to make a street drug purchase just a few hundred yards from here."

Unlike Gabriella a few minutes earlier, Sharon didn't bat an eye at Priefer's accusation that she had bought drugs on a nearby street corner. She looked directly at Priefer and replied, "Exactly what is this 'reason to believe' you're referring to?"

"That's irrelevant for now. What I—"

"There's nothing irrelevant about it, Detective. You just accused me of lying about where I was last Tuesday night. Either you explain what leads you to this conclusion, or this interview is over."

Priefer stared at Sharon for a couple of seconds as she met his gaze unflinchingly. *Well, this interview is going to be a bit different from the last one. This broad is a tough customer—certainly tough enough to be involved in this. She could be a more likely candidate than Donahue's daughter.*

"OK. We have surveillance video of an August ninth drug transaction on the corner of High Street and Halstead Street, and the buyer looks very much like you, Mrs. Rowinski."

"I want to see that video."

"I don't have it here. So if we could—"

"I'm not saying another word until I see that video. Your choice, Detective. Either we take a trip to the police station and watch this so-called evidence that I was out buying drugs, or we're done here. I'm not under arrest, so I don't have to continue this. I'll be happy to cooperate but not without seeing why you think I was out on a Newton street corner last week."

Priefer had to think quickly. Yes, the video's clarity was lousy, and there was no way to present it as iron-clad proof that Sharon was the blonde drug purchaser shown in it. But if she was indeed the buyer, the visual evidence of the transaction could be enough to shake her irritating confidence and force her to admit her role in the homicide.

"All right, I'll drive you to the police station, and I'll show you exactly why I'm doubting your story about last Tuesday night."

"No, thanks, I'll drive myself."

"That's fine."

Sharon and Priefer exited the interview room. A nervous-looking Dave was the only person still in the living area. Sharon gave him a quick wink and said, "I'll be back before long. I'm heading over to the police station for a few minutes."

"What? Why? Why are they taking you there?"

"They're not. This is my request. Don't worry. I'll explain it all when I get back."

"But—"

"Trust me. Everything's fine."

She gave her baffled husband a quick kiss, and headed for the exit, a few steps behind Priefer.

Heads turned throughout the police station as Sharon, dressed in stylish, form-fitting jeans and a black tank top, sauntered past the on-duty cops toward the viewing room. Sergeant Camp had not yet left the station to evict the woman with the eight cats, so Priefer asked him to set up the video again and queue it up to the moment of the transaction between Derek Underhill and the mystery blonde. Priefer left the door to the viewing room open to the main working area of the station, figuring that Camp would close it when he left after showing the video.

Sharon and Priefer took seats in the metal folding chairs facing the TV screen, and Camp fast-forwarded the tape to the moment at 10:36 p.m. when the encounter between Underhill and the unknown woman began. The three of them watched the recorded exchange wordlessly, and Camp hit the pause button when the two figures had walked out of camera view.

Camp asked, "Do you need to see it again?"

Priefer replied, "No, I think we've seen what we needed to see. Now, Mrs. Rowinski, do you still want to claim—"

Sharon cut him off with a perfectly calm, yet decidedly firm, query. "How tall is that drug dealer?"

"Excuse me? That has nothing to do with—"

"I want to know, now, how tall that man in the video is. If he's a known drug dealer around here, you must have had him in here at one time or another."

Camp immediately realized where this conversation was headed, and as the significance of Sharon's question began to dawn on Priefer, a sinking feeling came over him. Suddenly he regretted that Camp had discovered this video and shown it to him.

The woman in the video was at least five inches shorter than Underhill.

His face reddening, Priefer stammered, "I...I don't know exactly how tall he is."

Sharon turned her attention to Camp. "How about you, Sergeant? Do you know how tall that man is?"

Camp cast a quick, semi-apologetic glance at Priefer, and then replied, "He's about five-foot seven or eight."

Sharon slowly and dramatically pushed her chair away from the table in front of her and rose to her full height, facing Priefer. She announced, in a loud, deliberate voice that could be easily heard in the main working area of the station through the open door, "I am five foot eleven inches tall, in bare feet. The woman in that video, who you're trying to pass off as me, is easily eight inches shorter than I am. Nice try, Detective. This meeting is over." She grabbed her purse and took two steps toward the door before stopping to add at an equally room-filling volume, "One more thing, Sherlock. Gabriella Donahue is five-foot ten. You better dig up some shorter blondes to harass."

Priefer stared helplessly at the departing Sharon, saying nothing, sinking into his chair. Camp couldn't quite decide if he was more mortified or entertained by Priefer's screw up and just watched admiringly as Sharon exited the room. The collection of police officers in the main room of the station who had overheard Sharon's dismantling of Priefer's attempted interrogation managed to avoid displaying any overt reactions to the fiasco until Sharon greeted the room with, "You boys might want to go assist Inspector Clouseau in there. Last I saw, his testicles were rolling around on the floor." With a majestic shake of her long blonde hair, she strutted out of the station to howls of laughter.

CHAPTER 38

The atmosphere in the police station became instantly intolerable to Priefer in the moments after Sharon Rowinski's dramatic exit. A constant, merciless barrage of disparaging and off-color jokes soon chased the red-faced detective out of the building. In a largely ineffective attempt to save face, he claimed that he had to visit the Sussex County Medical Examiner's office to check the status of their examination of Denise's body and clothes—an update that could easily have been obtained by phone.

The visit to the medical examiner's office was brief, as the forensic pathologists assigned to the case could only tell Priefer that nothing new had been found to help identify who was in the room with Denise the night of her death. Nowhere near ready to return to the station to face more catcalls and bad jokes about Sharon's humiliation of him, Priefer pulled into a nearby diner for a long lunch. There he spent the next ninety minutes nursing a turkey club sandwich and several cups of coffee, alternately berating himself for his careless review of the video, cursing Sergeant Camp for bringing the existence of the video to his attention, and fuming at Sharon Rowinski for being such a smart-ass bitch. *Goddamn it, I really hope her husband is Blake's killer. That'll wipe the smirk off her face when I haul his ass off to jail.*

Priefer returned to the station shortly after 2:00 p.m. He was thankful that the cops in the main room seemed to have gotten over their desire to needle him over the morning's debacle, but his mood quickly darkened when the desk officer announced to him, "Hey, Skip, Chief Kehoe wants to see you immediately—and he asked me to emphasize *immediately*—in his office."

Priefer grimaced, mumbled, "This should be fun," and headed to the Chief's office door, which was closed. He knocked tentatively on the door.

"Come in."

Priefer opened the door to find Chief Kehoe behind his desk and Detective McDougal sitting in one of the two chairs facing the desk. McDougal had arrived at the station a half hour earlier after having finished his duties in court and had spent the past several minutes being briefed by the chief on the developments—or, more accurately, the setbacks—in the Denise Blake case.

"Sit down, Skip," Kehoe commanded, and Priefer complied wordlessly. "I've heard all I need to hear about your disaster in the video room this morning. What I don't know is, what the hell did you do out there at Total Immersion earlier in the morning?"

"I'm not sure I know what you mean."

"All I know is you've managed to piss off everyone out there so thoroughly that they're all threatening to lawyer up and refuse to cooperate any more in this investigation."

"I only interviewed one person out there this morning, aside from," he choked at the memory, "Sharon Rowinski. It was Donahue's daughter, Gabriella." He decided there was nothing to be gained by rehashing his altercation with Mark Donahue.

"Well, it must have been a doozy, because I got a phone call from Sharon's husband Dave late this morning, informing me that nobody there was going to speak to us anymore unless forced to with an arrest warrant. I eventually got them to agree to one more round of voluntary interviews tomorrow afternoon but only if you're *not* the one conducting them. For chrissakes, Skip, this is Police Work 101 here! Don't antagonize the people whose help we need to crack a case, especially one like this where we've got shit for physical evidence."

Priefer could think of nothing to say to effectively defend his role in the morning's events at Total Immersion and in the station video room, so he remained silent, avoiding eye contact with either Kehoe or McDougal.

Kehoe continued, "Jerry, you go out there tomorrow, do whatever damage control is necessary to get those people to open up about what they remember seeing or hearing around the time of the homicide. Take your time and be thorough, because this is liable to be our last easy shot at some of these folks. The band isn't going anywhere, but according to Rowinski, some of the others, including his wife, want to get out of there and will certainly be leaving soon. Right now we've got no grounds to stop any of them from doing so."

McDougal, having heard from several officers as well as Chief Kehoe about Priefer's ill-fated attempt to tie Sharon Rowinski to the surveillance video, knew full well that Priefer's hasty decision to lean on Sharon—and apparently Gabriella too—was all a result of his unwavering conviction that Mark Donahue or Dave Rowinski played a part in Denise's murder. McDougal recognized that Priefer's clumsy mistakes didn't eliminate either Mark or Dave as possible suspects, but he also realized that the day's gaffes by his fellow detective were going to make his interviewing job the following day more difficult. Still, he decided to throw Priefer a bone to help make his efforts seem like something other than a total loss.

"Skip, I guess your interviews with Gabriella and Sharon ran into problems today, but I'm sure you got some useful stuff from them anyway. Let's meet this afternoon to discuss what you learned and give me a head-start on my work there tomorrow."

Priefer glanced gratefully at McDougal and replied, "Absolutely. Glad to."

Kehoe then said to Priefer, "You are to stay away from Total Immersion, Skip. Your mission now is to figure out who that woman is in the surveillance video and whether there's any connection to this case. Also, follow up with the medical examiners and see if anything useful got plucked off the vic."

"I already took care of the medical examiner follow-up this afternoon. They found nothing."

"It figures. Damn. Then go find that blonde, that *short* blonde, in the video. Jerry, the people at Total Immersion are expecting you there tomorrow at 1:00 p.m."

At noon the next day, the dispirited group of Upper Hand musicians, family members, and associates gathered in the main living area of Total Immersion for a pizza lunch prior to the arrival of Detective McDougal. Mark, Dave, A.J., and Steve were all there, as well as Gabriella, Sharon, and young Justin. Cathy Ramello, who had come back to Newton the night before to lend moral support to the unhappy group, was also in the room, as were Sonny McCrae, Billy Cole, and Kevin and Wendy LaRoche.

As Cathy and Wendy started passing around paper plates and napkins in anticipation of the arrival of the pizzas, Justin suddenly decided that it was essential that he be wearing his New York Yankees cap while eating his lunch.

"Dad, where's my Yankees hat?"

"I don't know, Justin. Did you leave it in our room?"

Sharon said, "I know where it is. Justin, you took it off down in the studio when Sonny let you put on the big headphones last evening. It's in the studio control room."

Justin popped out of his seat and asked, "Can I go down there and get it?"

"No, I don't want you down there with all that equipment by yourself. I have to use the bathroom anyway, so I'll go downstairs and get it for you."

Sharon proceeded down the stairway leading to the studio just as the front door to Total Immersion opened, and Angelina Parducci entered carrying two pizzas. Right behind her was her boyfriend of the past nine days, Victor Rabin, carrying three more pizzas. Despite the summer weather, both were clad in long-sleeved black T-shirts and black jeans. Victor also wore a studded black leather vest.

As Angelina and Victor began placing the pizza boxes around the room, Steve cracked, "Got yourself a new job there, Victor?"

Victor gave Steve a sly smile and replied, "Just giving Angelina a helping hand. Hey, she's the only thing keeping me from dying of boredom around here. The recording sessions ain't exactly been electrifying lately. I'm betting I didn't miss a whole lot by not being here yesterday."

Mark grumbled, "Yeah, thanks for reminding us. Do us a favor, OK? Don't go blabbing to your uncle what a waste of time these past few sessions have been."

Victor chuckled noncommittally in response. At that same moment, Dave, who had been eyeing Angelina intently for several seconds, leaned over to Steve and whispered into his ear. Steve's eyes followed Dave's back to Angelina and went wide with revelation almost immediately. Steve quickly pulled A.J. aside and whispered to him. The process was rapidly repeated through Kevin and Mark, and suddenly Angelina sensed five pairs of eyeballs fixated on her.

"What are you guys staring at?" she giggled nervously. "Most of my tattoos aren't even visible today."

Dave asked Angelina evenly, "How tall are you, Angelina?" His question sent a shiver through the room. Only Angelina and Victor, neither of whom were aware of the existence of the surveillance video, failed to understand the significance of Dave's seemingly innocuous question. Now there were eleven people staring bug-eyed at Angelina, and in particular at her long mane of light pink hair.

"I don't know, about five-foot two, I think. Why?"

"Just curious. But you know what I'm really curious about? Why you were on the corner of High Street and Halstead Street late at night about a week ago, buying drugs from a local pusher."

Angelina's eyes went as wide as those of the people in the room staring at her, and a wave of sickening terror swept over her. "What... what are you t-talking about?" she managed to stammer.

"Don't say nothing, Angelina!" barked a suddenly tense Victor as Angelina scanned the room with her eyes to see the now steely gazes of ten people bearing down on her.

"That's right, Angelina. The Newton cops have a video of you buying all the stuff used to murder Denise—the heroin, the syringe, the date rape knockout drug. The pink hair threw them off—they've been wasting time looking for a blonde—but it's you, all right." Dave was bluffing about knowing exactly what was purchased from drug dealer Derek Underhill that night, as well as about knowing for sure that Angelina was the woman in the video, but his ruse worked. Angelina covered her eyes with her hands and began weeping. "I didn't know what it was gonna be used for!" she wailed. "I didn't even know what that flunitraz-whatever stuff was."

Victor grabbed Angelina roughly by the arm and yanked her over to him, bellowing, "Shut the fuck up, Angelina! He's just making this shit up to get you to say things you shouldn't be saying. Now keep your mouth zipped."

Mark and Steve arose from their chairs and started to advance towards the sobbing Angelina and the now menacing-looking Victor.

"What's it to you, Victor?" Mark yelled as he strode across the room. "Are you the one who sent Angelina out to buy those things? I bet it was you who stuck that needle in Denise's arm!"

"You're full of shit. Stay the hell away from me."

Mark and Steve continued to close in on Victor. Steve pointed his finger accusingly and growled, "You murdered Denise, you little prick."

Victor, still holding onto Angelina's arm with his left hand, reached into an inner pocket of his leather vest, pulled out a tiny, .25 caliber, six-shot Browning pistol, and pointed it directly at Mark and Steve. Angelina shrieked at the sight of the handgun. Mark and Steve stopped in their tracks, and a collective gasp arose from the others in the room.

Victor, trying desperately to figure out what to do next, now that he had dramatically raised the ante by pulling the gun, began barking orders. "Angelina, don't you go anywhere, got it? I'm letting go of your arm, but you stay right here. The rest of you—all of you—get over there in front of that wall, and stay there. I don't want to see any cell phones. And no hiding behind each other trying to make calls without me seeing you. Spread out along the wall so I can see all of you."

Victor was standing about fifteen feet from the wall where he had directed everyone to stand. No one said a word as they began gathering at the wall, except for Mark, who snarled, "Have you lost your mind, Victor? What the hell do you think you're going to do now, run off to Mexico and join a band of desperados with your little pop gun pistol?"

Victor had absolutely no answer to Mark's mocking question, so he simply yelled, "Shut up, Mark, or the next thing I'll do is put a .25 caliber part in your hair."

All of the adults except for Dave made their way to the wall as Justin, frozen with fear, sat motionless in his chair halfway between Victor and his captives. Dave took two steps towards his son to gather him up, but Victor leveled the handgun at him and ordered, "No!"

"What do you mean, no? I'm just getting my son."

"I said no. Leave him there!"

"Screw you, Victor!" Dave took another step towards his petrified boy. Victor pointed his gun in Dave's direction and pulled the trigger. The loud report of the pistol elicited screams and curses as the bullet sailed less than a foot over Dave's head and shattered a lamp across the room.

"I'm warning you, if you don't want anyone to get hurt here, start doing what I tell you. Justin's gonna be my insurance policy. He's coming with Angelina and me."

"*What?*" Dave and Angelina screamed simultaneously. Victor pointed the gun at a horrified Dave again to prevent him from making another attempt to grab Justin. He turned to Angelina and said harshly, "What? Do you think you're gonna hang around here and continue to deliver pizzas, ya dummy? You're cooked if you don't come with me right now. You have no choice."

Angelina stood sobbing as Victor stepped over to Justin, pulled him screaming out of his chair, and forced him to stand in front of him.

CHAPTER 39

Sharon emerged from the studio control room with Justin's baseball cap and headed toward the staircase leading back up to the main level of the building. As she reached the bottom of the staircase, she heard loud and apparently angry voices coming from the main living area. Climbing the stairs carefully and quietly now, she listened closely to the intense verbal exchanges emanating from above. The first sentence she was able to make out clearly was Steve hotly accusing someone in the room of being Denise's murderer. The next sound she heard was Angelina's scream at the sight of Victor's gun, although Sharon had no idea whose voice it was or why the woman was screaming.

Stunned and confused, Sharon crept silently up a few more steps until she could peer between the stair railings and see what was going on. Victor stood with his back to the staircase, brandishing his small handgun, and ordering everyone to retreat to the far wall of the room. Sharon witnessed her husband's attempt to retrieve their terrified son from his chair and barely managed to suppress a scream when Victor fired the warning shot over Dave's head. She had to fight off a paralyzing nausea when Victor announced that he was planning to take Justin with him as insurance.

Sharon retreated quickly and quietly back downstairs to the studio level, desperately looking for something to use as a weapon against her son's abductor. She came upon a row of four guitars on tripod stands: two of Mark's solid-body electric Les Pauls, a Martin acoustic guitar also belonging to Mark, and A.J.'s Fender Precision bass. The extra-long bass guitar was clearly too unwieldy, and she made an instant determination that the voluminous but hollow-bodied acoustic would lack the necessary heft to serve as an effective skull cracker, so she grabbed one of the Les Pauls. The guitar was significantly and disconcertingly heavier than she expected, but she convinced herself that she could swing it with enough force to incapacitate Victor with a blow to the back of the head. She tiptoed back up the stairs, gripping the instrument's neck with both hands.

Pausing when she reached her previous vantage point, Sharon saw a clearly traumatized Angelina being ordered by Victor to collect cell phones from everyone standing along the wall. She also heard Victor instruct Angelina to disconnect the telephone cords from the landlines in the reception area, living area, and studio, and to add them to the pile of cell phones. Justin was partially hidden from Sharon's view by Victor, but she could see that Victor had his left arm firmly around the weeping boy's shoulders, preventing him from running to the arms of his father.

Sharon knew she had to act quickly. Angelina would be heading down the stairway momentarily to disable the studio phone. She carefully kicked off her shoes to ensure that she would make no giveaway sounds on the wooden floor of the living area, re-gripped the neck of the guitar, crept to the top of the stairway, and launched herself across the twenty-five-foot expanse of floor between the stairs and where Victor was issuing orders to Angelina.

As Sharon closed to within ten feet of her target, Victor suddenly noticed the collective, involuntary movements of his captives' eyes as they reacted to the bizarre sight of the desperate mother, zeroing in on her son's kidnapper, wielding an electric guitar like a baseball bat. Victor whirled around just as Sharon began to swing the guitar at his head. He fired his pistol once, striking Sharon on the inside of her right elbow. The force of the bullet altered the trajectory of Sharon's swing; instead of striking Victor squarely in the head with the narrow edge of the guitar's body, the wounded Sharon bounced the flat back of the guitar's body off Victor's left shoulder and the side of his face.

Both Sharon and Victor crumpled to the floor, Sharon screaming in agony and bleeding heavily from the entry and exit wounds in her elbow, and Victor momentarily knocked senseless from the blow to his left ear and cheek. He stumbled over Justin as he fell sideways, landing on top of the howling child as the gun flew out of his right hand and skidded across the floor. It came to rest about eight feet away from Victor and close to twenty feet away from the group lined up along the wall.

Victor shook his head to clear the cobwebs as he shoved Justin out of his way and rose to his hands and knees, searching for the gun. At the same time, Dave propelled himself from his spot along the wall toward the weapon, and Steve and Mark, after a two-second consultation, took off in opposing arcs to attack Victor from the sides. Sharon rose to her feet, clutching her bleeding right elbow in her left hand, and staggered in the direction of Victor and her son.

Sharon watched in horror as Victor scrambled to the gun and picked it up while Dave was still almost ten feet away. Still balanced on his knees and his left hand, Victor pointed the pistol at the charging Dave. Sharon dove at Victor's left leg, managing to pull his ankle back with her blood-soaked left hand just before he fired. Victor's resulting loss of balance forced the angle of the pistol sharply downward, and the bullet zipped between Dave's legs, striking Cathy Ramello, who was still standing near the wall, in the shin. Cathy dropped to the floor screaming, and A.J. rushed to her. Dave, who had made a belated, awkward lunge to try to avoid being shot, flew off-balance past Victor and tripped over Justin, landing heavily on the wooden floor, fracturing his ankle in the fall.

Victor, cursing furiously, could now see Mark and Steve's flanking approaches from his left and right. Now up on his knees, he pivoted to his left to draw a bead on the fast approaching Mark. Sharon desperately pounced on Victor's right ankle, biting his Achilles tendon with all her might. Victor shrieked in pain and wildly fired two of his three remaining bullets, missing Mark with both. The first bullet slammed harmlessly into the wall, and the second one clipped the right side of Sonny McCrae's chin, sending him slumping to the floor, bellowing, and holding his bleeding lower jaw with both hands.

Enraged, Victor now wanted nothing more than to use his last bullet to kill Sharon. He rolled onto his back and tried to aim the pistol at Sharon's head. But before Victor could get the gun into position to fire, Mark and Steve converged on him like two onrushing freight trains. Mark announced his arrival with a savage kick to Victor's ribs, and a split second later Steve delivered an equally thunderous kick to Victor's head. Victor groaned and collapsed onto his left side, the gun falling out of his hand. Steve stomped on Victor's throat, as Mark retrieved his Les Paul from the floor, strode over to the incapacitated Victor holding the guitar by the neck, and prepared to slam it into his head.

"Mark, no, don't kill him!" hollered the crippled Dave from the floor a few feet away. "They need him alive to find out who put him up to killing Denise."

The rabidly furious, adrenaline-wired Mark, barely able to contain himself from crushing Victor's skull right then and there, paused, stared at Dave for a second, exhaled heavily, and redirected his swing of the guitar to Victor's back, making a sickening thud and drawing a low gurgled moan from the target of his wrath.

Once it was apparent that Victor posed no further threat, those who were not hurt in the melee began tending to the injured. Mark fished through the pile of cell phones, found his phone, and called out to everyone in the room, "Who has the phone number of the detective who's coming here this afternoon? Not the asshole who was here yesterday, the other one."

Wendy LaRoche, who was using napkins to help stop the bleeding from Sonny's face, ran to her purse, pulled out Detective McDougal's card, handed it to Mark, and quickly returned to administer to Sonny. As Mark dialed McDougal's number, Kevin LaRoche's eye caught Angelina, who had been standing paralyzed with fear throughout the mayhem of the past minute, attempting to slip unnoticed toward the exit. Kevin sprinted toward the front door to intercept her and caught her by the arm as she was about to push open the door. "Leaving so soon? I don't think so."

Angelina offered no resistance as Kevin hauled her back into the living area, just as Mark connected with McDougal by phone.

"Detective McDougal speaking."

"McDougal! Mark Donahue here. Get over here to Total Immersion right now, and send ambulances. There's been a shootout here, and there are...one, two, three...Dave, were you shot?"

"No, but I think my ankle is broken. Get help here for Sharon and the others."

"I'm on it. Detective, there are three gunshot wounds and one broken ankle. The shooter is in bad shape too, and his condition is liable to get worse if you leave me here with him much longer. And by the way, the shooter is also Denise's killer. So get yourself and those ambulances here, fast." Mark hung up before McDougal could ask any questions.

By 7:00 that evening, Sharon, Cathy, Sonny, and Dave had all been admitted to Newton Memorial Hospital, treated, and released—Cathy and Dave on crutches, Sharon with her arm in a sling, and Sonny with a large bandage over his chin. Mark, Steve, A.J., Billy, Gabriella, Kevin, Wendy—and even Justin—were all finished giving their statements to the police. Victor and Angelina were in custody, Angelina in a jail cell at the Newton police station, and Victor under armed guard at the hospital, where he was being treated for broken ribs, a damaged windpipe, a dislocated jaw...and a bite wound on his Achilles tendon. Victor was not yet capable of providing any kind of useful statement to the police regarding any co-conspirators to Denise Blake's murder, but McDougal arranged for the New York City police to bring Stan Rabin in for questioning.

Justin, exhausted and still traumatized by the events of the day, was upstairs napping, but the entire adult contingent was now gathered in the living area. A member of the police forensics unit was busy extracting one of Victor's bullets from the wall, but otherwise the police were finished examining the room.

About two seconds after everyone had finished issuing kudos and toasts to Sharon for her incredible acts of heroism—Mark described her "solo" work on his Les Paul as the best ever played on that guitar—and Steve, Mark, and Dave had accepted cheers for their bravery, Mark suddenly sat up straight in his seat. "Holy shit, we gotta call Jeff!"

Everyone went silent as Mark pulled out his cell phone and dialed.

"Hi, Mark."

"Jeff! It's over. You can come back."

"What do you mean? What happened?"

"Denise's murderer was Rabin's shithead nephew, Victor. We don't yet know why, or if Rabin himself was behind it, but I'll be damned surprised if he wasn't."

Jeff was immediately overcome with emotion, as gratitude over his bandmates' innocence intermingled with the sad reminder that Denise was still gone. "Oh, my God! Oh, my God!" he repeated over and over, tears running down his cheeks.

"Come on back here, buddy. We need you desperately."

"Of course. Of course. Oh, my God! I can't wait. Oh, my God! And Mark...I'm really sorry—"

"No, no, no! Stop right there. No frickin' apologies. If you even try to apologize to any of us when you get here, we're gonna slap you silly. Right, guys?" He held his phone up in the air, and shouts of agreement filled the room.

"Listen, Jeff, you were put in a horrible position. Everyone here fully understands why you had to leave until this thing was resolved. But now that it is, get your ass up here."

"You got it. I have one important errand I need to run, and then I'll be there. Funny, my wrist suddenly feels a whole lot better."

After giving a shocked Jeff a rundown on the dramatic events of the day, Mark hung up, and the room erupted in cheers at the news of Jeff's impending return.

CHAPTER 40

It took several minutes for Jeff to regain his bearings after the breathtaking news from Mark about the violence that day at Total Immersion and the arrest of Victor Rabin for the murder of Denise. Finally, he rose from his living room chair and walked into the kitchen. He rummaged through a cluttered drawer until he found a small slip of paper he had stuffed into the drawer shortly after he and Denise had moved into the apartment two months earlier. The name "Joanne Fisk" was handwritten on the piece of paper, along with the address of an apartment in the SoHo—"South of Houston Street"—neighborhood of Manhattan.

Jeff changed into a golf shirt and a decent pair of jeans, exited his apartment, and hailed a cab, reading the address from the slip of paper to the cabbie. The SoHo apartment building had a security guard posted behind a marble podium in the lobby. The guard, a heavyset, amiable man in his early fifties, was a rock music fan who immediately recognized Jeff.

"Hey, you're Jeff Britton! Cool!"

"Hi, how are you?"

"Great, thanks. Hey, we've got someone living right in this building who used to be married to one of your bandmates, Mark Donahue."

"Yes, I know. Joanne Fisk—that's who I'm here to see. Do you know if she's home?"

"Yeah, she's around. Do you want me to call up and tell her you're here?"

"It's sort of a surprise. Can I just go up and knock on her door?"

The guard paused for a moment. "Yeah, I guess that would be OK. We're not supposed to do it that way, but for guitar man Jeff Britton, I'll make an exception."

"Thanks. I appreciate it."

"She's on the third floor, apartment 3J. Elevator's right around the corner."

After signing an autograph for the accommodating security guard, Jeff, still limping but no longer wearing a soft cast or sling for his right wrist, rode the elevator to the third floor and found his way to Joanne Fisk's apartment. He knocked on the door with his right hand and was pleased to discover that the action caused no pain in his wrist.

The door opened, and Jeff was met by a striking woman in her forties, with large blue eyes, wavy, shoulder-length light brown hair, and a trim figure effectively highlighted by a pair of white pants and a turquoise sleeveless summer blouse. She greeted her visitor with a warm, welcoming smile.

"Hello."

"Hi. Are you Joanne?"

"Yes. I—wait. You're Jeff Britton! Oh, my God. Please, come in."

"Thank you." Jeff followed Joanne into her comfortable, brightly decorated living room and took a seat on the large, L-shaped sofa.

"I remember Mark telling me that you were a big fan of beer. I think I have a couple in my refrigerator. Would you like one?"

"Actually, I've been trying to ease back on those lately, but what the heck, if you've got 'em, I'd love one."

Joanne retreated to the kitchen, and soon returned with a can of Coors Light for Jeff and a glass of white wine for herself. Jeff accepted the can with a smile, thinking *this piss water isn't real beer anyway, so technically I'm being good right now.*

Joanne joined Jeff on the sofa. "It's nice to meet you, Jeff. I must say, though, it's also a little strange. During my time with

Mark, your name came up a lot, but not in particularly positive ways."

"That's sort of why I've come here."

"Well, at least you and Mark have clearly reconciled. I see and read things all the time about how well the Upper Hand is doing, and—oh, wait, there was something else in the news recently. Oh, my God, Jeff, wasn't it your girlfriend who was murdered at that recording studio?"

"Yes, I'm afraid so."

"Oh, I'm so sorry. Did they find out who did it?"

"Yes, just earlier today, in fact. Thankfully for me, it wasn't anyone closely associated with the band or with me personally."

"Still, my heart goes out to you."

"That's very nice of you to say. I appreciate it." Jeff paused to take a long sip from his Coors Light.

"Joanne, let me try to explain why I'm here. It's all a bit unusual, and I apologize in advance if this turns out to be a big mistake. Anyway, here goes—Joanne, even though you and I never met before today, I was a big cause, probably the main cause, of your breakup with Mark."

Joanne placed her wine glass on the coffee table in front of the sofa and stared quizzically at Jeff.

"Come again?"

"I know, I must sound crazy, but hear me out. I know that you're fully versed on what happened to me in 1990, and how the Upper Hand broke up because of my problems."

"Oh, yes, Mark brought it up many times while we were together. Many times."

"That's really kind of my point, Joanne. Mark was deeply, deeply affected by my stupid actions and the loss of the band,

and he pretty much spent the whole decade of the '90s and the first few years of this decade in an extended funk. Mark himself recognizes this now."

"How...how do you know this? You weren't around."

"We talked about it shortly after we got together again last year, and he admitted it to me. From what I understand, the other guys in the band, A.J., Dave, and Steve, finally got through to Mark and made him see how he'd changed since my meltdown and disappearance. The reunion of the Upper Hand, and my personal reconciliation with Mark, could never have happened without that effort from those three guys." Jeff drained his Coors Light and asked, "Could I bother you for another one of these? I'm just a little nervous here."

"Of course." Joanne rose from the sofa and headed to the kitchen, returning shortly with another beer for Jeff as well as the bottle of wine to replenish her glass.

Jeff popped open the can, took a sip, and continued, "Look, I know I have no business asking you about the reasons why you left Mark, but if it was his bitter, downcast outlook and personality that chased you away, I just want to let you know that his being that way was all because of me. He was never like that before 1990, and he isn't like that now. Joanne, what I'm trying to say is, *you never knew the real Mark Donahue.*"

Joanne placed her hand over her mouth, staring off into space, and said nothing.

"Maybe this was a mistake coming here to tell you this. I'm sorry if—"

"No, no. Not at all. I just need to process this. You're right, Jeff. Mark was never a laugh riot over the five years I was with him, but his moods just got darker and darker over time, until I simply couldn't be around him anymore. I feel like I'm a pretty positive person, but he was just sucking me into his...what was your word?...bitter world. It wasn't easy for me to make the decision to leave, because I saw many terrific qualities in Mark, but it became too much."

"Yes, Mark described you to me as a wonderfully upbeat, warm person."

"Really? Gee, that's nice to hear."

Jeff paused again and took two or three more sips from his beer. "I'm not sure if I'm doing the right thing telling you what I'm about to tell you, but since it's really the point of my visit, I'm going to do it. Please don't get too mad at me if this turns out to be a stupid idea."

"OK, I promise."

Jeff drained the second beer with two more long swallows. "Joanne, Mark regrets to this day that he lost you, and now that he has a grasp on why it happened, he dreams of a...I think his term for it was a 'do-over'...with you. I just felt it was important for me, as the cause of Mark's dramatic personality change during those years, to let you know this."

Joanne emptied her wine glass, and with a stunned look on her face, uttered, "I don't know what to say. This is quite a lot to absorb."

"I'm sorry if I've upset you. I know my telling you all this is more than likely going to lead to nothing. But I just had to let you know the facts. I'm going to play salesman here for just one moment, and then I promise never again to try to influence you in any way. The *real* Mark Donahue, who you've never met, is a warm, funny—and yes, *positive*—guy, who happens to think that you're the most terrific woman he's ever known."

He rose from the sofa. Extending his hand to Joanne, he said, "It was a pleasure to meet you, Joanne, and I appreciate you letting me dump all this on you. I hope you're not angry with me."

Joanne ignored Jeff's offer of a goodbye handshake, instead rising from the sofa to embrace him in a hug. She then stepped back and said, "Jeff, I think it was a wonderful thing you did, and you are obviously a special person and a special friend to Mark to have come here. I have a lot to think about. I'm a bit overwhelmed at the moment. I hope you understand."

"Of course. Again, I enjoyed meeting you. Good night."

As Jeff placed his hand on the doorknob, Joanne called out, "Could I have your phone number? In case I need to, well, you know."

Jeff's face broke into an ear-to-ear smile. "Of course."

CHAPTER 41

"He's here. He's here! The limo just pulled into the parking lot," Justin announced, running into the main living area of Total Immersion from the reception area. The exertion on his weakened lungs left the boy wheezing, and Sharon sat him down and patted his head until his breathing returned to normal. It was 1:30 p.m. on Thursday, the day after the bloody confrontation at the studio and the arrests of Victor Rabin and Angelina Parducci, and indeed, a limousine delivering Jeff from New York to Newton was arriving at that moment. A steel gray sky and a steady, driving rain could not dampen the mood of the gathering in the living area as Justin breathlessly delivered word of Jeff's arrival. Steve, Mark, and A.J. each grabbed an umbrella and ran out to greet the car and provide some V.I.P. bellboy service for their returning friend.

Jeff had been nervous throughout the trip about how he would react emotionally upon stepping back inside Total Immersion. Yes, it would be a tremendous relief to be back with his friends without having to wonder if any of them might have had a hand in Denise's death, but he had no idea how he was going to handle returning to the scene of the murder. He knew for sure that he would not be able to go anywhere near the second floor room he had shared with Denise and thus arranged for a room on the third floor for the remaining time the Upper Hand would be at Total Immersion. He consciously opted for additional physical stress on his injured leg over the emotional stress of walking past the room where Denise had died.

Jeff's trepidation about coming back to Total Immersion vanished when he spotted his three umbrella-toting friends splashing energetically through the parking lot puddles to greet the limo. "Greetings, sir, welcome to Total Immersion!" "May I take your bag, sir?" "Please step under this umbrella, sir. Your comfort is our only concern."

"Holy shit, I've never been called 'sir' so many times in my life! You guys are too much."

"Let's get inside, out of this crummy weather. There is a crowd of people in there who can't wait to see you."

Jeff was immediately mobbed when he stepped into the living area. It took him a full ten minutes to work his way through the happy crowd, exchanging emotional greetings, accepting renewed condolences for his loss of Denise, and listening to various perspectives on the frightening and violent clash with Victor just a day earlier.

He made a point of saving Dave and Sharon for last in his tour through the room. First approaching Dave, who was seated with his broken ankle propped up on an ottoman, Jeff grabbed Dave's hand, bent down to throw his arm around Dave's shoulders, and said, "I heard what you did, Dave. You were the one who figured out that Angelina was the drug buyer and got her to start blabbing about everything. Thank you so much. I've also been told about how incredibly courageous you were when that jerk-off, Victor, started waving his gun around and when the gun was knocked out of his hand."

"I tell you, Jeff, I don't think it was courage as much as it was sheer terror. I've never been so scared in all my life, especially when he said he was going to kidnap Justin to help him escape. Ugh, I still get sick thinking about it."

"I can't even imagine what that was like. But don't sell yourself short, Dave. What you did took pure guts. Anyway, what's the story with your ankle?"

"Clean break, gonna require about six or seven weeks in this cast. But hey, I don't need my foot to play keyboards. I'm ready to go. How about your wrist?"

Jeff held his right hand in front of his face and rotated his wrist back and forth slowly. "Take a look. The cast is off, and it feels pretty good. I'm probably three or four days away from being able to rip off any super-fast solos or leads, but I'm planning to start laying down some rhythms today."

"Excellent! Goddamn, we need you in that studio."

Turning next to Sharon, Jeff suddenly found himself choking up. "There she is, my absolute hero. I am in awe of you. Can I hug you without hurting your arm?"

"You better believe it, sweetie. Get over here." They held each other in a long embrace, Sharon keeping her injured right elbow tucked protectively close to her side.

Jeff said softly, "Some of these people wouldn't be here today, and we wouldn't be having this happy gathering, if not for your incredible bravery."

"I reacted like any mother and wife would, Jeff."

"No, you reacted like any mother and wife would *want* to under those insane circumstances. There are very few who could actually do what you did here yesterday. You're a special lady, and I'm shaking just thinking about what would have happened here without you."

"Thank you, Jeff. I'm just so glad it's over. How about you? Are you holding up OK?"

"Yeah, I think so. It helps knowing who to direct my hatred toward for the murder. I'll be very interested to hear if Stan Rabin put Victor up to it."

Jeff then pulled Sharon aside, out of Dave's earshot, and asked her in a near whisper, "Do you have a little time to speak with me alone, maybe in a few minutes when this little welcoming party dies down?"

"Of course. Is everything all right?"

"Yeah, yeah, I just have something I need to discuss with you privately."

Twenty minutes later, Sharon and Jeff were alone in the small side room where Detective Priefer had conducted his ill-advised interviews with Gabriella and Sharon two days earlier. Jeff was holding a manila folder containing several papers.

"Sharon, please excuse this very personal question, but I have what I think you'll soon understand to be a good reason to ask it. How much is it going to cost you and Dave for Justin's medical expenses over the next several years?"

Sharon's eyebrows shot up. "I...I don't know. It depends on a lot of things. Especially whether or not he needs a lung transplant."

"Let's hope it doesn't come to that, but give me your top-end, worst-case-scenario estimate."

"Oh, boy, let's see. A lung transplant operation can go from anywhere between half a mil to close to a mil, depending on whether it's a single or double. I think if Justin winds up having to go that route, it will be a double. With all the follow-up care involved, I guess we could be looking at well over two million dollars over the next few years. You can see why we're so glad the Upper Hand is back in business again."

"So, three million dollars could take care of pretty much all of your little guy's expenses for a good while."

"Yes, that sounds about right."

Jeff opened the manila folder, pulled out several pages of documents, and handed them to Sharon. "I'd like you to read this. It's Denise's will. I think you'll find it rather interesting."

Sharon began reading the will. Her eyes went wide, and she uttered "Holy crap!" under her breath several times as she learned of Denise's twelve million dollar fortune, and of the conditions under which Jeff would come into that money. When she was done reading the will, she slid the documents back to Jeff and said, "Denise was a unique lady, Jeff. Jeez, I had no idea she had that kind of money."

"Me, neither. It turns out there were a few things I didn't know about her. Anyway, you read that rather strange provision in the will about her ashes and that place in the Indian Ocean, right? Well, I fully intend to carry out her wishes."

"What, you wouldn't prefer to have the twelve mil put toward buying a boatload of Grey Goose L'Orange and dumping it overboard?" Sharon quipped with a smile.

"Amazing, eh? Anyway, here's the point of my nosy questions about Justin's medical expenses. I'm going to be quite tied up here for the next several weeks recording this album with the boys. I need someone to take care of all the details regarding Denise's cremation and the chartering of this boat to deliver her ashes to that place in the middle of the ocean. I'm offering a non-negotiable fee of three million dollars to perform these duties." He paused and grinned broadly. "Interested?"

Sharon's eyes filled with tears, and she stammered, "Oh, Jeff, are you sure about this? I mean, I don't know what to say! Three million dollars for Justin, are you really sure?"

"You bet I'm sure. It's a no-brainer for me. I can't think of a better use for part of this shitload of money I'm getting from Denise than to make sure that great little kid of yours gets everything he needs without keeping you and Dave awake at night worrying about it. Just make sure you get a big enough boat for everyone here to fit on—the whole band, Kevin, Sonny, Billy, wives and girlfriends. Let's turn this into a real proper send-off for Denise."

Speechless, Sharon rose from her chair, walked over to the still-seated Jeff, threw her uninjured arm around his neck, and kissed him on top of his head.

As Jeff opened the door to the side room and stepped back into the main living area, followed by a still moist-eyed Sharon, they were met by a newly arrived Detective McDougal, who had just finished shaking the water out of his umbrella in the reception area.

"Mr. Britton, Mrs. Rowinski, how are you? Mrs. Rowinski, how is your elbow?"

"It's doing OK, thanks, Detective. What brings you here?"

"We've obtained detailed statements from both Victor Rabin and Angelina Parducci, and I thought you folks would want to hear what they said. We now have a pretty good idea of exactly what transpired here and why."

"Of course, of course," replied Jeff. "Let me gather the troops."

Five minutes later a rapt group of twelve people—the band, Sharon, Cathy, Gabriella, Sonny, Billy, Kevin, and Wendy— sat silently as Detective McDougal recapped the results of the interrogations of Victor and Angelina.

"Victor Rabin has confessed to the murder of Denise Blake," McDougal began. "He claims that he committed this homicide at the direction of his uncle, Stan Rabin, whose record label business is, according to Victor, teetering on the edge of bankruptcy. Victor told us that Stan felt that Denise represented a serious threat to the health of Mr. Britton and, therefore, to the band and the album you're here to record." Jeff bowed his head and put his face in his hands.

"Victor further informed us that he was instructed, by his uncle, to make Ms. Blake's death look like a heroin overdose. Victor is apparently no stranger to heroin, but, not being from this area, he turned to his new friend Angelina Parducci, who also has admitted to some degree of familiarity with illegal drugs, to procure what he needed. Victor corroborates Angelina's claim that she had no idea that Victor wanted the drugs for anything other than personal use, and that she had no clue what flunitrazepam—the 'date rape' drug—was. She's not totally off the hook for the homicide, though. She apparently delivered Ms. Blake's dinner to her room that evening, knowing that Victor had spiked the glass of soda with the flunitrazepam. The prosecutor is still mulling over how to handle this. My guess is Angelina will get off fairly lightly assuming she testifies against Victor. Anyway, there was no glass of soda on the dinner tray we found in the room, because Victor disposed of it in hopes of eliminating any evidence that Ms. Blake had been chemically incapacitated. He clearly was hoping that the scene he left would, given Ms. Blake's history of heroin use, be accepted as an accidental overdose."

Dave cut in to ask, "Is Stan Rabin under arrest?"

"Yes, he is. He flatly denies having anything to do with Victor's actions, and this could turn into a 'he said...he said' case. He may have trouble getting around one thing, though. Stan arranged for ten thousand dollars to be transferred from a Signature Records bank account to Victor's personal checking account on Friday, August 12. That's after Ms. Blake was discovered dead, but before there was any suspicion of murder. Victor claims the ten grand was his payment for carrying out the homicide. Stan was apparently taken aback, and at a loss for a credible explanation, when the discovery of this bank transaction was revealed to him. He has stopped speaking to the police and has hired a lawyer who is in the process of trying to get Rabin out on bail."

Jeff looked up, and muttered softly, "Ten thousand bucks. So that's the price that son of a bitch put on Denise's life, to 'protect' me and the band. Damn." He turned to McDougal. "Did Victor say if Denise was conscious, if she struggled or suffered, when he injected her with the heroin?"

"We asked him that, and he said that she was out cold. The level of flunitrazepam found in her system strongly suggests he's telling the truth."

Jeff sighed and said, "I guess that's a good thing."

"By the way, Victor is also up on multiple charges surrounding yesterday's incident here, up to and including attempted kidnapping and attempted murder."

Steve called out, "I'd say that boy's toast. I just hope his scum-of-the-earth uncle goes down with him."

No one had any additional questions for McDougal, so the detective, relieved that the prospects for an easy last few weeks on the job were now dramatically improved—and twenty dollars richer after having collected on his bet with Priefer that morning—said his goodbyes and left.

Jeff sat staring off into space as various members of the gathering patted him on the shoulder and offered words of commiseration and encouragement. After a minute or so he suddenly sat up straight, exhaled deeply, slapped his hands against his knees, and rose from his chair.

"OK, I can't allow myself to wallow in this anymore. I just have to pull myself together and move forward. We've got a rock and roll record to make!" His face broke into a smile. "Let's go downstairs and listen to what a mess you guys made of things while I was away."

EPILOGUE

Steve stepped outside onto the rear deck of the sensational luxury yacht *Perth Princess*, accompanied by his latest girlfriend, a financial planner named Gail who, while of course stunning, was also, shockingly, over forty years old. To the amazement and silently hopeful approval of his friends, Steve actually seemed to be showing interest in establishing something resembling a stable, long-term relationship with Gail. Holding an oversized can of Foster's Lager in his hand, he let out a tremendous roar of general approval for the amusement of the other passengers on the ship, all of whom were gathered on the deck to soak up the sunshine and warm Indian Ocean breeze.

"OK," Steve announced to the group, "Someone has to explain to me why it's late spring here, when it's early December. I must have been out of school the day they taught that one."

"You didn't miss it. You were just too busy banging out drum rhythms on your desktop to learn anything in school," teased Dave. "It's a wonder you ever got your diploma."

"OK, wise guy, then *you* explain this upside down season stuff to me."

"It's very simple. It's all tied in to the tiltification of the sun."

Sonny extracted his bottle of Emu Bitter, a Western Australian brew, from his mouth and hollered, "*What? Tiltification of the sun?* Holy smoke, you must've eaten a lot of paint chips when you were a kid. Everyone knows the seasons are all tied in with the moon phases. The moon's gravitational pull is all backwards down here."

A.J. cackled, "I don't believe what I'm hearing. Goddamn, it's a good thing you guys all found careers in rock and roll, because it's quite clear that you don't know shit about anything else."

Joanne, Mark's former ex-wife and new bride, unlocked her arm from her husband's, retrieved her purse from a nearby table, and pulled out a pen and a piece of note paper. "Come here,

Steve, and you guys, too," she said, pointing to Dave and Sonny. "Let me draw you a couple of diagrams to show you what causes the seasons to be reversed here. Now, here's the Earth, which rotates on an axis with a twenty-three degree tilt..."

"Holy shit, she's smart too!" exclaimed Sonny. "Boy, oh boy, Mark. You owe Jeff big time for getting that little woman to take you back."

"Don't I know it," replied Mark, stepping behind Jeff and giving him a playful punch on the arm.

As Joanne completed her impromptu lesson for Steve, Dave, and Sonny, Kevin approached the group from the far corner of the deck, where he had spent the past fifteen minutes on his cell phone.

"Hey, guys, I know we don't want to spend too much time talking business on this trip, but you're going to be glad I paid to get the international connection for my cell phone when I tell you what I just learned."

"OK, let us have it," replied Jeff.

"First, the album—it's been in stores now for about four or five days, and I was told that *We Were Dead...But We Got Better* is a lock to top the Billboard CD chart next week. The single debuted at number three on the singles chart, and not only that, but 'Little Victories' is getting lots of FM classic rock airplay too—way to go, Dave—as is Jeff's solo acoustic number."

In an unprecedented move for the Upper Hand, the band had included on the new album a song consisting of nothing but Jeff on vocals and acoustic guitar, a plaintive tune written for and dedicated to Denise titled, "I Wish We'd Had More Time." The raw emotion of the lyrics and Jeff's stripped-down delivery, combined with widespread publicity surrounding Denise's murder, were driving radio program directors throughout the country to add the song to their play lists. At many rock stations, "I Wish We'd Had More Time" was getting even more airplay than the hot single, Mark's hard-driving "Seemed Like a Good Idea at the Time."

As soon as the raucous cheering subsided, Kevin continued his reporting on the good news from the other side of the world. "The really good news is that Signature Records' top managers are doing a bang-up job running the label and promoting and distributing the album and single while Rabin is cooling his heels in prison. And speaking of Rabin, every single one of his lawyer's motions—for case dismissal, for bail reduction, for change of venue—has been denied by the judge. And now that it's been revealed that Angelina overheard a key phone conversation between Stan and Victor the day after the murder, and is willing to testify to what she heard, there are rumors going around that Stan might be looking to make a plea deal. Stick a fork in that bastard. He's done! He's going to be selling Signature Records to his managers any day now to pay for his defense."

Kevin cast a mischievous look in Dave's direction. "And now for an update on the Great Dave Rowinski Indianapolis Ticket Give-Away Extravaganza!"

Dave covered his head in mock horror as the crowd hooted, and cried out, "I'm going overboard! I'd rather be shark food than face this unruly mob." He ran over to the railing and went into a diver's pose, with knees bent and arms and fingers pointed straight ahead.

"Relax, Dave. As it turns out, you dodged a bullet here. We ran a half-page ad in the local papers, as promised, offering free tickets at next March's show to anyone who presented a ticket stub from last April's show—"

The entire band groaned at the mention of the debacle of their April 3 concert in Indianapolis.

Kevin continued, "We received twenty-four hundred requests for tickets accompanied by *bona fide* ticket stubs, plus about five hundred with fake or questionable stubs. We've decided to honor those, too, just to avoid any negative press. So, all told, we're talking about two hundred grand in freebies—not too bad. But get this: the publicity generated by the offer caused a huge spike in ticket demand, a favorable article by Dave's reporter pal Hugh Gentry didn't hurt, and we've had to add a second show in Indy. We're going to come out ahead in that town, so you can step away from the railing, Dave."

"Well, that's how I planned it all along," exclaimed Dave, unable to suppress a shit-eating grin. This was of course met with a chorus of catcalls and boos from everyone.

One of the ship's crew members appeared on the rear deck, sought out Jeff, and informed him, "Mr. Britton, we are approaching our destination latitude and longitude. We'll be there in about five minutes." The festive mood of the gathering turned suddenly somber.

"Thank you. I guess I better get ready. I'll be right back, everyone."

Jeff disappeared into the interior of the ship and returned two minutes later carrying a box containing Denise's ashes, as well as two chilled bottles of Grey Goose L'Orange and a stack of small plastic cups. "I've sworn off this stuff for good, but this one last time, I'm going to have a snootful for Denise, and I hope you'll all join me."

Everyone, including Denise's number one antagonist, Mark, accepted a plastic cup from Jeff, and he poured out a shot of Denise's favorite libation to all: Mark and Joanne; Dave and Sharon; A.J. and Cathy; Steve and perhaps the first semi-serious girlfriend of his life, Gail; Kevin and Wendy; and Billy and Sonny and their girlfriends.

The yacht came to a halt, and the crewman called out to Jeff, "This is the spot, sir. There's no rush. You can take as much time as you need."

As Jeff removed the lid from the box of ashes and prepared to scatter them over the edge of the boat, Cathy called out, "Jeff, may I make a suggestion?"

"Of course, Cathy. What is it?"

"After you scatter Denise's ashes, why don't you sing that beautiful new song you wrote for her? You have an acoustic guitar on board. I can't think of a better way to punctuate this farewell to her."

Approval from the gathering for Cathy's idea was immediate and enthusiastic. Jeff paused a moment, and replied, "That's a wonderful idea. I just hope I can get through it."

Billy volunteered, "You stay here, Jeff. I'll go fetch your guitar."

As soon as Billy returned, Jeff stepped to the back of the boat with the ashes and his plastic cup of vodka, turned to his assembled friends, raised his cup, and said simply, "To Denise. I sure wish I could have had more time with her."

"To Denise," responded the group as they sipped their vodka and Jeff began to disperse Denise's ashes into the ocean. "Bye, babe," he whispered as the last of the ashes hit the surface of the water. "Please rest assured that I will never forget you."

Jeff then reached for the second, unopened bottle of Grey Goose L'Orange. Holding it in his hands, he retraced his steps to the spot on the edge of the deck where Denise's ashes still floated visibly below. He stopped, turned around to face his friends, and said, "I'm not sure if I should toss this bottle overboard sealed, or pull the cork out of it." After a brief discussion it was agreed that opening the bottle would allow Denise's ashes to intermingle with her favorite beverage forever, so Jeff extracted the cork cap and tossed the bottle overboard.

Billy handed Jeff his guitar, and Jeff successfully navigated his way through his wistful new song for his lost girlfriend. There was not an even remotely dry eye among the gathering by the time the song was over; even Mark was heard sniffling toward the end of the performance.

Jeff handed his guitar back to Billy, took one last glance over the railing at the spot where he had placed Denise's ashes and the bottle of Grey Goose L'Orange, and then summoned the crewman. "We're through here. We can head back to Perth now."

The astonishingly black, star-filled sky, and the full moon rising ahead over the ocean, left everyone in jaw-dropping awe as the *Perth Princess* cruised eastward that night back to its namesake Australian port. Everyone was out on the rear deck of the yacht, taking in the breathtaking view.

Dave and Jeff were standing together chatting, each nursing a Swan Draught, another popular Western Australian beer, when a contented humming sound drew their attention to Mark. He was reclined on a two-person cushioned seat and ottoman, with his right arm around Joanne and his left hand holding an Emu Bitter.

"It...does...not...get...any...better...than...this," Mark purred, as Joanne drew herself tighter against him.

Dave turned to Jeff and said, "You, my man, are on some amazing streak of good deed doing. First, your staggeringly generous gesture towards Justin's medical care, something I will never find the adequate words to thank you for, and then your orchestration of this reconciliation between Mark and Joanne. I just hope you feel as proud of yourself as you should."

"Thank you, Dave, I appreciate it. And yes, it feels good." Suddenly a scowl came across Jeff's face, and he stepped over to where Mark and Joanne were sitting. "But look at this, Dave. This woman is so good to this clown that she's turned him into a marshmallow. All we need is a cardigan and a pair of slippers, and we've got Mr. Rogers here." Jeff broke into a grin as Joanne hopped up and gave him a huge hug.

"Hey, he was already way mellower than he used to be, just as you promised. I just sanded off a few of the remaining rough edges."

"That's right," proclaimed Mark. "With perhaps a *slight* assist from my reconnections with you two, I now offer to the world a new, improved Mark Donahue with a personality and demeanor as smooth as a baby's ass."

"Aarrgh! He's still pretty insufferable, isn't he?"

"Absolutely, but I'm still working on him. I've only had three months, after all."

Mark stuck his tongue out at his tormentors and drained his Emu Bitter.

"You're a gem, Joanne," Jeff said, a bit more seriously. "I see exactly why Mark wanted so much to have a second chance with you." He started to walk away to leave Mark and Joanne alone, then turned back and inquired with a smile, "You wouldn't happen to have any single sisters like you back home, would you?"

Jeff's rhetorical, joking question was met with a decidedly non-joking reply that stopped him in his tracks. "As a matter of fact, I do. And she happens to be a big fan of the Upper Hand."

Mark chirped, "Oh, yeah...Cindy! She's hot, too. Really hot!"

Joanne made a face at Mark, smacked his outstretched foot, and exclaimed to Jeff, "Oh, my God, you two would be perfect for each other!"

Jeff started stammering, "Oh, no, I was just kidding—I mean, you don't have to—I wasn't trying to—"

"Nonsense. Just leave everything to me. Let's see, what time is it back in New York now? Around 10:00 a.m.? Perfect...*Kevin!* Come here a second. I need to borrow that international cell phone."

CPSIA information can be obtained
at www.ICGtesting.com
Printed in the USA
FFOW03n1725210915
16956FF